Crossing Mother's Grave

By
Jake Elliot

Damnation Books, LLC.
P.O. Box 3931
Santa Rosa, CA 95402-9998
www.damnationbooks.com

Crossing Mother's Grave
Sequel to The Wrong Way Down
by Jake Elliot

Digital ISBN: 978-1-61572-758-2
Print ISBN: 978-1-61572-759-9

Cover art by: Dawné Dominique
Edited by: Andrea Heacock-Reyes

Praise for the works of Jake Elliot:

"The world building here is pretty much on par with modern authors in the fantasy genre. Elliot has taken a bunch of traditional fantasy races and dropped them onto his world full of mystery, religion, politics and deception. I like what he has done with it, I like the way in which he communicates it to the reader through a mix of subtle referencing, descriptive visualization, and some overt story telling by an open campfire. Elliot doesn't let the world building get in the way of his plotting and characterization, it is there to be a cool setting that facilitates the motion of the story, and it does its job effectively."

—**Ryan Lawler**, at *Fantasy Book Review*

"I thoroughly enjoyed this adventure; it is a great read for fantasy fans. I just hope Mr. Elliot doesn't make me wait two years for each installment like Jordan did!"

—**Jeremy Kline**, author of *Lazarus Cane*

"*The Wrong Way Down* is a fast paced chase story, and Elliot does a great job of keeping his readers entertained while also keeping the scope of his novel simple and manageable for those who just want to be swept away on a fun adventure."

—**D. Robert Glixti**, author and book reviewer

*Dedicated to 'Scott' Wage,
Thank you for participating in the earliest stage of
what eventually became this book. Rest in peace
my old friend, the world misses you.*

J.E.

*I wish to acknowledge the rangers at Great Basin
National Park, specifically those at Lehman Caves,
and warm thanks go to the rangers at Carlsbad
Caverns who guide the lower caverns tour. Thank
you for enduring all my ultra-stupid questions
like "Could I pick up and throw stalagmites
like throwing knives?" or, "Could I swing from
stalactite to stalactite like a circus performer if
lava was boiling up from the floor?" I'm impressed
by how miraculously you maintained a straight
face—and this book is now better for it. I deeply
appreciate your help in making this story better
than what it could have been without you.*

*I also wish to acknowledge all the writing
professionals who helped me get a hand up; Kim
Richards, Andrea-Heacock-Reyes, Sally Franklin
Christie, Greg Chapman, Gary Olson, Tim
Marquitz and most particularly, my wife Becky.
I thank Ryan Lawler at Fantasy Book Review,
Jeremy Kline, and D. Robert Glixti, who had each
read The Wrong Way Down and given it an honest
opinion. All of your encouragements and words
of support are valued. I also want to thank all the
pioneer readers who bravely read The Wrong Way
Down. Crossing Mother's Grave wouldn't exist if
not for you. Thank you each and all.*

Prologue

The Day Before Everything Went Wrong

Between Capitol City and Dead Rik's Outpost, the ride had been long. The caravan of wagons arrived a day early, yet there had barely been time granted for a quick bath and a stretch for road-worn legs. Katia was already in the back of the last wagon and ready to move on. She sat in a cushioned rocking chair, her booted feet resting upon a locked box she'd peeked inside the day prior.

The lock provided yesterday's entertainment. Not surprised, she found the lock absent of spring-loaded blades, poison-coated needles, or even false bottoms hiding secret documents. Inside the locked box was a ledger with the neatest handwriting signing well-documented exchanges. There was no money inside—nothing but an expensive lock to challenge a good thief with no reward for the labor.

Katia wasn't going to rob the guy, at least not this early in the journey. She took nothing but a close look, as she had merely been curious of what the merchant, Gregor, would hide behind such a tricky lock. It impressed her to see a merchant as cheap as Gregor coughing up the money for such challenging locks, especially being used for nothing but to protect an honest ledger. It took her nearly ten minutes to figure out the right angles for her "key" to slide inside.

That was yesterday.

Having just arrived in Dilligan's Freepost barely an hour ago, the lead merchant was now expecting to leave before dusk. The next leg for the caravan would take two more days to reach Faradell Pass, then two more days to reach Pikonom Freepost, and finally two days to reach the Portown of Magistrey. If it were possible, the lead merchant would shave off another day of travel.

Gregor the Third—his full title—had permitted a ten-minute bath before calling the drivers to prepare the caravan for travel. Three drivers, four guards, Gregor, his secretary, another merchant named Ucilius, his wife and their two children, and lastly, Katia, were all hurriedly bathed, re-dressed, and back in their places.

Rocking gently in her chair, she was ready to go, but the others were still dawdling. From where she sat, she heard some of the caravan guards joking with the drivers between shrill screeches of Ucilius's kids running around somewhere out of sight.

Her eye caught a reflection in the glass, and it turned out to be her own. She glimpsed the blue scar running from her right ear to eye and then up to her hairline. Focusing on the blue tattoo in the window, she still saw the slave from Athania looking back at her.

Making a funny face, she pushed her fingers into the wooly hair sprouting atop her once clean-sheared head. Shaving was the custom of Athania. Her mother had showed her how when she was a child, and she had since kept with the Athanian tradition, being one of the only things she kept from her birthplace.

She rubbed the top of her head, disliking the feel of her coarse hair. Like the slaver's tattoo scarring her face, her hair was another part of Athania that would never go away. Beyond the window's reflection, more motion caught her eye. Adjusting her focus though the glass and into the general store, she saw Gregor's partner, Ucilius, paying for baths as well as the food for the next leg of their journey.

Outside the wagon and to her left, she heard a muffled voice calling, "Kat, are you here? Kat?"

To her surprise, she recognized the caller and quietly called back, "I'm only purring if you're petting, my dear."

The rugged-looking caller came into view. He wore a black vest over a long-sleeved white shirt that was stained with three days' worth of dust. His shoulders were thick, and the dirty white shirt seemed creased by the muscles concealed beneath. Blandly, his black hair shined oily with long sideburns joining his mustache. Dark eyes preluded a deep meanness.

Awaiting his approach, she calmly asked, "Stileur, what are you doing here?"

"Know that Darren is watching out for you," he said quickly. "I didn't expect to catch up with you here, but Darren said that if I found you to tell you we've got you covered. Just complete your assignment."

"What is going on?"

Still staggered by the death of his friends in Capitol City, Stileur blurted out, "Trevex is dead. It is too long and weird to tell you the whole story right now. That priestess you ditched in the woods? She hired a couple of heavies, and they're looking for you. I passed them somewhere on the road, but don't worry, Darren's gotta good plan to stop 'em right here."

The door behind Stileur opened, and Ucilius stepped outside. Katia tilted her head in the merchant's direction, giving Stileur a fair warning as her tone changed, "Well, it looks like we are leaving now; it was nice talking to you."

Turning, Stileur peered at the richly dressed, thirty-something merchant. He was wearing a brocade jerkin of olive green with gold threading, and there were elegant, lace ruffles wrapping his wrists. As Stileur saw it, such a show of wealth was a promise of easy prey. Stileur looked down at the merchant's scrawny little legs—like string beans in skin-tight, avocado pantaloons. By drastic contrast, it appeared as if the little guy had tucked a small melon under his shirt.

Stileur gave the shorter merchant a menacing stare before slinking away from the wagon. Katia stifled a grin, watching Ucilius jump from the unexpected display of hostility. Katia read the startled expression crossing his face as he advanced.

"Friend of yours?" he stated nervously. His hair had been cut near the scalp from the tops of his ears down. Up top, brown bangs remained long and had been greased back and parted on the right. A shallow nose accompanied by closely set eyes gave an impression the young man had been punched hard, and his face had never depressed.

What a pussycat, she thought mockingly before replying with an ice-coated tongue, "He looks at you dirty, and you think he's my friend? What does that say about us, Ucilius? I'm deeply hurt. I thought you and I were nearly in bed together?"

Stammering, Ucilius replied, "Errr, ummm. I'm married. Ummm, my wife and love…"

"Easy, easy. No worries," she interrupted. "Look, that soldier… he was off-duty and lookin' for love. I shot him down like you just shot me." She pursed her expression to make a dejected and wanton face.

Offering a nervous chuckle, "Well, then—I guess that explains it."

Observing the merchant's tight lips, Katia knew that Gregor must want something. The Third could never ask for himself. Ucilius looked deep inside himself, and not finding the courage or tact to tell her, he finally blurted out, "Gregor is concerned that if we have problems on the road, you won't do your part."

She thought, *I should slap the stupid right off your face.* Instead, she replied by saying calmly, "I don't understand what you are implying. I've paid a very generous amount to ride in the back of this wagon all the way to the Portown. Has there been some problem with spending the gold I paid for my ride?"

"No, no, no. Not that." Verbally, he scampered backward. "Gregor is concerned that if bandits attack, you won't help fight."

She snorted. "Is your wife going to fight? How about the book-keeper? Will *she* fight?" Ucilius held his hands up in surrender, reminding her that he was only the messenger.

Katia nodded slowly while easing into the cushioned rocker, "Well, you tell Gregor I'll do what I got to do. Nothing more, nothing less. I paid for this ride; do I look like a slave?" She paused before adding, "I dare you to answer that."

Ucilius stammered, and Katia stated resolutely, "I owe him nothing. He can give my money back and pay *me* some on top if he thinks I'm here to protect His Highness. You hear me, Ucilius?"

"It's okay. Don't get so upset." He kept his hands up while saying, "I'll tell him what you said. I'll tell him you'll do what you have to do. He'll just have to accept that as a 'yes'."

Chapter One

Day Eleven, 8:00 a.m.
The Day It All Went Wrong

Wynkkur had predicted rain would come, but it wasn't a far stretch for the imagination. Bruised and heavy, the clouds rolled across the sky since before dawn—ready to burst. Now, the rain fell over the valley and foothills at a gentle rhythm. At their elevation in these mountainous foothills, each dampening drop made it feel colder. Behind them in the lower valley, smoke curled like a tiny, black ribbon from the woods and into the background of ominous clouds.

Having reached the crest of an overlooking hill, the four riders took advantage of their elevated view. Miles behind them, they watched where Dilligan's Freepost burned. Sitting atop a black mare he'd stolen twice, Raenyl shook his head while looking in the direction from which they'd come. An Elvish longbow rested over one shoulder aside his backpack and quiver. Shaking his head again, words accompanied Raenyl's motion. "I can't believe it. Twice now, in the same week, I'm riding away from another burning building."

Priestess Popalia had never approved of the archer's unlawful skills, even if they were partially responsible for helping them escape from death—twice. Four days ago, to escape a violent situation in Capitol City, he'd broken into a livery and stolen the very horses they now rode. That was the first time their steeds had been stolen. This fact contributed greatly to why the freepost now burned.

Pointing at the priestess, Raenyl, the half-elf, objected, "Since I've met you, I've killed two hyorcs and a dumb boy, not to mention your good pal Stileur this morning. I've had to escape a burning building and break out of jail to dodge a death sentence." He held up four fingers. "I've been with you *four* days."

Popalia shook her mane of curly, red hair before pulling the hood of her white robe up and over. Around her neck and fitting inside nickel-eyelets, a blue silk ribbon ran the length of her robe's opening, tied together with a silver sash. As she tucked her hair underneath her hood, she also watched the smoke from atop her tan and white horse. She responded calmly to Raenyl's accusation. "Wynkkur and I were doing fine without violence and thievery before you came along. Don't try to pin this on us. Beyond Wynkkur's sword, we haven't any other weapons, and we were protected by the shield of faith."

Wynkkur rode upon a small messenger pony and stayed behind the others. He saw the smoke well enough from where he sat. Being a full-blooded elf, he stood nearly the same height as Popalia. Defensively, he said, "What would you two have done, hmmm? I didn't have too many options to choose from. It isn't Popalia's fault that Stileur set us up." Wynkkur emulated Raenyl by holding up four fingers, "Twice in four days."

The fourth rider present was Seth. Seth's steed, a powerful workhorse, would have been too big for any of the others to ride, but the steed fit the burly warrior well. His armor was crafted mostly of leather but had been reinforced at critical areas with iron bars and small plates. Seth wasn't the best armorer, but the modifications he'd added had kept him alive through a fair number of fights.

Adding to the conversation, Seth denied Popalia's claim. "The gang of thieves in Capitol City came with you, not us." Seth watched where the rain fell harder—right above where the smoke was starting to break up. Pointing at Wynkkur, he added, "Now that I'm thinking about it, it was *you* who started the fight back at the bar where we met."

Lightning arced from the sky to the distant plains as Popalia defended the elf. "If either of you had been in Wynkkur's shoes, you'd have done the same thing."

Raenyl shrugged. "Pick a fight with two hyorcs? I doubt it."

Seth nodded, enthusiastically agreeing with the priestess, "Yeah, you are probably right. 'Ascolan's Stick'. Ain't I right, Raenyl?"

Raenyl laughed, finding humor within his brother's statement. Not understanding, Popalia asked, "What is Ascolan's Stick?"

Grinning, the big warrior answered. "The orphanage where we grew up was called the Ascolan Home for the Wayward."

Raenyl's chuckle stopped, and he tried to explain. "Bane's Blood. I forgot all about 'Ascolan's Stick' until you mentioned it. That was the orphanage slogan, their mantra. They told us that truth is absolute and never divided. 'The truth sticks when the false slips.' Their philosophy was if Ascolan's wayward kids obeyed all their rules, they would be made strong."

Seth scoffed. "Stupid philosophy and stuff. It was actually the opposite. We'd break a rule, they'd beat us with a stick, and we got stronger. But god-pound all that bullshit, I'm just saying I'd have done my own type of damage to get you free, bro."

"Whatever," Raenyl snorted while pointing at the dark streaks in the distant sky where the rain could be seen falling out of the clouds. "That fire will be out soon thanks to the rain. Just look at it coming down. Commandant Benning and his Regulators are going to want revenge. I'll bet he is the type that will chase us all the way to land's edge...uptight prick."

"Bah!" Popalia waved her hand at Raenyl, dismissing his pessimism. "They'll be too busy rebuilding their barracks to chase us. We are the last of their problems."

Seth laughed, "Yeah, not to mention they'll need to go find all their horses before they can give chase. I'm agreeing with Raenyl, though. Let's put some distance between them and us."

Raenyl nodded. "Word will travel fast. We need to get through Faradell Pass before our reputation arrives. I doubt we'll be so lucky next time."

Wynkkur chuckled. "Well, since we released all their horses, word can only travel as fast as it can walk."

Popalia looked at the half-elf and said, "Raenyl, you need to believe me. If we can recapture Katia before Faradell Pass, we might never see another Regulator." Her eyes fell again to the shrinking cloud of smoke rising above the tree line in the distance.

Bitterly, Raenyl added, "I'm tired of thinking about the past and the pile of trouble that is following us. We're gonna need to stay ahead of a giant shit-wave to get this done. Once we have Katia, we'd better be holding your damn healing rod next."

"Do you have to use such foul language all the time?" Popalia criticized.

Raenyl turned his horse and looked up the side of the steep mountains, late spring snow still held high on the tip-top peaks. Unsure where Faradell Pass would be, he knew he couldn't see it from his current position. Instead, what he saw before him was an impassible wall, cold and eternal.

Frustrated by his thoughts and annoyed with Popalia, Raenyl replied, "Fifty pieces of gold will not make this mess go away. Your church will embrace you as their savior, Priestess Popalia. My brother and I, we're dead meat." His finger pointed in the direction of the smoke. "Very painfully, we will be left to pay your tab, again."

Wynkkur said nothing. He rubbed the side of his pony's neck and watched Popalia. Seth spoke up. "I can't pay for this. This isn't even our tab. We certainly didn't start it, so why should we pay for it?"

"Well," Popalia started to say, "sitting here on the road and looking behind us isn't going to solve any of our problems. Don't discount the power of the Great Mystery. As I see it, we're not dead, yet. When we get Katia, she can pay, because all of this is on *her* tab—she and her pal, Thorgen."

One of Raenyl's pointed ears poked up through his blonde hair, "You're just using us, now. My brother might be dumb enough to fall for your tricks, but I know what I smell upwind." The half-elf set his horse in motion.

"Don't call me dumb, Raenyl," Seth followed. "I know what is upwind, too."

Chapter Two

Day Eleven, 9:00 a.m.

Shivering, Popalia rode at the back of the line. It was mid-morning of the eleventh day since leaving her monastery. The rain remained steady, but not heavy. Raindrops glazed the road, wetting its surface and creating plenty of muck. Mud stuck to the bottom of the horses' hooves, coming off in clumps as they walked.

Seth, who was only a few horse-lengths ahead, peered over his shoulder at the priestess. He slowed for her to catch up and mentioned, "Cold, eh? This weather, it was so nice, yesterday."

Her hood dripped water, and her shoulders were soaked. Clean, white robes were what her church expected. Her robe bore mottled patches of dust, darkening as the cool water spread. Her lips appeared a shade paler. Shivering, she replied with a hint of amusement, "You want to talk about the weather? Okay. Yeah, I didn't see this coming. I should have bought a bigger pack at the market and stuffed more robes inside."

He rubbed the long stubble on his chin, "The rain is a little colder than I like, but I needed a shave and a bath. All I need is a little soap." Then, after a light chuckle, he admitted, "I didn't really want to talk about the weather. I just noticed you were cold, and I thought it was something we had in common."

Popalia giggled, "Thank the heavens for common ground. If you look real hard, you might find we have even more than 'being cold' in common."

He smiled and gave her a flash of blue eyes. "How hard would I need to look?"

Whatever intimate interest Seth had interpreted turned like an arctic puddle. Like the wind dropping from the peaks above, her voice chilled. "I am a priestess. You should look in other places for what you imply."

His smile faltered, and he looked away. "Sorry. Sometimes all I see is a pretty woman. I forget you have promised certain...ah... activities to your god."

"That's a little off the track, Seth Ascolan." Popalia shook her head. "I have not promised those activities to anyone or anything. I abstain. What I have received in exchange for my abstinence seems pretty fair. This is why I honor my commitment."

Seth admitted, "Well, I can honestly say I never want to live without sex. It is the greatest thing ever made."

Popalia smiled. "I agree absolutely. You have found even more common ground. Even without having had it, I agree that sex is the greatest thing ever made. Desire shared by a couple is among the highest blessing of the gods. All life comes from sex. People would never know the love for their children if they didn't first have sex."

"My parents forgot me in an orphanage," Seth reminded with a cool tone. "I love sex, but I don't want children. If producing children is the reason for sex, then I wouldn't have any, either. I think that's just dumb."

"I believe you," she acknowledged, "and many people probably even agree with you. One thing is for certain, if everyone agreed with me, there would be less children and a lot more priests and priestesses in the world." Grinning while thinking herself as clever, she tried to explain in a different way, "I believe that sexuality is a blessing. I've reserved that blessing in exchange for others, seeking greater favor from the Unknown Host."

Seth smirked, "You think the newer blessing is better than the one the gods have already given you?"

A green eye peeked up from under her wet hood and at the larger man, "Back when we were in the cell, it was you who said it best."

Seth's blue eyes flashed with curiosity, "What did I say? I say lots of things."

"You asked Raenyl if I could miss something I've never had." She paused as Seth remembered. Seeing recognition on his face, she added, "I don't miss what I don't know, but I know more than what you might think. You'd be surprised by what I know." She teased intentionally.

Seth nervously patted the neck of his horse as he said, "Well, I can't think of any blessing greater than sex, and I'd never give that up."

Popalia firmly stated, "Well, I suppose that is the end of our common ground."

Seth grinned uneasily and nodded. He pulled his horse ahead, and Popalia chuckled, "Hey, wait. I was just teasing you."

Seth slowed, "Oh, yeah. I know." He rode quietly, keeping his eyes forward. The soft rain pattered in the leaves of the trees and thudded against the road, adding more mud and deeper hoof-prints.

Changing the subject for one less tense, she asked, "So, Seth. What do you think of our current predicament?"

"Right now?" he asked. "Well, I think we are going to get Katia. She is on this road, and we are going to get her. That is what I think about right now."

"I didn't mean, 'What do you think we're doing?' I meant, "What do you think about how we got here?"

Seth gave an odd stare to the priestess. "Do you mean, spiritually, how did we get here? Like, heavy-thinking-stuff?"

"Are you avoiding my question?" she asked, slightly annoyed.

"I don't know what you mean, Popalia. I look at the space around me, and I decide if I am still alive or not. I'm alive right now, and I act or react—right now. I don't have time to dwell on old times. The past was bad, and I saw that elf turn an out-of-control fire into a firestorm. He burned that inn to the ground. Even if the lady who owned it was a bad lady, we didn't know it at that time. That is what I think of the past."

She nodded. "I don't think he did it intentionally. Wynkkur is my temple's wilderness guide. He is not a wizard. He'd told me learning magic was purely an accident. His excommunication from his tribe followed shortly thereafter. I do not believe he lit that blaze on purpose."

"Popalia, I only know what I saw." He held his hands out and smirked.

"Well, we are all in a bit of trouble over it. This is for certain," Popalia compromised.

"So, you really think this magic stick is going to fix it all?" Seth asked.

"You are referring to LeSalle's Grace as a magic stick?" Popalia watched Seth nod. She nodded slowly and replied, "To return LeSalle's Grace back to the temple would afford us many allies. You would be co-inheritor of the blessing from Grace. That is the blessing I am seeking. Do I think it will be a fix-all?" Seeing she had Seth's complete attention, she admitted honestly, "I don't know, but I have faith. You should have a little too."

Wynkkur held his hands up and out, loudly calling to everyone, "Stop, stop. Let's stop over in the grass and get off these horses for a minute."

Chapter Three

Day Eleven, 9:15 a.m.

Wynkkur stopped along the road, where the grass grew knee high and thick enough that their shoes would not get muddy. He tried to pull his foot over the saddle. His inexperience with riding showed while dismounting clumsily from the pony. Before escaping Dead Rik's, he'd only ridden on the back of the priestess's horse. Thoroughly awkward in his dismounting, he was pleased with managing to not fall.

Raenyl watched patiently, a grin stretching wide. Amused by what he saw, the archer asked, "Why are we getting off our horses?"

"I'm tired of being cold, and I'm going to dry off," replied Wynkkur. "The rain will be stopping at any minute."

Popalia rode her horse aside Wynkkur's, exclaiming youthfully, "Me first!" Using the front of her soaked hood, she wiped the last of the dirt from the jail cell off her face.

Raenyl and Seth remained mounted as Raenyl asked, "Why would you think it's about to stop raining?"

"You're half an elf. Is your nose too human to smell the change?" Wynkkur had not meant to be insulting, and despite the harsh-sounding words, the elf's tone reflected his intention.

Before him stood a youthful girl with chill-pink cheeks, her freckles mostly obscured by flushed skin. Wynkkur touched her shoulders while wording his quick spell. From the top of her hood down to the bottom hem, water and dirt repelled outward from Popalia's robe, beading before falling into the grass and leaving her instantly clean and dry.

Popalia thanked him before getting back upon her horse. Wynkkur crossed his arms to grip the rough wool of his gray robes. Speaking the words of magic, the water and filth that had soaked now splashed away from his clothing. He then called to Raenyl, "Come on. You are next."

"I'm telling you, this rain isn't—" Raenyl started to say but stopped mid-breath as the rain eased to just above a trickle. Raenyl looked around. "Well, that is weird."

Wynkkur shrugged. "The only thing weird is that you couldn't smell it." He looked at the half-elf. "Rain comes in three scents, *K'lyl* is the before-smell. Many humans can smell it, even if they don't name it. *Pah'lyl* is just rain-smell. *Ein'lyl* happens just before the rain stops." To encourage Raenyl off his horse, he clapped his hands and called, "Come down and get dry, so you don't freeze to death."

Raenyl didn't have the same enthusiasm as the priestess, but he got down, allowed Wynkkur to dry him off, and climbed back upon his horse. Wynkkur looked at Seth next. "Come down here," he requested.

Seth shook his head. "Uh-uh. It isn't natural. I don't like Popalia's magical food, and I don't like magically dry clothes, either." Seth ran a hand through his soaked brown hair. "Come to think of it, I really don't like magical *anything*."

Popalia sighed audibly. Repetitively, she had tried explaining that the food she offered was blessed and not magical. She knew no magic. By her request, her deity blessed their meals so that one bite would nourish the body for a day. It was not magic but a gift. Wynkkur shared in Popalia's frustration with the stubborn warrior.

Wynkkur shrugged. "It will be very uncomfortable to ride in wet pants all day. You'll probably get a nasty rash."

"Wank, I haven't forgotten about being blind only a few hours ago. What if drying my clothes is like stopping the fire back at the inn? I certainly don't want to explode in a ball of flame."

With both feet planted, Wynkkur stood his ground. "Your blinding was your fault for looking. My spell worked perfectly in blinding your guards. You should be pleased that I didn't have to kill or maim them. I promise our problems would be a lot worse if we'd killed any of the Regulators. Could you have done better if our shoes were exchanged?"

"Shoes?" Seth looked confused. "My feet are way too big for your shoes."

Popalia corrected, "No, Seth. He means if he was in jail and you were outside the cell."

Seth sat back in his saddle, replying with, "Okay, sure. I knew that. Well, I would have warned you I was gonna flashy-flash."

Wynkkur smiled warmly, "Flashy-flash? How could I have warned you without warning the guards? I barely had time to cast the spell."

Seth rocked from stirrup to stirrup, peering down at the smaller elf with judging eyes. "Okay, I agree. Killing the guards would not have helped us at all, but the fire at the inn? That was too much, man. It was out of control."

"Don't call me man." Wynkkur's voice grew sharp. "You can call me lots of things, but don't call me man. As for the fire at the inn, well, that had never happened before, and it was a fluke. I mixed up the symbols in my mind." He paused, then reminded, "Trust me. Making your clothes dry is twenty years of practice. I'd never tried to squelch an out-of-control fire someone spread by splashing burning oil everywhere."

Seth shook his head defiantly, cold eyes peering down at the elf. "You set that thug on fire first."

Popalia cut in. "Hey, you two. There is no reason for this. We are here now, we are all in it, and we need to work together if we want to get out."

Raenyl coughed. "That we are, sister—we are in it deep. Wank, just leave him be. The fire is by fault of Darren's gang. We can prove that with Katia. We'll catch up with her before the next Regulator encampment. Maybe even before nightfall."

"All right, then. Let's get on our way." Wynkkur broke eye contact with the armored warrior in soaked clothing and turned back to his pony. It wasn't that he was backing down. He was merely disengaging. They could pick it up any time after capturing the fleeing thief.

Stepping up to the pony, the small horse kept walking as he tried to get upon the saddle, forcing the elf to hop on one leg a couple of times like some strange dance move. Seth laughed while Wynkkur fought to get his leg over the testy animal. After tossing a dirty look back at the warrior, they were again on their way.

Chapter Four

Day Eleven, 9:30 a.m.

Clogging his nose, all he could smell was smoke and ash. Commandant Saviid Benning cursed in the rain. "Mayhem and madness!" The tall soldier wanted to sit down and catch his breath, but he knew there was no time.

He could feel the rain washing the sweat-salt from his cropped, dark hair and it felt good—a temporary relief. Wearing a grimace beneath his dark beard, he faced the clouds and let the large drops patter against his skin. His tan tunic appeared tiger-striped with lines of ash soaked into drenched creases of his elbow, armpits, and chest.

Fighting a losing battle, he and a skeleton crew of soldiers helplessly watched half of their home-base burn down. Dilligan's Freepost had stood for over forty years. Two commandants before him had defeated more than a few orcish hordes during their time of leadership, and now on his watch half of the outpost had been burned to the ground by one lousy elf. Saviid Benning was certain that this could only be the beginning of a bad week; the worst was definitely still coming. He'd have to own up for all of it. Such were the burdens of leadership.

The downpour had come as a blessing. The mess tent had been reduced to smoldering ashes, and the soldiers' barracks were a burning pile of wood, beds, and lock boxes of the forty soldiers who lived on the base. By pure good fortune, the rain denied the fire from leaping over to the hay bales by the stables.

The blacksmith and livery may have been spared, but where now would he house his men? Adding insult to injury, the escaped brigands had stolen all the unassigned steeds when they'd fled. He couldn't very well expect his own men to sleep in the stables until the barracks were rebuilt. No, the Commandant knew he would need to grovel for supplies from the general store, which was also spared from burning.

With all their food stores destroyed in the ashes of the kitchen and mess tent, he'd need to make a deal with the outfitter and his wife to feed his troops. He doubted there could be more than a few days' worth. It would be four more days until the next supply train arrived.

Commandant Benning called out upon seeing his subordinate, "Captain Snales." Captain Jorgan Snales exited the livery when Benning waved him over. Upon first glance, the short and stalky Captain Snales stood with an odd deformity—his chest looked wedged and boar-shaped.

Hyorc is the official term for domesticated orc hybrids. The expression "half-orc" is considered fighting words with most of the civilized hyorcs. Any orc breed who'd fight for the sake of king and kingdom was wisely referred to as hyorc. The opposite of a hyorc, the true half-orc roamed in the wilderness with the orc clans.

Awaking at the first alarm of the fire, he hadn't time to don his armor but instinctively grabbed his helm before leaving the officer's quarters to fight the blaze. Through the entire morning, his helmet remained atop his head. Through the helm's open face, he looked human, but the rest of his body, covered by clothes, was orcish. The helmet nose guard had been bent two years earlier by a war club, and his nose beneath tweaked in the same direction. Approaching Benning quickly, Captain Snales's eyes carried a meanness that had been bred into him—an anger that started at conception. Clicking his heels, he synchronized it with a quick salute. "Aye, Commandant. How can I serve you?"

"At ease, Captain." Saviid looked around the debris that was once his troops' barracks and asked, "Despite the obvious destruction to our fort, and that our prisoners have escaped, what is our status?"

The Captain stated facts only, "Corporal Maklo and his scouts returned thirty minutes ago. Maklo said he saw the smoke at dawn, and his team is the first to return. Medic Karl is in the stables, and he is badly burned. He says the civilian Stileur pulled him out of the flames after the first silo burst. Private Delgo wasn't so fortunate, and he'd burned to death—also caught in the grain-silo flare. That civilian, Stileur...his body was found at the gate house."

"Stileur's body?"

Snales nodded. "He'd been run through with a spear."

Squeezing the water from his beard with one hand, Benning replied, "The king is going to have my head. It is bad enough to have a dead civilian on my hands, but do you know the two men we had in our jail cell? Those two boys were Seth and Raenyl Ascolan."

"Ascolan," Captain Snales took off his helmet, revealing thick, brown hair that had been cropped short. He looked at the gate as two more scouts rode in, splashing mud across the soaked road and entering into the fort's bailey. "I've heard that name before, but I don't recall it being a bad thing."

"Well, turns out it *is* a bad thing. Those Ascolan brothers have been accused of robbing and killing a taxman north of Capitol City, and the king is very interested in speaking to them."

Whistling, Captain Snales reflected, "This is going to hurt us."

Saviid looked up to the sky, once again letting the rain freshen his face. Wiping his eyes, he said, "Look around, Captain. They've already hurt us. I hope our reputation can survive this, or the Regulators just might be laughed out of the history books."

"What would you like to do, Commandant?"

"Actually, Captain, I'd like to know what you'd do if this was your command."

"If it was my base and my reputation, I'd need to rectify this situation immediately." He tapped his fingers against the helmet under his arm. "They're only a few hours ahead of us. If they are wanted in Capitol City, they wouldn't go back that way, so they must be going east through Faradell Pass. We've got four horses, now. I'd give pursuit, and if they do get through Faradell, we can collect more troops there. We might even catch them sooner than that."

"What then? Arrest them?" Benning inquired.

"No," he stopped rapping on his helmet, "Bring their heads back in sacks. Leave their remains for the crows."

"You think like I do, Captain Snales. When this is done, I'm putting in the papers for your promotion. You will replace me as leader of the Regulators." Benning shook his head, "Once this mess is put back together, I'm retiring."

Snales rubbed his head vigorously, sending up a halo of fine mist. He reset his helmet upon his head. "Well, Commandant, I'll follow your lead until that day is done. How do you want to do this?"

"I must see to this personally. It is the only way to rectify the situation. Captain, I would like for you to come along."

"Yes, sir—indeed, sir."

"I'm placing Corporal Maklo in charge of watching the base until Sergeant Brody arrives. I have a few letters to write. With those letters, the Corporal must go to Capitol City to find a contractor to rebuild the barracks and a new mess hall. I also want the Corporal to inform the church about this priestess and her elf. We're going to need the church's understanding, since we are keeping her head." Commandant Benning continued, "We're taking those two bone-head privates, Joab and Clause. They are going to make this right or be dismissed from our ranks."

"Do you want to leave Brody in charge of the base?"

Benning nodded. "Yeah, I can't think of anyone better for the task."

Captain Snales chuckled and sarcastically quipped, "Brody will be pleased to inherit this mess." Saluting again, Jorgan added, "I'll have our horses ready as soon as possible."

"Good, Captain. I want to start chase within the hour."

Chapter Five

Day Eleven, 11:30 a.m.

Everyone rode at a fast trot. The road had swerved away from the side of the mountain and ran through a valley high in the foothills of the Glitchnod Mountain Range. Raenyl was determined to reach Katia before the caravan reached the pass. No one knew how close or how far the pass might be. They did not even know if the road split or if there were any signposts along the way to announce distances. So, they hurried without abusing their steeds.

The woods grew thick and tall on both sides of the road, giving the feeling of walking through a canyon. As the elevation continued to increase, bushy pines became more noticeable within the population of tall aspens. Now that the rain had stopped, the forest was fragrant with earthy scents from the various plants. Refreshed from a good watering, the woods were alive with color.

Suddenly coming up around another bend in the road, it became apparent something was not right. Three wagons sat unattended in the middle of the road, horseless and abandoned. Lying across the road in front of the lead wagon, a tree had fallen.

Raenyl understood what he saw before anyone else. "Shit, this is bad."

Raenyl climbed off his horse before the reality dawned on Seth, who quickly followed his brother's lead. "Get ready to ride fast," he said to Popalia as he dismounted. Pulling out his sword, he added, "This might get ugly."

Crouching, Raenyl held his bow with an arrow set on the string. To Seth he asked, "Want to check it while I cover you?"

"No," Seth reported, "but I guess I'm the one to do it anyway."

"Wait a second!" Popalia called from atop her steed, "This is Katia's caravan. Where are they?"

"Shhh, it's an ambush," said Raenyl, shushing the priestess.

With a weighty sword in one hand, he gripped his dagger in the other. Seth ran toward the back end of the last wagon. Deep footprints plunged into the muddy track as he charged. Mud squished beneath each footfall, then sucked each lifted boot, leaving open pock marks in the track. Pressing himself against the back of the last wagon, he flexed his sword's pommel while waiting for armed attackers to spring from concealment.

Raenyl kept his bow steadily aimed at the open area behind Seth. He waited for something—a sound, a rustle, an attack. Nothing came.

Glancing downward at his feet, Seth peeked quickly into the back of the cloth-covered wagon. Seth turned toward the rest of the group and shook his head. Creeping slowly around the side of the wagon, he shoved a hand through where the cloth covering had been cut open with a blade. He waved within the wagon to show the length of the tears to those who watched. He stood aside the driver's bench. Touching something upon the bench, he then showed reddened-fingers.

"Congealed blood mixed with rain water," Wynkkur deduced before climbing off his pony. He made it down with better agility than the time before. Stepping closer to Popalia, she remained upon her steed.

The woods were silent, except for the distant sound of little birds and the irregular drop of water landing somewhere in the forest unseen. Raenyl watched over both sides of the road with his bow at half-pull on the string and an arrow waiting to fly at the first sign of trouble.

Crouching low, Seth looked beneath the pines and into the woods. Not seeing any feet, his gaze turned up into the trees. Standing back up, he jogged toward the middle wagon. Embedded in the driver's bench, Seth yanked out a warped arrow and called, "Orcs, Raenyl. This was an orc attack. They're gone now, though."

"What?" Popalia expressed her surprise. "Are you sure?"

Seth nodded and Raenyl answered, "Blood remains, but without dead. Bandits always leave bodies, even their own."

"This arrow has a stone tip, and the shaft is warped," Seth added. "I'm pretty sure this attack wasn't done by elves."

"No elf would use arrows like that," Wynkkur voiced to demur. "That is embarrassing. No self-respecting elf would use a warped arrow." Heading toward the empty wagons, Wynkkur moved while holding his robe up at his hips to prevent dragging the hem across the messy road.

Easing on the bowstring, Raenyl put his arrow back in its quiver. "I don't think it matters really. Your Katia is gone, and so is your healing scepter."

"No," Popalia denied, "we are too close to finishing this. We need her to be alive. I'm sure she is still alive."

Knocking knuckles lightly against his head, Raenyl cut at

Popalia with words, "Once again, here is that thing I've been trying to tell you about called *reality*."

Popalia shook her head, "No way, Raenyl. My god did not liberate us from death only to deliver us back to it. That isn't how faith works. Here before us, a challenge is presented by the Unknown Host. The question is do we accept it or shirk away?"

Raenyl disagreed. "Your god did not deliver us from death, Wynkkur did. Wynkkur bought us a couple extra hours of life, and you sold us false hope that I never..."

Wynkkur was staring at the ground by the nearest wagon. "Wait!" the elf called out. "Quit fighting. You are both right, okay. Now, listen to me. I can see tracks here and over there." Wynkkur pointed from one impression in the ground to another. "The rain had covered all of the lighter tracks. I can easily follow what the horses left. If Katia is still alive, I can track to where she was taken."

"No way, I'm not chasing an orcish war party through the woods. Your thief is dead," Raenyl projected, "or worse."

Wynkkur exclaimed with a tone of hope, "Hold on, I got a new idea! You go tell the Regulators that we're really sorry for burning down their base, and we'll wait here for you to return."

Seth noted, "Raenyl, you might be rubbing off on our woodland friend. I think Wank is getting sarcastic."

"Don't gang up on me," Raenyl warned. "I am the voice of reason. Even if you are right and Katia is alive, how are we going to take down a war party? Neither Popalia nor Wank can fight worth a wet turd."

"We held our own with little challenge at the inn," Popalia snapped. "Wynkkur can blind them. Are you capable of handling blind orcs?"

Raenyl hurled back, "Why don't you just dazzle them with your wit? At the inn, we were attacked by boys! I am talking about orcs, not children."

Looking at the elf, Seth's jaw clenched tightly. "I really hated being blinded. I'm going to regret saying this, but how many could you blind?"

Wynkkur shrugged. "How many of them will look? If they all look, I can blind them all. The closer they are when my spell goes, the better their chance of becoming blinded. How many make up their war party?" Chuckling lightly, he added, "It could be the easiest fight you've ever had."

Raenyl's shoulders drooped, a sign of his surrender, "I'm not an orc-expert, but if this had been done by men, it would have taken at least twenty. I'd figure between four and six per wagon plus a couple of archers and the leader. Forty seems too many, too clumsy. A dozen would be very bold." Raenyl passed his eyes over the empty wagons and added, "Yeah, I'll bet two dozen."

Popalia informed the elf, "I remember seeing two merchants and two guards back at Dilligan's Freepost. Three drivers plus Katia, I can account for eight."

"I remember there was a blonde warrioress. There was another mounted guard." Seth rubbed his slightly damp hair, "I'm not sure, but I thought beside each driver was another rider, so that's nine including the thief in the back."

"Seth," Raenyl groaned, "warrioress isn't a word." Then, before Seth could remark, Raenyl turned a shade paler. "I swear I'd seen kids running around the wagons just before we were accosted by the gate guards."

Popalia inhaled sharply, "Oh, gods. I think you're right." Popalia focused hard, trying to remember what she'd seen yesterday afternoon. She nodded, "Oh my god, this is terrible. I remember the children, now."

Wearing a grim expression, Wynkkur asked, "How many do you think were taken prisoner? Of the eleven people, how many are still alive?"

The half-elf shook his head. "I don't have any idea. I don't even know if orcs take prisoners."

Seth threw into the mix, "They cleaned these wagons out. My guess is they put everything upon the horses—dead or alive."

Wynkkur looked over to the side of the road where he saw the ground torn by heavy horse hooves. "If the horses are over-encumbered, we could catch them by nightfall. The few spells I know are far more impressive at night—fire and lightning."

Raenyl sounded hollow, "This is stupid, and we are going to die."

Grimly, the elf replied, "We've been dead since yesterday."

Chapter Six

Day Eleven, 3:15 p.m.

Knee-high, the grass had been trampled and the soft soil crushed, revealing a trail obvious enough that the priestess could have followed while wearing a blindfold. Deep imprints and displaced mud cut across the ground. The valley ended, and the trail began to edge uphill. Looking as though an army had traversed the mountain's side, foot marks blazed an obvious pathway. Despite the clearly seen path, the steep terrain was becoming the more burdensome.

The steep mountainside had forced the pursued, as well as the pursuers, to switchback along the incline. Handling the track with sure footing, the horses traversed with ease, but the riders remained on a nervous edge. If a steed slipped, it would topple and throw the rider to be either crushed beneath the rolling horse or flung downward and into the trunk of an awaiting pine. The grade had become so steep that grass no longer grew—just a slippery shuffling over gravel-like stones.

After the tense couple of hours climbing the side of the steep hill and having reached the crest, they unanimously agreed they deserved a short rest. From here, the view was magnificent. The visibility of the valley beneath opened up with the absence of trees upon the limestone crest. A sharp breeze fell from the snow-covered peaks higher to the south. Popalia shivered before saying, "Without the smoke, it is hard to see how far we've come."

From their vantage, they saw the rolling foothills stretching out to meet the green plains on the horizon. For uncountable miles they saw trees covering the distance to the green fields of grain upon the northern horizon. Wynkkur pointed down and far away, "Is that the road back to Capitol City?"

"Sure," Raenyl answered sarcastically, "and over there is the city of Grissham."

"I've never seen this far before," Seth added with a boyish hint in his tone. "This is amazing."

"Savor it," Raenyl ordered. "This is a one-way trip."

Popalia's eyes sharpened, "Ignore him, Seth. We'll set camp right here with the rescued caravan before the sun sets."

While rubbing the mane of his pony, Wynkkur grinned at the optimistic priestess. "We better hurry, then. The sun will be setting in about three hours."

Seth grunted, "Yeah, let's just get this done. This Katia better be worth it."

Raenyl spun the black filly and began back on the trail, speaking over his shoulder, "These damn merchants better loosen their purses equal to how far we're sticking our necks out for them."

Another hour passed.

The hill's ridge was only sparsely dotted with an occasional tree. In its place, jagged limestone spires speared upward from the soft soil, some thrusting up from the ground equal to mid-thigh, but the majority remained the length of daggers and easily as sharp. The pathway remained obvious. Between the serrated teeth sprouting up from the ground, the prints made by the over-burdened caravan steeds were clear for all to see.

Hearing a din of flies buzzing off the trail, Raenyl stopped his steed. "Uh-oh. That's not good," he said while climbing off his horse.

Popalia looked around. "What is it?"

"Hear the flies? There is only one thing I can think of to attract enough flies to make that much noise."

Seth quietly agreed, "A body."

Raenyl nodded while stepping through the wicked stones. Two more steps, and a black cloud of flies erupted from the ground. Popalia watched Raenyl avert his eyes as the swarm of insects took to the air. She found it peculiar that an isolated limestone spike jutted from the ground the color red. As the swarm spread out, she realized it was more than just the one stone; the entire area surrounding the stone spike was a crimson pool. What she was seeing finally struck her as unintelligible violence. Turning her head to reject what she saw, she struggled against her rolling stomach.

"Oh, gods!" Seth pronounced as he climbed out of his saddle. Raenyl shook slightly as he walked away from the bloodfest left for the flies. Seth called, "What happened here, Raenyl? What is this?"

"I don't want to know." Pale, his eyes showed hollow thoughts. "Don't go there Seth, please just don't."

The big soldier needed to see for himself. "The blood is everywhere," Seth acknowledged. "A pool...a fly-covered pool." His face twisted with horror as he looked back. "How many people does it take? How much is this?"

"No," Wynkkur stated from atop his pony. Steering his pony closer to the paled priestess, he added, "It can't be made by a person, it is too much blood. A horse must have been killed for their evening meal. It has to be. We must be near their camp."

Raenyl looked up at the elf with relieved eyes as color rushed back into the half-elf's cheeks, "Maybe. That makes sense. They've probably set camp near here, unless they plan to run all night. Killing a horse to feed their band makes sense. They killed the poor beast away from their camp, so the flies would stay away. Good thinking, Wank."

"Well, whatever," Popalia began but swallowed before finishing. "This is just gross. Let's keep on."

Snorting, Raenyl slipped a foot into his stirrup and replied, "For once we agree, sister."

"This is a good sign, right?" Seth inquired as he pulled himself back upon his steed. "I mean, we are close. The blood can't be more than an hour old. It is still sticky on that rock and wet in the puddle. We could be done here by sunset. Then, we'll only need to get the stick-thing for Popalia's church."

Wynkkur snickered, "Stick-thing! I've heard LeSalle's Grace called a lot of names, but never that."

Popalia sighed, but otherwise ignored Seth and Wynkkur. "We should be careful. They could be very near."

Raenyl set the pace from the lead once again. "Twice now we agree. I don't know, Priestess, but maybe my good sense is finally rubbing off on you. In fact, I'd say when we get to the edge of this ridge, we scout a little way without the horses. If they're killing horses for food, I'd like my horse to be spared."

Chapter Seven

Day Eleven, 4:45 p.m.

Cutting through clothes and to the bone, a sharp breeze rushed from the mountain's peak as the sun lowered closer to the western horizon. The trees were now almost all pine, swooning briskly, and the cold wind whistled through the needles and branches with a comforting song. From atop the hill's ridge, nothing could be seen through the trees, but the orcs were down there and somewhere close by. Unseen, yet relatively near, a neighing horse emitted a warning from within the valley below.

Waiting in her saddle, Popalia shivered and wrapped both arms about her as the men crept into the valley for a closer look. She stayed behind with the horses, keeping the steeds a safe distance away from the ridge. They would need an element of surprise to keep any chance of rescue possible. She'd mumbled her praises aloud, thanking her deity that it was the orcs' captured horses and not their own steeds neighing. Had the noise been reversed, the chance for surprise would have also been inverted.

Pulling her robe tighter, the ends of her filthy, blue ribbon waggled in the breeze. Her cheeks stung when the wind was strongest, and her chin chattered slightly. She looked at the gray grime along the cuffs of what had once been starched and bleach-white. As a priestess, the higher priests of the Red and the Golden Orders insisted cleanliness was imperative to representing their god. Canon Shertlief's head would explode if he were to see the condition of the robe she had borrowed from the home chapel in Capitol City. Luckily, their paths would only cross if he came to her temple, and the big city priests almost never ventured out to her remote shrine.

From within the valley, a horse neighed, again. Her own steed snorted nervously. Popalia rubbed the mane gently, cooing soothingly as she brushed a hand across the animal's neck. She worried for her allies and hoped the rescue was moving with a blessing.

Knowing the source of her comfort, she began to pray.

Away from the ridge and the piercing wind, down under the cover of swaying trees, Raenyl and Wynkkur moved like whispers. Seth feebly tried to keep quiet, and watched his steps as best he could, knowing he'd never be as natural to the forest as

Wynkkur, nor would he ever be as deft as his brother. Luckily, the wind through the canopy of trees diffused the worst of his tromping. With wisdom learned from past warfare, Seth remained back a few paces. One hand held his heavy broadsword, the other his dagger.

At Seth's left, Raenyl held his bow with an arrow notched upon the undrawn string. The warrior grinned while watching the elf push bravely forward with his little sword in hand. Sure, the blade looked wickedly sharp, but Seth preferred the reach of his broadsword. Undoubtedly, the elf's silver-ribbed blade was a work of art but arguably not a weapon to fear.

Coming down the hill, they didn't need to walk too deep into the valley to find the horses. Raenyl passed Wynkkur, taking the lead while pointing him to take cover behind the trunk of a large, fallen tree. Wynkkur and Seth both moved in the direction of Raenyl's finger and concealed themselves as best they could. Wynkkur eased behind the felled tree, and the warrior slid behind a cluster of saplings. Raenyl pressed himself within the outstretched branches of a thick pine. He tilted his head down toward the lower valley, and the other two looked where the half-elf motioned.

The main war party must have set camp somewhere else. Here, there were only a couple of orcs unpacking eight horses. Short-legged with broad shoulders, the orcs stood equal in height to the average man, half a head taller than Wynkkur. Two thumb-length tusks protruded from their lower mandible, bordering an upturned and moist snout—reminiscent of swine. Their ears showed a similarity to elves, tapered and pointing upward. Unlike elves, the ears of orcs were higher on the skull and covered in coarse, dark hair.

Standing shirtless, the nearest orc wore pants with the leg-bottoms torn away and unraveling. Although its legs were shorter than the original owner of the pants, the orc's legs stretched the fabric. Thick, muscular legs extended from a stout torso. Clawed toes and long nails on hairy, mannish feet braced the ground as strong shoulders hefted a crate from horse to ground.

Unlike the variable outcome of hyorcs, the true-blooded orcs looked very similar in their physical make-up. Coarse, wiry hair—dark like their earthy skin beneath—covered more than just their ears and feet but also ran the length of their neck, covering shoulders and down the length of their man-beast arms.

Muscular shoulders rippled as the orc handed a large, wooden box over to the second shirtless orc standing nearby. Its chest was hairy, comparable to what a man's back sometimes is. Dense, black hairs covered sparsely over ribs and four small nipples. One of the lower nipples had been pierced with a silver hoop. Bulging arms took the wooden crate, setting it aside a tree and atop one of many piles being stacked.

There were several stacks of crates and locked boxes—a caravan's complete content. Upon the ground lay a small pile of looted clothes, rich and discarded like rags at the base of another tree. A hard stone's toss away from the working orcs, the three on-lookers shared a surreal sensation, like watching a dirt floor warehouse with tree branches providing the roof above. The last of the horses had been unpacked. Three wagon loads of materials lay in piles around the open forest, but there were no signs of any prisoners.

Beyond the stack of boxes and crates, a third orc led a nervously neighing horse to where the other unpacked horses were tied to trees by the reins. The horse-leading orc wore hardened leather chest coverings. At one time, the armor had been worn by a man. It wouldn't have surprised Seth to learn that the orc's poor fitting leather armor was a souvenir from a kill—a keepsake more than protective covering. Because of the boar shape of the humanoid's chest, the leather sides under each arm had been cut and then re-sewn, leaving a large area of ribcage beneath the cup-like shoulder pauldrons vulnerable.

Seth crept five paces to stand beside Raenyl. Trying to angle himself into the outstretched branches, he concealed his body as best he could from the sight of the working orcs. He crouched low, but it mattered not, for Seth was not easily hidden. Lucky for the watchers, the orcs were still busy, and they'd remained unseen as long as the beastly raiders continued working.

Quietly speaking so only Raenyl heard, Seth asked, "There is no one here—no merchants, no bald woman. What should we do?"

"By the gods, Seth. I don't know," Raenyl shot back above a whisper. "There are only three orcs. Let's take them down, and then we'll figure it out."

"What?" Wynkkur asked from only a couple paces away. "You want to attack...already?"

Raenyl grinned wide, telling the elf, "We are gonna drop those three orcs. I'll take the orc by the horses, and whichever one Seth doesn't want."

Wynkkur nodded with an uneasy expression, "What do you need me to do?"

Seth, now also grinning, suggested to the elf, "How about you sit and watch. This won't take but a couple a seconds."

Wynkkur smirked while returning his sword to its scabbard as Raenyl asked Seth, "Near or far?"

"Once I charge, I'm going for the closest one. I won't even peek at the other two unless you miss."

Scoffing, Raenyl added, "Stick to the right, and stay out of my way."

Seth pushed himself up and began moving at a soft jog. That jog quickly turned into a fast sprint, a fluid movement for a man so large. Ten paces away from his target, one of the two orcs by the crates heard the thumping footfalls of his charge and called out, "*Bee'lerck!*"

What began as a defiant warning became a pained grunt as Seth saw the first of Raenyl's arrows sink high into the orc's exposed chest. Seth bolted, closing the distance to the turning orc as Raenyl's second arrow found another stopping place in his target. Blood sprayed between warriors and spattered deep crimson across wooden crates.

The body of the first was falling as the second's hand reached toward a hatchet not far upon a crate. The clawed hand gripped the axe shaft as Seth's hurtling body closed the distance. Seth growled, swinging his heavy blade from down low and upward to avoid hitting the stacked boxes and chests. Up under the outstretched arm, the sharpened tip of the broadsword sliced into skin and crushed bone. The hurtling mercenary's heavy body slammed into the orc, forcing the hatchet to be dropped. The orc placed his good arm out to protect its head from smashing into the stack of crates.

Seth used the orc as a brake and took a short moment to regain his balance. Once he recovered his footing, he stabbed viciously into the orc's back as the orc tried to push himself away with his one good arm—the second splintered, useless from the broad blade and from being rammed into the crates. Jamming the thick blade through the orc once more, Seth held the beast under foot until hearing the last breath rattle out from his enemy's throat.

Seth's head spun as he looked up from his prey. A few paces away, upon the ground, lay the other orc—the one filled with Raenyl's arrows punched deep within its chest. Glancing over his shoulder, both Raenyl and Wynkkur remained unseen within the trees. On sure feet, the big warrior made his way around a pile of locked boxes. The horses exhibited a nervous curiosity while watching the mercenary approach. At the feet of a large draft horse lie the leather-clad orc. Deep into its snout an arrow-shaft protruded, the wound still pulsing blood. Seth saw the eyes flicker once then dim out.

Satisfied that all the guards were dead, Seth remained alert and walked back to the orc with several sword-sized holes pierced through its ribcage. While passing the pile of clothes, he grabbed a blue, silk shirt sized for a young boy. Seth began to wipe the blood off his sword, but silk was a terrible choice to clean the blade. He discarded it for a cotton dress sewn with fancy design.

He wiped the sword clean and returned it to the scabbard. His eyes set upon the hatchet at the edge of the dead's outstretched hand. Squatting down, he reached for the hand axe, peeking back to where his brother and the elf remained obscured in the trees. He saw Raenyl break from his position and slip around the tree he'd been hidden within. Raenyl vanished into the foliage as soon as he'd appeared.

Obscured behind saplings, Wynkkur warned, "Seth! Look out!"

Twisting to right himself, standing menacingly before him was a very different type of orc—not one, but two of them. These orcs stood equally as big as Seth, and both wore armor constructed from animal bones deliberately designed for an orcish body. Rib bones and vertebrae of men, deer, and various woodland creatures had been linked together as a primitive style of splint mail. Upon each head were helmets crafted by men. One wore a hard, leather cap and the other's helm was crafted from iron with an open face. The second had been adorned with two hand-length horns curving out over the wearer's eyes, adding a devilish visage to the tusk-jawed swine snout.

Seth looked into the pig eyes of the cap-wearing orc, realizing too late that the three easy kills had only been thralls. The dead orcs were a lower class, and before him stood two of the fighting orc-warriors that the Regulators frequently faced with deserved bragging rights. The orc was clutching a cutlass with a blade dulled by time, but the steel was now fashioned with serrated teeth to compensate. Within his other hand, he carried a shield. It was a round targe surrounded with nine sharpened spikes—protruding along the outer brim.

The second orc held a bone club—most likely a horse's leg, with the beating end wrapped in leather. Nails of varying lengths had been pierced through the leather. Primitive yet efficient, this club's design intended to tear the meat away from its victim before an agonizing death brought mercy. The second hand held a kite shield painted solid white with two thin diagonal red lines crossing the front. The pentagonal steel barrier had aged, and was now paint-flaked and rusted.

Having no time to withdraw his sword, Seth stood and spun while whipping his dagger from its sheath. Slammed while being off-balanced by the flat of the orc's shield, Seth's footing failed. Stumbling backward, Seth's leg caught against the side of one of the crate stacks. The crates didn't budge. Toppling backward, he watched both orcs advance on him. Laid out upon his back, with his feet still hanging in the air, Seth suspected this fight wasn't going to last very long.

Chapter Eight

Day Eleven, 5:00 p.m.

Wynkkur had watched Seth end the life of the first orc as Raenyl dropped the other two with an accuracy that could only have been bested by a full-blooded elf. Wynkkur doubted any human could use a longbow the way Raenyl handled his. He then watched as Seth checked the bodies before cleaning his weapon.

Raenyl admitted beside the elf, "I can barely see from here—too many trees in the way. I'm going to find a better vantage." Raenyl stepped away on quick feet and out of Wynkkur's view.

The elf turned back to watch Seth, surprised to see there were two orcs, bigger than the first three, quickly advancing on the kneeling warrior. Wynkkur warned, knowing it was too late. "Seth! Look out!"

Seth whirled quickly, rising up to the challenge, but short-lived was his defense. The club-wielding orc slammed Seth down to the ground with the flat of his shield. Wynkkur stood from his concealment and into the open as Seth slid backward across the dirt with both his feet hanging in the air.

Wynkkur took control of his breath, focusing his mind upon symbols of magic. Deciding in a fraction to use the lightning fragment spell, he worded the incantation with crisp articulation. Conjured symbols flashed within his inner-eye—three symbols he inherently knew. This time, he added one more symbol at the end of the sequence.

Two fist-sized fragments of scorching, white light leapt from the elf's extended hand. One seared the throat of the orc poised with his horse-leg club high above Seth, and the second hot bolt charred into the primitive breast-plate. Hair-singed smoke rose from fried and blistered skin, resulting in pig-like squeals of pain from the orc as he dropped his weapon to grasp at his seared throat.

Holding intense discipline, Wynkkur noted his experiment had worked. Before the orc could recover his stance, Wynkkur tried again. This time, he used the symbols for *Shock*, *Arrow*, and *Fly* and added the magical word meaning *Compound*. A second bolt flashed from his hand—this one twice as large as the first two. The orc burst aflame for a brief moment as the white-hot electric pulse seared its flesh. Badly burned, the beast-man flung away his red-striped shield, desperate to pull the smoking bone-plate over his head.

Swinging sideways from his prone position, Seth shoved the dagger's tip deep beneath the orc's navel. Seth yanked hard to the side, slicing a hole wide enough to disembowel. Spraying blood showered the rolling Seth, who narrowly escaped receiving a face full of intestines. The gutted orc fell forward with armor worn half over its head. Crumpling upon the ground while howling painfully, it fed the soil with draining life.

The second orc swung his serrated cutlass downward, barely missing the rolling Seth by the width of a slice of bread. With dagger gripped tightly in his hand, he reached with the other for the discarded kite-shaped shield and pulled it over his chest. The jagged sword slammed loudly against steel plating. Swinging again, this time at Seth's legs, the grounded warrior rolled right.

The swing missed again, slamming into gravelly soil. This orc learned fast and slammed a gnarled foot upon the back of Seth's boot. Held tight with his ankle pinned, Seth looked up to Wynkkur with desperate and hopeful eyes.

Wynkkur saw that Seth's end was soon, so he focused on the biggest light-flare yet. He summoned the symbols of *Shock*, *Arrow*, *Triple*, and *Fly*. He spoke the words clear and succinctly, and opposite of what he wanted, three tendrils of electricity sparked outward from his outstretched hand.

Horror and dread rushed in, as did the realization his misspell had cost Seth his life. Seth had been right in his earlier accusation. His magic was detrimental. Panic froze his mind as the flow of energy vaporized immediately. Like a fragile bubble popping, his magic retreated to nothingness.

With blood from the first orc dripping down his brow and into his short beard, Seth's eyes of hope hollowed into a face of doom. Fruitlessly kicking out with his free foot in hopes of breaking the one that was pinned, the aim of his foot lashed out clumsily. Seth tried rolling over, his dagger still in hand, but he knew the sword was coming.

Unexpectedly, the weight of the orc's foot came off Seth's ankle, and he was released.

Through blood-stung eyes, Seth saw Raenyl's boots atop a boulder barely twenty paces to his right. With Seth lying on the ground, the archer's shot was wide for the taking, and Raenyl didn't even bother aiming. Seth skittered forward, pulling himself on his elbows and knees as the orc above him fell backward with a vicious sneer under three-inch tusks. A single arrow pierced through the leather cap, clean through from orc ear to orc ear. Gravity pulled the last orc down beside the other three bodies, sprawled in a tangle of lifeless limbs along the stack of crates.

Rolling into a seated position, Seth's thanks were interrupted as Raenyl barked, "I turn my back for a couple of seconds, and you almost get killed." Anger dripped in the half-elf's words.

Seth stood up. Dirt and leaves were stuck to his blood-covered hand and dagger. "I looked over the area and thought we were alone."

"Perhaps you should leave the thinking to me," Raenyl degraded. "Your best thinking will get you dead!"

Wynkkur defended Seth by adding, "Keep your guard up. It isn't his fault. I think those two orcs were invisible."

Raenyl rebuffed with a snort, "Invisible orcs."

Looking from side-to-side, superstitious Seth muttered, "Witch doctor."

"No way," Raenyl debunked, his tone a little softer. "Maybe they came out of a tree."

Wynkkur moved toward Seth, but Raenyl remained upon the boulder, holding an arrow loosely against the string. Seth set the dirt-crusted, bloody dagger upon one of the crates and unsheathed his broadsword. Cautiously, Wynkkur walked around a cluttering of locked chests, speaking mostly to himself, "How do you see the unseen?"

Dryly, Raenyl teased, "Isn't that Popalia's expertise?"

Ignoring the half-elf's snide comment, Wynkkur's eyes followed the footprints of the orcs. The ground showed scuffs where more than two orcs traveled. Many feet had previously rounded a bush and tall pine. "I see a trail," the elf added as he circled the piles of boxes.

Seth closed in from the other side of the boxes and Raenyl remained stolid atop the rock, "Hey, if I can't see either of you, I can't see them."

Seth kept moving and circled the tree and bush, exclaiming, "Brother of Bane! It is a cave. It is a hole in the ground with a ladder down into lots of darkness."

Wynkkur took two more steps to stand next to the warrior. In the ground at Seth's feet was a hole bigger than if the warrior stretched his legs and arms out wide and lay outward. At the lip protruded the end of a rusty iron ladder. The hole went deeper at an angle, an angle promising only darkness. Wynkkur expressed, "Lo'Lyth's Grave! That's where those two orcs came from!"

Raenyl leapt from the rock and jogged closer, standing behind Seth. "Well, that would explain *invisible* orcs." Raenyl craned his neck behind them and said, "Gods pound all this. Let's take these extra horses and get out of here while we still can."

"What about Katia?" Wynkkur asked. "Popalia won't leave without her."

"Are you kidding me?" Shaking his head while rolling his eyes, Raenyl then added, "Okay-okay. I realize you aren't kidding me. Go get her, and we'll wait right here. If anything pokes up and out of that hole, we'll clunk it good and hold this area."

Looking from warrior to warrior, the elf turned his eyes to the bodies strewn about the ground opposite the crates and chests. Nodding, he left to retrieve Popalia. The elf never once looked back and headed up the hill to where the priestess was waiting.

Seth watched him disappear into the foliage before saying, "That is one weird little guy. Does he talk funny to you? I think he talks funny."

Shrugging, Raenyl removed his backpack and stepped up to the locked chests. "You watch that hole. I'm going to get into these chests. Shout if you need help." He set his pack on the ground.

Seth had a different plan. "Why don't you watch the hole while I drag off the bodies?"

Raenyl pulled from out of his pack a soft leather toolkit. Maple brown leather was wrapped around and over itself, then tied secure by a string in the center. The archer untied the leather knot with his fingernails while explaining, "I'm going to get into these chests. If we are lucky, the orcs stuffed the bodies of their captives in these chests, and I'm going to find them. If Popalia's god really deals in miracles, then Katia's head is in this box...or that box over there."

Seth shifted from watching the hole to looking at Raenyl, and then back again at the hole. Perplexed by deep thoughts—thoughts that were deeper than what Seth liked thinking—he finally asked, "Why do you want her to be dead? Don't you want to get out of this mess?"

With the leather case rolled open by his feet, several locksmith tools fit snugly in tiny leather eyelets. Withdrawing a probe, Raenyl answered Seth without judgment, "Look, I realize you're sweet on the girl, but we should face some facts together. She is a celibate priestess from a backwoods monastery, and we are in the deepest pile of shit we have ever been in. This '*Katia*' is dead, and the sooner Popalia gets it through her stubborn skull, the faster we can stop chasing ghosts and get back to surviving."

Seth nodded, "I agree, brother. We're on a nasty hook. We need to get out of Regulator territory, but if Katia is alive, she can clear our names." He paused before adding, "Or at least clear us of the mess back at Carouser's Inn and maybe even Dead Rik's. Bane's Blood! If she is alive, I'll beat on her shaved head until she gives us an honest confession. We are going to be hung without a fair testimony, and you know if she is still alive, we are still alive."

Tapping the lock pick against his open palm, Raenyl added, "Man, that priestess has you spun around her little finger."

"Do you really think Katia's head is in that chest?" Seth inquired with genuine curiosity.

Raenyl looked at the narrow point of the steel probe and sighed, "No. I think Katia's dead body and the rest of those dead merchants are in that cave. I think we should take these horses and some of this loot and ditch those two. Her church will save the both of them, but we're as done as a ten-copper whore."

"I heard you the first time! I'm not deaf, you know?" Seth repeated. "Popalia will get a pass, and we'll burn. I heard it already, but what if we *can* save those people? Wouldn't the end be different?"

Raenyl cursed before saying, "Hope is a four letter word." Raenyl surrendered to the warrior a little bit. "Help me retrieve what arrows I can from the dead, and I'll help you hide the bodies. Then, you can help me pick these locks and stash anything we can sell later."

Chapter Nine

Day Eleven, 5:30 p.m.

Wynkkur's breathing tore raggedly. "We...found a hole...in the ground...Orcs attacked...Seth...phew, I...this hill is too...steep."

Popalia fought against her own impatience. "Slow down, and catch your breath." She stayed upon her horse, keeping the reins of the three other steeds in her hand.

"Is everyone all right? I heard the sounds of battle below."

The elf nodded as he tried to calm his breathing. Withdrawing a water skin from his buckskin sack on the saddle of his pony, he squeezed a little into his mouth. Swallowing then returning the skin, he said while panting, "That hill...I know why they sent me...too steep." He looked up at Popalia. "Yeah, they are all right. We killed five orcs and found...their horses. Eight of them...eight horses."

Popalia felt dizzy for a moment as she asked, "Any survivors? Human survivors?"

Wynkkur shook his head, "No, but we didn't see...any dead, either. There is a big hole...in the ground. I don't like it...and I don't think Raenyl is too...pleased with this discovery."

"Of course he isn't." Her impatience won the inner struggle. "Well, let's go then, and let's hurry before it is too late."

Finally catching his breath, he urged, "Wait, Popalia. There is something else." He fit a foot into the stirrup of his pony and pulled himself into the saddle. "My magic backfired like it did back at the inn. The symbols got jumbled, and the spell altered. Seth almost died because of it."

"He is all right?"

"Raenyl saved him before he was harmed, but it was too close for my liking. We cannot have my craft backfiring in our time of need. My magic will get us killed."

"No, your magic has saved us many times," she rebuked. "Our lives have become the situation abnormal. Tell me what happened, and I'll ask the Mystery to guide you."

Wynkkur retold the battle as carefully as he could, trying not to linger on the details, but telling enough to paint a clear picture for the priestess. He finished the story by saying, "I tried to command a piece of lightning to strike the orc with three times the intensity, but instead, a fan of lightning burst from my hand like long fingers. It was reminiscent of what happened at the inn when I'd tried to temper the flames."

"Wynkkur, I'm sorry I don't understand. I will pray for the Mystery to unveil your secret, though." Curling her lips and displeased by her own answer, she continued, "I wish I could be more help than that, but your abilities amaze me and are vastly beyond my comprehension. I am sorry."

With a frustrated and accepting sigh, he replied, "No, don't be. I don't understand it, either. I am all alone with this—I always have been. I guess I should pray to Fenyll as well, since he is the source of elven magic." Offering a subtle grin, he complimented, "Thank you for being honest. It is better than giving false advice."

"Well, so far this adventure has been quite humbling. I've taken a few good kicks in my pride. With a couple more kicks like yesterday, I'll reach enlightenment before my next birthday."

Wynkkur chuckled while leading down the hill to where the mercenaries were waiting. Popalia first spied Raenyl crouching in front of a locker. With lock picks wiggling, he cursed under his breath. If Raenyl heard the horses coming behind him, he'd made no motion signaling his awareness. Wynkkur suspected the curse he muttered was this acknowledgement.

The warrior brother stood atop the far pile of crates. Seth had cleaned the orc's blood from off his face and his weapons. Watching toward the cavern entrance, he protected while Raenyl worked the locks upon the chests to no avail.

Popalia realized what the archer was attempting to do and asked, "Raenyl, what are you doing? Are you looting the prisoners?"

"Damn these locks!" he cursed. "I've never seen locks so complicated. I can't break inside even one of them."

Seth shot over his shoulder, "He thinks Katia's head is in the box."

"It is possible," Raenyl grumbled. "I need more sunlight to see inside the hole. The sun is too damn low for me to pick these god-pounded locks." Looking up at the warrior, he ordered, "Seth, hit this damnable thing with your sword."

Shaking his head, "It'll chip my blade, and I got a good, sharp edge right now."

"Use the blunt part. Just bash it good."

Still shaking his head, Seth added, "Use *your* sword. You got one, too."

Quietly, Raenyl whispered a foul word only Wynkkur's sensitive ears heard. Popalia stopped riding, but remained upon her steed. Looking around the area, she asked, "So, where is this hole?"

"It's over here." Seth motioned with a twist of his neck. He started down from his elevated post as both Wynkkur and Popalia climbed down from their horses. Seth held a closed fist toward Wynkkur. "Here. This is for you."

Wynkkur looked at the mercenary's fist, which was twice the size of his own. "A fist? For me?"

"No, Wank. Open your hand," insisted Seth.

The elf opened his hand, and Seth did the same. A white, translucent stone wrapped in an amber hue fell between hands. A milky white stem dominated one end of the water-smoothed stone. The milky-white ran through the stone's core, but half of the stone was enveloped with deep, golden crystal. The stone was as long as his little finger and about as thick as the knuckles of his thumb. "Pretty," he said while rubbing the soft stone between his fingers.

"It is yours," Seth admitted. "I'd be dead if not for you. Thanks."

"Really? Thanks, Seth." Wynkkur admired the citrine quartz. "This would sparkle nicely if there was more daylight. Where did you get this?"

"The dead orc we killed together. I kept its silver. I hope you don't mind."

Shaking his head, Wynkkur replied, "Not at all. Where are the—"

Looking over to Popalia who stepped near the cave mouth, Seth cut off the elf. "Hey, Popalia. Don't get too close. Two big uglies came up outta there, and pretty fast, too. Ain't that right, Wank?"

Wynkkur asked again, "What happened to the bodies?"

Raenyl stood up and kicked the locks on the chests, cursing loudly. "God-pounded master locks!" He kicked the lock, again. "Ouch! Seth! Didn't one of these damn orcs have an axe?"

From a few paces from the hole in the ground, Popalia shushed, "Do you have to make so much noise? We might still have the advantage of surprise without all this yelling."

Barking at Popalia, he did lower his tone a little. "I'm not going down there until I know they are still alive."

"Sadly, Raenyl," her face conveying genuine regret, "we cannot know if they are alive until we go inside."

Raenyl snorted, "By 'we' you mean brother and I, right?" Pointing toward the pile by the tree, "Seth already found bloody clothes in the pile over there, women's clothing to be specific. We don't even know if orcs take prisoners, I'd bet the odds they're all dead."

Popalia stepped away from the hole, "Women's clothes, like a dress?" Seth nodded, and Popalia shook her head. "Katia isn't the dress-wearing type of girl. I promise you Raenyl, the bloodied clothes are not Katia's."

Speaking through clenched teeth, Raenyl calmly repositioned. "How do you know? You were with her for barely two days before she got away from you."

"As a woman, it took me about ten seconds to assess Katia's style. She doesn't wear dresses, not ever. It'd be about as likely for her to wear the robes I wear." Not removing her eyes from the ladder jutting from the dark hole, she saw the bottom even with the shrinking light. "As for 'sending' the two of you into this cave alone—no chance. Not without me and Wynkkur coming. We are doing this together."

"You know what?" Raenyl laughed. "Come to think about it, Seth and I *will* go alone. If you and Wank get yourselves dead, who will pay us for sticking our necks out?"

Popalia shook her head within the hood upraised, "I'm the best insurance you have of getting in and out of there with your lives. It is not my time to die, yet. Both of you will be protected by the Nameless if you escort me."

Raenyl growled, "Grrr! You are impossible."

"And you are doubtful," she shot back. "Quit filling your cup with bitter wine, and refill it with faith instead."

Seth chipped in, "Don't worry, brother. I won't let anything bad happen to you."

Popalia grinned. "The Great Mystery will protect you as well, Seth. Wynkkur, what do you think?"

Staring down to the bottom of the ladder, Wynkkur answered, "It is a fitting place for Katia to be. It smells terrible in there, like over-ripe meat and old shoes. We've found Lo'Lyth's Grave—a place reserved for the damned." Calling over to the half-elf, "Raenyl, believe me, I want nothing to do with this cave. I just want to go back home. Escorting pilgrims through the woods is plenty of adventure for me. I'm sick of all of this, and it can end right here, if we are careful."

"This is so stupid." The archer shook his head, "We are going to regret this, all of you will see." Raenyl unrolled the leather casing to reload his lock picks. As he returned his picks to their proper holders, he commented, "Here is the only compromise—and there is no other way I'll go in there. Seth leads, I cover Seth. You two stay behind me, and Wank stays in the back behind all of us. If more than three orcs get within torch-throwing distance, Wank uses his flash spell to blind them. At the first sight of orcs, no one turns around, or else they get blinded." Rerolling the leather case, he held a cold stare with the priestess.

She nodded with a soft smile, "I agree. We will reassess our plan once we have freed the prisoners."

"What will we do about light?" Wynkkur asked.

Seth spoke up, "We found a couple torches on the orcs we'd searched. It'll get us a couple hours of light at least."

"I doubt it will take us an hour," Popalia stated optimistically.

Raenyl, the voice of pessimism, added, "If it takes that long, we'll be dead or dying soon after."

"I doubt it," she rebuked. "I'm not saying this is going to be easy. I'm only saying we will succeed. I do think we should leave our steeds unrestrained in case we come out of there running." She watched Raenyl smirk with his disdain before mentioning, "If it makes you feel better, I'll ask the horses to wait close by for two hours."

"You can talk to horses?" Seth scoffed incredulously.

Wynkkur chuckled. "She has a gift with animals. When she was a child, she would hand feed pine nuts to squirrels and chipmunks. More than once, a bird has chosen her shoulder as a perch."

Walking to where the orcs had tied the caravan horses to a couple of trees, she replied, "It scared the holy ancestors out of me the first time it happened. I think that silly bird was more startled by my panic than from where it had chosen to land. When it happened the second time, I realized my spiritual bond with animals." Looking back at Seth, she confirmed, "I can't really talk to them, though. Not like I talk to you."

Raenyl laid it right out, "I don't believe you."

"I know," she said while untangling the ropes that bound the workhorses to their trees. "But when we come out, and these horses are waiting to take each prisoner and all of us swiftly away, you will know then that the Nameless carries you in his hands. You will then believe me."

Each horse, as Popalia released it from its bonds, gave the

priestess thankful nuzzles. She bushed each mane once or twice, and when she'd finished, she went to the steeds they'd been riding. She wrapped their reins around the saddle horn, and again received what looked like kisses from each horse. It took her less than two minutes to free all the steeds and return to where Wynkkur and Seth watched over the hole. Popalia opened her hands at her sides, "Let's pray before we go."

Wynkkur took her hand then offered the other to Raenyl. The half-elf shook his head. "No way. I'm not talking to nothing for nothing."

Popalia stuck her other hand to Seth. "An unexpected blessing can't hurt, Seth."

Uncertain, his eyes darted to Raenyl. The half-elf smirked, and Seth shrugged. He took the priestess's small hand in his rough grip. He offered his hand to Raenyl, who shook his head once again. Wynkkur took the warrior's hand.

Popalia prayed, "Great Mystery, we need you to push back the shroud of darkness and bless us with light and illumination, so that we might best serve you. Don't forget Raenyl, even if he rejects you. Thank you. We accept your blessing." She released the hands she held.

"Hmmm, that is weird, I feel...eased," Seth remarked as he looked to Raenyl for acceptance.

Snorting, Raenyl scoffed, "You are such a—" Seeing that both Popalia and Wynkkur also appeared less burdened by stress, he paused, "Well, whatever. Let's just go."

Chapter Ten

Day Eleven, 6:00 p.m.

Looking up from the bottom of the ladder, Seth saw beyond the tips of the pines where once gray clouds swirled, appearing fuchsia in the sun's falling light. Their reflections promised deeper shades of dark to come very soon. The ladder's bottom was only ten feet from up top, but it felt like a mile. Seth reached back up as Raenyl released a lit torch. Catch complete, the burly warrior turned to face the black hole leading deeper into the earth.

Raenyl whispered down, "I'll be right behind you."

The tight space amplified Raenyl's words.

He nodded and turned to the hole in the earth. A couple more steps, and Seth would know darkness like few people ever will. The cave was carved into hard limestone jags covered by earth and had been supported and intertwined with snake-like roots from the surrounding pines. Many of the roots were cut away and shortened, but the tall blades-man was still forced to duck lower beneath the supporting stone.

Two thick lengths of log were wedged at either side just inside the cave mouth, giving more support to the entryway. The space between the two wooden pillars seemed to open like a throat belching foul air. Seth stepped into the narrow passage and paused. Catching the spoiled breath of fetid air full in his nose, he pushed the torch forward and bravely followed the light.

The causeway stepped down every two paces at a modest downgrade. Keeping the torch out before him and squeezing into the passage, he shuffled deeper and around a corner where the light gave way to a larger room.

Keeping eyes and ears sharp, his free hand rested atop the hilt of his weapon. One scuffle of foot upon stone floor or any motion caught in the torchlight, and the blade would rip free from its scabbard. The room was empty of orcs. No sounds scuffed and nothing darted. Regardless, dark shadows played at the fringe of the flame's range.

Tightening upon his sword's grip, Seth entered the small room. The torch led the way, pushing the darkness back. At the far corners, shadows slithered in the shifting light. Beyond the occasional scraping of his boots over rough ground and the occasional pop and fizzle from the burning end of his torch, the only sound was an ominous silence.

The light revealed three walls of the room without portals, but the furthest wall opened a passage deeper into the darkness. Sounds drifted steadily from behind him as he screened the items in the room. Popalia's voice echoed teasingly from outside the cave's mouth, "Raenyl, are you standing there for a good view up my robes?"

She was making too much noise. Seth ground his teeth together while noting chairs pushed out from under a table against a wall. Upon the table, a glittering twinkle bounced torchlight, and Seth stepped closer. Behind him, insult rang through the halls with his brother's voice, "Fine, come down without help."

The sparkle had arched from a pile of silver coins—six of them. Closer still, Seth saw a pile of copper coins mixed with what looked to be light brown beans. He scooped the silver and copper to the side of the table.

Hearing the soft steps of his brother's feet approaching, Seth spoke above a whisper, "Your voices are loud in here. Hurry. Scoop that coin, and put it in my pack." He waved the torch over the coins to catch the glitter.

Raenyl was quick to grab it up. As he put it in Seth's pack, he whispered, "This is where your invisible orcs came from. It looks like they were playing some sort of game. Here." Seth heard the coins clink inside a pocket of his pack. They'd both left most of their gear on the horses outside, bringing only the bare essentials.

Seth projected, "Aye, now all we need is these merchants to be real close, or something. We should check out the other hallway. It could be storage or a treasure room." Something caught the corner of Seth's eye, and his gaze shifted, but nothing was there. "Damn it! I hate the way this light makes the shadows come alive. Let's wait here for Wank."

As if Seth's words were a summoning, Wynkkur and Popalia entered the small room. Seth passed his torch to the priestess. He immediately regretted handing the light to Popalia, for the shadows grew longer and seemed edgy, now appearing more menacing than before.

Raenyl stepped back, his bow ready with an arrow notched on the string. The torch's light reflected off the walls, illuminating sparse furnishings. Still, the archer kept his eyes locked on the dark passageway leading somewhere beyond the little room.

Wynkkur held the second torch and looked around the room, "I don't like this. I think this room is natural." Holding his torch above the table's top, he asked, "Hmmm, are those beans?"

Seth was nodding, "Yup-yup, they're beans."

Raenyl added, "What do you mean by natural? Like, they didn't dig all this out?"

Wynkkur picked a bean up and rubbed it between fingers. Dried beans. He tossed it back to the table before replying to the half-elf, "The walls are solid stone not dirt. So yes, that is what I mean."

The elf set his torch on the table, and the flame's light dipped to a dull flicker, leaving only Popalia's flame for them to see by. Quickly opening his buckskin bag at the table's edge, he slid all the beans off the table. Behind him, Wynkkur heard Raenyl ask, "Why did you take those beans?"

"If we get tired of eating a bite of bread and carrot, we now can add a bite of bean to our meal choice." Wynkkur smiled, thinking he was clever.

Seth eyed Wynkkur and made an ugly face, "Orc beans? I'm never eating orc beans. Yuck!" He stood back up and added, "Who knows what they did to those beans."

Wynkkur's smile fell as he looked at his bag, then back to Seth. "I didn't think of that. Guess I'll take them out when we set camp, tonight."

"Seth, did you see this barrel in the corner? It is filled with torches," Popalia quietly called. "Do you think we should take some more?"

"If we plan to keep on this hunt, then yes," Seth was quick to answer. His quiet voice bounced around the echoing walls, "Stick as many as will fit in our packs, then light another one for my hand. I want my own light."

Popalia handed her lit torch back to Seth as Raenyl whispered, "Wouldn't you rather keep both your hands free for fighting?"

"I can't fight if I can't see," Seth replied with subdued attitude. "I've gone from blind at Dead Rik's to being blind in a stupid cave."

"Cave? If we are lucky, that is all it is." Picking his torch from off the table, Wynkkur's light expanded, again. His voice shivered with a deeper apprehension, "Pray—even if you don't have a god— you'd better pray we haven't found Lo'Lyth's grave."

"Yeah, whatever that means," Raenyl mused darkly. "With this barrel of torches, it's safe to assume orcs also need light. It makes us even, and we'll see them coming."

Popalia commented from behind the archer, stuffing his half-full pack with torches, "I don't like how quiet it is down here. My whispers echo."

"Count your blessings, sister," Raenyl stated as Popalia filled his pack with a couple more torches. "Maybe we can actually get out of here without too much trouble."

"Was that optimism?" Popalia quipped. "If you'd like to pray for a speedy exit, I'll pray with you."

Seth stood by the westerly passage, "Let's just go. Sooner we find them—dead or alive—the sooner we can get out of here."

Seth led with his torch into the downward passage. As they pressed on, they noticed the floors had been scraped of obtrusions, and the walls had been chipped smooth. Seth's shoulders nearly rubbed against the sides of the cramped space, his head bent with a crook so as to not bump the ceiling. Fighting in such confining quarters would be fatal. He couldn't swing his sword. His elbows already nearly grazed the sides of the walls.

Behind Seth, dread filled Raenyl as he recognized his brother blocked 80 percent of his view. If orcs came from deeper in the darkness, it would be harder to miss Seth than hit anything else, not to mention the challenge of finding space to use his bow. Longbows were never designed for tunnel crawlers.

From the back of the line, Wynkkur griped, "I don't like this; we are making too much noise." The only sound was the scraping of their feet and an occasional tiny rock being kicked down the tunnel. The air felt thick and heavy, its weight oppressive and echoing every soft sound any one of them made. Smoke from the torches bounced along the top of the shaft, slowly making its journey to the outside world behind them.

From the front, Seth informed, "There is a wider offshoot from this tunnel coming up on the left."

"Take it," Raenyl ordered.

"Hey," Popalia's tone rang agitated, "Don't I have a say?"

"Not this time, sister," the half-elf addressed. "We can't fight in this tight of a space. We need more room."

"Well, for the record, I would have said to take the path of least resistance. Let the will of the Unknown guide us. So, I would have said go left."

"Shhh, it would be nice to hear the orcs first, instead of helping the orcs hear us," Seth reminded sensibly. Seth's uncharacteristic wisdom bore enough truth for both archer and priestess to fall silent.

Seth led the way into the wider pathway. He felt it more than he heard it. Bouncing off the walls, there was a faint vibration—a sound from deeper in the wider cave. He stopped as did the rest of the group behind him. Eye contact between brothers said all that was needed.

Raenyl nodded and said barely above a breath, "I can hear it, too. I wonder how far it is."

Several paces forward, the sensation grew into a rolling squall of multi-tonal echoes. Silently creeping closer still, Raenyl heard with clarity as soon as Wynkkur factually stated, "Swine."

"Orcs," Raenyl corrected. "You all stay here. Hand me a torch so I can see. I'm going to scout forward since I'm the sneakiest."

Seth agreed, "Since I'm not sneaky, I'll stay right here."

Popalia thought aloud, "Don't you think they will see you with the torch?"

Raenyl's voice gruff, he barked while whispering, "Maybe, but if I can't see what might be on the ground in front of me, there is no way I can be sneaky." He dropped his backpack by Seth's feet. "Right now, it's either Bane's Blood or Fortune's Kiss. It's about fifty-fifty as I see it. Damn these odds right down into the Abyss."

"You both keep saying Bane's Blood. What does this mean?" Wynkkur asked. "I don't understand."

Seth handed the elf's torch to Raenyl and said, "You're kidding? I thought you were kidding last time you asked. Doesn't everybody know Bane's brother?"

"What a clever diversion," Raenyl muttered while moving away. "You three keep making all the noise."

With that said, all chattering stopped. They watched Raenyl continue up the path with a torch burning in his hand. It did not matter how quietly he moved, the light he needed screamed far too loud. Up ahead a little ways, the tunnel curved to the left. Around the bend, the half-elf slipped out of sight, but the reflection of his light stuck to the cavern walls a lot longer.

Chapter Eleven

Day Eleven, 6:15 p.m.

Raenyl moved steadily on soundless feet. The tightness of the cavern seemed to be intensified by the radius of his torchlight. He hated the damn torch, and he hated this damn cave. If anything waited in the shadow at the end of his light, his silence would be pointless. "Damn this stupidity," he muttered under his breath.

He'd travelled beyond the bend maybe seventy, or a hundred paces, when his thoughts struck him. *Why hadn't they ditched the stupid and annoying priestess*? The two of them should have split as soon as they'd seen the empty caravan. *Good luck, priestess, but we got to go...*but here he was–down in this rotten cave and looking for dead people.

Arguing with himself, he knew exactly why he was here. The priestess had manipulated all of them into this shit-deal. They had good reason to run for their lives. The Regulators would come for them. You can't burn down a military base without retaliation. It was like smacking a beehive with a stick—you were going to get stung.

Raenyl looked deep within himself. Shaking his head, he knew Seth had been right. He knew if there was only one survivor from that caravan left in these caves and he and Seth just walked away...

No, that weight would be far too heavy to carry. Even if his last day was approaching soon, thoughts like that would haunt him until his final sunset. His conscience had dragged him here. Popalia only fanned the flames.

Conscience did not stand alone; there was also the terrible seed of hope. Once again, the fault lay at Popalia's feet. Curse her and her feeble hope. The variable promises of "what if" rattled in his mind; Seth had made it clear *what if* also bounced around in his own skull. *What if* Katia was still alive? *What if* Popalia's church could free them from their death sentences? *What if* crawling in this damn cave could alter their inevitable fates?

Raenyl did not believe one bit of it. It was a steaming pile of dung—all empty promises—and Popalia was leading them to their deaths. *But, what if*? They certainly couldn't go backward. They could not go by way of Dead Rik's and on back to Capitol City. That truth could not be abandoned, no matter how desperate his need might be. So, *what if* forward is the only direction to move?

Raenyl stopped and glanced over his shoulder. He may have come 200 paces or 2,000, but he'd never know. The torchlight's radius ended at around thirty paces. By the closing sounds of orcs ahead in the distance, he knew he'd better do something with the torch. He didn't think they were coming though. They sounded stationary.

Aside him, he noticed a narrow fissure in the cavern wall at eye level. He set the torch handle into the crevice space where it could hold the torch for him. He knew it was impossible to use his bow and hold the torch at the same time, so maybe leaving the torch here would keep the cavern lit as he crept forward.

"Bane's Blood, this is stupid," he whispered while leaving the torch behind. After ten more paces, he realized that the torch's light traveled further than he'd expected. He could actually see at a further distance than he could with the light in his hand.

After forty paces, he was comfortably in the shadows, while the torchlight continued to cast a minimum of reflection across the gray walls. Granted, anything in the cave ahead of him would see his silhouette like a cut-out target, but the soft light eased his mind, letting him believe he was hidden.

Ahead, he saw a soft wavering light of a deep-red hue. The light ahead seemed to drench one wall of the cavern. The pig-like squeals of the orcs added a hellish ambiance. Close and clear, Raenyl knew there were several orcs in the space ahead.

He could smell burnt pine and something even sweeter on the air. Sliding against the wall, he could still see by the far fringes of his own torchlight. Was that beef or horse? Did orcs eat swine? Raenyl's mouth began to salivate. He hadn't had a good cut of meat since the night the priestess had become his problem. Mixed within the smoky scent, he distinguished meat cooking over an open flame.

Deep in the shadows, feeling forward along the wall, Raenyl was careful nothing fell over. Sliding his feet softly so nothing knocked across the walkway, he moved slow, fearful a tiny pebble could echo down the long hall and call unwanted attention to his presence. He looked backward again, relieved he'd left the torch so far behind. The light now served as a candle along a windowsill showing the way home on a dark night.

Slowly easing another ten paces, he gained a little better orientation. The red wall was light reflecting from within a larger cavern. Only a few more steps, and the wall he crept along fell away and down into a bigger, fire-lit cavern. The pathway he followed continued beyond the exposed trail where another black-mouthed tunnel waited, swallowing deeper into the sunless unknown.

Approaching the fall-away wall, Raenyl duck-walked the last few paces until he saw down into the cavernous room. Peeking with one eye around the wall, he saw the room easily could fit a hundred orcs. Below, the cavern glowed, alit by three widely spaced fire pits made up mostly of glowing coals.

Many orcs were gathered but not close to a hundred. Counting quickly, he saw eight ugly females, each with four swollen breasts; Raenyl observed some must be nursing mothers. Eleven little orc-offspring scurried in the low light, not including the rare orc baby tied in furry carriers that rested on a hip within breast range. Raenyl counted six males within the room—two of them being the big warrior types. Upon seeing the little orcs and the nursing offspring, hair stood upon the back of Raenyl's neck. This was no raiding camp—this was the raider's entire tribe.

A female with a crying baby on her hip tossed a log onto a fire. By the fire's light, he saw through the murky smoke trapped in the high ceilings of the big room. Smoke used the tunnels as an exit out. Raenyl looked down below at the nearest pit. Aside a pile of wood at the nearest fire laid a naked and bloodied body of what his mind defined as once being a young woman. It looked as if her chest had exploded outward, and one breast was a mangled mess.

Raenyl felt his heart leap. He'd first thought it was Katia, but then one of the larger orcs lifted her over his shoulder. Long, dark hair fell from the lolled head. One of the female orcs brought over a long, iron bar. The woman hung like deadweight, and the stronger orc strained to support her battered body as the female orc tied the woman's hands to the top end of the iron bar. Once done, horrified Raenyl watch as the dead woman's feet were tied to the bar. Another male, one of the smaller males, was setting two forked poles into holes on opposite ends of the fire pit.

Raenyl's mind began to flitter as he understood what was happening. The smell of cooked meat all made sense, and he felt instantly sick. Looking further toward the back fires across the room, other bodies roasted over their own personal fires.

There was only one thought in Raenyl's mind. They had better be far away before this tribe added them to tonight's meal.

Chapter Twelve

Day Eleven, hour 6:30 p.m.

Whispering, Wynkkur said to Popalia, "This is crazy. We should go look for Raenyl."

Popalia answered, "He's only been gone a few moments."

He sighed, "Are you sure? It seems like we've been waiting forever. I might not understand Bane's Blood or know his brother, but I know about Lo'Lyth's Grave. We are at the cusp of madness, and we should leave mother's grave while we still can."

Seth stood his ground. "Not without Raenyl, but to ease our wait, I'll tell you all about Bane if you tell me about this grave you keep saying."

"Speaking, not saying, Seth." Popalia grinned, thinking how she'd become Raenyl's backup when correcting Seth's poor speech. Remembering Seth as being a terrible storyteller, she offered, "Seth, would you rather I tell it?"

"Naw, I can tell one of the Bane tales. I even know which one I'll tell." Seth looked both ways into the darkness, "If anything comes though, I'll need to stop."

"If anything comes, I might run." Wynkkur also looked from dark cavern to dark cavern. "Keep it to a whisper; I've had enough of orcs giving us the surprise."

Seth sneered menacingly. "If an orc comes, we'll make our stand right here. I'm not leaving Raenyl. Got me?"

Reluctantly, Wynkkur nodded, so Seth continued, "Well, here is the story. Bane was a man with great ideas and big dreams. One day, Bane dreamed of being the greatest fisherman. Living in a fishing village on a lake, there were many great fishermen, but Bane's dreams were much bigger."

Popalia interjected, "Hold on, Seth. Let me explain a little bit to Wynkkur. All the stories about Bane begin like that. Bane is a folk-tale character. He isn't real. All the stories about Bane begin with Bane was a man with great ideas and big dreams. Bane can be a cartwright, a blacksmith, a farmer. Anything a man can do, so Bane can do, understand?"

Wynkkur asked the priestess, "Why haven't I heard any of these stories?"

"These are cultural tales with no religious origin. The church wastes no words on hearsay and folklore. The church leaves such fancy for the commoners. We have sacred text to commit our memory—not folk-tales, understand?"

Seth huffed, "Can I tell my un-churchy story?"

"Sorry, go on."

"Bane went to the village docks where the fishermen had gathered for the day. One man held a net weighted with stones at the edges. Throwing the net into the water, he pulled the net out and there were two fish within. The next man had a spear and stood upon a rock, still and waiting. As a fish swam by, the man thrust the spear into the water, impaling the fish. Then, Bane watched a man in a boat, and clutched in the boatman's hands was a stick with a string. The man jerked upon the rod, pulled a fish out of the water, and into his boat. Bane was impressed that with nothing but a stick and string, the man caught a fish. For the whole day, Bane watched as the boatman pulled fish after fish from the lake into his boat."

Seth paused, "Do you have any water in your bag? This story-telling stuff makes me thirsty."

Wynkkur retrieved the water from his bag, and Seth drank. Handing the water back, Seth added, "Keep that on top. I may need more soon."

"What about yours? Where is your water?"

"I'm saving my water for when I'm not telling you a story. Call it payment or storyteller tax. Anyhow, as the fisherman came in to dock for the evening, Bane went to the fisherman and praised his amazing accomplishment. The fisherman pulled a hook from a fish's mouth, explaining to Bane how the fish had been caught. This gave Bane a great idea. That night, Bane went to work in planning how he'd become the greatest fisherman ever."

"The next morning, Bane woke up before the fishermen had gathered to start their day. He went out upon the lake in the fisherman's boat while the rest of the villagers were preparing their nets. Bane had designed a hook as wide as his hand, and for his bait, he used half a slice of ham. Throwing the ham into the water, he shouted to the fishermen upon the shore, 'Watch as I catch the biggest fish in this lake!' And the fishermen watched."

"There was a bubble. A big bubble burst, and then there was a tug on his line. Bane yanked his string as the lineman had showed the day prior. He felt the hook snag, but the fish was too powerful, and Bane was pulled out of the boat. Bane had done it—he'd caught the biggest fish in the history of the village. Bane held tight, and the fish dragged him down deeper into the lake, and no one ever saw Bane, again."

Seth bowed his head before saying, "That is it. That is a story about Bane."

"That's it?" Wynkkur stated incredulously. "That is a dumb story."

Popalia chuckled, "They are all like that. The point is that Bane is a fool. Bane's Blood, or Bane's brother, is an insult, claiming the accused as being akin to Bane. This is the other reason why you would not hear the priests of the monastery speak such expressions."

"Yes, I understand, now, but I still think it is stupid."

"It isn't stupid. It tells us sometimes we just got to let go. Sometimes, the prize is too big. Well, anyhow, you now owe me a story about some grave." Seth motioned to Wynkkur with his hand, "Gimme some of your water first. I'm really dry after all that storytelling."

"What? Get your own water. I need my mine, since I have a real story to tell you."

"Come on, Wank. Don't mess around, and gimme some water. Mine's at the bottom of my pack under all the torches, and it is hard to get at while I'm armored."

"Look, squat down, and I'll get your water for you. I need mine."

"Come on, Wank!" Seth teased. "You don't need that much. Look how tiny you are compared to me. Popalia will use her god-magic to make it bite-sized like she does with carrots and bread. Besides, your water tastes better than mine."

"Shush you two!" Popalia whispered. "There's light coming from the tunnel Raenyl went down."

Both Wynkkur and Seth looked to the cavern Raenyl had traveled down. Seth withdrew his sword, and Wynkkur did the same, but the elf stepped back to give Seth room.

Raenyl came into view from the nearest bend. "I heard you talking from way up in the tunnel. How every damn orc in this place hasn't heard you surprises me." He looked to Popalia, adding, "Let's get out of here while we can. This suicide mission is over."

Popalia's head spun with hearing this, "What? Did you see Katia?"

The half-elf stammered, "I—what I saw—forget it, let's just get out of here. This isn't a war party, this is the *tribe* of the war party." Raenyl passed the priestess and kept moving toward the exit. "I'm out of here now, as I should have left you after finding that caravan this morning. Stay for dinner if you want. Come on Seth, we're going."

Popalia stood her ground as Seth looked from Raenyl to the priestess. She rebutted, "Did you see her? If she is dead, then hope is lost, and I cannot believe the Great Mystery would leave us without a lead."

Raenyl did not stop. He led the way, even if no one followed, yet. Speaking over his shoulder, he added, "Do whatever you want. I'll tell you what I saw. I'll tell you when I'm on my horse and away from here. I'm leaving."

Popalia looked to Wynkkur with a frustrated gaze. The elf understood her plea but stated, "I'm sorry, Popalia. Being here is courageous—and stupid. The Unknown will need to find another way to get LeSalle's Grace." Then to Raenyl he said, "Wait up. I'm coming with you."

Seth shrugged, "Me too, brother. Me, too."

"I can't do this alone," the priestess added as she followed the big warrior.

Raenyl snipped, "You're not alone; your god goes with you."

Popalia growled her displeasure but followed all the same. Seth invited her to get in front of him as he stepped into last place. As she passed, he claimed, "You have to admit, this was a bad idea."

Saying nothing, only offering a frustrated smirk at Seth, she held her torch high and followed the fleeing Raenyl.

Chapter Thirteen

Day Eleven, 6:15 p.m.

"Well, doesn't this just make everything worse," Commandant Benning said to no one in particular, his eyes scanning the sight of the stripped and abandoned wagons sitting horseless in the middle of the road. "Private Clause! Private Joab! Ensure our security. Captain Snales, stay at my side."

Dismounting quickly, both enlisted soldiers started their parameter sweep. Unstrapping his shield from off his back, Private Arty Joab pulled his sword from its scabbard in one quick movement. Wiry and light, the soldier moved with a purpose.

Being a seasoned Regulator, he'd expected a raise in rank to Corporal up until seventeen hours ago. He'd been with the outfit for six years—ever since he'd turned nineteen. Having been in three battles alongside the Regulators, he'd gained some respect among the officers, up until a few hours before dawn.

When the Ascolan brothers had been captured with their gang, the elf had escaped using magic. He and Private Clause were ordered to protect the three prisoners until the elf was found. Everything changed for Private Arty Joab when that damn elf blinded him and Private Clause. They'd found the elf all right, burning down their base and setting the prisoners free while they both fumbled around sightlessly. By the time their fellow soldiers came to the jailhouse, both Privates were locked inside the cell and the prisoners were long gone.

Private Joab did not like being the brunt of a joke. He believed that the elf blinded the two of them, because they were watching his bandit friends. Arty Joab didn't understand the word "irony," but he understood "humiliation," and he did not like having the ground whipped out from under his feet.

The mystery to him was how the elf had gotten the drop on him. He was a seasoned Regulator, but it didn't matter now—fate's gale-force winds had stolen his promotion like a Dandelion spore. More than he wanted his lost promotion, Private Joab wanted an elf's head on a stick. It would serve as suitable redemption for his flattened pride.

On the other hand, Private Eugene Clause was not a seasoned

Regulator. He was twenty years old and had not yet established a reputation to have it lost. He'd been with the Regulators for barely over two months. Hired with great promise and expectation, he'd failed and embarrassed his entire outfit.

Eugene, a handsome young man, kept his face shaved clean and his thick, chocolate hair groomed short and even. Where Joab had earned a little leniency, and always appeared slightly unshaven, Private Clause shaved daily, his rotund cheeks presenting a boyish look, all but in his eyes. Eugene carried mean eyes. They were honest eyes, but beneath his youthful features he hid a deep, unsatisfied cruelty.

Holding his spear at the ready, Private Clause charged into the forest thick, knowing if he failed now, his short career as a soldier would end. He'd joined the Regulators for the promised opportunity to kill lesser beasts, and having just missed his opportunity to kill an elf, he'd been humbled—but only a little.

He knew how deep his trouble was with the Commandant. He'd been told to go back to his father's pig farm if he couldn't properly atone. Orcs and pigs may look similar, but killing a dumb pig with a mallet wasn't the same as impaling a beastly orc on the end of a sharp spear.

To keep his chance to kill orcs, he must first kill a slippery elf. Less than a man, but more than an orc, Private Clause looked to the challenge with relish. Especially since the elf they hunted had already bluffed the entire garrison.

From atop the saddle of his horse, Commandant Saviid Benning watched as Private Joab crossed the road before vanishing into the underbrush. Shaking his head, he conferred to Captain Snales, "How much you want to bet this caravan is the same one the Ascolan brothers were after? I got ten gold that says this caravan is the same one that left Dilligan's, yesterday."

"I'd be a fool to take that bet, sir." Dismounting, Captain Snales turned to where his battle axe was attached to the back of his saddle. "Do you think the Ascolan brothers did this?"

"Unfortunately, I doubt it," Commandant Benning projected. "This is by far the worst situation for our needs. The brothers Ascolan are opportunists—they'd continue fleeing up the road. They know their only chance for survival is to get through the pass before our messengers arrive."

Jorgan Snales unhooked his axe from the leather sheaf that covered the dual wedges. Holding the long shaft in both hands, he gave his commander a snide grin, "Only we haven't sent messengers to Faradell Pass. They probably ride like the sparrow flies."

"We need to catch them before they get there." Commandant Benning cursed, "Dammit! This complicates everything. I should have brought more men."

"We could send one of the privates back for a squad to investigate this while we go after the brothers."

"I'd send you back if that were the case. Those two bone-heads need to make up for letting that firebug embarrass us." Commandant Benning's tone humbled. "Honestly, Captain. I don't think I can take down the brothers without you."

Captain Snales grinned from ear to ear while setting his axe over his shoulder. "You give me too much credit and not enough to yourself, sir."

Watching the thick woods where the two privates had disappeared, Commandant Benning doubted, "I've been leading our army from an office for five years, Captain. Your hands know the grain in the haft of your axe. My hands haven't felt steel in five years. My sword arm is so rusty, it squeaks."

Encouraging with his wide grin, "It's like riding a horse, sir. I'd bet my life that your blade hasn't forgotten the feel of your hand."

From one side of the empty caravan, Private Joab called, "All clear." Private Clause called from the other side of the road, "Here, too."

Wearing chainmail with steel plating over their chests, and steel pauldrons cupping their shoulders, both privates examined the last empty wagon. "It was orcs, sir," Arty informed.

Snales nodded and spoke in low tones for only Benning to hear. "I bet it is the same band we'd had problems with last spring and fall. They've got to have a camp somewhere close by."

"Ha-ha," Private Clause pointed at the ground with the tip of his spear, "They didn't even bother to cover their tracks. The rain compromised their retreat."

"What are we going to do, sir?" Captain Snales asked.

Commandant Benning understood exactly what his subordinate implied. Saviid knew his answer but didn't want to own it. Instead, he said, "We are going to clear this road and set camp. It has been one curse of a long day, and I want to eat and sleep."

Chapter Fourteen

Day Eleven, 6:30 p.m.

Wynkkur kept pace right behind the archer. They quickly approached where the caves intersected. Leading, Raenyl stepped out into the exit tunnel. He'd made a critical mistake.

Rattled deeply by what he'd seen, he didn't think or even look. He just stepped out into the exit cave. In his mind flashed the stripped woman and the bodies being prepared for cooking like turkeys on a spit. Stepping out into the narrow cave with his torch held before him, Raenyl strode right into the single-file path of several approaching orcs entering from the exit.

Marching through the cramped passage approached two of the big warriors wearing tribal armor. Behind the leaders followed a torchbearer. Further back and following the first three were even more orcs, but other than the light radiating from their torches, they remained unseen in the tight space. The first two stopped, surprised by the half-elf in the middle of their annex. Fractured seconds passed by. Half-elf and orc looked at each other in stunned disbelief, giving the archer enough time to fully realize the depth of his folly.

Gripping the thick shaft of a primitive battle-axe, the first orc planted his feet. The axe blade, a chipped stone-wedge tethered to a forked club, seemed the less sinister compared to the muscular warrior sneering through piggish lips. The sound of metal blades being drawn echoed from behind the first orc.

"Damn this! Go back!" squealed Raenyl. Wynkkur, unaware of the battle-ready orcs, ran directly into Raenyl's back as the archer leapt backward and out of sight from the gang blocking the exit. Raenyl cursed again while intentionally dropping his torch, "No, too late!"

As Wynkkur fell backward, the archer pulled an arrow from his quiver. The bow's string hooked between the arrow's notch as Raenyl drew his powerful weapon. He felt the familiar strain in his shoulders, chest, and wrists. Releasing pinched fingers, the oak bow vibrated in his hand. A second later the arrow reappeared deep inside the barrel-chest of the nearest warrior. The hurling wooden shaft led by a razor-steel tip punched between ribs, then lung, and then pushed back out again through ribs.

Expressing either an emotion of alarm or angered violation, the other orcs squealed shrilly as the pierced orc fell against the side wall howling. The second warrior whipped two short swords in his hands and charged forward as best he could in the confining tunnel, shoving his way past the first orc staggering against the cavern wall. Carrying the light for the running warrior, the torchbearer pursued.

The other orcs stopped to tend to the one sliding down the wall. From deeper within the abysmal corridors of pure blackness, echoing calls howled back from everywhere and nowhere. Behind the half-elf, Seth pulled Wynkkur back upon his feet. Raenyl, not realizing the elf had been knocked to the ground, pulled a second arrow from its holder.

Growling with determination, the charging orc sprinted faster. Sighting down the arrow, Raenyl lowered his aim before release. The determined growl shifted to a high shriek as the arrow penetrated underneath the orc's belt-buckle and above its groin. The torchbearer leapt over the writhing warrior as the group of orcs who'd stalled for the injured picked up the chase. The torchbearer, being smaller, was unhindered by the cramped hallway and moved swiftly.

"Go!" Raenyl ordered as he stooped, snatching up his torch. Popalia was already running, rushing deeper into the cavern from where they'd just come. Wynkkur offered to take the torch from Raenyl, which the half-elf surrendered. Wynkkur ran between priestess and archer, but Seth waited behind with his broad blade held low in both hands.

Rounding the blind corner, the orc stopped suddenly, pierced through the bowels by Seth's hard-shoved sword. As the blood-darkened blade shoved out between back ribs, Seth yanked violently, removing his sword. A strange wheezing sound gurgled between stubby tusks as the orc braced against the pull of gravity, its clawed hands plugging the hole in its abdomen. The sound of blood pattering across the stone ground, accompanied by its scent, made a strong presence in the annex.

Palming the orc's sweaty forehead, Seth gave a hard shove before spying down the hall opposite the exit route. More orcs were coming; he saw two more torch-wielding groups on their way. Having no time to count, he noted there were several males in each group. Seth was already running as the bleeding orc hit the back wall before curling to the floor.

By the dim light given from the grounded torch behind him, Seth pursued Raenyl. The warrior saw the light from Wynkkur's torch giving his brother's sprinting form an outline of orange light. Slowing a little, Seth looked over his shoulder as the next group of orcs leapt over the blood-spilling body of the torchbearer. Another group of four joined from the opposite bend, so Seth turned his focus on Raenyl's glowing shadow and ran faster.

Ahead of him, Popalia passed the first bend where the cavern narrowed again. Wynkkur was next around the bend and the light source went with him. Raenyl's shadow became illuminated against the side wall as he stepped into the bend. Two more steps, and Seth began cursing the invading darkness. Before he could round the bend, the darkness was consuming everything.

Terror rode Seth's shoulders until he made the bend, then relief returned with seeing the elf and priestess carrying the light so many steps ahead of him. Feet slapped stone, bouncing a din of echoes everywhere, altered only by their own ragged breathing and the howls of those who pursued. Seth watched the leading priestess look to her left where the wall fell away. Popalia slowed as did Wynkkur. Seth was relieved that he was allowed to catch up. He hated being between the ever-invasive darkness and the hostile orcs seeking revenge.

Up ahead, the elf reached out and gently shoved the priestess forward, saying, "Move! Move!" Popalia's lip curled under her nose, making a mask of revulsion. Looking away, she began to flee from whatever she'd seen below. Continuing forward, the path enclosed again, and there Popalia and Wynkkur stopped, motioning for the brothers to hurry.

Raenyl sprinted through the open area and Seth heard the telltale crackling of arrows bouncing off the wall beside his brother. Long, wooden slivers fired from bows slammed their heads against immovable stone, but none found flesh. Raenyl got by, and Wynkkur called to him, "Run, Seth. I'll blind them as you pass!"

Running and watching for archers, Seth saw what disturbed his brother so deeply and caused the lip-curl on the priestess. Glancing into the open area, he spied the spit set over the fire and the charring remains of what was once human. Down in the tribe's dining area, the floor swayed with life and long shadows. The swaying silhouettes were orcs, and a great many—old, young, male, female, fat, and skinny—each of them uniquely ugly and all of them snorting petulantly with the interruption of their gruesome feast.

A bee's sting bit into Seth's arm. There was an audible thump and knock as something hit his armor. An arrow found him, piercing through the meat at the back of his arm, pinning his left arm to his side. Yelping more from surprise than pain, his adrenaline overrode any agony. He was far too high on endorphins to feel the bite of puncture and torn flesh. Passing the elf, he clenched his teeth as the sorcerer's magic flash offered temporary daylight.

For a quick instance, Seth saw that the tunnel before him was long. The tunnel walls were beige-ish brown, spotted with black, and running for a great distance before eventually splitting. As suddenly as the light appeared, it faded—a lance of uncontrolled light, wasting the darkness for one brief lifespan. As the darkness returned, Seth heard the crackle of diminishing magic that cooked the air around the elf's sword. Seth spun around with the encroaching darkness to see the final fade of red-hot light absorb into Wynkkur's blade.

Seth attempted to move his left arm while surveying the blinded orcs behind him. His arm spiked with sharp pain and remained immobile, pinned into his armor. Simultaneously, an orc shrieked, having stepped too far and falling over into the feeding area. Seth felt with his fingers around the wooden splinter as warm blood squirted from the hole through his arm. A soft pattering touched his ears as the spray hit the wall beside him.

Seth couldn't fight with an arrow pinning his arm, but at the moment, it wasn't an issue. All of the orcs who made up the first group had become blinded and now squealed with their fear and surprise. Seth realized none of the orcs knew he was bleeding, but his trail would be easy to follow once they did.

"Let's get out of here," Raenyl said as he released an arrow into an orc stumbling at the back of the line of pursuers. Raenyl's arrow pierced right beneath his protruding sternum, and the beast fell hard upon his backside before rolling over and onto its side. "More are coming."

"I'm hit," Seth added with a small hint of embarrassment in his tone.

"You are a big target to dodge arrows," the archer stated as he shot an arrow down into the feeding room. Another pained squeal returned from somewhere within the fire-lit room. "Is it bad?"

"It isn't good," Seth answered. "My arm is pinned to my side, and I'm bleeding, but I think my armor stopped it from being any worse. We need to go—and now."

Popalia promised, "Once we are safely away from these orcs, I'll take care of it."

"Yeah, away from here, but where is safe?" Raenyl added while patting Wynkkur's shoulder as a quick way of saying thanks.

Popalia, who was already on the move, stated, "The only way we can go right now. We go deeper until they give up."

"Gods pound it," Seth cursed as Wynkkur stepped behind the priestess. "That—or until we are cornered and slaughtered."

Still, he followed the priestess as did Raenyl. Clearly, travelling back the way they had come would not be survivable anymore. A larger group would be coming after them, now. He tugged his arm lightly, and the pain screamed enough to clench his teeth and water his eyes.

Popalia led, holding the torch before her. Like the terrifying sounds from some infernal punishment, behind them reported a seemingly endless squeal of blinded orcs echoing in the halls. Popalia ran until the tunnel turned right. It was the first turn to present itself.

As they ran, the awful smell of cooked bodies dissipated, but the memory never would. The further from the feeding area they ran, the deeper down into the earth they placed themselves. Seth hoped Popalia led them away from the cooking pits, but by spraying his own blood droplets across cavern walls like a dog marks every bush, he doubted their own end would fade any differently.

Chapter Fifteen

Day Eleven, 7:00-ish p.m.

Popalia took another right at a junction where a second tunnel intervened. "Wynkkur, give me your torch."

He handed her the torch, which she heaved down the left-hand tunnel. It sparked fiery embers as it hit a bend, bouncing into the unseen crook, and dimly glowing in the tight corner. Pointing down the darker cavern they'd just entered, she said, "Into the darkness, quick!"

Everyone scurried quickly into the darkness as she called, "Deeper, I can still see you." As soon as she could no longer see Seth, she dropped her torch in the four-way junction. Praying for her ruse to work, she ran into the vacuous darkness until she joined her allies. No sooner had she stopped moving when the first pursuing orc arrived at the junction. To muffle her labored breathing, she pushed her face into her robe. At her right, she heard the strain of Raenyl's bow being drawn.

The orc was joined by two more—one muscular orc holding a knotted club towered over the other two males. Examining the torch on the ground, he squealed what must have been orders to one of the smaller ones. The smaller orc uttered protesting sounds until the big one slammed a heavy fist atop his head. Popalia saw the blow carried enough force to rattle the protester. The big orc grabbed the other torchbearer, and the two of them sped down the decoy tunnel. The smallest of the trio remained rubbing his head in the grounded torchlight.

Popalia silently prayed for the orc to leave so Raenyl would not need to release his arrow. Sound echoed through the tunnels as more orcs announced they were coming. Popalia's fear was reaching for the limits of madness. Popalia counted four more as the next hunting party arrived. Three of them were the big warrior type. If the orcs decided to split up, they'd be as good as caught.

Why hasn't Raenyl fired? She questioned, confused by the archer's patience and amazed by his strength at holding the powerful bow ready for so long.

The biggest in the second group squealed at the shorter straggler, who pointed in the direction where the other two had gone.

Nodding, the big one hit the little one with more force than what would be considered playful on the piggish flat of his nose. As the little one squealed in pain, all of the others guffawed.

Moving all together, the orcs followed the first group down the decoy tunnel. Raenyl slowly eased the string of his weapon to its slack position. As the sounds of the group echoed down the opposite hallway, Raenyl expressed barely over a whisper, "Bane's brother! I can't feel my arms."

"Mine hurts like unholy wrath," Seth said through clenched teeth.

"I don't think I can take much more of this," started Popalia. "Praise the Blessed Mystery for how we did not get caught."

"It is good we didn't take the bait," Seth stated above a whisper. "The scout had left that runt there for us to kill, and then the second group would have caught us."

"How did you know that?" Wynkkur asked.

"I didn't," he replied. "I'm figuring it out as we go."

"It is strange to imagine that such beasts would have a regimented social hierarchy," Wynkkur wondered aloud.

"Now isn't the time for chit-chat," Raenyl barked. "We need torches lit, Seth's arm bandaged, and then we need to get out of here."

Wynkkur spoke a phrase of what sounded to be gibberish, and before anyone could question, the area was washed with apparent torchlight. Only it was not a torch. It was the elf's hand engulfed in flames. He replied, "Show Popalia your wound."

Raenyl stared at the elf's hand aflame and asked, "Doesn't that hurt?"

"Not for the first few minutes," Wynkkur answered as Popalia tended to Seth's impaled arm.

"This'll take more than a few minutes, Wank," Seth coached from experience. "Can we do this on the move? I don't want to be here when those orcs learn we tricked them."

Raenyl removed his backpack as Popalia examined Seth's arm with a gentle touch. Informing Seth of what she felt, she said, "What a blessing. The arrow is caught right between where the chain armor and the leather pads overlap. Half an inch in either direction, and you'd have a hole in your lung."

Unsnagging the blood-coated arrowhead from out his armor more by sense of touch than by Wynkkur's lit hand, she asked, "How's that? You're set free."

She glanced at Raenyl pulling two torches out of his pack. She asked, "Could you remove the tip of this arrow for me? Wynkkur's hand is busy." Setting the torches on the corridor floor, Raenyl removed a sharp knife from a sheath kept tied against his upper thigh.

He clipped the arrowhead from the shaft with one strong twist. Seth reacted, "Ow-oow! My arm—ouch, please!"

"Shhh, quit it," Raenyl ordered while examining the stone arrowhead in his palm. Wynkkur lit one of the torches, doubling the amount of light.

"This is only going to hurt for a quick moment," Popalia rose and then lowered his blood-smeared elbow. "Relax. I need you to relax, and—" She yanked the headless arrow back up and out of the hole through his arm.

"Grrph!" Seth painfully muttered as a large pulse of dark droplets spewed from the reopened wound.

Popalia placed both of her hands over each of the holes and began to pray. While asking for divine favor, her voice exhibited a commanding presence, "Praises to the Unknown. This brother's arm was injured in service to you. Please use me as your vessel to heal by."

For Popalia, it felt as if someone had stabbed her through her left arm. She whimpered audibly, and let go of Seth to tend her own phantom pains. Upon her knees, she laid her head against the rough stone floor while biting her lip against the pain. Then, it was gone, fading as quickly as it came.

Raenyl lit one of the torches from Wynkkur's flaming hand before saying, "What is with all the dramatics? Does the sight of blood—" Stopping mid-sentence, he began a new one, "What happened to the hole in your arm?"

Wynkkur extinguished his hand with a single magical word before saying, "Popalia healed it, but not before taking Seth's pain."

Whimpering softly, Popalia added, "It is the sacrifice expected in exchange for my gift."

Raenyl grabbed Seth's arm and rubbed over where the hole used to be, proving his eyes weren't fooling him. Seth only smiled. With a euphoric glaze in his eyes, Seth stated, "Man, I feel great."

"It's all the blood you lost. Look how much is on your sleeve and pants." Raenyl's granite rationality wasn't bending with this puzzle. He'd cut the arrowhead himself, he knew the wound had been there. Yet, now it was gone.

Popalia sat up and wiped the tears out of her eyes, "You were touched by the Nameless; that is why you feel so good. My god cleansed and healed your wound, but like Wynkkur said, I needed to feel your pain in exchange. That is how healing works."

"You shared my pain with me," Seth said with deep surprise and admiration.

"And you shared my god with me," she added, "but now let's get out of here before the orcs realize we'd tricked them."

Upon standing, Raenyl heard a blur of an echo rolling from the darkness behind them. Raenyl shushed, and a second later, it was there again. They all heard it the second time. Each of them waited, holding their breaths. All ears were fine-tuned, waiting for whatever rolled through the dark halls.

Deep from within that darkness, a woman's voice could barely be heard, "...no...," and quickly after a man's voice bounced in the vacuum, saying either "stop" or "help", and finally the voices were punctuated by a high-pitched shriek.

Simultaneously speaking, both Seth and Popalia expressed, "Survivors!"

Raenyl slung his bow and withdrew his longsword, "Let's be quick about it."

Rounding one bend, the tunnel widened. From deeper in the darkness and around a future corner, they heard a woman's cry for mercy, "Don't do this," and then the shrill voice pitched, "Stop it!" Before the tunnel's next bend, light reflected from a torch burning on the other side of the curve. A woman's echoing scream wailed, "Noooo! Noooo!"

Seth was first to make the bend, and seeing by the light of a large orc's torch, he witnessed horror redefined. Standing with their backs against the wall, there were three people shackled against the walls. The corridor revealed another bend, and from there, a man's voice called, "Leave her alone, you nasty beast!"

Two out of three visible bodies hung slack against their shackles; the first was male with disheveled, greased hair and wearing rich clothes. With head slumped forward, a long string of drool hung off his chin. Dangling aside him was a second slack body, a woman whose clothes had been removed, save her boots, which were still strapped tight. Her legs were bent at unnatural angles. Her blonde hair smeared and blackened to the tips where they'd soaked much blood. In the torch's light, dark-staining blood streaked down the woman's muscular body, collecting in a pool beneath her sprawling legs.

There, in the middle of the hall and squatting with its back to

Seth, a brutish jailor looked up and into the face of a terrified woman. His hand was unseen and blocked by his body. As Seth rushed the distance, the terrible picture became clearer. The woman's pants had been yanked all the way down to her ankles. The kneeling jailor held the hips of the resistant woman while vigorously rubbing his other hand between her legs. Piggish sounds, reminiscent of chortling, over-powered the girl's frightened whimpers.

Seth charged, making the last few paces before the molesting orc turned its head. Seth thrust with his sword and sharpened steel slid across the jailor's throat beneath the jawbone, slicing all the way to the opposite jawbone. A geyser of orc's blood fanned across the warrior, the wall, and evenly splashing all three prisoners. Swine eyes bugged outward as dirty-nailed fingers withdrew from within the woman, grasping at the gurgling tear at its throat.

Seth brought his knee up swiftly, pounding against the orc's chin, knocking the beast upon its back as a torrent of blood and bubbles leaked from a sword-torn throat. Blood pulsed through clenched fingers with a sickening gurgle. Seth shoved his sword downward, entering the orc between its ribs before cleaving down into its heart.

Looking from the dead orc directly into the crotch of the molested girl, he saw no sign of blood or injury—or hair for that matter. Wide eyes shot upward to the girl's face. Seeing the dark V tattooed across one side on her face, he remembered what Raenyl had said the day before, "Bugs on top—then bugs below."

The woman, teetering upon the edge of hysteria, responded as if doused with ice water. "What did you just say? I was gonna say thank you, and I may even a'shared some love, but not now shoog...not now."

From the other side of a rounded corner, where the tunnel again wavered—this time to the left—a man's voice shouted. Sounding both frightened and relieved, he called out, "People? Praise Stranoss, we're saved! Can you get the key and let us out?"

"You are Regulators, right?" A deeper male voice called from the unseen side of the prisoners' hall, "Please! Tell me you killed 'em all?"

Even with her pants at her ankles, she spoke boldly. "Not Stranoss. You're praisin' the wrong god, Gregor. Big man, you come with the princess. Ain't I right?"

Seth turned to look around for Popalia, "What...princess? Hey, wait. I thought you were a priestess."

Stepping around the bend, Popalia ignored Seth's confusion,

"Somehow Stileur must have tipped you that we were coming."

"He did tip, but I never thought you'd be fool enough to come all the way down here looking for lil' ol' me." Seeing Raenyl for the first time, she switched to a sweeter persona, "Well hello, handsome. I hope you brought better manners than your friend. Maybe you'd help me by getting the key out of the dead one's pocket. I'd like to stop showing the wide world my good spot."

Without a word, Raenyl knelt down and began patting the body for anything useful. Wynkkur stayed in the bend, where he could watch down to the other end of the long hall. Seth walked around where there were three more prisoners. Two were men— one around thirty, the other appeared older, maybe fifty.

Seth noticed the shackles were iron cuffs looped around a long chain fed through thick, rusted eye-loops that had been pounded into the wall. The elder man nodded at Seth, "You got the keys? I'm Gregor. I'm in charge of this caravan. I own it."

The younger man was stocky, his face sheathed with a full beard. Seth appraised him to be in his late twenties. The younger man denied, "Not now, Gregor. Not anymore. You own nothing, now. You are a king of nothing."

Between these two men, a third woman hung from iron cuffs. The woman's face shined with a mixture of relief and harried frenzy. She appeared to be in her middle-forties and a little plump. Seeming grandmotherly, and unlike the other women, she remained fully clothed and seemed physically uninjured. By her aura, one could expect sweet treats upon being greeted at her front door. Now chained to the wall, bedraggled, dirty, and on the brink of madness, she pleaded, "Please, get us out of here. Please, sir. We beg you."

"Now-now, Bennae. This young man is here to free us," Gregor stated as if it were fact. "We'll get Enga and Ucilius back to the Regulators, and they'll be okay." Looking over the thick-muscled Seth, the merchant added, "Free me first, and I'll pay you well, young man."

Seth bent around the corner as Raenyl pulled his hands from patting down the orc, muttering, "This one has no key." Looking around, Raenyl asked, "Where else could the jailor have put it?"

Panicking, Bennae stated, "Oh, by Stranoss. Please, find that key."

Checking the pockets and belt of the dead orc one more time, Raenyl shook his head. "Are you sure this orc has a key?"

Gregor reported, fear growing on his tone, "Dammit, it must

be the other one with the key. There were two, but these foul orcs all look the same to me."

"Orcs and Athanians, I bet they all look the same to you, Gregor," Katia slighted before offering to Popalia. "Hack my chains free, and I can open all their cuffs with a hairpin. These are simple locks, and we can be out of here in a minute, tops."

Shaking her head in disbelief, Popalia made a comment to Raenyl, "I think your skills are needed once again. It is funny how the Mystery moves."

With a grin, he offered his back to the priestess. "My set is rolled in soft leather. They're right in the top pocket of my pack. Just get 'em for me, and we'll be on our way."

Popalia pulled the lock picks and handed the bundle to the archer as he said, "By the way, apology accepted. When we get outside, and our horses are waiting, it'll be my turn to eat crow pie—all the way back to Dead Rik's."

From the back of the hallway, Wynkkur darkly reminded, "I think we should keep on to Faradell Pass. Our reception might be a little warmer."

Nodding, Raenyl withdrew the narrow tools he'd need to open the cuffs as Katia remarked, "What an inventive little Princess. I see you brought your own locksmith. Could you unhook me first, so I can pull up my pants and stop promoting my sweet spot?"

Popalia protested, "Not Katia. Free any of the others, but not her." Popalia knelt and began pulling the woman's pants up from her ankles and worked them back up and over her blood-splattered hips. Raenyl rounded the corner, and Popalia heard, "I'll give you a gold coin if you let me out first."

"Eat dung, Gregor. Your money means nothing, now." The other man ordered, "Hey, locksmith. Spring me first, and I can help fight."

"You can fight?" Raenyl observed the man was in great physical shape. As the man nodded, Raenyl began to unlatch the shackles. Katia was right. The simple locks were a matter of catching one small hook, and then the cuffs popped open. He was working on the second cuff as he asked, "What's your name?"

"I'm Westin. The unconscious girl is Enga. She is my partner. Gregor hired us to protect him years ago, but today is our last day with him. We quit, and when she comes to, she'll agree with me. We are done."

Raenyl popped the second lock from around the mercenary's wrist, "I hate to bear bad news, but your partner quit first."

"No, that can't be." He crossed around the wall where the naked and blood-leaking woman hung from her bonds. His footing slipped on the blood puddled beneath her slack body. Westin's knee banged hard against the ground, but he ignored any pain he may have felt. He lifted her chin and brushed aside her red-stained hair.

Seth looked over Westin's shoulder at the smashed and torn flesh of Enga's face. One-half of her face was recognizable, and Seth remembered seeing her before. Less than a day earlier, he'd seen her strong and beautiful. Sitting tall upon a regal horse, she was leaving Dead Rik's at the same time he was being arrested. In the limited torchlight, the half of her face that had not been brutalized reflected a lifeless gray. "No, Enga." Westin kissed that side of her face.

The grandmotherly woman, Bennae, cried out, "Enga! No, gods. No! This cannot be—she was alive only a little while ago." Shaking her locked cuffs above her head, she pleaded, "Please, get us out of here."

Gregor asked with a dry voice, "What about Ucilius? Is he still breathing?"

Katia answered, her voice hollow, "He is next to me. He's no worse than when we were chained here." Quieter, she muttered, "No better, also."

The third man—the one called Ucilius—was still alive of sorts. His body had remained unbeaten and unmolested, but light had faded from his eyes. It was as if he'd become hollow, as if the spark once shining there had been snuffed out. Slumped down, the chains bit into his wrists, and his hands appeared blue in the flickering torchlight. A long drop of spittle drooled down the side of his lips, connecting to his chest.

Raenyl started working on the eldest woman's cuffs as Gregor remarked, "Excuse me, son. Did you not hear me? I said I'd pay you gold to get me out of these shackles."

Raenyl nodded, "I heard you, but did you ever hear of 'ladies first'?" By this merchant's presumption that he was for sale, Raenyl immediately decided not to like him. Unhooking one of the lady's wrist cuffs, he said, "One done."

Smiling appreciatively at the half-elf's acknowledgement, she said, "Thank you. My name is Bennae Kobblepot, and I'm Gregor's personal scribe. If I can return any favor in any way…"

"Hold your thanks a little longer," he grinned, thinking about her suggestion while using his probe to open the second cuff. "We are not out of here, yet."

Bennae shook her numb wrists, hoping the blood would flow back into them. "Thank you for freeing me."

Raenyl asked Popalia, "Who is next?"

"Free the merchant, then he can help with Ucilius. Leave Katia—leave her for last, if we even free her at all."

"You prissy bitch," Katia stated. "I've converted to believing in the Unknown. I'm like your sister, now. So unhook me next, damn it!"

Popalia shook her head, "Ha-ha, right. For a chance to escape, you will kill us. I am sure you won't give me a chance to catch you, again."

Katia snarled back, "You are here, because I asked my god for help. Say 'Hay'ah' to the Great Mystery!"

"Hay'ah?" Popalia scowled, "Do not blaspheme, Katia—dare not make false praise. My god's wrath is rare, but do not tempt."

"Don't minister to me, sister," Katia remarked coldly. "All the dirt comes out with a'washin. In the end, all that is left is an ugly truth." Her eyes shot at Ucilius hanging slack-jawed across the cave, and repeating a little softer, "Always an ugly truth somewhere."

Freed, Gregor moved closer to the catatonic man, assisting him upright so that his wrists could be relieved from the bite of the cuffs cutting into his skin. Gregor said to Katia, "It is funny hearing you speak about truth. Ucilius had asked if you would fight before leaving Dilligan's Freepost. You said yes, and now look at him, poor boy."

"No, Gregor. That's not what I said. What I said was, 'I'd do what I haft'a do.' That's what I told Ucilius, and he said, 'Gregor will just haft'a take that as a yes.' That is what we'd said."

"Please, I knew it was a bad idea to take you along. You were bad luck from the beginning. We'd have made it without you." Then to Raenyl, he encouraged, "Come now, boy. Come unlock Ucilius."

Seth crudely stated, "He's been jelly-brained. We're not really taking him, are we?"

"If he is breathing, he is coming," Popalia claimed.

"Please. Enga, too," Westin beseeched. "I'll carry her, but I can't leave her here."

"How will you fight and carry her?" Wynkkur asked from aside Popalia.

Westin's dark eyes turned into cold, little stones. "I'll fight. I'll fight until death so you can get away, but I'm not leaving her here. Not after what they did to Lissa, not after..."

Gregor found an edge in his voice. "Don't you dare talk of Lissa's indignity." Gregor spoke in a voice sharks use before choosing where to bite. "You can despise me, but do not ever disgrace my daughter."

"Indignity? Disgrace?" Westin scoffed. "Indignity is gassing at a dinner. Disgrace is how you killed Enga long before today began. Lissa's end was horror!"

"Shush, shush!" Katia whispered. "Save if for outside! Westin, I'll help you carry her."

Seth barked, "Well, I'm not carrying 'Useless' over here!" Lowering his voice, "Of course, Gregor, if you'd like to pay me..."

Popalia spoke, "Listen to me, all of you." Whispering a little louder—loud enough to hear her whisper echoing down the hallway—she repeated, "All of you."

Everyone quieted, and she continued, "Katia, I've made a decision as to what to do with you. I'm chaining you to me. Our fates are now equal. If I die, you can drag my body around with you until you find someone to unlock us. I'll trust you won't kill me—it will be easier for you not to. Everyone comes out with us. Ucilius, too. I can help him as soon as we get out of here, but we need to get safe first."

Westin's eyes begged, "What about Enga?"

Popalia empowered, "She is your responsibility. We will unhook her, and then you can decide from there what to do. She is your charge."

Seth informed Westin, "If you need a weapon to fight with, take Wank's."

"Not my sword," Wynkkur protested. "I need my sword."

"Seth, you're a dumbass," Raenyl corrected Seth's speech. "Westin needs a weapon to use, not to 'fight with'. The orcs have weapons for us to 'fight with'. Westin, you can use my longsword until you get your own or until we get outside...hopefully the latter."

Westin nodded, "I'd appreciate that. I'll take it until I find a spear. I'm pretty handy with a spear."

Seth glowered down at Raenyl, "You're a dumbass."

"Big-bodied idiot," Raenyl shot at Seth before turning back to Westin. "Let me finish unlocking everybody, and I'll hand it right over."

Chapter Sixteen

Day Eleven, between 7:00 and 8:00 p.m.

The way out was temporarily closed. Bound together—yin like yang—clergy and thief led the others into the unknown with a torch out in front. Bennae and Gregor ran side by side a couple of paces behind the leaders, separated only by Ucilius. One arm of the comatose merchant draped over the shoulder of the scribe, and the other arm hung around the neck of the caravan owner. Dragging the incapacitated man made them slow. They'd be caught in the next few moments if not for the men waiting back, giving the non-combatants a fair start.

Seth, who was leading, destroyed two of the smaller thralls at the junction to the way out. Their corpses lay leaking in the intersection, but he couldn't kill both of them before one shrieked. All the orcs in the tunnels now knew their prey had been found. It was time again to run, and if anyone was going to make it out alive, the men must stand and fight. Distant torchlight reflected off the wall at the crux of the next bend, announcing an advancing group.

Wynkkur urged Gregor and Bennae, "Move faster or leave Ucilius. They are coming."

Gregor grunted and pushed forward as Bennae whimpered in resignation. Wynkkur turned to Westin, who carried Enga's body over one wide shoulder. Black streaks of dried blood marked where it had run freely down her legs.

"Time to fight," Raenyl gloomily stated.

"Right here?" Westin looked to the nodding half-elf before questioning, "Why here? We can't fight in this tiny a space."

Holding his torch angled over his head, Wynkkur tilted his head in the brothers' direction. "We will give them this space, or at least the illusion of space. It'll give time for the slow ones to escape."

"Wank, are you're gonna fight, too?" Seth prompted, "Shouldn't you be protecting Popalia?"

Wynkkur's almond eyes blinked once before he stated, "I am protecting her by protecting you."

Raenyl readied his bow, offering an emotionless shrug. Westin chortled, and Seth's grin grew wider. "Looks like the elf is going to show us people a thing or two."

"Yeah, I'll show something. Just keep your eyes watching on the coming orcs—and not on me." Wynkkur withdrew his sword.

Westin set Enga's body upon the ground and griped, "It is too tight here. I can't swing a sword without—"

"This will be easier if you'd just trust me," Wynkkur interrupted.

Raenyl knew there was no time to explain and said, "They're coming. We just need to hold them for a moment. Keep your head low, and I'll sink the first one." On Raenyl's last word, the first orc saw them standing in the junction and charged faster. He was a beastly orc—more than a head taller than the three that followed.

Making up the front line, Seth and Westin squatted low as Raenyl drew his bowstring tight. The bone-armored orcs charged with swine-like shrieks, the broadest of them wielding a crude spear. Raenyl's shot zipped through the air above and between the two squatting warriors. As the arrow hit the lead orc in the chest, Westin emitted a surprised, "Good shot."

With Raenyl's arrow protruding from its chest, the large orc stopped running but stood defiantly. The archer set another arrow as fast as it could be pulled from his quiver. The second orc passed the staggered leader, then the third and fourth stepped around the large warrior. A feathered shaft sunk above the new leader's piggish-nose and between both eyes. Falling forward but a few steps from the junction, the orc's head smashed into the ground with a hollow *thunk*, and the arrow's shaft cracked loudly as it broke. The other two continued their relentless gait, stepping over the fallen warrior.

The big one with the arrow piercing its chest lumbered forward. Another orc passed the one that stumbled in a mad dash at the human and elvish intruders. As they all closed in on the junction, the nearest of the orcs leapt over one of the bodies Seth had dispatched. Westin growled through bared teeth as he and Seth braced for contact.

Wynkkur's sword flashed brightly. The mottled gray and beige walls of the cave reflected the sudden pulse of light, and three pairs of yellow eyes mirrored back tiny, glow-like starbursts. As suddenly as it flared, the flash was gone, and three orcs rubbed their eyes while squealing frightfully. One tripped over a dead body on the ground, falling with his palms to his eyes as the others felt their way along the wall. Chuckling, Seth stepped forward, running his sword through the nearest orc against the wall, ending its life quickly.

Grimacing with a deranged stare, Westin stabbed into the orc crawling on the ground. Westin pulled his arm back, and the bloodied blade followed. He thrust forward, again. Pulling the blade out, he plunged the point in a third time, then a fourth, and repetitively thereafter, stabbing into the orc's back with Raenyl's sword. The coppery stink of warm blood permeated the air as the crimson spilled, appearing black in the torchlight and pooling in the depressions across the stone floor. Westin turned to the third blinded orc and stabbed it multiple times in the back.

Surprised by Westin's disturbing display of grisly violence, Raenyl fired between the two men, punching a second arrow into the injured and final warrior feeling his way along the wall. This time the arrow pierced the orc's thick skull, dropping the blinded warrior lifelessly to the floor. In the distance, more orcs could be heard.

Looking at the pile of cooling bodies lying about the junction, Westin casually stated, "Not much room here, anymore. I guess we got 'em all." Nodding over to the elf, the broad-shouldered guard complimented, "Your spell helped serve these two-legged pigs their rightful desserts." Westin spit upon one of the orcs he'd mutilated, but Wynkkur was already running in the same direction as Popalia.

Another mob of approaching orcs was coming—the torchlight being first to show itself at the end of the tunnel. Reaching down, Westin picked up a javelin from a dead orc. "It's a little small, but it'll work for now." Westin used his pants to wipe the blood off of Raenyl's weapon before offering it back, pommel first.

"Thanks, let's go," the half-elf exclaimed while re-sheathing. Westin lifted the dead body of Enga from where her morbidly naked body sprawled across the floor, and fell in pursuit of the eagerly retreating Wynkkur. Seth picked up one of the torches burning on the ground. Raenyl took up a swift jog, following the light of Wynkkur's torch ahead.

They stayed ahead of the group of orcs, even with Westin hustling to keep pace. Raenyl occasionally looked back to see the pace of the orcs remained steady but not overcoming. They came around another bend and sight of the orcs was blocked. A few paces further, Wynkkur came to another cross in paths. He stopped and looked at the ground.

Seth asked, "What way?"

"Right," he said and turned into the right tunnel.

"Are you sure?" the warrior asked.

"Yes, Popalia will always try to choose the *right* path."

"She said the path of least resistance," Raenyl remembered.

In the light of his torch Wynkkur saw what he looked for, a black swipe across the side wall. Pointing his torch at a black streak scraped along the tunnel, "She used her torch to mark the way for us. See, the right pathway."

Westin caught up as Raenyl said, "We need to lose these orcs."

Sweat drenched Westin's face, and his breath was labored while speaking, "If we are lucky, we can face them here."

Tossing his torch down the opposite tunnel, Wynkkur shook his head while saying, "We need to catch Popalia. Tricking the orcs worked well last time."

Everyone silently agreed and ran a little faster, giving no mind to their burning muscles or their ravaged breathing. The trail ran straight a short ways before bending to the left and down steeper into the earth. They made the bend before the orcs had reached the junction behind them. With a little luck, the orcs would choose the other pathway.

Continuing swiftly with gravity's pull and reaching the tunnel's lower bend, they saw what they hoped to be Popalia's torchlight. The runners reached the second bend, sweating and panting. It was Popalia, but hope vanished upon seeing the end of their chance for escape.

Popalia, chained to Katia, stood upon the edge of a cliff looking down and over. The tunnel's path had flattened and leveled out to a plateau overlooking expansive darkness. Above their heads, the ceiling vanished into black. Pointed spikes hung from unseen foundations, their tips reflected in the torchlight.

"Lo'Lyth's mad realm!" Wynkkur's head spun with visions of doom. "This is the end of sanity!" The chamber of darkness beyond the wide shelf they stood upon drove the uneasy nail of fear deeper into the souls of all who looked. No one needed to know Lo'Lyth or her fate to know they looked into the mouth of madness.

Popalia looked over her shoulder at the sweating elf, "I think I can see the bottom. It is only twenty feet lower, maybe thirty, but no more than that."

"We can't get down there," Bennae protested. "Ucilius can't get down there."

A panting Seth barked, "Then, we leave him. We can't stay here."

Westin set Enga's booted body down at the cave's mouth, resting her against the wall. His words came in sharp gasps. "No one...stays. All...go."

"Ucilius is alive." Gregor added, "I'll pay you, big man, if you help me get him out."

"I can't carry him and fight." Seth wiped his arm across his saturated face, "Look how tired Westin is."

"Seth," Raenyl began, "did you bring that rope?"

"Aye, fifty feet of it," Seth answered. "It is in my pack, under the torches."

"Kneel so I can get it." Seth squatted lower, and Raenyl dug inside. The rope was bundled neatly, but two of the torches fell out with the rope's extraction. He picked up the torches but thought twice before returning them. "Popalia, let me see your torch."

"It's almost burned out." She handed the torch to the archer. Raenyl lit one torch and handed the new one back to the priestess. He tossed the old one over the cliff edge. The flame sputtered angrily while spinning into the darkness below. Embers sparked as it hit the floor. Pillars of what appeared to be melting stone rose from the ground in the cavernous expanse below.

"Good guess," Raenyl complimented the priestess. "I'd say it's about twenty-two feet to the bottom. We'll let Gregor down first, and then we can lower Ucilius to him."

"No," the merchant rebuked. "I don't know what is down there. You or the big man here should go first."

"Spineless worm," Katia cut at the merchant. "Unchain me. I'll go first." The chain was wrapped around both women's shoulders and locked between their shoulder blades. Four feet of links was all the distance separating them. Each link of the chain was thick as fingers curled and inter-connecting.

Popalia denied, "You and I share our fate, now. I can heal Ucilius, and then we go."

"No," Wynkkur protested. "No way."

"What?" Popalia faced the elf.

Gregor agreed with Wynkkur. "The elf is right. Our families praise Stranoss, not fickle gods like yours."

Wynkkur quickly changed the subject, "I can hear the orcs coming. They will be here sooner than we can get down."

Raenyl nodded, "I can hear them, too. Damn it. We will need to face them with our backs to the edge."

"At least we'll have room to swing swords here." Seth removed his wide blade from its scabbard.

Clutching his acquired javelin with both hands, Westin offered, "If we can pin them at the bend, we might survive this."

"I agree," Raenyl chipped in. "With Wynkkur's flashy-flash, we might survive this."

Weakly, Wynkkur admitted, "You might be on your own this time. I'm spent. I haven't slept in two days."

"You think we slept last night?" Raenyl added. "We are all spent."

"You don't understand," Wynkkur said while shaking his head. "Magic is like a daily candle. The wick is only so long, and I'm out of wick. That last spell was like scraping the bottom of the honey jar." He nodded toward the tunnel, "They will be here soon. Let's get ready."

Seth growled, "Then, get your sword ready. We all fight, or we all die."

"We can't fight!" Gregor exclaimed. Bennae nodded aside drooling Ucilius.

"I'll fight. Gimme your sword, elf-boy," Katia taunted. "You swing like a girl."

Popalia handed her torch to Katia and eased down to her knees. The cave floor was hard, and she tucked the edge of her robe under her knees to pad them. Between thief and priestess, there was barely enough slack in the chain for Katia to remain standing. Popalia inhaled deeply, and Raenyl barked, "What are you doing? We all fight, or we all die!"

"If we are going to survive the next couple of minutes, we will need the blessing of my god," she peered over at Gregor, "whether you like it or not." Leaving her palms open and at her lap, she closed her eyes and began to pray in silence as the first light of the approaching orcs illuminated the bend in the tunnel.

Pulling his bowstring tight, Raenyl whispered a curse as he waited for the first orc to show. He stepped back and in front of the priestess as Seth scampered close to the inside wall. Westin held the javelin low, bracing for the coming attack standing to the left of the archer.

A thrall with a torch rounded the corner, squealing alarm to those who followed. Raenyl's arrow forced its way into the skull via the eye-socket. The force popped the orc's eye out, pushing the dangling orb out and to the side before slamming solidly against the back of his skull. Blood, like a dark tear, dripped down the side of the beast-man's swine-like snout. The torch dropped from twitching hands as the body crumpled to the cave floor.

A second orc rounded the corner on fast feet. Snarling, the second thrall charged as Raenyl reached behind for another arrow. Westin stepped forward, holding the short spear out like a horseman's pike. Noticeably stockier than the other betas, this orc was still not as large as the tribal warriors. With a shortsword and a small, wooden buckler held at the ready, it sneered, spying Westin though piggish eyes.

Leaping from concealment at the cave's mouth, Seth swung a cleaving blow as the orc stepped into the open space. Smashing the sword arm with the mighty swing, a muffled, wet pop sounded as bone snapped underneath muscle and flesh. The arm bent awkwardly, and the small sword clattered over by where Wynkkur stood, protecting Popalia's right side.

The orc spun around, bringing the small shield up to deflect Seth's second blow, its blood-spewing right arm hanging limp and inoperable. Seth's second blow came as a quick knee to the groin. As the orc dropped to his knees, Seth exploited the top of the orc's skull with the blunt edge of his blade near the sword's hilt. Pig eyes rolled up as the beast passed out.

Two more orcs, both armored alphas, forced Seth to jump back a pace and then step back two more. Two other orcs appeared behind the two alphas. One reached down to grab a hold of Enga's arm and pulled her bloody body back into the tunnel.

"No!" Westin yelled as they reclaimed his partner's body. A second thrall grabbed a handful of blood-starched, blonde hair, pulling the battered woman even further into the hall.

Hurling his javelin, the bone tip of the primitive weapon pierced into the lower spine of one orc pulling Enga. Releasing the woman with a howl of pain, the orc touched the short spear hanging in his back as another two orcs appeared from around the corner, each grabbing an arm of the dead woman, yanking her into the cavern and out of sight.

The orc with the spear in its back squealed painfully as his weaponless partner yanked the javelin. Black sprayed across the grounded torch's flame, sizzling and dimming the light. Westin, now a weaponless fighter, cursed as the closest alpha lumbered closer.

As two larger orcs moved in, capturing still more space, the shelf became noticeably tighter for everyone. Bennae squealed with terror as one of the warrior orcs slashed outward with a longsword, missing quick-footed Westin by a baby's reach. Raenyl fired his second arrow at point blank range. The arrow pierced deep through leather armor, a mere third of the arrow's feathered shaft remained exposed.

Seth tried to push the other alpha back a couple paces as the big orc that swung at Westin made a pained, yet determined sound. Westin was forced to step another length backward and closer to the cliff and non-combatants. The half-elf stepped back in the other direction, exposing an opening to praying Popalia.

The orc with the arrow pierced into his side lunged at the half-elf with his long blade. It was an effort to either run through or knock him over the edge and into the chasm. Wynkkur stood by, completely ignored as if he were merely a useless thrall of the human warriors. Wynkkur leapt forward, shoving the tip of elvish steel at the orc pushing at Raenyl.

Through some sort of miraculous luck, the short blade of silvered-steel sliced through the lacing between thick leather plates. The smaller sword cut into the skin, sliding under the ribs and deeper into an already skewered lung, not a palm's width distance from where Raenyl's arrow had punctured through cured leather.

Backhanded across his face, Wynkkur saw stars swirl while being thrown to the floor by the reactionary blow. Dazed and with his head resting over the cliff's edge, Wynkkur managed to keep grip on both his sword and torch. At his feet, he heard the hollow thump of a head knocking against limestone floor.

Wynkkur heard steel clashing with steel as Seth's sword deflected an attack from the other alpha. From where he lay upon the floor, he listened to Popalia mumbling the words of her prayers while awaiting the spots swirling over his eyes to fade away. Katia was calling to Seth, "Get him!" Also calling out was Gregor, "Stranoss, please!" As his eyes were regaining focus, he gave ear to Bennae's terrified whimpers. Twisting his head upright, the elf looked over the body of the orc he helped kill.

There were still four thralls, two warriors, and one other who'd just arrived. Wynkkur felt the aura on the newest arrival, and the elf's skin prickled. Upon sight of the newest arrival, the light curled into a surrounding shell of shadow. It was as though the light was being strangled, but refused to completely die.

Hovering up and over the shoulders of the shorter orc were the severed wings of a great raven, stretching as if they were becoming of the orc. There was an ash-blasting painted across the new orc's face. Even his tusks were blackened, but above his snout, the eyes seemed to glow with a possessed fire.

A feeling deep within Wynkkur tugged his eyes to fix upon the orc's belt. At the orc's belt rode a leather case shaped into a cube. From the cube's center swayed what Wynkkur first believed to be a drift of smoke. It was not smoke but a faintly glowing spirit. The ethereal being clung by several moss-like appendages, wrapped into the back and shoulders of the winged orc.

The parasitic soul had its shrunken head and impish face pressed against its host's ear, cruel lips whispering commands to a mindless, obeying host. They were forever connected. Tiny waif-like chains bound the glowing wisp to the cube upon the orc's belt. Wynkkur observed the spirit's head, which appeared with a twisted and malformed face, constantly dripping and resurfacing from within itself.

Shouting out in terror, Westin warned, "Witch doctor!"

Seth was having his own assortment of trouble. His adversary put up a ferocious fight. The blades-man barely held his space and fought purely on the defensive, whipping his heavy blade and having only enough time to deflect and parry. A second warrior moved in to flank and finish Seth.

Raenyl had one ready arrow and three targets. He needed to choose between witch doctor and the two attacking his brother. He knew which target to take, yet he chose the second. *Ascolan sticks.*

The flanking orc howled as Raenyl's arrow drove through the side of one buttock, exiting the tip of the arrow out the other cheek. The maimed orc slid belly first across the ground as Raenyl reached for another arrow.

Ducking once to avoid a wild swing, Seth lunged forward, driving the warrior he fought back a couple steps. Steel slammed into steel, echoing with a vibrating ring. Peripherally noticing the grounded orc thrusting outward with a rust-spotted dagger, Seth leapt onto one foot, avoiding the slash at his ankle. With a raised foot, he slammed down violently with his heavy boot, crunching his heel between orc tusks and crashing a quick stomp upon the orc's face. Lights out.

Seth, in what appeared to be an unstoppable frenzy, moved in upon the last of the warriors. Sword high and anticipating a final strike, Seth suddenly stopped. The cringing alpha held his sword angled in defense, but Seth's swing faltered as his eyes bugged wide. Voluntarily dropping his sword, the broad blade bounced noisily across the ground.

Stepping back while clawing at the side of his armor, Seth rasped, "I can't breathe."

The chain shirt that was the base of his armor tightened around him like constrictor coils. Seth feebly grasped at the catches of his armor, his face growing dark in the torchlight. Desperately needing to escape, his leather and chain protection had turned against him. The remaining thralls gathered by the witch doctor and made elated sounds—piggish chortles of promised victory.

Raenyl struggled internally as the orc warrior swung mightily. All Seth could do to avoid being cleaved in half was fall backward. Seth's only focus now was upon the life and death struggle with his own traitorous armor as Westin rushed weaponless between Raenyl and at Seth's attacker. Westin threw himself forward, slamming into the bigger orc, and they both fell to the floor in a tangle of pummeling arms and legs. Raenyl pivoted, turning his aim toward the witch doctor.

As Westin and the alpha rolled ever closer to the ledge, two thralls rushed to where snarling human and grunting orc wrestled for life or death. Two more betas dashed at Raenyl with his one arrow.

Fear and hopelessness filled Wynkkur. The elf cowered, stepping to the side as both orcs, neither much taller than he, ignored the elf while sprinting closer to the half-elf. Consumed with paralyzing fear, all Wynkkur heard were his thoughts screaming how they were going to die. Peripherally, the witch doctor uttered victorious squeals while the attached spirit continued whispering malice in his ear.

"Do something, Wank!" Raenyl fired into the face of the closest thrall. Grabbing the arrow through its snout, the orc tumbled forward like a sack of thrown meat. Still, the elf stood frozen as Raenyl screamed, "God pound it!"

Raenyl set another arrow's groove against the string, pulling the bow tight. There was no back step for him. Behind the archer, the priestess knelt, mumbling pointless prayers at the edge of a twenty-foot drop. Standing close to the fear-frozen elf, the witch doctor snapped clawed fingers. Simultaneously, Raenyl's bowstring severed. Powerful oak whipped straight, no longer arched by strong sinew.

"Argh!" The broken string lashed against the archer, slicing a bleeding line across the half-elf's cheek. The charging orc lunged at Raenyl as he reached for his sword. The thrall without a weapon bit deep into the top of Raenyl's shoulder. A stream of warm blood shot from the orc's mouth as an agonized shriek ripped from the half-elf.

Wynkkur, mesmerized in his state of horror, observed the orc biting into howling Raenyl. It held the archer's arm down, keeping his blade trapped in its scabbard. The orc's other arm reached up for the archer's throat. Raenyl intercepted the arm, fighting to keep his footing from toppling over Popalia, who would fall along with Katia into the darkness below. Frozen Wynkkur watched Seth gasping on the ground, his face turning purple in the flickering torchlight. Bennae screeched Westin's name shrilly as two thralls tore Westin from the warrior he wrestled. The stocky guard defiantly slammed his forehead into the alpha as the two smaller orcs pulled him up and back. Wynkkur stood motionless, knowing they were all about to die.

The witch doctor emitted a noise sounding as close to laughter as a pig could make. It was a sickeningly cruel sound, a sadistic noise. The spirit at his side licked at the inside of the shaman's ear, its forked-tongue waggling.

Wynkkur suddenly snapped, "No!" Pointing his torch like a wand at the possessed sorcerer who had beaten them, the elf spoke the names of the symbols he saw dancing in his mind. Wynkkur recognized the magical words as being the same he'd accidentally spoke at the inn.

The torch, not quite as exhausted as the elf that held it, burst into a jet of searing flame. The flare seared the shaman's already blackened face, his hair vaporizing into pin-prick embers across his head, the chortled laughter shifted into a flame-inhaled choke. The wreath of flame surrounding the witch doctor's head dissipated as swiftly as it had erupted. The spirit by his ear was unharmed—being both incorporeal and immune to pain. The wicked soul dove into the ear of the inflamed orc.

With raven wings aflame, feathers singed and burning, the spell-user looked upon Wynkkur with hypnotic eyes. A deep and throaty sound, like canvas being torn slowly, the noise now commanded in Elvish, "Kill my swine, and I'll serve you. Kill this foul dog, and take my cube from his belt. I will serve you far better than I could ever serve this blood sack. I promise joy no greater..."

Wynkkur did not see Westin, held up by two thralls. He did not see the orc-warrior rising up for the kill. He could not see the bruised color flushing from Seth's face as his armor loosened. From what seemed like miles behind him, he heard the half-elf curse, his voice gritty with pain.

Wynkkur closed the distance, his only focus upon the demon speaking within orc-flesh. Wynkkur fully intended to oblige the demon. Elvish steel flashed in the light of burning wings. The blade whipped over inflamed shoulders, like scissors snipping at a paper doll. The orc's head rolled backward, falling away from the neck that once bound it to body.

Its vile heart still beating in a body not accepting its own death, a violent spray of blood in a variable pulse fountain, shot out from vessels now detached. Much like the recall of a spinning yo-yo, the demon spirit retreated back into the box upon the orc's belt. Knees unlocked, and the decapitated orc toppled backward. Upon hitting the ground, a geyser of blood shot across the cavern shelf toward the cave opening. The wooden cube popped from out of the orc's belt, bouncing into the expanding puddle of dark red.

Westin, held up by two orcs, rose on both legs and kicked hard against the warrior orc. Stumbling, the alpha fell over the edge where the wet sound of meat being slapped came from the lower cave. A gurgling sigh followed a second later.

Still in shock, Wynkkur looked behind him, as Katia shoved the tip of her torch into the eyes of the orc biting into Raenyl. The half-elf had changed grip from sword to knife, stabbing his blade forcefully and repetitively beneath the arm of the orc, now on the losing side of what began as a clear victory. Seth scrambled, re-covering his sword while the two thralls that held Westin decided that running was truly the better part of valor.

Wynkkur let them pass, his eyes fixed upon the wooden cube lying in the glistening pool of blood. The elf kicked the little box at the fleeing orcs who never looked back. The box bounced against the cavern wall, ricocheting into the tunnel behind the two sur-viving orcs.

Chapter Seventeen

Day Eleven, between 7:00 and 8:00 p.m.

Raenyl sat down upon the cavern floor, the bloody dagger slipping from his fingers. Reaching up to his wounded shoulder, it hurt like liquid fire had been poured deep inside. Cursing the darkness, he could feel the blood spreading through the front and back of the material of his shirt, but he could not see the severity of the bite into his flesh.

Concerned Seth, who had unlatched the hooks along one side of his armor, asked, "Are you all right, brother?"

"I was about to ask you the same thing," the archer replied.

Seth reported with restored confidence, "I can breathe, again, and I'm on my feet, but I heard your scream. Are you sure you're all right?"

Wynkkur helped Popalia to stand. She asked, "What happened? Is everyone alive?"

Gregor spat, "While you were cowering behind the archer, we almost died." To Wynkkur, he complimented with a nod, "Good show with that flare, truly."

Releasing Wynkkur's hand, Popalia stated with incredulity, "Cower? I hardly think I was cowering."

Katia attacked verbally, "You stupid old man. You were pissin' your pants, and she was seeking true help." Raising both hands outward in gesture, holding the torch burning bright, she offered, "Thank you, Mystery. Thank you!"

Popalia's tone rattled like snakes and sharp hooks, "Katia, you better stop mocking my deity."

Gregor sneered, "What do you mean by I did nothing? *I* did nothing? Look at yourself."

Raenyl defended Katia, "She saved my life—which in turn, saved yours."

Bennae spoke up, "Quit fighting! Everybody is alive. Thank Stranoss, we can get out of here, now."

"Stranoss?" Astonishment dripped from Popalia's lips. "Stranoss was busy ensuring the snow on the mountain was melting. I believe all his priests were counting money, or chickens... eggs, or something equally mundane while we came to save you."

Bennae's eyes narrowed, "That is just mean-spirited. I don't insult your faith."

A disbelieving mask spread from Popalia to Wynkkur, who shrugged, saying, "Let's tend to the wounded."

Popalia added, "No kidding, and let's not tend to the ungrateful."

"Well, I'm thanking you," Katia added with a neutral tone.

"I'm sure you are," Popalia added mildly sarcastic.

Westin, who looked down into the darkness of the lower cavern, asked, "How do you suppose we get out of here?"

Gregor stated elementary, "We made right turns the entire way here, so we make lefts the whole way back."

Seth was helping Raenyl out of his backpack, "Ow, god pound it! That hurts!" The big warrior apologized while sliding the strap over the half-elf's blood-soaked shoulder.

Setting the pack upon the ground, Seth answered Gregor, "That way is locked down. Now that Wynkkur killed their witch doctor, the two that got away will tell the tribe, and then an even bigger group will come for us."

Westin stood over the edge where the orc he'd kicked had fallen. Agreeing with Seth as he tossed a burning torch to the bottom, "Those orcs are expecting us to go back; they'll be waiting for us to come." As the torch hit the bottom, he turned away, making a sour face, "There are spikes growing out of the ground down there. Take a guess where that orc I kicked had landed?"

Raenyl spoke while unbuttoning his shirt with one hand, "I'm out of the next fight. Seth and Westin are the only fighters left in our group."

"I'm exhausted. I need sleep before I can help anymore." Wynkkur added, "I don't even know where the power for that last spell came from."

"Think it is a *Mystery*, huh?" Popalia begged the question. She then agreed, "We all need sleep before we can get out of here. I'll heal Raenyl, but then I'll need sleep, too. Seth, can you make it a little longer."

"I'm asleep on my feet," the warrior answered as he helped Raenyl out of his shirt. "Oh gods, brother. That looks really bad. Katia, hold that torch closer. It is really bad, Raenyl."

"Yes, I know it is bad! It is *my* arm," Raenyl replied. "This arm is...useless."

Bennae, who'd been wobbling on the edge of hysteria, shrilled, "We cannot wait here! If Westin is right, they'll be back, bigger and tougher, and we'll be dragged down the tunnels like Enga!"

Shaking her head, Popalia denied, "That's not going to happen."

Wynkkur agreed with the scribe, "If we are still here when they get back, we won't be so fortunate a second time."

"Westin," Raenyl called, "in my pack, there is a small, leather pouch. It is down at the bottom, under all the torches. It is a small bag about the size of Seth's fist. It'll feel like there are a bunch of nails in it. Pull out the extra bowstrings. They are just inside the pouch."

"Want me to re-string your bow?" Westin looked baffled.

Raenyl shook his head, "No, I just don't want them lost."

Westin rummaged through Raenyl's pack as Popalia plotted, "We can use Seth's rope to get down into the bigger cavern. Down there, we will find a place to hide. Bennae, we all need sleep if we are to survive."

"How can you even suggest sleep?" protested Bennae. "Can you sleep? They want to rape and eat us!"

Shaking her head, Katia mocked quietly, "I'm pretty sure they won't rape *you*." Only Raenyl and Popalia were close enough to hear her.

Westin withdrew a small pouch, "Is this the one?"

"Yeah, that's it," nodded Raenyl. "Open one end and after removing my bow-strings, fling the contents into the hallway. It'll slow down our pursuers."

"What is it?" Wynkkur asked.

Westin smiled, "Caltrops."

"Caltrops? What are caltrops?" Gregor inquired.

Katia chuckled mischievously, "Nasty, nasty—tiny spike traps. Barbs—when stepped on, they'll stab right through the bottom of shoes. It'll come as a rude surprise for barefoot orcs."

Westin stepped over the cooling corpse of the headless shaman. The stink of seared hair still lingered over the body. Avoiding the blood puddle, he stepped close to the cave opening and flung the sack outward. A second later, the sound of tiny prongs tinkled across the cavern and into the dark hall.

"Hey, rich boy," Raenyl called in his best Gregor impersonation––which was still awful. It may have been because he was speaking through clenched teeth. "Be a good lad, and search the dead. Your scribe can help, too. Seth, Westin, and Wank, find the easiest way down while Katia and Popalia bandage my arm."

"Rich boy!" Katia chuckled dryly. "I like that. You're funny."

"It's exhaustion, I'm sure," Raenyl slurred.

"Or blood loss. You're usually not funny at all," Popalia

remarked. "Katia, bring the torch closer so I can see."

Not liking to be ordered around, the merchant resisted, "Do you know how much these clothes are worth? Westin, you do it. I'll help the elf find a way down."

"I told you, Gregor. I don't work for you, anymore." Westin turned away from the merchant.

Raenyl enlightened Gregor, "You work for me, now, and your payment is you might get to live if you do what I say."

"You only have one arm. What is the worth of a one-armed archer, hmmm?"

"I have three arms," Raenyl expressed. "Seth, take Mister Moneybags and throw him over the side. We came here for Katia."

"Really?" Surprise washed Seth's face in the flickering light. "Oh, you mean like what Clarence said about Malthrak and Oliev."

"I'll throw him. I'll be your extra hands." Westin advanced upon the merchant quickly, grabbing the merchant from under each arm. Westin wrestled the struggling merchant closer to the edge as if he planned to toss the man over.

Apparently, Bennae believed the caravan guard would throw the merchant into the darkness below, so she shouted, "Westin! Stop it!"

Gregor, the weaker man, was helpless in the arms of the trained fighter. He stammered, "No! Westin, please. Gods help..."

With one hand pressed against Raenyl's shoulder in an attempt to slow the bleeding, Popalia turned to the two men, one pushing and the other being pushed. Behind her, Katia affirmed, "He's gonna do it."

Popalia's tone snapped with the firmness of a disciplining mother—"No! Westin, stop!"—and he did, right at the edge, holding the merchant inches from his own life.

Westin emitted an aura of unfathomable rage as Popalia altered her tone to one of calm understanding, "I don't know what happened to you this morning, but we cannot afford to turn on each other. Raenyl is right—Gregor is going to search the dead for supplies. What money he may have means nothing right here and now."

The elder man begged, "Please, listen to her Westin. Please?"

Westin, who stood upon more than one edge, claimed, "This... all of this is his fault. Enga, Lissa, the kids, and all of our dead friends...it is all his fault."

"I lost a lot, too, Westin. Please, don't kill me. You know what I lost!" Panic animated the merchant's expression as he held his breath, waiting for life or death.

Popalia spoke softly, "If it is his fault, then let him live. Your revenge will only win you his guilt." Westin stood holding Gregor, whose toes hung on the corner before the nothingness below. Clenched teeth barred beneath sneering lips, Westin eyed the old man with hateful intent.

Popalia snuffed another angry flame. "We will be out of here soon, and Gregor will no longer matter."

Electric, a very tense couple of seconds passed, and Bennae sensitively reminded, "Please, Westin. Think of all the years and not just what happened, today."

Westin sniffled, pulled Gregor back from the edge, and released the merchant. Westin turned to wipe his eyes, and Bennae took the warrior in a gentle hug. Caressing his shoulder, she whispered gently in his ear as Gregor took three swift steps toward the nearest of the dead orcs. Squatting down beside the orc Raenyl had been bitten by, the merchant asked, "So, what am I searching for?"

Seth volunteered, "I'll help him. I'll show him how."

Foreseeing Raenyl barking at Seth, Wynkkur offered, "I can find a way down without Seth's help. It won't even take long." Raenyl nodded and remained quiet.

Katia lowered the torch closer to Raenyl's shoulder. "Oh, that is a nasty bite. I'm no doctor, but that is gonna need more than just a bandage." Blood pulsed through a puncture made by one of the orc's tusks. Teeth markings were imprinted in the inflamed meat between his neck and shoulder. Each time his heart would beat, the blood ebbed through the gash—his life dribbling down a defined chest.

"I can heal this, Raenyl." With a shiver, Popalia added, "It will be no worse than fixing up your brother earlier."

"No, I don't want anything to do with your god. We told you that when this whole mess got started, Seth made *our* point very clear." Raenyl watched all the blood dripping from the wound to his belt. *It was like a tiny stream*, he thought. "Just wrap it, and let's go. I'll manage until we get back to Dead Rik's."

"You want to go back to Dilligan's? You have far more faith than you let on," Popalia charmed. "Thought you said that was suicide."

"This is suicide. Coming into these tunnels was suicide. Bane's Blood! Arguing with you to bandage my shoulder is suicide. We got your precious Katia, and we are free to go back, now. So, start bandaging my wound...please."

Katia's voice sounded slippery sweet, "For real, you really did come in here just for me? I'm flattered." Her voice harshened, "Here I thought these chains meant something else, altogether." Like an ice pick, she spat, "Reminds me of working on my momma's farm."

At the other end of Katia's chain, the priestess remarked, "You know why we came for you. Nothing has changed between us over the last week. We want LeSalle's Grace."

"Well, Princess. You are chasing the wrong fool for that prize. You *know* I ain't got that. And at the rate we're moving, it's gone, baby. It's gone!"

"You're going to get it for us, and you will remain chained to me until it is back in my hands. It is mine, and I want it back!" Popalia saw herself throwing one mouthy thief over the edge as her own rage began to bubble.

Louder than the two girls, Raenyl barked, "Shut up! Will you two shut up and patch me before I bleed to death?"

"Shush!" Bennae scolded. "Don't draw more of them to us. Be quiet."

Popalia whispered, but it was a harsh and angry whisper, "Fine, Raenyl. I'll patch you. I'll heal you without your permission, and then I'll heal Ucilius next, despite Gregor's protests."

"Damn you, Popalia!" Raenyl protested, but he did not stand up or pull away.

Setting her hands upon his wound, she felt his warm blood pulse through her fingers. Popalia tried to focus but was off-centered. Her connection to the source of her power was severed. She could not touch her god.

Shaking her head, she spoke a prayer, but it fell weak from her lips. "Great Mystery, the Unknown Host. Heal Raenyl, please, so we can all get out of this cave." There was a hum in her mind as she imagined the power that should be there. There was no tingle in her hands, nor pain in her shoulder, only Raenyl's sticky blood pushing through her fingers.

"Some healer," Katia spat.

"I'm bleeding a river!" Raenyl's patience was at its end. "Gods pound it. Will you bandage me, now?"

Popalia began by saying something completely out of character, but exactly what she needed to say. No words could be truer for her in that moment than, "Damn it! I can't heal the unwilling, and I can't heal when I'm angry." She spat, again, "Damn it." It felt good to say it, so she added two more, each louder than the first,

"Damn, damn!"

Moving quickly to her side, Wynkkur grabbed Popalia's arm at her elbow. Both Raenyl and Seth were chuckling, amused with her outburst, but all others shared an expression equal to Ucilius's. Wynkkur whispered in her ear, "This is not the best time or place for a breakdown. Pull yourself together, Priestess of the Blue Order."

Katia smirked in her torchlight as Popalia stared at the dark blood on her hands and what soaked into the sleeve of her once-white robes. Catching Katia's cynical expression from the corner of her eye, Popalia heard the deeper wisdom of Wynkkur's remark. His words, like the crack of a whip, pulled her together. Remembering the last lesson given from her father, as a priestess, she must remain in control of her emotions and not be controlled by them.

Sighing deep, she took new control over her panicked tone, saying, "I will not fight you, Raenyl. I should trust my god more than your abilities as an archer. I doubt with that wound you could even re-string your weapon, let alone pull it if someone else re-strung it for you. You can carry a torch with your good hand, and we will still get out of here...somehow."

Turning to Wynkkur, she requested, "With that sharp blade of yours, could you cut my robe at the elbows so I can bandage Raenyl?"

"In Seth's pack," Raenyl informed, "there is a wooden box filled with cotton bandages and an ointment to prevent infections. You don't need to make your robe sleeveless."

Katia added with what sounded like true concern, "You need more than ointment and bandages. You need to be sewn up. You're gonna bleed out, man. You'll be dead before we see daylight."

"I've got needle and thread, compliments of Carouser's Inn," Popalia informed. "It's in my pack, but we need to get out of here. We've got to get off this ledge and deeper into the darkness before more orcs come.

Nodding, Raenyl agreed, "Even with the caltrops as a deterrent, I'd feel much better being anywhere but here."

Chapter Eighteen

Day Eleven, 8:30 p.m.

Relaxing aside the fire, Private Joab lay upon his bedroll—his armor, weapon, and shield all within an arm's reach. Watching through an opening in the trees, the clouds drifted across shining stars. His booted feet rested upon a rock outside the fire pit. He could feel the fire's warmth through the soles of his boots.

Captain Snales sat across the pit, scraping a whetstone across the wedge of his dual-bladed axe. He sniffed once, then looked across the flames, "Private, I think your shoes are about to burst aflame."

Private Clause, who was curled up and nearly asleep, mumbled, "I thought that was Arty's shorts I'd smelled."

"These are not my shorts, nor are these my boots. They are Regulator boots," Arty Joab teased. "Nor is this my sword, armor, or shield."

"Oh, yeah," huffed Jorgan Snales, "well, if Regulator boots burst aflame, it will be Regulator gold deducted from the wearer of Regulator-issue shorts."

Muffled coughs of laughter came from the huddled young man aside the fire. Private Joab pulled his feet away from the flames, adding his own comment, "Pound that! I lost enough, today. I'll keep my coin, thank you very much." Noticing the tips of his boots were smoking, he asked the Captain, "Sir, how far do you think the Commandant went?"

"Why, do you want to go hold his hand? He might be lonely out there without you, Private. He might need someone like you to help him wipe," The hyorc chuckled. "If you rub nicely, you might even earn your raise back."

Propping up on one elbow, Private Clause griped, "Come on, you two. I haven't slept since yesterday morning. I'm tired."

"No one has slept since yesterday," Jorgan's scything tone cut at Eugene. "Had you killed the elf when he blew into our jailhouse instead of letting our prisoners breeze out through the front gate, *we* wouldn't be here."

Clause pleaded with his officer to listen. "Please, sir. We would still be sleeping on the ground by our burned-up beds even if we *had* killed the elf. The fire had barely started before that elf charged in with his damnable, blinding light. He might even have passed the messenger heading back to fight the fire."

Snales scoffed, "Bah! You two were playing hide the weasel and got busted cold!"

Joab shook his head, "Sir, no sir. You might find Clause cute, but he's not curvy enough to get a rise out of me."

Seeing too late that now was a bad time to tease his hyorc officer, Arty retreated, "Seriously, sir. We hadn't even time to lock the door, but there is more to it than that," his voice lowered to barely above a whisper. While pointing to Clause, "We think that priestess wasn't a priestess at all."

"Now you're gonna blame that crying, little girl? Shame on the both of you. Especially you, Private Joab," Captain Snales sneered. "You had the heads-up that the elf was coming, and he beat you both like he was beating children."

Joab looked to Clause while licking his lips nervously. Clause sighed and spoke up, "Captain, sir. I know I haven't been a Regulator long, but ..." He sat upright, "I swear that girl hexed us. She put a witch's curse on us seconds before we were told about the fire."

"Sir, he's not lying. It was the creepiest thing I've ever seen."

Transparent doubt washed the Captain's face, and a sigh followed, "Private Clause, you haven't been a Regulator long enough to fill my ears with bull dung." Raising a finger to his lips, he whispered, "Shhh." Looking then to Private Joab, he said, "Tell me what happened, Arty. Tell me what you think happened this morning."

Rubbing the stubble on his chin, Arty Joab started, "That big one, Seth, was trying to get us all riled up enough to open up the cell. He'd been taunting us for hours, but we're better than that. Eventually, he gave up and sat in the corner next to the girl. We went back to playing cards, waiting for our relief to come."

Jorgan Snales could smell the scent of the Commandant. He was close by and waiting within listening distance. Quickly deciding the Commandant's interest in the privates' story should also be his interest, he set his axe and whetstone nearby. "All right, then. Tell me about the creepy part."

Arty nodded, "Well, that's just it. I'll tell you, but you won't understand. Damn, sir. I don't understand. After sitting in the corner for hours with her hands tied behind her back, she rose up to her feet like when a puppeteer picks up his puppet. She was limp and nothing. Then, she was up on both feet, walking just like one of those wooden marionettes." Eugene nodded but remained silent, his eyes wide in agreement.

Arty continued, emboldened by Eugene's animations, "Captain, I swear by my mother, she looked like a dirty clown who crawled out from the sewer. She had these dark streaks beneath her eyes down to her chin, but both her eyes were alit, like there was a lantern in her head. In a weird but sweet voice, she says to us, 'You should let us out now or face the consequences,' or something like that. So, Eugene tells her we can't let them out, and I ask her about setting Capitol City on fire. She admits they started it, claiming it was an accident. In some sort of weird trance, she even admits to stealing the horses."

Seeing the Captain's skepticism, Private Joab emphasized, "I'm not jerking you, sir—it was like the very air had changed. My hair could have stood on end. She then says we've made our choice, and she goes and sits back in the corner, again. Not one minute later, Private Holker informs us of the fire in the mess tent, and not even a minute after that, the elf flings open the door and flashes our eyes with an awful, blinding light. Sir, I fully agree with Eugene. I think she cursed us."

Commandant Benning stepped out into the fire's light, and the privates looked surprised by his return. Saviid Benning admitted, "Whatever crimes they committed in Capitol City no longer concern me. Her god-pounded elf burned down my base. My base! We've been disgraced and are no longer a respectable army. We look like circus buffoons. I'm embarrassed to wear my uniform."

His dark eyes gleamed angrily in the firelight. Saviid continued, "We have not been so badly humiliated since the day Rik Carver was betrayed by the Order of Might. More than anything, I want their heads on spears, but it matters not. This witch already humiliated us. We will never recover, and I resent this fact."

Quietly, Private Clause asked his Commandant, "You heard us, *and* you believe us?"

Commandant Benning rubbed the back of his neck forcefully. "I don't know what to believe, anymore. I sent a letter with Corporal Maklo to be delivered to the Church of the Unknown. If this girl was their servant, we'll demand answers. If she wasn't, then I may as well believe your story. As it stands right now, it makes as much sense as any of this shit-tide we're wading through."

Private Joab dared to ask, "We *are* going after them, aren't we? I mean we have to get them."

Commandant Benning watched Captain Snales ease himself lower onto his bedroll. Without expression, he replied cool and suggestively to Arty, "Go to sleep, Private. Just as always, you'll get my orders in the morning, but this time you *will* follow them."

Chapter Nineteen

Day Eleven, sometime between 7:00 p.m. and 9:00 p.m.

"Who is going down first?" Raenyl asked everyone, scanning their faces. "Come on, quickly! Who's first?" Gregor stepped back a pace as Bennae shook her head. Ucilius stood between the two of them, drooling with hollow eyes.

Wynkkur stood at the edge, looking down to where a burning torch lay. It was only twenty feet down, but it felt more like a mile to the bottom. Radiating a limited amount of torchlight, the glow reached out from within a miniature forest of stalagmites. Dark shadows surrounded where the light was consumed between calcite teeth.

For all negative appearances, Wynkkur had done well with finding a way down. Viewing from top to bottom, the decline was less steep than anywhere else along the ridge, and all the way down were obvious foot and hand holds. Through the darkness, the climb down would challenge even the most fit. Still, no one scoffed. Wynkkur's path down couldn't be matched anywhere else along the ridge. This would just have to do. Never averting his stare to the jagged stones below, emotionlessly he stated, "Welcome to the realm of madness. Lo'Lyth's lair begins here."

Seth interjected, "I thought you said it started back there?"

Wynkkur looked out into the pitch, speaking morosely, "That was before we got here."

"I'll go first," Seth volunteered. "I don't know what a lowlith is, but I'll get bragging rights for bagging one, I'm sure."

Raenyl shot back, "Who will hold the rope if you're down there? I can't do it. Not with this hole in my shoulder."

"Let Popalia heal you." After a slight pause and a quick flex of his grapefruit-sized left bicep, "It feels good, brother. No fear..."

Katia cut in, "I'll go first." Looking over at Gregor, "Spineless Gregor should wear fancy dresses. Unlock me, and I'll even mark the way down as I go."

"No way," Popalia denied. "We'll go together. You'll run away if I let you go."

"What!" Katia interrupted. "Where am I going to run to?"

Popalia refused to look at the woman chained to her, "We live together, or we die together. This is your only out." Turning to Raenyl, she stated, "She is right, though. We will go first."

"No women are going to show me a coward," Westin growled. "I'll go first. Besides, I can fight if there are any orcs down there."

"No, Westin," Popalia argued. "This isn't about cowardice; it is about getting away safely. Katia and I have four arms together. I can hold on while Katia sets torches."

"I still don't like making a woman go first," Westin admitted.

"Two women," spouted Katia, "or one woman and a girl."

Raenyl began to chuckle but cut it short. He then nodded, "All right, but if even a hint of trouble, hang onto the rope, and Westin and Seth will pull you up. I'll watch the way behind us for any returning party."

There were no more words spoken of it. Like a spider with two heads—Katia behind Popalia—they climbed down to the lower chamber. Westin had tied them together, so they could best achieve the tricky goal before them. Awkwardly, they began their journey down, but the confidence of both women got them to the bottom. They'd climb together, four feet and four arms holding on and then stopping. Popalia gripped the sidewall as Katia raised one torch to Gregor. Gregor lit the torch and Katia planted the torch in a crevice, grinding it into place. They'd climb together, until Katia could barely reach the torch above. She'd then pull a torch from Popalia's pack, light it from the torch above, seeking to find a crevice in which to plant the torch.

The journey down started out clumsy and menacing, but soon after beginning, the challenge lessened. It took more time to plant the three torches than it took to climb down tied together. Katia's feet were first to touch the lower floor, and she began loosening the knots binding her tightly to the priestess.

As soon as the women were untied, Seth asked, "Is everything okay?"

Fire illuminated the vertical path back up to the big merce-nary. Popalia nodded, "Aye, we are fine. Send Ucilius next."

"Wait, wait, wait," called Gregor. "Who will protect him down there?"

Seth regarded Gregor with disbelief, "Who is going to protect him up here? The first orc that comes around that corner, I'm tossing 'Useless' to them before I get down there." Gregor grew quiet and backed away from the edge.

Ucilius rolled against the sides as he was lowered. Lifeless as a bag of apples, he reached the bottom and slumped to the ground.

The girls untied him, and the rope went back up. Then, Gregor came down, followed by Bennae, and then Raenyl.

They had lowered Raenyl slowly, yet Popalia insisted, "Let me see your shoulder."

"It is still bleeding." His body language said no.

"Sh—sh-shush!" Westin called from up above. Everyone fell quiet. Then, after a brief silence, a drop of water plopped into a dark pool out in the unknown space. Then, there was another plop echoing somewhere else in the darkness. Westin's whisper returned, sounding loud, "Wynkkur says orcs are coming."

"Dammit," Raenyl said with little surprise. Louder, he called up to the two fighters, "Westin, come down, then Wank. Seth, can you make it without a rope? We can't leave the rope for them."

Popalia added, "The climb looks worse from where you're standing."

Westin didn't waste time answering and quickly wrapped the rope around his chest and knotted it in the center. Seth held the opposite end of the rope stepped back and braced himself as Westin clambered over the side and scurried down. Westin moved fast and got down to the floor. He was untied in seconds.

Seth pulled the rope back up. As the end slipped over the ledge, he looked over his shoulder to where Wynkkur watched down the tunnel. The big man called, 'Hey, it's your turn."

Wynkkur left his post while warning, "I couldn't see any torches yet, but by what I heard—" He shivered, "Many are coming."

Seth looped the end of the rope. "How many?"

Putting both hands together so Seth could round the rope, he answered, "Too many, and it sounds like they are coming quickly."

Seth nodded, "You're not climbing. I've seen you climb, and we'll both die before you get down there." Seth yanked on the rope to ensure it was tight. "Just roll over the side and I'll drop you down quick. It'll be bumpy, but I'm coming down right behind you, so get out of my way." Not exactly a comforting gesture, his large hand patted the elf's shoulder.

Wynkkur got near the edge and lay down. Inhale deep, exhale deep. "Into the mouth of madness." He rolled, falling over the side, and Seth was quick to feed the rope. Wynkkur banged his elbow once, then his knee, but then he was on the ground, sitting on his butt. He was together in one piece, a little sore, but clearly remembering Seth's words. He hadn't bumped his head. Looking up, Seth tossed the rope down.

Flipping over, Seth slid down until his foot touched the first torch. Then, just as he promised, he came down quick. Using the torches first as a foot stop, and secondly as a hand clutch, he'd remove the torch and drop it to the ground below as he rapidly clambered—more like a controlled fall—into the lower cavern. No sooner did his feet touch the ground than a howl of sheer pain erupted from the space above.

Then, there was a second shriek, and a third following almost as fast. Darkly, Raenyl chuckled. Westin grinned, saying, "Caltrops." The next shriek hollering from the upper tunnel was not pained, but a sound of pure rage.

"Let's run," a stressed Bennae suggested.

"Yeah," Wynkkur agreed. "Let's." Holding his torch high, he moved away from the coming orcs and deeper into nothingness.

It was not nothingness. The ground was treacherous with multiple spikes, like needle-teeth sprouting up from the cave floor. There were large formations resembling melting stone with a sickly sheen reflecting the torchlight. In the valleys between the larger stalagmites, the floor collected water in ankle-breaking puddles and shallow pools. Wynkkur sought a pathway within the nightmarish realm, but there was no trail to follow.

Wynkkur hurried through the grand chamber with everyone keeping his quick pace. He looked up but saw nothing except darkness. Looking to either side, darkness waited outside the fire's short range. Quickly up and over a small incline, the other side became smooth and without so many of the jagged cavern spires.

Raenyl called from behind, "Stop, stop. Hold up." Everyone slowed but no one stopped. Raenyl ordered firmly, "Gods pound it. I said stop!"

"We've got to get away!" Gregor spoke for everyone.

"Yes, and running with these torches marks us." Raenyl offered his hand, "Give me your torches." Bennae and Wynkkur handed theirs first and Raenyl dropped them each into a puddle. Hissing a final protest, two lights blinked out.

"What are you doing?" Gregor panicked.

"Put out your torch, or they will see us!" Seth understood and set his torch into the water. Popalia followed, but Gregor refused.

"Put it out, old man," Raenyl snapped.

"No! How will we see without it?"

"You're going to get us killed, you old fool. Put it out!"

"We can't see without light. We will be caught!" Gregor argued.

Raenyl growled, "If I had two arms, I'd snatch it…"

Westin grabbed the torch in the merchant's hands, but Gregor resisted with a death grip. Westin broke the merchant's grip by punching Gregor in the jaw with a quick left. The last thing anyone saw was Gregor's hand covering his mouth as Westin extinguished the final torch.

Blackness swallowed all. Gregor whined from nowhere, "Ouch, curse you Westin. Now we are all going to die!"

"Shut up, Gregor," Raenyl whispered from nothingness. "Be quiet and watch the way we came."

Someone was breathing heavily, and someone's boot scraped the ground. Someone bumped Popalia, but she thought it was Katia. Then, all they heard was the dripping of water. An occasional sounding of "plop" rang through the cavern, then nothing. The breathing eased, and then, "plop," another drip in the distance. They had left a couple torches burning on top of the cliff, the only light in the eternal black. At a distance of barely 400 paces, they saw high upon the ridge they'd scaled down.

Both Wynkkur and Raenyl heard more. Up there, muffled from human ears, they heard the sounds orcs made. It was coming from the tunnel, and there were many gathered. The light increased from the cave opening. The orcs had cleared a path through the caltrops.

They were on the ledge; their own torches glowing beacons, announcing their presence. Their snorts echoed through the cavernous space, tinged with almost human emotion. Sounds resembling shock, and snorts resembling sorrow echoed from the ledge as they gathered about their fallen. Some of the orcs stood along the edge, waving their torches and hoping to see what hid in the darkness below. They were checking the ledge to see if anyone hung there. A random orc made a sorrowful whine, as did several others soon after.

Wynkkur held his breath as he watched in suspended animation. An orc approached the edge and threw his torch into the cavern, illuminating the darkness as it flew. Spikes, like the ones on the ground, could be seen hanging above from the ceiling. All shadows wobbled as the torch flickered through the air, but it was immediately extinguished with an angry hiss upon landing.

It seemed that the orcs on the ledge parleyed. Their piggish snorts sounded enraged, as if two leaders argued. Then, one of the noisy orcs subsided, leading some of the others to leave. Wynkkur was not sure, but he thought it looked as if they were beginning to take the dead back to the tribe.

They all watched from the shadows as the orcs drifted back

down the long tunnel. No one was sure how many orcs had come, but later, they would agree that it must have been over a dozen. As the last orc left, the light of the torches dissipated into sublime darkness.

A snide tone, Raenyl was first to speak, "All right. Let's find someplace to fall asleep."

"I can't keep going, Raenyl. I must rest," the elvish dialect painted Wynkkur's voice in the pitch black.

Shaking, old and male, "We need light. This is too much."

"Mmmm-hmmm," a female response sounded from the same direction.

Elvish dialect retuned from the blackness. "This is exactly why I must rest. I cannot provide light, now. The well is dry." The tone had an edge.

The first voice returned, "I can provide light if we need it. Though, I think Wank here is right. We should get some sleep."

A female voice, wobbly and insecure, "They'll come for us as we sleep!"

"No, Bennae," the voice's owner sounded strong and sure, "They would already have come down if they believed we were here. We are safe." The confidence faltered, "...er...well, safe from the orcs at least."

Old, yet childish, "You didn't need to punch me!"

The strong voice returned, "Yeah, I did. At least I didn't kill you. She is right, the priestess—you should have to live with yourself."

"I provided for you."

"Only gold, Gregor. You took everything else."

"Hey!" a new voice boomed, powerful and commanding, "Whatever bad blood is between you two, you're gonna hav'ta put it in your backpacks or something. It's got to wait 'til we get outside."

"Well said, brother. I love your metaphors."

"I ain't got no metaphors. I ain't got metaphors."

"Big man, that is *my* leg you are touching." Female and bitter, "I still got bugs on top, so don'cha touch."

A woman's voice, almost arrogant but not, "I'll need light to sew by. If I don't stitch you up right now, Raenyl, you will sleep forever if you fall asleep ignoring that wound."

Small and humble, almost expected of an injured boy, in a voice frightening to the priestess, "If I asked," then, a long pause. Seconds were swallowed by absolute sightlessness, "Would you heal it?"

Silence. Darkness. Inhale. "Absolutely, Raenyl. I can heal that bite completely."

Chapter Twenty

Day Twelve—Sunrise

Private Arty Joab felt a tickle across his cheek, but sleep still held him. He moved his hand to brush whatever away, but nothing was there. Then, the tickle returned, this time awaking Arty.

Sitting up, his eyes opened and blinked to clear them of sleep-crusties. As Arty's eyes gained focus, they recognized black leather boots stuffed with green pant legs. One long pace away stood a grinning Captain, who teased, "You sure are cute when you sleep."

"Aw, Captain. That's really creepy," Private Joab's speech slurred while rubbing his eyes clean. "Waking up to you ogling me makes me worried."

Captain Snales pursed his lips into a kiss as Commandant Benning's voice boomed from above and behind him, "I sent the Captain to wake you, Private. We are all ready to go, and you are still snoozing."

Private Joab sprung from his bedroll as if doused. He first picked up his boots and sword before realizing his armor had not yet been donned. Dropping his boots, then the sword, he pushed his shield to the side to pick up the breastplate and chainmail.

As Private Joab prepared himself for travel, Commandant Benning addressed his troops, "Years ago, I'd met our king when he was still a prince, and I swore to his father that I'd see to the protection of these roads. In honoring that commitment, our mission has changed."

"By the end of this day," Saviid pointed at the nearest wagon, "we will know where these raiders are camped, or the Regulators will disband and be released from service to the crown. Today shall be the Ascolan brothers' second lucky day."

"Sir?" Private Clause inquired, "If the Ascolan brothers are wanted by the king, would not their capture redeem us?"

Captain Snales chuckled, "The brothers haven't gotten away. After we find this orc camp, we can tell the king the brothers slipped by while we were doing our job. He is the king. He'll get the Ascolan brothers, just not through us. Remember Private, this trail you found along the side of this mountain is paved with redeeming glory and not just for you."

Benning educated his troopers of the out-laying geography, "From Faradell Pass, the only city of worth is Portown Magistrey. The northeast is unoccupied by civilized men. Magistrey is in the middle of a desert and pressed up against the ocean. Southwest of Portown is a religious community, and then nothing is inhabitable all the way to Athania. Athania is not welcoming of fugitives."

"Why didn't you just tell us all this last night?" Joab wrestled his head and arms through his armor's respective holes. Once his limbs were through, the chainmail suit rolled heavily down to the top of his belt, leaving only the pauldrons to be adjusted.

Commandant Benning did not need to be loud to prove his word was absolute. "Don't test my authority, Private. I was not certain of my decision last night. That is why I left *glorious you* in suspense. Now, hurry up. You're holding up my army."

Arty Joab retrieved his sword and shield as Captain Snales withdrew the long stick he'd kept hidden behind his leg. It was a skinny switch he found fallen from aside last night's fire—a stick with one end charred and blackened. Tossing the stick out and into the bushes, it slapped many leaves, making a fair amount of ruckus.

Turning to where he'd heard the stick clatter, Arty asked, "What was that?"

Eugene, seeing Arty's face for the first time chuckled. "It sounded like a squirrel to me."

Benning also saw the black whiskers the Captain had drawn from nose to cheek on both sides. He uttered a jovial laugh, "Or a cat!"

"There're no cats out here," Private Joab scoffed.

Jorgan Snales, still grinning, winked and added, "Sure there are. Big ones, too. Now, get your helmet on and move out, Private."

Chapter Twenty-One

Day Twelve, Unknown hour

In the darkness, Wynkkur listened as a woman whispered, "I'm not going to wake him. He's a wizard. He could turn me into something...unnatural."

A male voice, "Miss Kobblepot, I want light to see by. He can light our torch, so feel around until you find him. Go on, now. Go."

Amused with what he heard, Wynkkur listened. Was anyone else awake? Popalia would have informed them he was incapable of turning anyone into anything "unnatural" if she'd been awake. He didn't even know what "unnatural" would be. Quietly enjoying a dark theater, Wynkkur listened to the same male voice call out from the black vacuum, "Miss Kobblepot, here. Take this torch. That way, he can light it and go back to sleep if he wants to. I wouldn't want you to be turned into anything without hands, so make sure to be polite."

"What torch? Oof!" Then, slightly peeved, "Okay, I got it." Wynkkur heard scraping across the rock floor.

Then, there was another voice. "Kugh! What?" Certain it was Katia waking, the next comment made it absolute to the elf, "Big man, you best let go of my leg!"

"Sorry, I'm sorry. I can't see! I'll go the other way."

"Shhh!" Groggily, Seth's voice called from a different area of darkness. "I'm sleeping—damn sun's not even up."

"What's going on?" Popalia called sharply.

"Confound it. I'm sorry. I'm just trying to find the wizard," Miss Kobblepot announced.

Sounding miffed and slightly violated, Popalia added, "Well, those were not *the wizard* you were just grabbing." Raenyl's dry chuckle rang out, and Westin sniggered.

Seth boomed, "Quiet, I'm sleeping!" Quieter, he muttered to himself, "Ouch, on a god-damned rock." Then, there was a skipping clatter in the deeper darkness, moving away from the listeners.

Startled, Gregor asked, "What was that?"

"I'm sorry," Bennae pleaded with everybody. "Sorry, sorry. We just want light. I didn't mean to wake everyone."

"Well you did, Miss Kobblepot! You seem to have awakened everyone *except* the wizard!"

"I have flint and steel in my pack," Raenyl's voice chimed, sounding uncharacteristically happy. "Gimme a moment to fish it out, and I'll give it to you."

"He can't use it," Westin added sarcastically. "He can't even wipe his own bum without calling, '*Miss Kobblepot, Miss Kobblepot!*'"

Bennae sounded genuinely hurt. "Westin Weller, I have a far better practice than to be so foul." Humbled, the caravan guard apologized with a resounding grunt.

Wynkkur remained silent, finding it challenging to stifle his laughter. Wynkkur assumed he was hearing the half-elf rifling through his backpack, and then Raenyl spoke, sounding friendly, "Gimme the torch. I'll light it for you."

Although this darkness was something terrible, Wynkkur found the sounds ringing throughout as being overly humorous. Chuckling once, Wynkkur spoke two words of magic, hoping to override his rising fit of laughter. With his hand aflame, the biting light caused him to squint. He realized the light blinded nearly as much as the darkness.

"Here," he extended his flaming hand toward Bennae, who had been feeling across the ground in the wrong direction over behind Popalia and Katia's area. "Light your torch off that." The scribe stood up, hurrying to the elf's side. As she lit the torch, he teased, "I could never turn you into anything unnatural...well, except a pile of smoldering ash." Wynkkur smiled and shook out the flame from his hand, while Bennae recoiled and drew the lit torch away.

Gregor's white wig sat upon his head, twisted just enough to make his face appear uneven. His bottom lip was swollen and bruised. He added, "You heard us and didn't offer to help? Why?"

Wynkkur shrugged, "Did you ask me for help?"

"We're all awake, now. Thanks, Wank," Seth grumbled.

"Sure, Seth," Wynkkur answered pleasantly. He then shivered and said, "Glad we all woke up. How we are not dead surprises me, being where we are."

"Darkness doesn't kill," Raenyl stated with a slight grin. "Those orcs gave up after finding all their dead friends on that cliff."

"Orcs are now the least of our worries," Wynkkur informed. "This is Lo'Lyth's realm—this is her exile."

"What is a Lowlith?" Gregor touched his mouth and grimaced. He shot a sneer at Westin before saying, "I'm very well read, and

I've never heard of a Lowlith."

"Wait, wait," Seth rubbed his eyes. "You said this was Lo'Lyth's grave yesterday, now it is Lo'Lyth's realm." Fearfully superstitious and childlike, he asked, "Is Lo'Lyth undead?"

Wynkkur peered around at everyone who was now awake and sitting, stopping his gaze on Gregor. "You never heard of Lo'Lyth because Lo'Lyth has never been written, at least not in human books. You will be privileged to hear the story of Lo'Lyth's Grave from me. Normally, I would not tell you the tale, but now it is important for you to know where you are." He gazed at everyone. "Listen up. You all need to know this."

He began, "This story has been passed from generation to generation so that we will never forget, and so we elves never make the same mistakes as our beloved, sacred mother."

"After the world had been created by the gods, they created one elf, Lo'Lyth, and she was to cultivate and care for the land. She could commune with the gods, and the land began to tame under our mother's guidance and direction. She was the god's perfect creation, and she was given immortality as proof of her perfection."

He continued, uninterrupted, "In each of their respective seasons, the gods would visit and give counsel, but they could only come when their reign upon the land was strongest—on the day of the full moon of the respective equinox or solstice. Rynon the Sculptor came in the freeze of winter, Fenyll came on the hottest day of summer. Mah'taow, god of the winds, knocked the autumn leaves from trees as Wythra rolled spring rains across the sky. For one day, at the peak of their reign, each god would visit our mother.

"Our mother was given the heart of the gods, and she also shared reason and longed for the few days spent with the gods—one day with each god, one time per year. She waited through all the other days with loneliness as her only companion.

"No elf knows how long the land had been blessed with our mother, for we did not yet exist. Time holds no concern when there is no death. Loneliness though, is its own sort of slow death—grim and prolonging. Fenyll, god of fire and of fruit, eventually leads to Mah'taow's season of seeding.

"It is unknown to the elves, for we were not there, but somehow, Lo'Lyth had convinced Fenyll to bless a watermelon. It is rumored that she had claimed wanting the melon's harvest in the year to come to be bountiful, for even today all elves will agree that a cool watermelon fished from a cold spring is best eaten on a hot day. She'd promised the god there would be much to share in the year to follow. Soon after, the god left, his day having passed.

"The translation is hard here, please give me a moment." Wynkkur shook his head, his eyes distant as he remembered tales from his childhood. "Lo'Lyth was cunning, and she had no interest in planting the blessed seeds into the ground, but instead planted the seeds within her womb. One by one, after the spring rains and Wythra's time had finished, forty-two sons and forty-two daughters had been born. Upon the day of Fenyll's return, his visit was first met by the sound of eighty-four elvling cries.

"Fenyll, displeased at being deceived, cursed Lo'Lyth's womb so that everything born from it would die after a time upon the land. Angered, he left. All the gods, equally angered by their chosen's clever deception, agreed to never touch the land with their feet, except Rynon, sculptor of the mountain tops.

"Lo'Lyth cared none at all. She raised her elvlings to adults. She showed her offspring the secrets of the land, the nature of the trees, and the order of the animals. Knowing her womb and her elvlings had been cursed, she paired the first sons with the first daughters, so that they too could continue living forever.

"Lo'Lyth never knew death until one son did not awaken. His breath had stopped in the night, and his body was no longer warm to her touch. An eternal grief took her as the days of her elvlings faded, yet she remained. The same fate then befell her grand-elvlings, and then again to her great-grand-elvlings.

"The immortal soul became so ravaged by grief, it poisoned Lo'Lyth's mind. She abandoned the first tribe for the untamed wilds, desperate to tend to her broken heart."

Wynkkur continued telling the story of Lo'Lyth as Popalia took half a loaf of bread and began to break it into nine bite-sized pieces. "The fourth generation of elves searched the forests for Lo'Lyth, but it was as if she had been swept away by the winds. With the Mother gone, they continued living off the land and producing their own children. The fifth generation of elves did the same as did the sixth. By the time of the seventh generation of elves, Lo'Lyth's name had been forgotten."

"The Mother's name was not the only thing that had been forgotten, but also what the Mother had taught her first children. The land no longer bent by the direction of elves, the wilds had become forgetful of the time when elves were a director and a friend. Elves began to breed in bad seasons. Without guidance, they bred too much and too often. By the ninth generation's time upon the land, elves were reduced to barely another animal upon the land. The tribe had gotten so large, elves found themselves eating wild grasses and gnawing on tree bark like the beaver; for all the game had either been over-hunted or had moved far away.

"The gods' names were forgotten by the elves. At the birth of generation ten, they knew not the purpose of Wythra's rain, let alone her songs. Fire warmed the elves on cold nights, but praise spoken to Fenyll for the light on dark nights would never be worded.

"The tribe had become so large that one elvling would never be missed, but one elvling was missing. The mother and father searched behind rocks, in trees, along the shores of a lake, but their elvling was gone. A week later, another elvling vanished, and this time, another family searched the area for their young. The tribe had become so large as to not care for so few. Another elvling, sent to fetch water, never returned. A fourth elvling sent for burnable wood was never seen again. A group of young would play in the woods, but one would sometimes never come home."

Popalia handed out the ration of food to each person, then passed her water-skin around so all could wash down their bite of bread. Everyone listened as the elf continued, "The oldest and wisest elf remembered his grandmother's stories told from her grandmother about gods and their names. It was he who remembered that water rushing over rocks would often gurgle the word 'Wythra,' and leaves in trees often announced 'Mah'taow' in their rustling. He begged the others to remember the names of their creators. He believed the gods had taken the elvlings, and he called to the mothers and fathers of the missing to honor the names of the old gods.

"Mothers were the first to pray, fathers joining next, followed by brothers and sisters, then aunts and uncles; the names of the gods spread from lips to ears, but elvlings still vanished. The entire tribe was called to join in one great call for the gods' mercy. It was the dark season, the cold season—the season of Rynon when the tribe gathered, more than 100 score of elves. And they prayed. Unknowingly, they'd gathered upon the day of solstice, the day that the gods were the closest behind the veil of reality.

"An eagle, a great messenger, flew high up to deliver the cries of the elves, and their laments were heard by the gods. The eagle flew down to pass the message of the gods. In the tribe center, circling over the elves with heads humbly bowed, the eagle screeched, ordering their attention. The great eagle flew barely above the heads of each elf, calling all to watch before landing upon the central hovel within the vast tribal grounds.

"Imbued with the message of the gods and a beautiful voice, the eagle sang, 'Praise be to the gods, whose names you have forgotten and now remember. Upon this day, elves accuse falsely, for the gods have always honored the sacred laws promised to rock, tree, wolf, and elf. Nothing is born but by the power of their mother—always hold respect for the mother. The gods have done no harm against the elvlings, for it is also law to never injure the youth, as the young are sacred to the future. This is the eternal will of the creators. So it has been, and so it shall always be.' The eagle fell silent.

"The elder then asked, 'Great eagle, with your keen eyes and superior wisdom, where have our elvlings gone?'

The eagle answered, 'They cannot return from where they have gone, for it was Lo'Lyth who has taken your young, and she shall continue, unless a pact be made with the gods,'—and all the elves inquired.

"The pact was made clear by the avatar. The mother tribe must split into four clans and move away, so the injured land could heal. Each new tribe must praise the names of all gods but seek the lessons of one god and honor the chosen god's ways. Lastly, no pairing of elves shall create more than three offspring in honor of all mothers and offspring everywhere. Keep the cycle true.

"The eagle, having stated the desires of the gods, launched high into the air by the beats of powerful wings, flying off to fulfill the will of the creators. Soaring high, over the tallest pine upon the highest mountain peak, the eagle spied a hole surrounded by snow. Spiraling downward slowly, the eagle spotted what once had been the grave of Lo'Lyth's first born, now exhumed. Closer still, lying within the grave and upon a bed of bones, the mother slept.

"White bones, spread like a wreath around her sleeping form, Lo'Lyth stirred as she heard the beating of wings in the trees. Looking up and seeing the great eagle, she shirked away, knowing the bird represented the love she had failed, the honor she had soiled. The chosen herald called, 'Lo'Lyth, sweet Lo'Lyth, favored soul of the gods. Look now to how far you have fallen. The bones that surround you are your own flesh and blood, the mortality you could not accept. Your own offspring, which you have abandoned, have now become your game. You feed like the spider, choosing your own kin.'

"The ground beneath Lo'Lyth gave up the secrets she'd tried to hide. The elvlings she'd hidden popped up from beneath her bone-bedding like ambitious potatoes. Her grave contained the bodies of elvlings planted, and there had been many elvlings planted.

"She was then marked by the gods. Her fair skin faded to ebon-black, and her honeycomb hair bleached cold like snow. Fangs sprouted from her incisors as if a manifestation of her sins. Lo'Lyth's grave opened up, growing ever deeper. Then, the earth above covered it, and the mad mother was absorbed into the ground. Lo'Lyth has since been kept, and for as long as elves honor their pact, then deep down within the hollows, Lo'Lyth shall remain."

There was silence after Wynkkur finished his tale. Bennae was first to speak, "Stranoss, my god. That is horrible! Had she killed those babies?" She began to sob. "Why would you talk about that? Eating babies..." The sobs exploded.

"Miss Kobblepot," Gregor's tone softened, implying a sordid concern, "I'll take the torch, so you can wipe your eyes." Taking the torch, he then peered at the elf. "Shame on you, telling camp-fire tales after all we've been through. Keep your ghost stories for children."

Wynkkur's face froze, he blinked once, and once more before answering, "No, you misunderstand. What I just told you is sa-cred. This is the event marking the beginning of our culture—the event of Lo'Lyth's terrible fall. Her madness split the elves into clans, which began the Elven Calendar. We can follow the moon cycles backward to the exact day the avatar came and banished the Mother."

Bennae cried with her hands covering her face. Westin moved to her side, covering her with a protecting arm. Westin spied Wynkkur with a wry smile, "Your story says you came from watermelons."

Wynkkur shook his head, "No, I didn't. I said Lo'Lyth's off-spring came from blessed watermelon seeds. I was made by my parents' joining."

"Well, I think your story was well spoken," Popalia cheered. "For the record, I thought it was a wonderful story, even if it doesn't fit our predicament as you said it would."

"Yes, it does," Wynkkur defended.

"No, it does not," Popalia stubbornly refuted.

After a frustrated and long sigh, the elf spoke, "She was

banished to the hollows of the land. We are now in the hollows of the land. She is immortal and insane, and she is down in here with us."

"Wank, my little friend," began Seth, "we will protect you from crazy Lilith, all right?"

Wynkkur corrected, "Lo'Lyth, not Lilith. All of you shouldn't take this so lightly."

"Sheesh, whatever. Now you sound like Raenyl." Seth turned to his brother, "Speaking of, you are being quiet this morning, or whatever time it is. What time do you think it is?"

Raenyl nodded; there was a grin spread wide across his face. Looking at his hands, he said, "I think it is time to go, so lend me a moment to restring my bow." He nodded again, apparently pleased with his own idea, but instead admitted, "I rhyme."

Popalia's tone carried genuine surprise, "Raenyl, are you okay?"

"I feel great. Good as new." Smiling, he reflected, "Is this what new feels like? Anyhow, I feel fine."

Popalia then realized and laughed, "You are still elevated from the healing last night...or, whatever time that happened. I agree completely. Let's get out of here."

Chapter Twenty-Two

Day Twelve, 11:15 a.m.

Private Eugene Clause gulped as his heart pounded against his ribs. His stupid horse nearly killed him, but somehow the horse managed to find its footing and brought both of them atop the hill's peak. Breathing sharply, he looked over his shoulder and down the breakneck grade of gravelly soil, imagining he and his horse flipping end-over and into the trees at the end of a fifty-foot roll. He shivered, imagining the sound his skull would make upon contact—a sound like "Thwack!"

Shifting in his saddle to face the private, Commandant Benning said, "Looks like fortune smiles upon you today, Private. That there was the wrong way down."

"You saw that? My horse nearly fell, and I thought I was dead," Eugene chuckled dryly. "Getting down will be even harder for these horses. That grade is unnerving."

Captain Snales dictated, "Once we've found our mark, we'll seek out the optimal route for an offensive. It's SOP, so quit snivelin'."

"Captain, I nearly fell, me and my horse..."

Barking louder, Jorgan Snales cemented his expectation, "This isn't 'boy-bonding day'. I don't care how you feel. Mess up again, and we could all get killed. Understand, Private?"

"The horse slipped, Captain." He looked to Arty, who unknowingly still had four black whiskers drawn across his cheeks. Private Joab shrugged.

Snales glanced between Private Joab and the commander before prodding, "It's the rider, not the horse. All our horses are combat steeds—the best trained in the kingdom. Your riding is sloppy boy, just like how I'd expect a farmer to ride."

Incensed by the insult, Eugene's voice spoke differently, "Sir, yes sir. I will ride with more care."

Benning lowered his hand for Snales to ease a little, "The Captain thinks you should be more wary, soldier. I cannot agree with him more. This tribe we are closing on is slick and has evaded our most talented scouts. They attack with speed and precision, time and time again. This is not a combat mission, soldier, but one of reconnaissance. If they see us first, we fail. If we make too much noise, we'll trip an ambush." Commandant Saviid allowed his words to sink in before adding, "I agree with Captain Snales that killing yourself now *would* be best for the rest of the group." Benning's eyes chilled like frozen coal.

"Sir, Commandant! I will be more careful. I'll buff up, like right now...see?"

Ice black hollows peered into Private Clause, "Don't make me regret letting you live."

Private Joab then asked, "Sir. Captain, sir. Are you suspecting this trail will lead to that gang we fought last spring?"

Chuckling, "You mean the ones that gave our ballista some practice? Yeah, I think so. They've got a smart leader; he'd sent a sacrificial team to check our guard. I'd bet your future children that there were several orcs watching from the forest edge while the assault team died. Remembering how scrawny most of those orcs were, they were most likely overflow from the tribe. The orcs we're looking for have hit these roads four times between us and the Pass. They've been dormant since last fall."

"Eugene, my comrade," Private Joab urged, "as far as first missions go, this is as rotten as they get. You can't blow this one."

Eugene Clause's stare narrowed. He nodded, "Right. I may be 'country', but that doesn't make me blind. You're trying to pin yesterday morning on me." Shooting a glance to Saviid Benning, he pleaded, "I'll do by your lead and your lead only, sir." Back to Arty Joab, "You are as guilty of yesterday's failure as I am."

Jorgan Snales nodded, "You are right, Private Clause, but Arty's score with the Regulators is six wins and one fail. Can you remind us of your score?"

Private Clause recognized being in the corner. "All right. Okay, so tell me what you want from me to make this good? I'll prove my worth. Just tell me what to do."

Commandant Benning spoke up, "Take point. Private Joab will cover our flank. If you are noisy or sloppy, the Captain and I can handle damage control."

Private Clause eyed Private Joab with fire. Private Joab felt the heat and remarked, "Rank and file, brother. SOP." Eugene tapped his heels, and his horse launched forward. He looked away from Arty and took point without offering another word of protest or conviction.

Private Clause led silently and observed the terrain. There were very few trees atop the ridge. The ground was too stony and the soil too harsh for anything to take root. Jagged limestone teeth poked upward, and through these rocky teeth the trail continued for the better part of an hour. Following the trail atop the edge of the mountain, the peak leveled, and the path overlooked the valley from where they'd come.

Clause watched to the right, toward the higher mountains. His eyes, ever perceptive, were quick to see upon the ground a circular area of crusty black. He held his hand up for those who followed to stop. Continuing forward, he rode through the sharp spikes jutting up between ankle and knee height.

Commandant Benning requested, "What goes, Private?"

"Dried blood, sir, and lots of it." He swallowed, "Sir, I've killed five hogs in one day for my pa, and this would be nearly the same size puddle. It is all over the place."

Captain Snales nodded, "We're very close, then. Orcs kill their prisoners outside their camps and leave them to drain. The meat becomes lighter and thus easier to haul the rest of the way, just like what you used to do with the hogs."

"Sir, if we are this close, wouldn't it be wiser to leave the horses here and continue afoot?" Private Clause implored.

"Now, you're beginning to think like a Regulator," Captain Snales complimented.

In the distance, just over the lip of the hill, a horse neighed in a valley below. Emitting his excitement, Private Joab added, "Shit! We are close."

"They kept the horses." Commandant Benning's face stretched in puzzlement. "That is very arrogant. They neither covered their trail, nor slaughtered their stolen beasts. Something isn't right—Regulators, dismount."

Chapter Twenty-Three

Day Twelve, Hour Unknown

The cavern they walked through was immense. There had to be a wall someplace in this hollow, but they hadn't come to any stops since leaving where they'd slept. No one would agree as to how long they'd been walking. They could not see the sidewalls of the cavern in which they traveled. Popalia's plan acknowledged the fastest way from the orcs was in a straight line, putting the orcs at their backs.

Gregor called over to Seth, "Come closer, boy. Help me keep Ucilius upright."

Seth walked with a raised torch in one hand, his sword lowered in the other. "Where did you send Bennae? I thought she was helping you carry Useless."

"Don't call this boy such rotten things," Gregor replied. "Ucilius is a brilliant mathematician, simply brilliant. Please, help this old man and have some compassion. I can't keep up and carry the boy all by myself."

Sheathing his weapon, Seth growled as he looked over the "boy". He was easily his elder by eight years. "Take this." He handed the torch to Gregor and looped an arm around the catatonic man. "If Raenyl sees me, he'll be mighty pissed."

"I'll stand true by you, son. I'll inform your partner that you are protecting the group by moving us along at a swifter pace. Your partner seems a sharp fellow. I'm sure he is prone to reason."

"Reason or not, he'll still be some sort of pissed. I know him as good as myself." Seth's given support did help speed the pace of the stragglers. Raenyl was all the way to the forward, leading the group within earshot of Popalia's requests. Westin and Wynkkur walked a few paces in front of Seth and Gregor. Bennae quickly moved up the line to speak with Popalia.

Gregor chipped in, "Well, then. I'll sweeten the pot. When we get out of here, I'll contribute two gold coins—one for each of you. How can anyone be angry about gold?"

Seth chuckled with Ucilius stumbling along, "I got a better idea. Let me have the two gold coins, and I'll just deal with Raenyl's grief."

"So, you will help me with Ucilius, then?"

Shaking his head, Seth answered, "When Bennae isn't helping you, I'll help for two coins of gold. That is as close of a deal as you will get from me."

"You drive a hard bargain." Gregor nodded, "I'll agree to your terms, but only if you stop calling him Useless."

From a few paces up the line, Westin growled, "Two days ago you said Ucilius was as practical as the last tit on a boar. Why this sudden change of heart?"

"Pah, ignore Westin. There has always been banter between Ucilius and I. He is my son-in-law. All this mess has changed lots of things for both of us. Ucilius is a good boy, and I mean a real good boy. So are you for helping out—this is too much for an old man to carry." Whispering, he added, "Westin has been deeply wounded. He and Enga worked together for years. They were very close. I wouldn't bring it up—clearly he has become quite addled."

"Well, I don't want to start any problems," Seth replied without whispering. "We came for that woman, Katia. Once we get out of here, we'll be on our way. No point in sharing our troubles for too long." Seth took notice of Gregor's swollen lip and added, "If the orcs come back, I'll need to let go of Usele...I mean Ucilius, so stay near me until Bennae comes back."

About six paces forward of the business deal taking place, Wynkkur held his own torch as he walked a few paces aside Westin. He believed they had been walking through the dense darkness for hours, but without seeing the sun, it was impossible to tell. The torches cast orange light above and below, radiating off the longer stalactites above and marking the stalagmites growing from the cavern floor—some of them like melting pillars dripped from ceiling to floor.

The cavern floor was pocked with cup-like impressions filled with water. Occasionally, a drop of water could be heard landing with an echoing "plop". Wynkkur was mindful not to step un-evenly. Popalia might be able to heal a broken ankle with just a quick pain for herself, but Wynkkur felt there had been enough excitement since this journey began. Needless to say, he watched his footing.

Westin, who carried an acquired spear, stepped closer to the elf. His spear had been fashioned by humans. The steel blade extended as long as fingertip-to-palm, affixed to an ash wood pole reaching as long as Westin was tall. It was as thick as a gold coin was round. Although the tip was sharply pointed, the blade had dulled due to neglect and overuse.

Lowering his weapon to the side, he whispered so that only Wynkkur heard, "Trust me when I tell you, Gregor is a serpent. When you get a chance, warn Seth before he becomes ensnared so deep as to never get out."

Watching the edge of his torchlight, Wynkkur responded, "It would be unwise of me to spread gossip. Seth respects you more. I assure you, he does not trust me."

Westin, who was caught flatfooted by the elf's statement, replied, "Teams don't work on distrust. I may not be part of *your* team, but the two of you seemed very trusting yesterday, or whatever time that was."

Wynkkur didn't feel like talking. "It was last night," the elf said curtly. Ahead of them, Bennae began speaking with Popalia and Katia, and he wanted to listen. His relationship to Seth and Raenyl shouldn't be in this guard's interests. He responded with saying, "We are very committed to keeping each other alive, but beyond that, our ideals are in conflict. It is complicated, and I don't feel like explaining. We are quite determined to getting out of here alive. Trust me. As sinister as you imagine Gregor, he is only human. I promise, Lo'Lyth is a far more dangerous serpent." He looked out to the deep black as if merely mentioning the eternal mother would invoke her. He shivered.

Westin didn't like the way he felt. There was a wall of ice crystallized between them. The elf seemed pricklier, somehow. Westin nodded, "I'll be sure to speak with Seth later, if I get a chance." Tapping the spear's blunt end on the floor, he stepped back out and into the shadows.

Wynkkur hadn't meant to come off as rude, but he also didn't really care if he did. Six paces forward, Wynkkur focused his keen ears to listening. Bennae sometimes turned her head as she whispered to the priestess, and the sound of her whispers carried in the same direction. It may only have been small talk, but having an older sister and a mother, Wynkkur knew when females spoke to each other, often times there were other agendas.

Upon the land, there were only two humans Wynkkur trusted completely. His loyalty was not to the church, but only to Head Priest Ellund Saiwel and to his daughter, Popalia Saiwel. They had given him a place in the world when his world had exiled him. Westin could mock the tale of Lo'Lyth if he wished, but Wynkkur had a deeper kinship with the mad mother. His very name was viewed as traitorous among elves—Wynkkur translated into *"dominant hand pushes outward"*, or by an even closer translation, *"one-hand against"*.

Ellund, lead priest for the Temple of Dawn's Mystery, had accepted Wynkkur when no one else would. Wynkkur remembered twenty-two years back being fearful and lost. In the upper valleys of the Phildok Mountains was where his old clan, the Heigh Clan, lived. Having been banished from his tribe, Wynkkur ran, expecting to be killed by the beastly kobolds that inhabited the lower mountains. He'd somehow bypassed the larger hunting parties and made it into the forest in the mountain's shadow.

Once he was off his mountain, the trees had changed and the forests seemed wilder. Humans called the area Darkin Woods, but within the thickest of the forest were tribes of the Whood Clan. Halfheartedly he hoped the Whood Clan would take pity upon him and allow him to stay, even with his mark of a bad name.

Stumbling through the wilderness, he'd heard the cry of what he'd thought must be a very young elvling. Creeping ever closer, he'd found an oddly built construction. He'd wondered, did the Whood Clan build with stone? It was square and built up from the ground by square, gray bricks adhered with mortar. The roof of the odd construct was as tall as the Giant Rynon, and he wondered if this was the Whood Elves' version of the communal lodge named Rynon's Home.

It was not built by elves, and the smells should have announced that fact. This was the place where an exhausted Caundiss Saiwel had just given birth to her daughter.

Finding an open window, Wynkkur peeked up and through, expecting to see elves within this stinky stone square. He gasped upon seeing the large human holding such a big baby in her arms. The smell, an awful reek, forced a reactionary sneeze. The male inside in the dark corner of the cubed room had heard Wynkkur's sharp sneeze as did the woman who drew the stinky baby close. Running out through the front of the stone building was another young human that Wynkkur would later learn to be named Marcel. The two white-robed men gave a futile chase as the spry young elf used the woods to escape capture.

Driven by hunger, Wynkkur came back a day later. Hungry was a poor word—famished, emaciated, starving were all better fitting words. He'd remained unseen that day and let himself into the hennery and took several eggs. He used magical heat to cook inside their shells. That night, he found the back stables where cows' milk cooled in metal urns. He drank freely until falling asleep in the hay. He'd prayed to his abandoned gods for the humans to be merciful and kill him while he slept.

Wynkkur knew he could never go back home. Barely a moon into his adolescence at exile, he knew his choices were to die in the forests, be bludgeoned by club by his own tribe if he went back up the mountain—assuming he could get through the hunting grounds of kobolds—or die at the hands of the humans with the bad-smelling offspring. One-Hand Against chose death at the hands of the humans.

His projected death never came. The beautiful scent of cooked bacon welcomed him the morning he'd hoped to wake up dead. The plate of bacon left at the door outside also included two slices of bread and half of an apple. There were no humans and no death. Wynkkur ate, and upon finishing, he ran away, deciding to die another day.

Upon the next morning, he returned, and in the same place was another plate of food beside a cup of fresh milk. This time it was waiting for him upon the Temple's stone steps. Cautiously, he advanced. He waited for a trap, but none came. He ate bread and bacon for the second day in a row.

By day four, Wynkkur had accepted these humans were not going to kill him. The big man with the white robes and red sash strapped around his neck and down his chest kept calmly repeating, "Ellund, Ellund," while taping his chest. This was the first word Wynkkur learned in the human-speak.

Coming back to the present, Wynkkur looked from the cavernous darkness and to the human females walking within the torchlight. The elf knew his loyalties were to Ellund and whatever came from Ellund. With that thought, he took a quick step forward to hear better of the older woman's words.

Chapter Twenty-Four

Day Twelve, Unknown Hour

While holding her torch over her head, Bennae Kobblepot asked, "Madame Priestess, in what direction do you think we are traveling?"

"Madame Priestess. That sure sounds classy," interjected Katia. "I like the ring of that."

Ignoring the woman on the other side of the chain, Popalia responded, "Please, Bennae. I am only a servant of the Unseen Truth. I would prefer to be called something humble, like Popalia. If you feel that is too informal, then referring to me only as priestess is sufficient."

Katia helped by sniping, "She don't like bein' called Princess too much, either. So, don't call her that."

Bennae's judging eyes fixed hard on Katia, "You have been chained to the priestess since they found us, but none of us know why. Will you tell me why?"

Popalia nodded at Katia, "Since you wish to waggle your wicked tongue, why not tell Bennae how we've become so close and intimate?"

Katia's eyes narrowed, but she chose silence.

"Right, then. If Katia wishes to expound, she may. She helped steal something that my church wants to have back. Katia is going to help us, despite her immoral loyalties."

"I was unaware Katia possessed any loyalties at all," Bennae stabbed. "She told Gregor she would help in the events of an ambush, but when the orcs came, she was nowhere to be found."

"You old sack," Katia spat. "Go put your gossipy mouth on your old man's money handle! Gregor and I had no such agreement! You act so chaste—thinking you got yer'self a holy hole. Do ya..."

Popalia interrupted coolly, "I still have that gag from our last meeting. I'd kept faith that I'd get to use it, again."

Equally cool, Katia replied, "I got a torch in my hand. Think of that pretty, red hair..."

From a few paces behind, Wynkkur's words pierced like an ice pick, "I'd curve the flames to scorch your face. The last time you threatened Popalia, I blinded your eyes. This time, I'll peel your skin." Pausing for two heartbeats, he then added, "Why don't you hand the torch to Popalia."

He knew she would do it. Katia bad-mouthed everyone, taunted and mocked them, but she barely poked at him. She was afraid of elves. Thinking back to that fateful first day at the temple, she had at once started ridiculing him, but upon lowering his hood to reveal his face, she'd since averted most of her poison away from him. He didn't know why she feared him, but like he ordered, Katia surrendered the torch to the priestess.

Raenyl called from the front, "Is there a problem, Wank?"

"The problem has passed." Wynkkur's voice was like a sheet of ice.

Popalia, with torch in hand, smiled politely at the merchant's scribe, "To answer your original question, I don't know what direction we travel, but I do know that it is away from last night's trouble. I suspect this cavern will eventually narrow, and then we can follow that tunnel back to the surface. We need only remain steadfast and faithful."

Sounding surprised, Bennae retorted, "Some rescue plan. Surely you joke with me."

"I hardly feel this is the time or place for jokes."

"This cannot be," she lamented, addled severely by this unexpected news. "You're leading us where? What odds of success do you think your plan has?"

Giggling confidently, Popalia defended, "I am a follower more than I am a leader." With zeal, she continued, "The Great Mystery guides me, and I follow. If you want odds, pray to Kranias. He rules over gamblers and luck. As a servant of the Unknown, I share with you the Divine truth that our chances are always fifty-fifty—either we do it or we don't. I plan to push on until I can no longer push on, but I'm sure we'll find a way out of this place. We just need to look carefully."

Expressing without hiding her disdain, Bennae squawked, "This isn't an answer. This isn't an answer!"

"No, but at least now you are aware of the question," offered Popalia as if philosophical truths would prove consoling to the accountant. "The Mystery wouldn't be mysterious if the answers were always obvious. Life is an opportunity not a promise. Please, find some comfort in knowing this predicament wasn't part of my plan."

The older woman's face altered with something between disbelief and revelation, "We are lost. I mean, for real lost. There isn't a way out of here."

"Now, now Bennae," Popalia sweetened her tone to soften the reality. "Being as we are still alive, perhaps the Unnamed desires something beyond our deaths."

Realization won over disbelief. "We are hopelessly lost and have no way of getting out of here. Why are we following you? This is madness, just like the elf said this morning—or I mean, after we awoke."

Katia jabbed, "What you mean to say is after *you* awoke all of us."

Popalia took pause. The priestess thought it was common knowledge among the group what Bennae had just grasped. "Yes, Bennae. The fates drove us to find you, and now the fates have blown us over this way. Have faith, and a new way shall be made."

"The priests of Stranoss warn us that your god is slippery and tricky. I should have sought my own way before following yours." Bennae stepped back in a panicked retreat. She bumped into one of the large calcite deposits—a drooling stalagmite. Tripping backward and down upon her backside, she held the torch before her in a death lock.

"Oof!" she emitted, standing up quickly.

Katia giggled while Bennae scampered up the line to where Raenyl scouted at the forward edge of light. Seeing the half-elf in her torchlight, she approached swiftly, saying, "We're lost!"

"We sure are, Miss Kobblepot," he answered calmly. "We are in the deep stink of it."

Deeply frazzled, she'd been able to convince herself that her heroes had an exit plan. Her patron god Stranoss was a god of absolutes, and by her own faith, she was convicted. When reality found its grasp, the truer fear consumed her mind. Her whole life had been about numbers. Every day had an order, but now she screamed madly, "You don't have a plan!" He voice echoed from ceiling to floor in the vast cavern.

Raenyl looked into her eyes, seeing the radiance of her terror. "We had a plan, Bennae, but living became more important than our plan. We've reacted, and now we are alive but here. Did you hear me, good lady?"

Raenyl grimaced. That sounded so wooden. Did he really say that? Good lady? *What a moron.*

"I am a good lady, and I don't deserve this. This is bad! Stranoss, why?" Her eyes burst with tears as she clutched Raenyl, burying her head against his firm chest.

Awkwardly placing an arm over her shoulder, Raenyl reflected this was way beyond his comfort level. He tried to sound sensitive, but his tongue turned to wax. "The worst has got to be over, Bennae. It can't ever be as bad as with the orcs. Our spot isn't good, but it is better than it was with the orcs."

"The orcs!" With eyes wet, she glared at Raenyl. "Those babies, Ucilius and Lissa! Oh, those poor babies...those orc made us watch as they...we all had to watch, and now here we are." She scanned the darkness beyond the torch flame. "We'll never get out of here. The sun is gone forever!"

Raenyl tried to hold her together, but he watched the last grip of her sanity slip. Bennae fell inside herself and was gone. The lights went out, her mind fractured like a glass mirror. Releasing the archer, she bolted and ran off away from the group.

"Aw, crap!" exclaimed Raenyl, looking over to Popalia. "She just went snap—crazy." Turning on his heel, he began to give chase, calling her name.

"Well, damn," snickered Katia. "I didn't see that coming."

Popalia chased after Raenyl, so by default Katia needed to jog also. Seeing the front of the line begin running, Wynkkur and Westin took pursuit. Then as Gregor pushed next in the hasty dash, Seth was left pulling along an uncomprehending Ucilius.

Bennae didn't run too long before finding a wall. Resembling a row of shells, the wall appeared to melt. A wet sheen reflected the light as Bennae changed course, running aside the barrier. Deft for her age, she maneuvered through the wet potholes and over the occasional sprout of a calcite stalagmite. It wasn't so much that she outran those who gave chase, but they allowed her to go. Loud sobs burst from Bennae with every dashing step. The others allowed her to travel with unhindered direction.

Finally, as she stopped running, her foot kicked something long and thin, equal in length to a broken arrow and equally as thick as an almond is wide. It skittered noisily, clattering and echoing through the dark. Bennae bent over, one hand pressed against the wall and the other held her torch outward. She cried freely and without reservation as the whole of the group began to arrive, Raenyl first.

"Bennae. Whoa, girl," he cautioned between gasps. "Hold on right here. You found a wall. This is a good sign. Don't run anymore, okay?" Crouched, she still sobbed, but at least she had stopped running.

Popalia and Katia arrived, then Wynkkur, who decided to

remain back a couple extra paces. Westin closed in a little closer still, calling out, "Bennae, please. I know this is all wrong. We should be at Faradell Pass, waiting for our ten minute baths and a bite of stew. We should be halfway home, but we are here instead. Please Miss Kobblepot, pull through this. Please, Ucilius needs you...as your friend, I need you, too."

Gregor arrived next, panting with the exertion, "Good job, Miss Kobblepot! You found the wall. All we need do now is follow it out. Isn't that right, Priestess?"

Popalia didn't exactly agree, but she agreed that she should. "Yes, sure. It is as sound a plan as any. It must lead somewhere, and that is a lot better than where we were heading."

Bennae wouldn't look up at anyone. She moved her foot from a puddle of mud, streaking raw earth across stone. "You think...you think I did good, Gregor? The Third believes I did well?"

"Oh, dear Miss Kobblepot," Gregor cooed. "Above your head, I can see a blue spot." Sounding amazed, he asked, "Can anyone else see it?"

"Don't tease me Gregor, oh please. I cannot bear it." Bennae lit up like religious zeal. Her eyes rimmed red from crying, now aglow with enraptured joy. "Is it a sign, a marking of Stranoss?"

Gregor pointed up above Bennae's head, "I'm serious, Bennae. Can anyone else see it, like a blue soft light? It is up between those hanging arches." Excited now, Gregor exclaimed, "Bennae, you may have found an opening in this cave! Maybe even a way out!"

Seth, still hauling Ucilius, strolled up behind the merchant, "What is that? It looks like a dull light. Is it a way out? Raenyl, can you see?" Seth pushed the catatonic man toward Gregor, "Here, take Ucilius, and I'll take the torch back."

"I bet it'll be easier to see in the dark." Gregor barely prevented Ucilius from falling face forward, but he caught him and rested his son-in-law against his shoulder.

Katia chuckled, "Well, I'll be a..." Squinting her eyes to see better, Katia added. "It isn't like any light I've seen. Wait, is that even light?"

"Of course it is light," Gregor disputed. "It glows, so it is light."

Bennae shifted her footing, and there was a crackle beneath. Looking down, she realized the dirt she stood upon was old cloth. Beneath the brittle and decomposing cloth, old and age-brittle sticks broke upward with small puffs of dust. The rock beneath her left foot shifted, and she stepped back awkwardly. Cloven in two but with one half gone, the stone was not stone, but bone. Half of an orc's skull—a hollowed eye outlined yellow in the flickering light.

"Wait!" Raenyl exclaimed. "Are those bones?"

Bennae looked up, the light of her torch revealing she stood directly between the tips of four angles, evenly distanced in the ceiling above her. Pushing her torch upward, she first thought she saw a single obsidian sphere dangling from within the odd angled stalactites. The black orb blinked—it was instead an eye stalk observing her. Multi-focal lenses, like the eye of a cyclopean fly reflected the torch light in her hand. The bulging eye was connected at the edge of a long and narrow crevice. Opening like some grievous wound, the crevice transmuted into a jagged maw filled with sharp, predatory teeth.

She began to step away from the open mouth as it spat a gob of goo. Spraying across Bennae's torch-hand, and then quickly dribbling down along the side of her head and landing upon her shoulder. Tendrils of milky white and sinewy tissue could be seen inside the regurgitated goop, giving a membranous and mucus-like film adhering upon the eldest woman.

"Oh, god Stranoss! What is this?"Her hand holding the torch was stuck within the sticky slime. In her panic, she swiped her free hand across the pasty drool on her shoulder, but her action made only for worse. "Oh god, both my hands are stuck!" She pulled, and sticky tendrils stretched but held her hand trapped.

Above Bennae, it suddenly became clear that the four angles were crab-like legs that clung into the ceiling, holding the long body against the cavern's roof. Along the length of it, underneath the one bulbous eye, the jagged mouth ran across the majority of its body. Comparatively similar in girth to that of the average man's torso from neck to pelvis, it appeared this monster's body existed purely to support its mouth.

Attached to the mouth's body, four arm-like appendages came out from concealment. There were no hands upon the ends of these small appendages, only a pointed spike at the end of each arm. Hard and shell-like, each of the tiny arms possessed two elbows joints. Two of the arms spun together rapidly, raveling up the sticky snare, lifting the screaming woman upward at a swift rate.

"No, Miss Kobblepot!" Westin shouted with no time to act. The scribe's horrific shrieks rang for miles within the dark spaces, piercing the ears of all who stood helplessly close by.

Reaching back over his shoulder, Raenyl drew an arrow.

Westin stepped forward, knowing he would never arrive in time. Everybody else stood shocked, gripped by sheer terror and mesmerized by the nightmarish spectacle. Raenyl had an arrow on his string, but Bennae's body was now in the way of any shot. He didn't even know where to aim his arrow.

Westin stopped two paces away as the two unused appendages struck, shoving deep into the shrieking woman like a scorpion's stinger. The thin spikes gouged into Bennae's soft, suspended body—one darting beneath her outstretched armpit and puncturing far into human flesh. Bennae's screams muffled and lost power as her lung was torn internally. Pain choked through her throat as the second barb ripped into her skin above her hip. Her body was caught and lifted swiftly closer to the awful mouth with sinister teeth.

The torch, caught in the sticky secretion, now hung within the slime while the two arms fished Bennae ever closer. From the floor, everyone stared horrifically into the torch-lit teeth, wide and shark-like. Shoved within the stretched mouth beside a single bugging eye, the carnivorous hole sawed deep into Bennae's living flesh.

Warm blood dripped like a heavy rain, splashing across the stone floor. The sound of tearing, shredding meat echoed though the hollow cavern, accented only by a horrible gurgling sigh. The tiny needle arms held Bennae suspended at the mouth. Blood poured freely, pattering like buckets of water being dumped from atop a roof.

"Run!" Wynkkur addressed to everyone, but his words were focused at Popalia. "We can do nothing for her now. Run for the sake of everyone who still lives."

"The way out!" reminded a numbed Gregor. "Bennae had found the way out."

Seth, still holding onto Ucilius, nudged the elder man away from where his personal scribe was being eaten. Everyone but Westin moved away from the suspended horror dripping life-blood like some macabre waterfall. As the others took flight, a lone tear streaked the guard's face, running through the hairs of his beard. He kissed his hand before extending it to what had once been the mother of the caravan, now reduced to quivering meat.

Yes, as Gregor had said, Bennae found a way out.

Chapter Twenty-Five

Day Twelve, Unknown Hour

Raggedly breathing, Katia spoke, "No, Gregor. It was a trap. You saw that blue coloring on the side of...of it? That blue color, it was a reflection of our own light." Turning to the priestess, who was also quite winded, she added, "Thank you for stopping, I almost...almost fell."

Carrying the awful vision of Bennae being devoured, they'd all dashed into the eternal black. The sound of her final gurgle, the fast pattering of dripping blood, the wet-ripping sound as her clothes were penetrated—these were sounds echoing within the survivors as they ran. Trusting blindly, Popalia had run into the first alcove, which in turn was actually a narrower tunnel. No one protested leaving the grand cavern. A wide, smooth tunnel trailed at an upward grade. Needing to rest did eventually outweigh the lingering horror of what they had just witnessed.

Taking the moment to refresh his burning muscles, a perceptive Westin asked, "What do you know about traps? I agree with you. That thing ambushed us, but why would you call it a trap?"

Boldly, she announced, "I am a security consultant for private companies. I know a lot about traps."

Chuckling, Raenyl jibbed, "And I'm a locksmith with a zeal for excitement. Security Consultant...that sounds respectable."

"I'm hired by companies to challenge various securities," Katia's eyes cut at Raenyl. "There should be honor among like associates, not treachery—even if they do work in different companies."

Popalia slashed, "Your 'company' murdered a close friend of mine and stole a priceless memoir from my home. Both were loved—the item stolen was equal to my friend whom you cut down."

"I didn't kill nobody!" Katia shot back. "You don't know nothing! No, you know less than nothing—you think you know a lot, but you don't know diddly. I never kill nobody! My job saves lives, but some lives just aren't good enough for you. Ain't I right, Princess?"

Popalia cut with her words, "All life is precious, Katia, but some people throw their lives away with the nightly chamber pot, but that is by decision of the one who made the waste. I am not responsible for your life-decisions. Some people give to the greater part of life, and other people only take from it. You only need to know within yourself, Katia. Do you give life, or do you take it?"

Turning back to Westin, she ignored the priestess and informed, "Mother Nature makes the best traps. Oftentimes, you'll find snake and spider venom used as trap responses. Good trappers will use a lure, trick bait—you get it? That rock-crab-thing used a lure. Its shell bounced the light and glowed for a moment. Maybe it was only reflecting our light, but Bennae was already under it. If she hadn't already been under it, once we'd seen that light, one of us would have gotten under it, anyway."

Gregor didn't care about traps. Shaking an accusing finger, he seethed, "I knew by all that gold you'd paid something was wrong about you! You thief, how much did you steal from me?"

"Not one copper. You sleep with all your gold in your pillowcase," Katia responded while chuckling at the merchant's hollow anger. "All you got in that fancy lockbox are financial records, and I admit I was shocked by what was in there."

The merchant's face flushed red, "My books are clean!"

"No shit, old man...spotless, even. I've never seen books so clean. Legible and easy to read. I'd think by what I'd seen, you'd be missing Bennae more than what you are." Katia waited a second before stabbing, "Your gold might be completely honest, but your heart is filthy dirty." Recoiling with a hiss, Gregor withdrew his finger.

"Finally, someone else can see," Westin rejoiced. "He is such a snake."

Snecring, Gregor looked like a weasel that had been backed into a corner, "You have no right to hold what happened against me, Westin! Orcs took her, I didn't. I favored you. You can't see it now, but you will. We should be working together to get out of here."

"No!" Westin rebuked harshly, "It *is* your fault we are here! It is so much your fault, it should have been you raped by the orcs. You will pay for Enga and for Bennae! Have you forgotten the names of the drivers, or what about your own daughter and grandkids?"

The merchant bellowed, "Quit it!" The words echoed through the tunnel, "*quit it*" before echoing again even deeper away, "*quit it*". How far back would the protest ring in the hollows of the grand chamber behind them? Quieter and with exhibited control, he said, "Just stop, okay? If I'd let you marry Enga, nothing would have changed." With more conviction in his voice, he repeated,

"Nothing would have changed."

Gasping, Popalia asked, "What? Married? I thought she was your partn—ohhhh." She'd had no idea. She'd never been exposed to love in such an unorthodox way. Her own mother had grown cold as her father's lover before her adolescence had even begun. All Popalia knew about love was shared between her father and the other members of her temple. Awkward, Popalia felt dense and ill-equipped for helping either man through this problem.

Katia understood, "See, country Princess. I told you. With a little scrubbin', it'd come out in the wash. Truth always does."

Westin seethed at the old merchant, "Nothing changes behind the castle walls preserving your denial. Maybe I wouldn't hate you—not this much—and that would have been different."

"Please, have mercy, Westin?" Gregor found Ucilius's hand and squeezed it. "Look at my boy, here. He watched his wife die the other day..."

Westin interrupted, "Your daughter died! We all watched, Gregor! We all watched her die!"

Gregor waved off the young warrior and surrendered, "Well, go on. Tell them all what happened. If you think these strangers need to know what horrors we've endured, then you go right on ahead and tell them. Relish in your revenge."

Nervous laughter proceeded as Raenyl butted in, "We really don't need to know. We got the idea, plus we've seen our own portion of bad things we'd rather not share with you." He looked around at everyone. "What good can come from it?"

Katia turned her eyes away, looking deep into the darkness before them. "Let's just get out of here. I remember more than I want." A moment of tense silence remained. The chained woman with no chance for a positive future quietly repeated, "Let's just get out of here."

Popalia was still trumped by what she'd learned of Enga, and she weakly offered, "If any of you want to speak privately, I'll listen. Even if it just eases the burden from weighing on you, let's talk."

Using his spear for support, Westin rose upon his feet. "Katia is right, let's get. The sooner I see sunshine, the sooner I can put Gregor behind me."

Chapter Twenty-Six

Day Twelve, 1:00 p.m.

Unknown to Commandant Saviid Benning was the definition of the word "serendipity". Also unknown to the officer was that Seth Ascolan had ducked behind the same fallen tree only twenty hours earlier. Over where Privates Joab and Clause pressed together in the thickest branches of a conifer pine was the same place where Raenyl shot the first of what would eventually be many orcs.

Captain Snales peeked over the tree husk right beside his superior officer. He did not know the stacked boxes remained exactly as they had been the day before. By the tree, on the ground, a pile of clothes still lay like they did the day prior. Stacked boxes, coffers, and crates, but the Captain saw no orcs. He could, however, see two of the heavy draft horses used for the caravan, plus a tan and white mare. Somewhere behind the obscuring bushes, another horse neighed.

"The horses look bound, sir," Captain Snales remarked barely above a whisper, "but there are no orcs within sight. It is likely they dumped their goods here and kept on moving."

Commandant Benning swore, "Bane's Blood, Captain. Either we've been duped by a decoy and walked right into a trap, or this is just a random supply drop. If this trail is cold, we've lost both the Ascolan Brothers and those damnable orcs." He rubbed his eyes through the small T-shaped opening cut into the face of his helmet. The cropped horsehair plume sprouting from the crown of his helm had been dyed green—a symbol that he was a high-ranked officer. While rubbing his eyes, he asked, "Have you ever come across orcs so cunning, Captain, or am I losing my edge?"

"This makes no sense, sir. This is way outside the norm. There must be sentries guarding this supply dump. We're going to need to flush them out."

Saviid Benning's eyes were now red and agitated from being rubbed. His eyes passed from tree to tree, looking deep within the branches, "This stinks of ambush."

"Yes," Snales agreed, "but it is all wrong. This isn't the place for an ambush. We passed several waypoints that would have been optimal for an attack—the road or at the peak of that slippery hill-top were both better than leading us all the way here."

"Aye, this is odd. Still, this valley is prime for defending."

Jorgan Snales grinned wide, "Well, sir. I don't see us turning back, now."

"No, but now I wish we'd brought along a couple of crossbow-men." With a gloved hand, he signaled for the privates to come closer, yet remain low.

Crawling close enough to hear, Commandant Benning ex-plained, "Something is wrong about this place. It reeks of ambush, but if we are going to keep on this trail, we've got to get through this spot. Private Joab, I want you to take Private Clause around to the left. Watch in the trees as much as you need to watch the ground. The Captain and I will sweep right. We will meet at the crates once the perimeter is free of orcs. Private Clause, this is life and death, now. Stuff your bad blood with Arty. Without him, your life is forfeit."

Smirking, Private Clause rapped Private Joab's pauldron and chipped in, "We'll fist it out when we get back to base, but right now, my brother is my keeper."

With a small chuckle, Arty Joab recanted the troop's slogan, "Side-by-side to death or life."

"Hoo-rah," whispered Captain Snales as Commandant Benning saluted the privates.

Breaking in two different directions, all of their senses fired at high alert. Watching the two privates vanish through the trees, Benning had never questioned his own decisions before every-thing went mad yesterday morning. No longer were the tactics the standard charge and maneuver. That damn elf turned every-thing upside down, and now these crafty orcs were twisting him around, leaving him wondering which way to wear his helmet.

Right then, he decided this would be his last ride. Once this mission was over, he'd hang his sword and shield. Captain Snales will make an excellent replacement. Jorgan Snales was un-equalled in combat, and his confidence stood upon a solid rock. He loved his men, and the men loved him. A commander cannot doubt himself, or it puts all his men in potential harm.

Pushing his thoughts behind him, Benning listened with all intensity. The wind swayed, and the branches creaked high above. In the valley's center, the wind was accompanied by a quick snort of a horse sneezing. Saviid instinctively stopped and held still. He'd heard a sliding of shale stone rolling over grounded pine needles nearby. Seeing Jorgan tapping his nose, Saviid understood if the Captain could smell orc, the orc could most certainly smell both of them.

Across the valley, a frantic sliding of stones echoed rapid movements behind the trees. "Damn!" a voice sounding like Arty's called out. Quickly following the expletive was a sound familiar to the old soldiers, the sound of a shield repelling an arrow—*Donk-crack!*

Both Jorgan and Saviid froze—experience held them, waiting for whatever happened next.

The sound of quick-paced feet scampered across the valley, followed immediately by a crackling of branches snapping within a pine or shrub. Neither officer needed to see in order to know the noisy crash of a shield meeting armor. A heartbeat later returned an inhuman squeal, stifling quickly into a muffled gurgle. Along with the short thrashing from behind the trees, both officers heard a shifting of rocks as soil was being displaced.

Quickly following was another skittering of rocks, this time from the opposite side of the tree where the officers stood. The second orc scrambled right into the officer's view, in both hands a short bow with an arrow notched on the string. The orc stood with oxen shoulders and hulking biceps—a giant—but he did not have eyes behind his ears. He saw neither Jorgan nor Saviid, nor did the orc witness their shared smile of good fortune.

Balancing on the side of the hill, Jorgan lifted his axe high and swung with braced legs. At a slight angle downward, the full wedge bit, beginning between clothed shoulders, and then cleaving past skin and muscle, ripping through ribs and severing the orc's spine. The orc's body dropped without resistance due to nerve-severed legs. His arrow went flying into free space.

Jorgan pulled, feeling the powerful suck of the biting axe as the orc collapsed forward. A wretched and agonized squeal broke from the paralyzed orc while sliding face down in the loose gravel. Jorgan stepped out from cover, swinging with a silencing, and skull-splitting whack.

Jorgan Snales needed to move fast. There could be another unseen archer watching from the trees. Foot soldiers he could handle with ease, but any more archers would be difficult to handle with only an axe. Scanning both sides of the valley and taking particular interest in the trees, shrubs, and rock outcroppings, he could not see any archers pointing death his way.

Allowing momentum to carry his next move, he leapt forward,

bridging the open space to cover behind the trunk of a thick tree. Looking back at his Commandant watching him with hawk-like eyes, both his sword and shield held at the ready. Snales protected himself with his back against the tree. He faced the direction of the privates and spotted Private Clause lying beneath a bush, who in turn gave a thumbs up.

Snales pointed two outstretched fingers at his eyes, and then thumbed in the direction on the other side of the tree. Eugene spied for signs, but finally showed the captain a thumb-to-finger zero. He nodded but waited all the same. He signaled the privates to continue their sweep while he stayed positioned behind the tree. He was in a good place to protect the privates if there was another archer.

It didn't matter—he knew there weren't any more archers. Jorgan lived with the demon of orcish rage. Needing to wrestle with it daily, he knew the full-bloods lacked the human trait of patience. If there had been a third orc watching over this cast-off junk, he'd have already made himself known. He'd have broken from cover at the same time the orc with the now-split skull had. Jorgan knew he only needed to hold for a few more seconds. There could be a half-orc in this tribe, so a second or two spent waiting would prove prudent.

As long as he'd been a Regulator, he'd known the thin line between hyorc and half-orc was cultural conditioning. That was the only separation between what he was, and the monster he could have been. Full-blooded humans generally judged both as being the same. It took years of discipline to achieve the level of respect he'd earned. Those couple of extra seconds of waiting with his back to a tree was proof of the difference.

Satisfied with his team's safety, Captain Snales stepped out into the open announcing, "All clear."

Commandant Benning sheathed his sword, as he gave praise, "Captain, your actions confirm what we'd discussed yesterday morning."

"Just doing my job, sir." Jorgan Snales meant it. Speaking up, "Privates, are you two all right?"

Private Joab called out, "I killed number fifteen, but just barely."

Private Clause chuckled, his eyes glowing with signs of an adrenaline high, "It was wild, Captain Snales. That was truly wild."

Arty Joab pushed his way between the branches of two trees,

saying as he approached, "We came in from above that orc and had the full advantage. We were upwind and at about ten paces off, he spins with his bow ready. I got my shield up and 'Whack!' His arrow bounces off. We charge—Eugene and I are charging, but he gets the second arrow and goes for Private Clause at point blank."

"I jumped!" Eugene smiled. "I jumped into the bush, and the arrow whizzed by my ear!"

"I got 'em.' Private Joab slapped the side of Eugene's shoulder. "Good moves. I thought you were done in."

"Good job," Commandant Benning commended. "That's two less predators to bring trouble to us later. Let's go through this stuff and see if we can pick up their trail before it goes completely cold."

"Wait!" Captain Snales suddenly said, and then a little quieter he repeated, "Wait a moment. I remember something. When you first told me about the Ascolan brothers, and I told you I'd heard that name before, I now remember where."

Benning's face revealed amusement, "Don't you think it's a little late? We're hunting orcs now, Captain."

"No, sir. This is significant."

Benning shrugged, "So tell."

"Those two boys are war heroes."

Benning laughed, "From what war could they be heroes, Jorgan? There hasn't been a war within the kingdom since Dilligan's conflict."

"There was the Blackmire Uprising just east of the Imperial Garrison. I remember now, there were only five survivors. They saved all those farmers at Blackmire Hamlet during the goblin surge. I remembered their names, because two were brothers—two out of the five survivors. I am sure it was Ascolan. Absolutely positive, sir."

"Absolutely sure? Please tell."

Pointing at the tied brown and white mare, the Captain said, "I checked that steed into the stables two days ago. It's the same one they repossessed yesterday to escape. That's the priestess's horse, or I'm a full-blooded orc."

"Sacred Mother Asunna!" Benning choked. "Do you think…?"

He hadn't time to finish his statement as Private Joab called, "Commandant! I found a bunch of bodies!"

Benning felt dizzy, "Who is it?"

"Who? No, it is a pile of orcs…lots of them." Arty's nose

wrinkled. "They're still fresh, less than a day old. Plenty of flies, but the bodies barely got any stink on them."

Both Jorgan and Saviid rushed over to where the Private stood aside two bushy pines. Behind the low branches, the bodies had been piled one atop the others. The mass of flies that had feasted upon the blood puddle the day prior had now found their way to the rotting bodies piled grotesquely—an orgy of interlocking, hacked-up bodies. Private Joab added, "I heard the flies before I smelled the bodies. How many do you think there are?"

"Bodies or flies?" Captain Snales jibbed.

"They are all orc," Benning replied out of shock. "Fifteen, or maybe even twenty dead. Captain Snales, how could I have been wrong about the Ascolan brothers?"

"They burned down our base, sir," Captain Snales reminded. "They are wanted for robbing our king."

"Yes, Captain. I am merely reflecting that I'd expected them to run, not try and save this ill-fated caravan. I guess they were determined to get that mulatto woman after all."

Private Clause, who had been looking around the stacked boxes, called loudly, "Sirs! There is a big hole over here. Right here behind this tree!"

"What?" Benning's brain inside his skull may as well have been a child's top by how fast it spun. He'd been hunting and killing orcs and bandits for over twenty years, and he'd been a Regulator for eighteen of them. He'd seen piles of orcs before, but it was *his men* stacking the bodies.

Another thing...why were these orcs digging holes? He'd never heard of orcs that bury their dead. With his upper lip curling in disbelief, he expounded upon his surprise, "What kind of hole?"

Private Clause looked inside. "No, not a hole, but a cave!" The other soldiers were approaching as Eugene stepped up to the edge. "I think there is a light in there."

From within the cave's shadow emitted the soft twang of a bow string snapping straight. The arrow's stone-tip pierced six inches outside his groin, scraping against the inside of Eugene's hip bone. The pain forced a gasp and beneath him his knee buckled. Falling at the edge of the hole beside the ladder, he kept a tight grip upon the shaft of his spear.

Exiting from out of the cave's shadow sprung an orc with vengeance shining in its eyes. Private Clause angled his spear, shoving the sharp tip at the approaching orc. It was an awkward attack and easily dodged by the defender. The orc leapt up and took ahold of one of Eugene's feet. Eugene rammed his spear down again, this time piercing through the buckskin jerkin the tribal warrior was wearing. The sharpened, steel tip sliced through muscle between shoulder and neck, dramatically spraying what seemed like a lot of blood, but was actually no more than a deep laceration.

Private Joab was first to arrive and reached his hand out for his injured partner. Arty tossed his shield to the ground as he called to his friend, "Take my hand!"

Eugene was busy kicking at the orc trying to pull him down. Then, a second arrow pierced through the Private's chainmail, just beneath the breastplate. The arrow did not penetrate more than an inch deep into his side, but the wood and stone projectile inspired a web-spreading of pain. Dropping his spear, he reached for Private Joab's offered hand.

Their eyes and fingers touched each other at the same time, but hope was lost on both of them. The orc with the injured shoulder yanked Eugene Clause down into the hole before Arty could get a solid grip. As Eugene's body crashed against the hard ground below, Arty watched as two new orcs rushed forward as one pulled screaming Private Clause into the darkened cavern by his outstretched arms.

Eugene's shrieks could be heard echoing from within the hollow as time stopped for Arty Joab. Revelation flashed like a blinding light, remembering the priestess's curse and her saddened tone. It became clear to him, now. Had he and Eugene freed the priestess and her gang, both he and Eugene would be back in the stockade right now. He and Eugene wouldn't have been here, about to die. The priestess wasn't a witch—she'd tried to save them from the fate they'd both chosen. They'd chosen loyalty to the Regulators and not to the spokeswoman for a god.

Reality whipped Arty Joab as he shouted at the bleeding orc climbing up the rusty ladder, "You be damned!" Private Joab swung downward with his sword, his blade shearing a large chunk of cheek and snout from the burly warrior. With an agonized squeal, the orc released the ladder, cupping its hands over its sword-sliced face. Blood oozed freely through tightly pressed fingers.

Private Joab turned toward his discarded shield. Both Commandant Benning and Captain Snales were motioning for him to clear away from the cavern entrance when the hidden archer stepped out from the darkness. Arty was bending away from the cave as the arrow left the bowstring.

Arty Joab felt and heard the projectile hit his breastplate at an angle before bouncing off and grazing the side of his neck with a stinging scrape. As he reached for his shield, a spray of crimson peppered the shale stones, pine needles, and across his shield. Instead of grasping his shield as he'd intended, he cupped his neck where he felt the warm jet of his own blood splash.

Captain Snales, with wild and urgent eyes, grabbed the journeyman soldier and pulled him away from the opening. Arty exclaimed with a manic fear resonating in his voice, "The gods, Captain! I can feel my heart pulsing!"

"Hold your hand over it! Don't bleed out, son!" To emphasize, he pushed Arty's blood-saturated hand harder against his neck. "Hold on. The Commandant and I will get you out of here, but you've got to hold out, Private. That is an order."

"That priestess! Captain, sir!" Arty gasped in his panic, his eyes rolling frantically in his head. "She was right. Please, Captain. She was right!"

Jorgan Snales misunderstood Arty's variable meaning. "Nonsense, Private. Don't give up." Captain Snales patted Private Joab's side and stood up to join his superior officer for the fight that was coming.

Benning stood at the edge while Snales looked down at the bottom where a small orc—one of the thralls—stepped out from the cavern below. Blood dripped from his hand, and Saviid wondered if it was Eugene's. The orc held something raw and blood-soaked—something that looked skinned or removed. In the hand that didn't drip blood, resting in the palm, was a small, wooden cube. To Commandant Benning, it looked as if a trail of smoke streamed up from the box and roiled around the blood-covered orc's ear.

Commandant Benning turned his attention back to the orc trying to climb up the ladder. The orc Arty had cleaved lay at the base of the ladder, cupping his hands over his spurting face wound. As another uninjured orc began to pull himself up and out of the hole, Saviid slammed his shield into the swine nose, hearing the crunch and sending the orc back down and atop the wounded.

Stepping back with battle-heightened agility, he pulled away just as another arrow shot up from out of the hole and over the head of the wild-eyed thrall. *Was he laughing? Can orcs laugh?*

That one filled Saviid with an unnatural dread. He felt compelled to kill that one, but the archers in the darkness were going to make it impossible to assault this opening. As Commandant of the Regulators, he recognized this no-win battle before them. Holding his shield up to deflect incoming arrows, Saviid looked back to the grounded Arty Joab.

Weakly, Arty called out, "Leave, sir! Please, just get away." Arty Joab pinched the gash in his neck but knew it was a critical wound. It may only have been an inch of flesh removed, but the vein that had been severed would never be stitched in time. He rolled his head to the side, both to close upon the fatal injury and give him a moment longer, but more so he could watch the men who'd been his family for the last six years just one last time.

Dizziness, with an accompanying tiredness, pulled at Arty Joab. Arty, saddened far more than he was frightened, wished only that his friends would flee. As the world seemed to shrink and grow hazy, he saw the Captain split the head of the next orc trying to climb up and out of the hole. Cursing as he leapt backward, Jorgan Snales yanked his axe from the orc's fractured skull, "God-pounded archers!"

Arty's eyelids weighed exhaustingly. His heart stung for his friend Eugene and silently, he did something he hadn't done since he was a child. Praying to the Great Mystery, he asked for mercy for his friends.

This was not how Arty Joab expected to leave the world, not this calm, not so understandably. Sleep stole him away to some-place less hectic. Arty learned the meaning of peace.

Chapter Twenty-Seven

Day Twelve?, Unknown Hour

Wynkkur held his torch up, but he watched his feet as he walked. Wondering to himself about how dirty his robe could be, the flickering torchlight altered all the shadows making it hard to discern. He also pondered how odd it was that he couldn't smell himself, but he could very clearly smell everybody else. He was certain he must stink, too. Everybody stinks, especially after as long as they had gone without bathing.

After six days through the wilderness since leaving the Temple of Dawn's Mystery, they'd arrived at the big temple in Capitol City. That had been his last opportunity to bathe. That was Popalia's last bath, too. If Raenyl and Seth had bathed, they had also done it before the fire at the inn, and how long ago was that? Wynkkur was confused. What time was it now? How long had they been walking through this darkness? Had it been five days since leaving Capitol City or five days since the morning they'd escaped Dilligan's Freepost? His best guess was it had been twelve days since leaving the monastery, so yesterday must have been when they'd left the freepost.

He bent to sniff his robe, and he thought he saw something sparkle down lower. Looking at his belt, he moved the torch, and a narrow reflection danced across the pommel of his sword. Masterfully set within the hilt of his sword, at the bottom of the hand grip was a small, polished piece of malachite. He moved the light again and what looked like a symbol caught in the swirls of the multi-hued green stone.

Unexpectedly, his head hit the downside of a slight protrusion in the ceiling. He bit his lip hard enough to cause his eyes to tear. Wynkkur's sinuses stung. "*Be'lail*!" he cursed in Elvish while rubbing the tender spot beneath his crusty, blonde hair. He could feel the grind of grit against his now-bruised scalp. The grit wasn't new. He'd collected a head full of dirt beneath the soldier's barracks while he hid at Dilligan's Freepost.

Westin walked behind the young sorcerer through the tight cave, his spear held out and to the side. "Are you all right? Do you still have all your teeth?"

"My teeth are still in one piece...it seems my lip cushioned them." Wynkkur slipped a finger across his lower, inside lip. Pulling out his finger from his mouth, he saw blood within the saliva. He flicked his lip with his tongue and felt the gash, tasting copper from the dirt on his finger. "Damn this cavern of the damned."

Westin snorted, "Me, too. I've had about enough of this. Walk up a long tunnel, then walk down a long tunnel. Follow the tunnel right, follow it left. It doesn't matter. This tunnel just keeps on going."

"Thankfully there isn't a third option; then we'd have *real* trouble," Wynkkur included.

That sounded funny to Westin, so he implored with a faint chuckle, "What do you mean by a third option?"

"Right now, we go either forward, or we go backward. If we hit a branch in the trail...well, do you see?" Westin's cinched brows said he didn't see, even though he nodded absently. So, Wynkkur concluded for him, "If we come to a crossroad, we'll need to make a choice, and that would require potential regret."

"Oh, yeah," Westin got it. "Now I see. Yeah, that would be hard. What if we choose the wrong way? We could still hit a dead end, and then we'd have to go all the way back."

Wynkkur nodded and gave the human a little subtle guidance, "We should try and avoid 'what if' scenarios. Right here is where we are. Hitting my head was a result of not focusing on right here. We have done something right, and as a result, we are still alive."

"Enga isn't still alive, and that isn't right."

"That is a topic for a priestess to answer," replied Wynkkur. "Right and wrong are her area of expertise. I am only a guide."

"Don't you work for the temple?"

"Yes, but as an elf, I have other gods."

"I don't trust the Unknown Host," Westin whispered. "There is no temple in Magistrey...only one to Stranoss and one to Asunna. Somewhere close by the portown, I heard there is a temple for Shaelowe, but I won't go near it." Westin got back to his point, "I'm asking you for your guidance, because you are not the priestess."

Rubbing the swelling nugget on his head, he surrendered, "I'll entertain your question, but you are making a mistake by talking to me. Elves are very different from humans. All the same, I will be honest with you."

"Thank you. It is all I want." Westin's shoulders eased with having someone to talk to. "I went to work for Gregor the Third about eight years ago. The militia pays their troopers one gold piece per month, but Gregor sweetened the pot and offered two gold. Literally, it was twice as much coin for half the work. I worked twelve hours for six days a week, but all I needed to do was sit at the gate house at Gregor's estate with another guard. Sometimes, I'd accompany Gregor to the docks, so he could yell at someone without fear of getting hit. Other times, I'd escort Lady Ophena to the market. She's Gregor's wife.

"I was relieved from escorting Lady Ophena once Enga was hired. You see, she was hired for in-house protection. Enga's father is a Sergeant in the Militia, and Enga was quite the fire-brand." Westin smiled with the memory, the warmth of the grin exuded the deeper character of the man. "The first time we went out for a drink at the pub, she got in a little spout with some big knotter from off one of the fishing ships."

"I thought I was gonna haf'ta fight, but she clobbered the poor guy good. He hit back, she hit even harder. They brawled across tables and onto the floor, and I couldn't get a foot in edgewise. She was on top when the city guard arrived to pull her off. Ha-ha, that fisherman had to leave town after having his reputation so shattered." Westin laughed harder before adding, "I knew right then I had to make her mine."

Wynkkur wanted to get back to the sparkly he'd seen on his sword. Pretending to be patient, softly he asked, "Is this what you want advice on?"

A swirl of emotion danced in Westin's eyes. All points of the emotional spectrum showed a quick rotation: surprise, hurt, anger, and finally a quick acceptance. He said, "Of course, I'll move forward." Pausing, he then added, "No, you are right. I should just go to the priestess. You're not even human."

"Westin," Wynkkur addressed, "I gave to you my promise by giving my word. You sound derogatory, but you speak no greater truth when you say I am not human. Like you, I do have emotion. Advice comes from the mind, not from the heart. From the heart comes experience, but never advice. They are the north and south of the spirit."

Wynkkur saw the wheels begin rolling in the warrior's mind. The elf then added, "Right now, the axis of those two points is spinning. When those points stop, you will find your center. At the same time, you will find your answer."

Westin didn't get it. "What? What are you talking about...some magic formula? I don't understand."

Wynkkur looked down at the small malachite stone in the pommel of his sword and thought, *How can I explain this?*

Holding out his hand with the torch, he slid it down to just beneath the first hint of heat. "Where the fire is represents your mind—these are your thoughts," and then the other hand he balled into a fist around the bottom of the torch. "This hand represents your feelings, and these come from what we elves call a heart." He grinned, realizing the warrior missed his subtle joke. Shaking the torch with both hands he added, "The mind and heart are connected."

With deft hands, Wynkkur rolled the torch over the back of his hand, catching the torch with no more than an inch separating skin from flame. "This is what your heart and mind are doing right now." He rolled it one more time and said, "For you, it is happening a lot faster than this, and when your mind and heart stop spinning, you will find your answer."

"That isn't what I'd come to ask you."

The elf, possessing dry and emotionless features, stared into the warrior's eyes. With impassive, almond-eyes blinking, Wynkkur replied, "Of course it is. I am not off by my diagnosis or conclusion. Would you correct me where my observation is wrong?"

Nodding, the guard eased back a pace, "Well, let me think on it, and I'll get back to you."

Wynkkur smiled a false-friendly expression before walking away.

Westin watched him go. To the guard, the elf appeared to be doing some strange and uncoordinated march. With his attention focused downward, occasionally, he would wave his torch from the cave's ceiling to down by his hip. The elf gave a serious stare downward and at the side of his leg while he walked. Westin shook his head, wondering why he had even asked the elf anything at all.

Westin was moved to pray under his breath, "Stranoss, should I begin praying to the mad-god Kranias? My actions show no reason."

His heart ached. *Perhaps it is not reason but desperation.*

Chapter Twenty-Eight

Day Twelve?, Unknown Hour

"So, Princess. Howd'ja find me?" Katia asked from a short pace behind the priestess. "The last time I expected to see you, you were making cute little moany-sounds in your sleep. I admit my deepest surprise in seeing your pet at the river later that day. Then, I saw you again at Dead Rik's—that was something else. You were the last person I'd expected to come up behind me like that."

Katia just began looking for Popalia's buttons a moment ago. Popalia ignored Katia's banter and focused only on the tunnel ahead. Once again, the pathway arched to the right while bending upward. Sometimes, the upward bending was sharp enough for the priestess and her attached personality to need assistance from either Raenyl or Seth. A little while earlier, Raenyl had pulled Popalia and Katia up into a new pathway. They'd needed to scale up six feet to reach a new off-shoot tunnel, traveling off in another unknown direction.

"Your elf is loyal like any dog I've ever seen. 'Good boy, Elf-boy!' Hee-hee," Katia chuckled. "Don't miss the point, now. The point is—I waved to your elf-boy from the other side of that river. I know you had to find a way around that river 'cause there ain't no way you'd get in that water. That water was too cold for a princess like you to climb in. Honestly, a prude would never show herself before a man, even if it is only an elf-boy. Not to mention that current and those robes would've dragged you down." With an intended pause, she added, "Come on, how did ya find me—and so fast, too?"

"Well, it's like you said, Katia. You prayed to the Great Mystery, and we appeared just in time to watch you flirt with that orc."

Katia pressed, "Awww, I'm just tryin' ta be friendly, and you're tossing dung balls in my face. Come on, now. How'd ya do it? Come on wit it."

Raenyl, who walked at the edge of Popalia's light, warned, "She is trying to trick you." Ahead of everyone, he watched the blackness ahead. His bow held an arrow, but it was relaxed on the string.

Katia's childlike chuckle was innocuous and brief. "Trick you?

I'm chained up to the girl without a key. I might do a trick for you, maybe...if the princess would turn her head." Katia made very suggestive sounds.

"I had two days of her fine company just north of Darkin Woods," Popalia informed before agreeing with the archer. "She is not only tricky when captured, she is slippery when free."

"I could be slippery for you, too, Raenyl," Katia licked her lips while suggestively making a hungry groan.

Raenyl looked over both women. Popalia's once curly, red hair was now a matted, oily mess atop her head. Her white robes were an ugly gray, and her sleeves and blue ribbon were splattered with crusty specks of dried blood—his blood and perhaps even a little bit of Seth's as well.

There beside her stood lithe Katia. She wore black, form-defining pants, with laces meshing up each side and drawn at her hips. The dark brown blouse she wore was both wrinkled and dirty, but still politely advertised the athletic gifts held within. Next to the finely shaped burglar, Popalia appeared so inadequately simple. Raenyl smiled wide as he acknowledged, "I bet that'd be really nice."

"Oh, it is," she pouted with her eyes.

"Would you trade ten gold coins for it?"

Her eyes recoiled to the priestess, "Wow, am I worth that much? You pay good."

"Pays well," Raenyl corrected. "You are worse than Seth."

She spied Raenyl, and her suggestion changed, "My friends are very rich."

Raenyl's voice turned cold, "Your friends are dead."

"What?" Grief wobbled across Katia's normally brave face. Quietly, she muttered, "Stileur?" Had the caverns not been so notorious for amplifying noises, no one would have heard. Facing the priestess, Katia heard the sing of steel leaving a scabbard a couple paces behind her. She added, "Easy there, boy. I just want to know if this is true."

"It is," the Elvish accent cut cold.

Katia sniffled, but her face held straight, "I want to hear it from the priestess."

"Your friends attacked us while we slept, and we beat them at our own disadvantage," Popalia stated confidently.

Weakly, Katia mumbled, "That was Trevex."

Raenyl snorted before correcting, "If Trevex was the half-orc, your half-orc friend tried his best to turn my head inside out while

I slept. He'd even taken a cheap shot at my goods with that damn club. Then, I ended his life."

"Stileur said he'd stop you at Dead Rik's." Katia brave face was back on. "I looked out the back of the wagon and watched you being arrested. I know his plan worked."

Raenyl kept his eyes on the tunnel ahead. "You know how fickle luck can be. Later, as we tried to leave, Stileur thought he'd be a problem for us. I stopped that, too. Be relieved in knowing he died quickly."

"I thought it was your—"

Raenyl completed her statement, "My brother? No. He is *your* truest hero. I killed both your friends."

Popalia added, "Darren chose the fate of your gang by trying to prevent the inevitable. If we'd caught you before reaching Dilligan's Freepost, Stileur's ending may have been different. We certainly wouldn't be here right now."

Distant and remembering her friend, Katia shook her head and rebuked, "You got no right putting the dead on me." Her eyes steeled as she restated, "Trevex, Stileur, and the entire caravan. I will not carry any of that. I paid for my ride, more than paid..." Her tears fell freely as she turned her head so Popalia could not see them. With a weepy voice, she cursed, "God pounded orcs!"

Popalia remained quiet. She left Katia alone to mourn for her friends. Raenyl continued scouting the dark spaces ahead while the thief sobbed without reservation. Softly, Wynkkur returned his sword to his scabbard and dropped back a pace.

When Katia's tears were done rolling, she concluded, "Your god cursed us when Thorgen killed that priest. That is what you think. Isn't it, priestess?"

Void of any warmth, Popalia's voice seethed, "As sure as the world is flat, you stole the gift my god gave to our land. It was free for all, and you stole what holds our world in balance. It has protected the realm of men, and the world cannot afford to pay for its loss."

Reflectively, Popalia added, "Pray for the Unknown's mercy. Pray to Asunna, too. Pray that Shealowe does not fill the empty space Thorgen tore into the void. Believe this, Katia. More than just Darren's schemes will be damned."

Chapter Twenty-Nine

Day Twelve?, Unknown Hour

The tunnel widened gradually, and as Wynkkur had warned Westin, their problems multiplied. Before them, the tunnel split into two dark unknowns. Two pitch black holes led in two separate directions, and neither revealed any hint of salvation.

Shaking his head, Raenyl looked from tunnel to tunnel, "This is bullshit." While running his fingers through greasy hair, he cursed, again, "Gods pound it. One path is as hopeless as the next."

Popalia rebuked the half-elf, "Don't call the gods in vain. We need their help, not their vengeance." Optimistically, she enlightened, "On the bright side, they may both lead to the outside. Maybe this is a blessing."

"Well, I still think this is bullshit." Raenyl, the non-believer, retreated a little. "I apologize if I've insulted your god, but this is a damnable mess, however we look at it."

Wynkkur nudged Westin with his elbow, "Now you will see what I mean. We've come too far to go backward, and now the path before us is beset with uncertainty. This is where a leader must lead and followers must follow. Watch closely to see the true leader."

Westin looked from Raenyl to Popalia, and finally over his shoulder as Gregor walked up carrying a torch. With a sour tone, Gregor stated, "I realize you all think I am a rotten man. I'm used to it...my intentions are often misunderstood. Regardless of all your judgments, I stand by my decisions with integrity, and when I am dead, my deeds will weigh heavy on the scales of Stranoss. Westin is not the first person to hate me for the hard decisions I've made, and when it is over, he will thank me for standing true to pure ideals."

Popalia nodded. Understanding Gregor's stance, she warranted, "I'll receive your council."

Gregor continued, "You all think I am cold—that I have ice in my veins. In the end, Stranoss will know I made decisions for the betterment of all and not just for myself. Decisions can be made with a clear mind and conscience and without fickle, emotional impulses."

Raenyl sighed along with an immature eye-roll, "What would you decide for us all?" The dark line from where the bowstring had cut his cheek looked like an exclamation point.

Gregor then offered, "There was a way out of this conundrum. It is back somewhere by where Miss Kobblepot died. I saw light by that thing. It is obvious we should go back the way we came."

"It would take us a day of walking to get back there," Popalia reminded. "Even if there is an exit back there, that thing might be hungry, again. Wisdom would dictate against going back into harm's way. Instinct warned us to run, and we ran. Life always moves forward, and never backward."

Gregor removed the wig from his head. Stubble, equally as long as on his bruised chin, circled around his head. Upon his crown and stretching to his forehead, all saw the large bald spot where no hair had grown for years. Swiping his hand to remove the sweat that gathered, dark streaks smudged his scalp where he'd wiped his dusty hand.

Looking back at the priestess, Gregor's stare and tone carried an intended mockery, "Priestess, leadership isn't a popularity contest. It is a position for those who can make hard decisions and live with what happens after making them. The consequences should be to the benefit of the whole and not for the few."

"I agree." Popalia, still nodding, added, "Absolutely I agree. Impulsive decisions will lead us in the wrong direction. My decision by your council is that we take inventory of everything we possess, then we sleep. As a whole, this group can make a decision in the morning...after the whole has rested. Assessing all of our frayed emotions, now would not be the best time for making major decisions."

Gregor chuckled, "Priestess Popalia, it would be just, and it would be fair, to admit this rescue hasn't gone well. Experienced leadership is available. You are a woman—barely a woman by the looks of you. Do you think all these young men follow you because of your experience?"

Popalia looked from Raenyl to Wynkkur. Wynkkur shrugged. Raenyl raised his hands in surrender and announced, "I'm an employee of the church. I'm in this for the gold. But if we *do* get out of here, I want an advance."

Popalia smiled lovingly at Raenyl. By keeping her smile, she may as well have backhanded the old merchant, "Your eyes tell you the truth. I am a woman—and just barely. My church made me a full priestess, because they believed I possessed the qualities necessary for the job. I will admit that *this job* is quite a bit bigger than I ever wanted, but as a leader I am not alone. Without your insights and advice, we wouldn't have gotten this far. I'm not just saying that. I mean it."

Popalia's tone stayed sweet, "Understand, Gregor. I do not lead any more than I follow. My god leads and right now, it is time to rest. You are your own free man and have been since you were unlocked from your shackles. Maybe some of these young men will accompany you if you want to leave. Feel free to ask them, but I'm betting they will stay and rest, and in the morning they will stay and eat. I hope these reasons are more important to these young men than what you've suggested."

A sneer stretched beneath his pointy nose, and Gregor angrily replied with wild hand motions, "Look before you. Nothing is there except death. We all know there is a way out behind us. The orcs won't be expecting us to get back out that way. We don't even have to go back that far." Desperate to be heard, but feeling completely ignored, Gregor's tone begged, "There is a way out by where Bennae fell."

"Gregor, we are all tired, and that will be tomorrow's decision." She looked around, "Does anyone oppose this plan?" No protests were uttered. "That is the consensus, Gregor. We will check our inventory, and then we'll sleep."

Gregor wasn't letting it go. "You are young and foolish, and at the expense of us all. Your leadership got Bennae killed."

"What?" Raenyl barked, "You shut your mouth!" Popalia raised her hand to quiet Raenyl, but his words boiled over, "Your dumb mouth is going to get *you* killed!"

Waving her hand to break their line of sight, Gregor ducked to hold eye contact with Raenyl. The priestess moved her hand, maintaining a broken view from each other. Gregor's jaw opened as if to say something, but he only grew more frustrated with Popalia. She snapped her fingers, saying, "This conflict is between you and me and has nothing to do with Raenyl. Outside of Katia, no one here is being kept against their will. You don't have to stay with us if you don't want to."

Popalia's eyes glazed razor-sharp, pushing Gregor back a pace. Her voice rang solid and without bias, "I do feel that if I am providing nourishment for you, I should receive a bit more respect from you."

Gregor took Ucilius's hand and eased the absent man to the floor. He then sat against the wall alongside his son-in-law.

"Whether I stay or go, I'm damned either way." Gregor sat still, Ucilius his mirror.

"I wish we hadn't left half our gear on the horses," Seth stated as he and Raenyl removed their packs.

"I regret leaving the jerky on my horse. I doubt the horses will eat it," Popalia said, having difficulty removing her tiny pack.

Wynkkur helped Popalia get free. Her pack was dainty in contrast to both mercenaries. Within her small pack, she still had one and a half ceramic vials of blessed water, her silver prayer tiara, a third full waterskin, a prayer book, a padded prayer board, two carrots, a loaf of bread, a tiny but bulging coin-pouch, and four remaining torches.

Raenyl scoffed, "Seth, just yesterday you told me you were glad all your gear was on the horse."

As a part of Raenyl's pack, he included his quiver, which currently held two dozen arrows, its intended capacity being forty. Inside his pack's side pocket, he stored a whetstone, flint and steel for fire starting, and the main pack held sixteen remaining torches, his lock picks, and an empty pouch that once held a handful of caltrops. Beneath a change of clothes was a fist-sized coin-pouch, an almost empty waterskin, and a couple of wrapped bowstrings.

The warrior growled, "That was yesterday. Yesterday, I was running for my life."

Seth's pack provided an armor repair kit, several various lengths of leather each at a different thickness, narrow pliers, a half-full water-bag, the bloodied clothes he'd worn the day of entry into the caves, four tent pegs, and fifty feet of rope. In a side pocket hid a whetstone and tiny bottle of blade oil. Thirteen torches remained in his pack.

The elf found Seth's words to be funny, "Ha-ha, now we just walk for our lives."

When Wynkkur opened his buckskin sack, he withdrew several books of various sizes and thickness—five to be exact—two blankets followed by two small pillows, thirty-eight torches, and two waterskins—one was empty and the other two-thirds full. He shook out the bag and thirty-two small, tan beans fell out with a couple handfuls of dirt and several coins—ten gold, eighteen silver, and three coins of copper.

Gregor noted as the silver and gold coins tinkled on the stone ground, "That is a fair bit of money."

"How do you fit all that in there?" Westin asked while shaking his head.

Wynkkur replied, "There are a couple of pockets inside for easier storage."

"Come on, Elf-boy. Tell us." Katia was truly asking, even if it sounded as though she'd given an order.

"This is an Elvish holding-bag." He fluttered it open, but only darkness could be seen. Popalia brought a torch closer, but the elf closed it quickly. "It is made to assist elvish hunters. There was a hunter who'd once put over a hundred rabbits inside his. If they were small hares, I might fit forty inside mine, but still, it is handy."

Surprised by the elf's revelation, Popalia asked, "Where did you get that?"

Patting himself with one hand before tugging the tip of one ear, he stated, "I'm an elf." Shaking the bag, he repeated, "This is an Elvish holding-bag."

Seth laughed. Then, he looked at Popalia and laughed again, harder still. Popalia asked what was so funny, to which Seth answered, "And you think *I'm* dumb." He broke into more laughter.

"I lived with Wynkkur my entire life!" Popalia defended, "He always does this! Twenty-two years, and he now let's me know he has a magic bag!"

Wynkkur shrugged as Seth's laughter was waning. The elf replied, "It is just a holding-bag. Like I said, it has extra pockets inside." He began to stuff one of the blankets into the buckskin sack.

"Hey, elf?" Gregor licked his lips. "Why not let us use the blankets and pillows? Why put them away?"

"Because there aren't enough for everyone. That is why." Wynkkur stuffed the first one in and began with the second. "One pillow is mine, and the other is Popalia's. I'm not sharing my pillow with you—or anyone for that matter. It would be rude to use a pillow and deny the rest of you, so it goes back into the bag. Elves share in liberty, and elves share in sorrow."

An image flashed in his mind. Elanya-Mora, the Zef'Lut Medicine elf had told him, "*When in dark times, remember first that you are an elf.*" Were those her words? He wondered, but he was certain it was very close to what she'd said. Times were now dark indeed.

"We are not elves," Gregor said, still hoping to get a blanket.

Wynkkur put all the books back except one. Smiling at the merchant, he replied, "Then you should have brought your own pillow." Changing the subject, "Since you are going to bed, I'll take that torch off your hands. I should read before falling to sleep."

Westin had already curled his arm beneath his head, his eyes weighing heavy. "How can you read? Are you not exhausted like the rest of us?"

Wynkkur agreed with the guard. "I'm tired, but not as bad as yesterday. This book is my spell book. Most of it makes little sense to me, but I keep hoping to understand its combinations, to unhook a little more arcane knowledge. By our current position, more knowledge can't hurt."

Chapter Thirty

Time Has Been Lost To Darkness

The torch flickered and faded, at last extinguishing. Darkness supreme, true ruler of the caverns, won once again. Wynkkur put his book away as the light was failing. Nearly asleep, he heard Katia ask softly, "Princess, you awake?"

"Murr, umph-errr," was the closest retort compared to language. As close to sleep as Wynkkur was, he swam back up to consciousness. His dominating worry being that Katia was up to no good, he'd need to be ready for anything. Quietly, he fought against his own overdue slumber.

Katia whispered, "Raenyl. Raenyl, wake up."

What is she up to? Wynkkur thought, but he remained silent and still.

"Maah, what? What is this?" an awaking Raenyl muttered.

"Raenyl, it is me. Shhh."

"What, what is it Katia?" Raenyl cursed, "Damn this darkness."

"I just...I just need to know. You didn't hunt down my friends, right? They came after you?"

"Seth and I were hired to recapture you and retrieve the scepter Thorgen has. We're not a death squad—just soldiers for hire. After the incident at the inn, we almost quit."

"The inn?" Katia led.

"That's where your hyorc friend and his gang ambushed us. It was ugly."

"So Trevex and Stileur, they both attacked you first?"

Frustration laced Raenyl's tone, "Yes, Katia. Yes. We're not even to harm Thorgen if we can avoid it. All Popalia wants is her scepter back. She doesn't even want you, but you just happen to know how to find Thorgen. She wants her scepter back—that is all. Get it?"

"Sorry for waking you." There was a pause in the darkness, and then she added, "Thanks for being honest with me."

Raenyl grumbled, but then a moment later, he added, "Katia, your friends died to protect you, and they fought fiercely. It came down to their life or mine. Do you understand?"

A moment passed in the thick black, "I'd have done the same

for them."

"If you were wearing my boots, you'd have done the same as me." There were no more words from either Raenyl or the thief. After a few more moments of listening to silence, Wynkkur allowed sleep to roll him someplace else.

Chapter Thirty-One

Time is lost to darkness

"Why do we always turn to the right? Hmmm, priestess?" Gregor challenged.

"Not always." Popalia's hair hung around her face in clumps, greasy and without life. The weight around her eyes showed a soul frayed by pressure and stress. Having her prisoner chained to her while trying to sleep on the stone floor made for an unpleasant respite. Her tone revealed her growing impatience with the merchant's constant grinding as she explained, "Philosophically, if you always turn to the right, you can only go in a circle. Right has proven correct for the last couple of turns."

"What do you mean, 'proven'? We are lost, as we were two days ago. This isn't a philosophical problem, priestess. This is real." Gregor was on the attack, "Theology and dogma aren't going to save our lives—only sound decisions will."

Raenyl stood beside the elf and chided Gregor, "Quit with your antics. We all know you want to go back to that thing that ate Bennae, so just say it instead of trying to be clever." They'd made the decision that morning to take the right tunnel, and Westin would take point for the day—if it was day. Seth and Ucilius remained at the back.

Gregor looked at the archer, and realizing he could get hit again, he altered his tone, "I just wonder why we didn't go left. We went right in the orc's area, and we almost died on that ledge. Bennae ran to the right, and right into that thing. The last tunnel was also right. By her argument, we've gone in a complete circle; shouldn't we be getting out of all this mess by now? If her philosophy was reliably accurate, that is."

Popalia pushed forward, following Westin's steps. "Deciding whether you're going to stand on your left foot or right foot every day is a fool's charade. Only by the desire of the Great Mystery will we ever see the light of day. You may as well sit at the crossroads contemplating the right and the left while waiting for another rescuer to come if you're going to second guess every tunnel we've chosen. Or better yet, what would Stranoss do?"

Katia chuckled and added, "Now, that's funny. Good shot,

Princess."

Westin called out from up front, "Stranoss would want us to eliminate the most obvious wrong first. Only Kranias deals with chance and odds. Stranoss seeks logic, and I think He'd smile upon your logic, priestess."

"Why thank you, Westin. Believe me when I say the Mystery is not at odds with Stranoss. Stranoss provides many answers for many of the Mystery's questions. The Unnamed's main purpose is to fill the spaces between the gods—not just one, but all of them."

"I didn't know that," Westin admitted. "The priests of Stranoss say the Unknown Host has no loyalty and can side with Kranias or Asunna in the time of one breath. Is that true?"

"Only by a rigid perspective is that true." Popalia explained her answer, "You may not know this about the Unnamed—although historically considered to be a neutral god, the Mystery will always seek the side of righteousness when the balance is uneven. As our beloved Paladin, Kravin LeSalle once wrote, 'If the land should fall into darkness, the beauty of the rainbow should be forever lost.' I've never seen more proof of those words than right now."

"Great, more philosophy," Gregor snipped.

Raenyl, in his growing frustration, shot back by saying, "You are not a hostage here. We will give you one-eighth of our torches, and you can go on your merry way. Maybe there is an exit back by that monster. No one here will stop you from leaving."

"I have no food or water," protested Gregor. "How will I get Ucilius back there or even out?"

Seth, who carried the second torch in one hand and led a stumbling Ucilius with the other, offered, "After you pay me, you can take Useless here anywhere you want. You can even feed him to that thing, so you can get out."

"I wouldn't dare!" Gregor's tone rang genuine with horror.

Seth inquired with a sharp edge in his voice, "Wouldn't dare what? Pay me?"

In an odd way, Westin defended Gregor, "He pays his debts, and he pays them on time, too. Though, he would serve Ucilius to that thing on a golden platter for the opportunity to squeeze his way through a weasel's hole."

"I am not the villain here, Westin. Despite all of your meaningless accusations, I'm a respected tradesman. I've never said anything about wanting to leave this group."

Katia chastened, "Then, shut your mouth, old man. We are all tired of hearing it."

"Here, here," chimed Raenyl.

They walked for a ways longer. The tunnel gradually climbed and then dropped steeply for several yards. The tunnel veered left then rolled right before splitting, again. To entertain Gregor, she took the left tunnel, which after walking for what seemed like several miles, the tunnel ended where it had collapsed upon itself. Nobody said anything, but there were a couple of evil eyes given to Gregor. They made it back to the break in the tunnel and continued to the right after six torches had been wasted on the wrong turn.

The second tunnel, the one on the right, turned upward. The angle sometimes climbed as challenging as fifty degrees and made for exhausting work. Delicate and careful, everyone traversed the difficult tunnel. One slip, and whoever trailed behind would tumble all the way back to the bottom. Seeming to make matters worse, the walls were closing in. Within an hour into their climb, the tunnel where two people could walk side-by-side now narrowed only wide enough for one person at a time.

Katia, on the short chain, remained intimately close to the sour-smelling priestess. Katia mentioned Popalia could turn the snout of an orc. Popalia responded that unlike the others, they had four arms and four legs to prevent slipping. If they had fallen, all but Westin would have tumbled in a tangle of bodies to the bottom.

At one point, the grade became too difficult to lead the stumbling zombie, Ucilius. Seth awkwardly adjusted his position to keep Ucilius pinned to a wall with his knee, while with amazing dexterity and balance, removed his backpack with one hand. Switching the torch to his opposite hand, Seth worked open his pack with one hand. Raenyl climbed down to help the pair.

Seth removed the rope bundle from his pack. Strapping the catatonic man to his back, he then thanked his brother for the help. He tied the other end of the rope through the straps of his pack and let the pack drag behind him. "This isn't worth two coins of gold," he grumbled as he hauled Ucilius up the narrow incline.

Battling the path for the duration of two torches, eventually the tunnel leveled. Exhausted and hungry, they'd rounded the crest. Its width remained snug, and it would be uncomfortable sleeping in a single file line along the corridor. Having survived another day in the land's dark bowels, they joked together and celebrated life endured. What they'd decided to call "day three" had come to an end, and they vowed to cherish every day they managed to survive.

Chapter Thirty-Two

Time Is Lost To Darkness

"How much water do we still have, Priestess?" Gregor asked with his usual condescending barbs. "Half a skin?"

Raenyl rolled his head from shoulder to shoulder, stating, "Not today, Gregor. Every day you do this, but not today, all right?"

Seth added, "Yeah, the troop morale is bad enough, and here you start, again—every morning, like a kick in the sack."

"Excuse me for my concern. I think it is a good and fair question," Gregor mocked while pointing low and in Popalia's direction. "Her god can bless the water, but when we run out, what then? Hmmm? We can't even drink our own pee. Who has urinated last? Or better yet, when was the last time any of you needed to go?"

Popalia spoke up, "We have two skins that are half-full of water. It is enough for today and tomorrow. We don't urinate or relieve ourselves because of the blessing. Our bodies are sustained on the most miniscule amount, but once the blessing is removed, the starvation and dehydration is equal to the days without food or drink."

Raenyl and Seth burst out almost simultaneously, "What?"

Katia tittered, "Uh-oh, here is more of that washin a'comin' out."

Popalia admitted, "I've heard of priests fasting for one complete moon cycle with only one bite of dried bread and two gulps of water, but what we are doing is too much. To pray and meditate for almost a month takes a toll on the priest. He isn't running, fighting, climbing, healing, or arguing with someone who only sees the worst of life. Before rescuing the four of you, the four of us hadn't had a real meal since leaving Capitol City. If we lose the Mystery's blessing, we will wither and die within a couple hours."

Seth barked loudly, "I knew your magic food was bad! I said it on the first day!"

Westin understood Popalia and defended, "No, no Seth. This isn't that bad. It is good. Look, as long as the priestess has some food and water, everyone is okay. How long will you be able to maintain everybody's nourishment?" His gaze fell upon the priestess.

Wynkkur and Raenyl answered simultaneously, "Two days."

"If we find more water," Popalia added, "twenty-eight days is the longest I've seen anyone go without a regular diet."

Raenyl shook his head, "This just keeps getting better and better. Where are we going to find more water?"

Gregor pointed backward. "There is water only two days back, in the main cavern."

"He is right," Seth remembered. "We could make it right on time."

"No," Popalia stated firmly. "We have not been led this far to turn back, now. We would be further along if you had just trusted me, yesterday."

"Led? Led where and by whom?" The older man denied, "Certainly not by your mysterious god. Look at this. We are going nowhere." He flung his hands outward for emphasis and slammed the tips of his fingers against the wall. "Ouch."

Popalia chuckled. "We are in a rather tight spot. You should be careful." There were intended multiple meanings to what she'd said. As Gregor sucked at the abrasion on the tip of his middle finger, Popalia added, "I suspect that we will find clean water ahead. I could bless dirty water if I need to, but I'm not leading us back into the hopelessness behind us."

"You are leading us to hopeless deaths before us," Gregor stated quietly.

Wynkkur reminded the stubborn merchant, "You were already dead when we found you. We bought you a couple more days of life, and you are still ungrateful. You should be in the bellies of orcs right now, if not orc feces atop a refuse pile. Lead on, Popalia." Reluctantly, the brothers nodded in agreement.

Westin spoke up, "I'm still with you, priestess. I don't want to deal with those orcs, again...or that thing that got Bennae. Certain death is behind us with potential death up front." He shrugged, "Guess Enga and I will reunite sooner than later." He began walking. "I'll lead if no one else minds."

Popalia clapped the broad-shouldered warrior on the back. "My god leads to safety for only those willing to trust. We have two days' time at least, and much can change in two days. For all we know, we could be out of here in another hour."

"This is hopeless," the merchant stammered.

Following Westin, Popalia said, "Like the old cliché, it is always darkest before the dawn."

Wynkkur reflected on Elven Mythology and the tale of Lo'Lyth before saying, "Only here, it is always dark, and there will never be dawn." Raenyl uttered a grim chuckle and followed Wynkkur. Gregor grumbled under his breath and held the hand of stumbling Ucilius. A very unhappy looking Seth carried the back torch at the end of the line.

Keeping with yesterday's agreed upon rule, only two torches burned at a time. This was to conserve light. Popalia carried one for the front, and Seth or Gregor shared a torch in the very back. They walked through the narrow tunnel, and only after one torch began to flicker—just before it extinguished—they would retrieve a replacement and light it. For obvious reasons, no one told Gregor there was only two-and-a-half days' worth of torches left.

The confined tunnel remained level, but gradually the tunnel grew stricter. Westin didn't notice that he was walking at a slight angle until armored Seth called from the back of the line, "My shoulders scrape the walls if I don't twist." A few more paces and Seth called again, "Are we getting bigger? My head rubs against the ceiling if I don't stoop a little."

Wynkkur, an inch shorter than Popalia, stated nervously, "I don't like this. The walls are shrinking."

Feeling the spread of everyone's unease, Popalia prayed loud enough for Westin and Wynkkur to hear. She prayed only for the power to change their attitude about the situation. "Blessed Mystery, the enlightened and unnamed. Hear my faithful prayer. Stay with us and grant us courage to continue pressing on in absolute trust."

Westin found the resolve to push forward as the tunnel continued getting smaller. The earth was shrinking. Both Westin and Seth had to walk sideways, and Seth's armor frequently scraped the wall upon one side or the other. Walking in front of Seth, Gregor pulled Ucilius and pleaded, "Let's go back before this dead ends. We've wasted all of yesterday, now today is ruined, too."

"Shhh," Westin called from the front. "I hear something."

From the very back came Seth's frustrated voice, "Is it the sound of me getting stuck?"

"What?" Raenyl asked with unabashed fear tickling his tone. "If you are stuck, we are all stuck."

Everyone who could turn their head scrutinized the end of the line as Seth shook his head. "Sorry, brother—bad joke."

"That isn't funny, Seth," scorned Popalia.

"I said it was a bad joke, but let's get a move on."

"Wait, both of you! Be quiet," Katia growled. "For real, I hear something, too."

Everyone was quiet, and Wynkkur excitedly admitted, "I can hear it, too. It's water, rushing water, like a stream...an underground stream!"

Westin's eyes lit up, "Is it?" He couldn't tell, but he wanted to believe.

Katia nodded, "I think elf-boy is right. It might be rushing water."

"We just need to get a little further through this tunnel, and we can get our skins filled," Wynkkur said with a smile.

With renewed zeal, they pushed forward. As tightly pressed as they were, the tunnel began to bow. The pathway began to warp, awkwardly bending into a tight crevice contorting to one side. Westin led, his knees bent, and his back arched. He couldn't turn his body around, because the tunnel was now too tight. Scooting forward by sliding his feet, he barely kept his balance as he led the group while arched backward.

Bent like the quarter moon, he managed to twist his head around, scraping the tip of his nose on the encroaching cavern wall. Fear shined in his eyes back at the priestess, who had luckily entered the crevice positioned the other way, with her butt bent out. Kissing the bowed stone, Katia faced the same direction only a short pace behind.

The elf was right—it was water and more than just a trickle. It sounded like a rushing flow, and only a little ways forward. Westin learned the echoes in these tunnels were misleading, but the water sounded as if it was within 100 paces. It had to be close, and he knew it was close. Could he make it? It seemed the bully that was fate held wonderful candy just beyond their short reach.

Popalia asked, "Westin, are you okay? Can you move?"

He swallowed hard and then replied, "I want to turn around, like you, but I can't move. It is too tight for me to roll over. When I turned my head to see you, my nose scraped the wall."

"Give me your hand, Westin. Please, just touch my fingers if nothing else." With his left hand, he reached out. She took his hand and ordered, "Fear be gone!"

As if shocked, Westin released her as soon as she spoke her command. "Whoa!" Then, he turned his head, scraping his nose to face the darkness ahead. With his head turned, he admitted, "I can get a little further." And he did.

Shuffle, shuffle, shuffle, and then he called back, "The cave opens up in about three more steps. It gets bigger, again."

Four shuffles more, and the corridor opened into a larger room. Westin pushed through and sat upon the ground. He moved out of the way so the others could get by, muttering praise the whole time, "Oh, my god Stranoss. Thank you."

Popalia squeezed through with Katia right behind. Katia gave the priestess an awkward hug, "Let's not go back that way. A'right, Princess? I don't care where we go…Blackmire Garrison. I don't care. Just not through that, again."

Wynkkur came out next and wiped his filthy sleeve across his lightly perspiring forehead, smearing long, dark streaks. Raenyl added a few select curses as he stood up straight, again. He looked behind and saw a much-stressed Seth holding his torch behind frozen Gregor and Ucilius. Gregor's eyes were closed, and he lay with his face and chest resting on the curve of the corridor. He had his arms spread wide, as if giving the wall a warm hug.

Seth called out, "He's stuck, and I'm not much better."

Raenyl swore, "Buggering bullshit!" He sighed before pretending to speak calmly, "Gregor, you are almost out of the tunnel. Just ten more steps, and you'll be out of there. Look at me. Here, open your eyes. I'm standing upright." Raenyl did a little jig as the merchant opened his eyes.

"I can't…it is too hard," Gregor wailed in his panic. "We should have gone back, but now I'm stuck."

Raenyl traded looks between Popalia and his brother, "I don't have the patience to deal with him. Seth, just push the old fool out of your way."

"I don't think I can, Raen. I'm—well, my armor is scraping on both sides, now. I could get stuck if I push too hard."

Wynkkur spoke quietly, "I can get him. I can do it."

"Really?" Raenyl admitted his surprise. "How? I could barely move in there."

"If he won't move when I get to him, I'll chop him into pieces small enough to drag out." Wynkkur didn't sound like he was joking. "Did you hear me, Gregor? I'm coming to help you, but if you don't want to come out of there, I'm chopping you into pieces."

Popalia rebuked, "Wynkkur, that is awful. Tell me you won't!"

He shrugged and slid himself back into the awkward space. Shuffling closer, the elf called, "Reach for my hand, and I'll guide you out."

"No," Gregor whined. "You are going to cut off my hand."

"I'm going to lead you out of here. If you don't want my help, I'll cut you to pieces, so Seth and Ucilius can live. So, take my hand or die."

Gregor reached out for Wynkkur's hand, and Wynkkur took it. "I've got you, now slide your feet. Good, now again." Wynkkur stepped back and Gregor followed, as did Ucilius sliding along behind him.

After the three got out, Seth heaved through the tight space with strong legs. To make it past the last hard step, Seth exhaled completely and pushed through. The leather and steel of his combat suit grated the walls in protest. Then, he popped free.

With the relief shining in Seth's eyes, he joked while rubbing the hardened leather codpiece affixed to his armor, "Thank you for saving my ass, alongside all else I hold dear. Phew! Thought I was about to lose my good things back there."

"You were going to kill me," sneered Gregor. "Nasty little elf."

Wynkkur retorted. "You've been our biggest problem since the orcs, and I'm sick of you. We all are. You were stuck in the tunnel, you made your choice, and I honored it."

Here in the spacious cavern they could stretch outward with both hands and still have a foot of space on either side. Above their heads were hundreds of calcite stalactites, a few as long as swords, but most of them no longer than rounded daggers. The flickering flames from the torches cast teeth-like shadows across the ceiling; everyone watched overhead for stones set at angles evenly apart. Nothing above resembled the goo-spitter from two days earlier. Relieved, they all moved beneath the spike-hung ceiling toward the sound of rushing water.

The glistening of moisture reflected the light. Another pace and the wall came into view. The cavern ended. At the back, from a hole in the ceiling of the back wall, a stream of water gushed out from a hole as wide as Wynkkur. It splashed against the back wall and ran a semi-steep angle down into a chute that led deeper into the world.

Popalia was the first to utter an elated cheer, "Ha-ha, Gregor. It's fresh water. Oh, thank you, Mystery. Thank you for your blessing."

Sour Gregor was quick to remind, "This is a dead end. Sure, we got water, but we are further from an exit than we were a few days ago."

Seth shook his head, "Man, haven't you ever anything good to say?"

Westin grinned at Seth as Raenyl added, "Bane's Blood,

Gregor. We found drinkable water in the middle of nowhere, and you're gonna piss in it."

Katia followed Popalia closer to where the water fell freely, saying to the merchant while watching her footing, "I was right. Your heart has problems." The priestess handed the torch to the thief and stepped upon the smooth rock beside the steady falls.

Gregor nervously adjusted the wig upon his head, "Wait, please. I am happy we will now have water. Truly, I am. But I was hoping we were getting out of here."

"We all are, Gregor. Do you think any of us want to be here? Are you really that self-centered?" Popalia asked as she withdrew a skin from her bag. Removing the stopper from the bag's mouth, she held the bag into the path of the falling water. "We might have to go back to where Bennae died."

"Well, why did we come way out here? There was water in the cavern where my scribe was killed." Gregor seemed to be turning purple in the dancing lights. "We came here for nothing."

As the skin filled, she stopped it. Twisting to put the skin in her pack, her foot slid a little. "Whoa!" Popalia patted her chest.

"Be careful!" Wynkkur ordered as he stepped a little closer.

"It is nothing, Mama Hen," Popalia teased. "Here, just give me your empty skins."

"Hey! I want answers!" Gregor barked. "Don't you ignore me, little girl. I'm the Third!"

Popalia smiled while taking the waterskin Wynkkur offered. Wynkkur shook his head concerning the merchant, but the joyous sparkle in Popalia's eyes overrode the elder's belligerency. He understood, after finding fresh water, nothing could dampen her spirits, now.

"Yawn, you are the Third," Westin taunted. "Your 'title'—it means nothing in this place. When will you finally get that, old fool?"

"Gregor, I've told you many times. My god looks to you to find answers. My god only provides the questions. Every time I ask 'why,' all I get are more questions." She filled one of Wynkkur's bags and traded him for his second near-empty skin. She stretched across with one leg to brace against the wall as she reached up to fill the skin. "The deeper my gratitude, the more is revealed for my understanding."

As the water splashed over her hands and into her face, she pivoted her weight to look over her shoulder at the angry man. "I'll tell you what. We will go back to where you think you saw light, and we will check for an exit."

"What?" Katia expressed her dissatisfaction. "I don't want to walk backward two days! You said forward, never backward!"

Shifting again to tie Wynkkur's second skin, she looked down at Katia, "We've gone as far forward as—" Her foot slipped.

Right off, her foot abandoned the rock she'd used as an anchor, her knee landing painfully hard against a rock in the rushing water. Cold water soaked swiftly into her robes at the same time her knee slipped beneath her along the slick chute.

Katia uttered a noise that sounded like, "Grunk!" as the chain connected to the priestess yanked against her body. Popalia's wet weight dragged the thief down. Katia followed the pull of her bonds as the slick, stone slide whipped the priestess along. Face-first, Katia lost her footing, her own arms flailing out and feebly grasping at slippery rocks while the priestess yelped, "Oh, god. No!"

Wynkkur looked up from where he'd been returning the first skin to see the priestess slipping down with Katia sliding face-first in pursuit. Crying out in disbelief, "Fenyll's fire!" he leapt forward. His hand shot out in hopes of catching, but he only succeeded in touching the booted heel of Katia as the two women were flushed into the hole of the earth.

Wynkkur gaped at his betraying hand. The tips of his fingers relayed the sensation of the missed boot. The whole point of any of them being in this cave had just followed the priestess into the mouth to nowhere. Seeing her go, down into the great nothing, he dropped his torch and stepped closer.

Seth stood equally stunned as all the others, only he knew what no one else did. Before Wynkkur could react in his shock, Seth reached out and grabbed the sorcerer's robes. Wynkkur protested, "No!" As Seth pulled the spell-slinger in close, the elf voiced pure anger. Wynkkur shouted up into the face of the warrior, "No!"

Seth squeezed the squirming elf, holding him firmly. Genuine sorrow clung with wicked claws in his tone, "Wynkkur, they are gone. Popalia is gone."

Chapter Thirty-Three

Time Is Lost To Darkness

Seth dragged Wynkkur away from where the earth had sucked down both reasons why they were there. Surrounded by Seth and Westin, Wynkkur knew he couldn't force his way past the two soldiers, so he tried to convince them to let him pass, "She needs our help! We can't let her go without us. We have to go after her!"

Shaking his head, Raenyl's tone was dour, "Where they've gone is a one-way trip."

Gregor began to stammer something but quieted himself, instead. He took Ucilius by the hand and led him to sit down. Wynkkur looked from half-elf to blades-man, then to the other men and said, "No way. She just went down that hole, and I need to help her. She is very scared." Looking to Seth with pleading eyes, "I need to get to her."

"No way. Uh-uh," Seth firmly stated. "She is gone, and you need to get back to your senses. You can't just—" With his fingers fluttering, he pulled his hand away from the side of his head, "you know...just go out of your mind."

"What?" Wynkkur gasped.

Raenyl nodded, "I'm sorry, my fr-friend..." Raenyl looked away. He couldn't say anymore. Wynkkur didn't deserve this, and with that revelation, Raenyl realized Wynkkur really was his friend.

Wynkkur shook his head, again. "No, she is down there. Look, I know you're all scared, so I'll go first, okay?" He looked between the two warriors at the hole where the water poured through. "I saw her torch go out when it hit the water. Wherever she is, it is really dark right now. It is a night with no dawn."

"Poetic, mister elf. How very poetically put." Gregor brushed Ucilius's hair aside. "You know, I made some mistakes with Ucilius. I never appreciated him for all the—"

Seth snarled at the merchant, interrupting, "We don't care about stupid mistakes you've made! Our employer just got sucked down into—" After a brief pause, and not being sure which word he wanted, he decided on, "no-place-land."

Raenyl went over beside the hole and yelled inside, "Popalia, can you hear me?" Behind him, through the twisted tunnel they would soon travel again, he heard those words echoing. Putting his head as close to the water as he could without getting wet, Raenyl listened.

Everyone listened.

The only sound was splashing against the wall, and the roaring din of splashing water ricocheting down the chute below. No other sound could be heard. Raenyl called again equally loud. After a moment of waiting, he said to the elf, "I have good ears, Wank—almost as good as yours."

Calmly, Wynkkur replied, "Let me come closer, and I'll listen. I agree your ears are elvish, but I want to hear for myself."

"No, brother," Seth called to Raenyl. "He'll try to jump."

Wynkkur assured, "I won't. I just want to listen."

Raenyl nodded, "Come closer, but no tricks. I want Seth to keep one of your hands."

Seth added, "Like the one you hold your sword with. I don't need you cutting off my hand, so you can go kill yourself."

Wynkkur's tone resembled sincere hurt, "Seth, know with all my words that I would warn you first. I have that much respect for you. I promise to let you know with enough time for you to quickly decide."

"Just gimme your sword-hand," Seth took Wynkkur's hand, encasing it in a grip of meaty steel. They may as well have been cuffed together. He wasn't going anywhere without Seth's permission.

Raenyl called into the opening again, his loudness reverberating off the walls and down each tunnel. Wynkkur waited. He listened intensely. He heard the echoes of Raenyl bouncing further in the halls than any of the humans were capable, but there was no sound of Popalia coming anywhere from down below. Wynkkur shrugged, "So, she is down further than I thought. That, or the rush of water is blocking any sound from reaching our ears."

Westin set a hand upon the elf's shoulder, "Wynkkur, I know this is hard to accept. When you love someone as much as you did Popalia, it is really hard to let it go. You were right about what you said the other day, about my mind and my heart. It doesn't matter whether Enga and I were married, as it does not matter that you are elf, and she is human. Our love and our loss are equal."

"I know what I said to you the other day was right." Wynkkur tried to pull his hand from Seth's, but the warrior held him firmly. Sighing, Wynkkur said to Westin, "Actually, my feelings for Popalia are very different from yours and Enga's, not to mention the fact that Popalia is still alive. I know this, because I am still alive."

"That is crazy talk," Gregor interjected. "We are alive, because we didn't slide through the hole in the world."

To Seth, Wynkkur said, "Let go of my hand. I'm not jumping, yet."

Seth regarded Raenyl, who responded with a shrug. Seth released the elf, and the elf rubbed his freed wrist. "Thank you. As you know, we have gone with only a bite of food and a couple gulps of water, per day, cumulative for nine days. I'm an elf—Popalia's god means less to me than any of you—but I do believe in Popalia. She has proven herself to me."

Looking at Gregor and then Ucilius, Wynkkur continued, "She has been greatly blessed by whatever gods there are. She is our connection to life, and it is only through her faith that we've been nourished."

Staring deep into Westin's eyes, the elf continued, "If she were dead, we'd have lost our blessing. We'd immediately have felt fatigue and hunger, and our bodies would have become emaciated. It is her bond between us and her god that has suspended our death. She is our bridge between life and death."

He let his words sink in before stating, "She is down there, in the darkness, alone with only Katia—our enemy. If she dies down there, so do we." He looked around the cavern at each of the men gathered. "The choice is yours. I'm going down looking for her, and I encourage you to come with me. I'm not expecting any of you to come with me, but you will not stop me from going."

"You are crazy," Seth said stepping back a pace. "I'll get stuck in there."

Raenyl added, "Even if your crazy idea is true, we'll be in the same bad place as Popalia. If we jump down there with you, our torches will be soaked, and we'll have no light. We can still get out of here. We just need to go back, like Gregor suggested days ago."

Wynkkur stepped closer to where the water poured and stood beside Raenyl. With both hands, he touched each of the archer's shoulders. "You are not bound to me. I'll give to you all of my torches as well as all the coins in my bag if you think you can make it out of here before starvation sets in. All you'll need is a full meal to counter the consequences of Popalia's blessing. Once you have eaten, your body will return to its normal functions. It only takes one meal."

"What are you going to do for light?" Westin asked.

Wynkkur withdrew his short blade and muttered a couple of unrecognizable phrases, and the silver-ribbed weapon burst aflame. The light wasn't much, but it was enough. "I learned this from my spell book the other night. Just in time, I think."

Seth sounded like he was thinking along Wynkkur's lines, "What if I get stuck? I'd go with you if Raenyl would go, but I don't want to get stuck."

Not very consoling, Wynkkur offered, "We'll tie ourselves together with your rope. What happens to one of us will happen to all."

"You can't go!" Gregor stood up. Both warriors turned to face the merchant, and their body language spoke volumes. His tone softened, "I mean, I—I haven't paid you your gold, yet. If you leave me here with Westin, I'll even double your wage."

Westin laughed, "Wynkkur, I'll go with you. Maybe Gregor will finally understand that I no longer work for him."

"Thank you." Wynkkur nodded, "I must inform you. You've only gone four days without food. You'll be ravenous, but you could make it back out the other way if you can avoid the orcs. I'll even give you this full waterskin to help you."

Westin shook his head, "My Enga is gone. If I die with you, I'm gone, too. I've decided I'm with you all the way."

Seth shook his head at the merchant, "I can't spend your gold if I die before receiving it. I liked that weird girl a whole lot more than your gold coins."

Nodding, Raenyl turned to Wynkkur. "I don't like Gregor enough to die with him. If we die and Popalia was already dead, I'll find you in the next life and beat you like an orphaned hyorc."

"What about Ucilius?" Gregor pleaded, "You can't just leave him here to die!"

Seth chuckled, "Well, then. Looks like you are coming, too."

Chapter Thirty-Four

Time Is Lost To Darkness

The water rushed the two of them into the mouth of the unknown. Popalia had barely enough time to inhale as her hands slipped across slick stones while being whisked into the void. She held her breath in the darkness as the water flung her around inside the stone chute.

Five seconds can last forever when expecting the absolute end. Popalia was flung outward into oblivion with the water spraying in all directions. The chain between the two women snapped tight. She was now free falling through the forever black, and so was Katia. Popalia heard the sound of water slapping water approaching from below.

Ker–plunk! The priestess was submerged. Her soaked robe wrapped with heavy iron chains became a dangerous burden in the darkness. Terrified and thrashing in the blackness, her robes would eventually drown her. She kicked around and splashed frantically, throwing her head up to the surface above the black water, drawing in a desperate gasp.

A tough hand reached out and grabbed her, pulling the priestess upward. Katia's voice followed, "Quit thrashing! It isn't even four feet deep!" Holding Popalia's arm with one hand, Katia's other hand found the priestess's butt and pushed downward while stating, "Oh, lordy-lord. Was that *your* behind I touched? I'd expected it to be softer on a princess."

The constant tumult of cascading water made it difficult to hear anything, with the exception of Popalia's shrieking, "What are we going to do?" Standing up, Popalia yelled, "Why aren't we dead?" From multiple points in the blackness, echoing reflections bounced back with the request, "*We dead? ...Dead? ...Dead?*"

Katia shook Popalia firmly, her voice steady, "What? Do you wanna die? I don't want you dead, not yet. I'd need ta' pull your stinking corpse around wit' me. Now, be quiet! Your loud and crazy screaming Ain't gitten' us out'a here!"

Popalia grappled against Katia—her fear her only reality. She cried out, "I don't know what to do." In sheer panic, she said it one more time as if confirming it for herself, "I don't know what to do?"

"You got to calm down, girl," Katia ordered. "By sake of the gods, you are a priestess. Pull it together."

"This darkness—yet, I can see light flashing in my eyes!"

"We've been in this black ever since you found me. This ain't no new darkness, just the same ole' pitch. So, screw your tight-ass down before I slap you around!"

Popalia released her grip, and out of pure shock, started removing her backpack, admitting without lucidity, "I have torches in my backpack, but I dropped Wynkkur's waterskin after I fell." As if her phrasing made sense, she concluded, "Now, I'm all wet and in the dark."

"Yeah, we're in a bad spot," Katia sounded harrowed. "Although, we're in a far better spot than having an orc's fingers stuck up inside us. Where is all this faith you talk about? Or are you hurt? Are you injured from the fall?"

"No," Popalia's voice broke in hysteria. The pure black was evil. Swirling shadows danced in the darkness of her mind, reflected on the sightlessness in her eyes. "No, I'm all wet! I'm all wet, and the torches are, too. My backpack is all—"

A hand-sized sting whipped across her cheek, and the echoing crack sounded louder than the cascading water pounding the underground lake.

"You hit me!" Popalia stated in surprise.

"I swear I'm closin' my fist wit' the next one sister, you hear me?" Katia's voice turned icy, "Where is your god? Here you're sleeping in a wolves den and playing the fool."

Katia's words sounded familiar. It was from some sort of spiritual story, a tale Popalia had heard as a small child—something her mother had told her. A fragile answer followed the realization. Popalia's courage was a wet, paper tiger. "My god is here. I just can't see."

Then, with a stronger voice, she replied, "I don't need eyes to believe."

Katia cooed, "Right, what we need is a miracle. That's your business. Mine is keeping cool when the shithouse walls fall down. So, you tell me when your faith shows up. Or is this too much for a princess like you?"

Finding her faith, Popalia steeled and sounded confident, "My god is always with me, especially when the darkness surrounds." A snickering Katia stated, "Ha, maybe there *is* a priestess here after all." Allowing Popalia no time to backslide, "So what do you suppose we do, now?"

Popalia proclaimed, "We must get out of the water and dry off." Her tone changed from confidence to question, "Did you hear that?" Not waiting for Katia's answer, she said, "It sounded like someone calling."

Katia whispered, "I think it's the Great Mystery telling you to take a bath."

Softly but not demanding, Popalia shushed. They listened to nothing...and finally, behind the rushing water, a small and weak sound like, "*Can you hear me?*"

Elated, Popalia cried, "Oh, my god. It is Raenyl. I'm sure of it!" she shouted. "We are alive! Help us, Raenyl!"

Katia shushed the shouting priestess, "I can't hear!"

Quietly, they waited, and within the water rang Raenyl's voice, "*Popalia, can you hear me?*" If Raenyl said more, the rushing water blocked it from being discerned.

Katia sighed. After a moment of listening and hearing only water cascading a couple stretches away, Katia attempted to sound confident, but weakness slipped out of her mouth, "We may need to find our own way out."

"We need light," Popalia reminded everyone, as if it were a new observation.

"I've disarmed spring-loaded needles that had been dipped in poison—this here is just dark." Katia quipped. "We can find a wall, and that'll lead to dry land. We can feel our way out'a here." Katia's confidence surprised the young priestess. "That is crazy. We need light."

"Well, you just open that little heart of yours, and let the sunshine out, all right?" Katia began to shuffle in a direction.

Popalia felt the slack tighten between the two of them as she noted, "That is part of a hymnal, 'Open your heart, and let the sunshine out. You're in safe hands. Shoes on the road, guiding my route.' How do you know this?"

Katia didn't hear Popalia, or she ignored the question and said, "It seems as if there is a slight grade upward over here. Come on. Maybe it'll lead us out of this water." Popalia did not resist and Katia added, "You should wash yourself first. You stink, and more than a little."

"I stink?" Popalia started, but then agreed, "Yes, I probably do. You're no rose, yourself."

"Well, we got plenty of water." Then, sharply she yelped, "Ouch! Son of Bane!"

"What?" Popalia asked. "What is it?"

"The ceiling gets low over here."

"Well, you wanted a wall." Popalia found a chuckle-worth of humor in the statement. "Really, are you okay?"

"Yeah, I'll be all right. I'll accept any blessing, even at the cost of my poor forehead. Left or right?"

"What?"

Rubbing the knot growing on her head, Katia asked, "So, do you want me to follow the wall right or left?"

"What does it matter? It is all blackness to me. I now understand why Kravin LeSalle emboldened our church away from its neutral stance; he'd said Shaelowe's darkness would cover the world if the Great Balance didn't take the side with Asunna's light."

Popalia then asked the thief, "Did you know the Great Mystery used to be called the Great Balance? Isn't it funny how the definition of a god can change by only switching one word?"

"That is really heavy." Katia's tone relaxed a notch, "You know, I haven't been mocking you and your god, right? I am changing— or at least I'm trying. I have been for a little time, now."

Popalia stayed quiet.

After a second, Katia mumbled, barely loud enough to be heard over the constant splash and echo of falling water. "This mission I'm to do, it is my exit mission. Darren said '*do this one thing*,' and he'd kick me out of our family. You see, you cannot be 'retired' from our thing. Retired means dead, but if rules are broken, family members can be estranged."

Katia's tone frosted a little bit, "That is family business, not yours. What pertains to your business is that I regret the part I played. I promised your god I'd change, and I know you don't believe that. It doesn't matter to me what you think. I don't care."

Katia actually did care, and Popalia heard it. Feeling skeptical, the priestess inquired, "Why make a promise with the Unknown? Why not Kranias?"

Chuckling, Katia admitted, "Back with the orcs, I put a prayer out to him. I even put one out to Stranoss—believe that." Deciding what direction to move, she said, "I'm goin' right, but for no good reason than because it's the opposite of wrong."

"Sounds fine to me. Like you're saying, we can always change direction later. Perhaps if I'd changed direction earlier, we wouldn't be here, now."

"Now-now, Popalia. Here you are wrong. This right here, in our face, is fate. This ain't chance, or a bad decision, or 'a punishment' like elf-boy thinks." Leading along the wall, Katia recalled, "It is like you'd said on the way to the garrison. I have to make right for what I did. I'm being honest wit' you, now. I had no idea what Thorgen had come to steal. I thought it was those gold candlesticks in that round room. I knew nothin' about that jeweled scepter—nothing."

Sliding another step into the eternal black, she continued speaking, "I was angry at him for killing the priest, but we still had to finish the job. So, I checked for traps, and I found none until elf-boy's sneering face appeared in the smoke. That scared all my holy-holes tight, you hear me?"

Popalia explained, "That's just an illusion to keep the pilgrims from getting too close. It only happens if a priest isn't in the room. It wasn't a trap, merely a chastening. Do you understand?"

"Well, I thought it was going to bite my hands off. So, as fast as I could, I snatch up that scepter." Her tone lowered, "Now, I know that rod is more than somethin' pretty to look at. I...I touched your god."

She paused for a moment, and Popalia wondered if she was making this all up. Katia continued, sounding confident, "I know it, now. When I touched the scepter's handle, your god touched me. I ain't neva felt nothin like that before...no good-hard sex... no nothin' ever felt like that. It was pure ecstasy. When your priests found me, I was numb with pleasure, but I still knew what Thorgen and I had done was bad—real bad. I didn't know then I had to make this right, but by the time I'd gotten back to the city, I knew I couldn't continue living like I have. I'd changed inside."

Popalia doubted half of what she said was truthful, if any of it. Yes, Popalia knew she was in with wolves, but she wasn't a fool. Young? Undoubtedly—but foolish? She asked the thief, "How do you expect to make this right? What is your plan?"

"Well, I thought long and hard about it while chained to that wall. Oh, it looks like this is the wrong way. It is getting deep."

"What is getting deep? Our subject or the path?"

Chuckling, Katia felt with her foot, and the water deepened by more than a foot. "Both, but you need to lead back the other way, unless you want to start swimming." Katia's voice sounded out, "Watch your head."

Popalia had already been feeling along the ceiling so as not to bang her head, "Got it." The water was about waist deep along the wall. Her submerged robe flowed around her legs while walking back the other way. "So, let's say you caught up with Thorgen. How do you intend to make your past right?"

Katia, right behind the priestess, admitted, "I don't know. When I'd seen Darren, I was hot about bein' abandoned by Thorgen. Then, Darren said Thorgen never returned. Thorgen burned us all. He tricked us, you see? He used the family to help rob your temple, but now he's keepin' the scepter for his self. I ain't liberal to say how our family operates, but Darren pays us good— all contracts are pre-agreed. Thorgen is clearly playin' for all the cookies and ain't sharin' with none of us."

Popalia was getting frustrated with the snail's pace of their movement. She asked with a hint of gravel in her tone, "You suspect he has a different buyer."

"Most definitely," Katia's tone chimed. "He has skill, but Thorgen wasn't a member of our family. He and Trevex are old friends. One day, Trevex tells Darren his buddy's got an easy mark, and Darren should get in on the fast coin. Thorgen said to Darren that your temple had a bunch of gold and nearly no one guarding it. He'd said the hardest part would be finding your temple, but he had good information on how to find it. He'd come to Darren 'cause he needed someone who was good with traps. He'd split the fence even with my family—fifty percent was his for finding the mark. That's how I got involved, you see?"

Popalia stumbled on a submerged protrusion but did not fall. She judged by the sound of the falling water that they may have moved fifteen paces total since they'd fallen into the pool. In her frustration, she remarked, "I don't think we are getting anywhere."

Katia must have misinterpreted, "I'm getting there. Thorgen knows the rules. We don't kill. We might like the finer things in life, but no one wants bloodied hands touching their crystal goblet, right? Soon as I got back, I'd told Darren what happen't. Darren was beyond pissed off, and he put me up with Gregor's caravan. He told me to intercept Thorgen and steal our prize back from him. I told Darren I intended to kill him for what he'd done to me. I said it was the least I could do after leaving me in the position he did."

Popalia interjected, "Do you suppose this would make things right?"

With a snort, Katia accepted. "Not right, just even. I didn't know how to make it right, but I wasn't goin' to give Darren the scepter. I know that much. I hadn't figured that far ahead, yet. I'da said I got Thorgen, but he'd sold it, but then I'd need to come up with some gold to prove. I didn't like that option, either. Darren had always been good to me. I didn't do my friends like that, and Darren never done me that way."

The floor was lowering, and the waterline advanced to just beneath Popalia's breasts. She continued forward with the hope that the water would again lower in the next couple of steps. Katia asked from in the black, "What are you going to do with me?"

"Well, Katia. You have probably noticed this rescue hasn't worked out too well."

After a dry cough from the thief, she then remarked, "Ya think?"

Popalia felt her face flush, but there was no alteration in her tone. "All I ever cared about was returning our scepter to my temple. I don't care about Thorgen, Darren, his gang, or you for that matter. Once I'm holding LeSalle's Grace in my hands, everyone else can walk away. I'll make sure Seth and Raenyl are justly compensated and that the church clears all our names of what your gang has done. I can forgive and forget, but I cannot make promises on behalf of the church."

Katia's surprise was not masked, "You would just let me go if you got your prize?"

Popalia nodded but realized she was invisible. "When Grace is held within both my hands, I will share a little of it with you. I'll turn my back and let you walk. Again, I do not know what the church will do, but *I* will not be after you."

In two steps, the water rose up to her armpits. She could feel a gentle change in the flow of the water. There was a current underneath, pulling at the hem of her robe, out and away from the wall.

Katia asked, "Can you feel that? It is pulling out into the deeper water. I don't hear anything over the falling water. Can you?"

"No. I don't like this." Not masking her frustration, Popalia prayed, "Please, Unnamed. By your sacred text, you promised to be our light in dark places. I can't foresee a better time for you to keep your word than right now."

"Hay'ah," Katia added.

Unexpectedly, within the contrast of continuous black, a faint silver hand-shape appeared. Popalia saw her hand set against the dark stone. It was a vague differential, but undeniably true. She could almost see. Popalia turned her head toward Katia, and both women simultaneously recognized they could each see the faintest outline of each other above the shivering plane of water they were standing within. The very air seemed to vibrate in the weak but indisputable light.

Turning quickly in hopes of narrowing down the source, the light ended before their shoulders and heads could fully rotate. A new fear pinged within each of their souls. Something else was with them in this darkness—something capable of controlling light.

Barely over the crashing of the falls, Katia's voice trickled nervously, "I'd like to get out of the water, now."

Chapter Thirty-Five

Time Is Lost To Darkness

Waist deep in black water, with the tumult of the nearby falls crashing in their ears, both women's senses were rendered useless in the pitch darkness. Due to the nearby falls, all they could smell beyond their own soaked and spoiled scents was the cool vapor in the air. Katia had grabbed ahold of Popalia's arm with such intensity, she could feel ten points of rigid fingers digging into her flesh. In her own chest, she could feel the adrenaline beating though her heart. In her mind, she heard the fearful whimpering of her own inner voice. *It is Lo'Lyth! Wynkkur was right! She is here, and she knows we are here!*

Katia rasped the same thing in her ear, "It must be that crazy elf Wanker talked about!" The fear was paralyzing, crippling, and both women waited for whatever dreadful event was to befall them.

Popalia recalled the sacred texts, "*Unknown to the baby in the womb is the world outside, yet despite fear, life must re-birth.*" Rising up from within the whimpering little girl, a tenacity renewed by holy appointment, priestess Popalia conjured a sunburst of divine courage.

"Lo'Lyth, I rebuke your insanity! I encourage you to take my hand so that your madness may be removed! By the will of the Great Mystery, I'm here to heal and not harm—nor will I be harmed!"

With a strange reversal of roles, Katia shrilled, "What are you doing? We cannot beat this!"

Popalia placed her hand upon Katia's back, where she could feel terrified heartbeats bumping. Popalia commanded, "By power Unnamed, your fear is replaced with peace." In the pitch black, a relieved sigh sounded over the crash of the falls. Both women waited for the unknown, and then, the unknown came.

A shrill voice, sharp and bone-scraping, "The creature Lo'Lyth does not speak with a human tongue. If you have come here seeking the one called Lo'Lyth, she is beyond the reach of the sane. This fact places your sanity in question. Who are you?"

Katia gave a soft pat to the priestess's shoulder, so Popalia stated, "I am Priestess Popalia, and we are lost."

From the black, at an unverifiable distance, the shrill voice replied, "We know you are human. We saw you. We will not be fooled easily! You are very far from where you belong. Why are you here?"

Katia bravely answered, "We fell down the waterfall. We were getting water, and we slipped. That is how we got here." There was no sound for a moment. Then, the moment stretched, and Katia called out, "Are you still there? We cannot see."

High pitched and reedy, "We do not believe you. Even if your pleas for help sounded sincere, you cannot get this deep without light. No animal from the surface could get here without light. How did you get here?"

Popalia answered, "We have become separated from our group. Our torches are now wet. Our group is above us, and we need to get back to them."

Shrill and piping, "Torches? How primitive! You travel with flame, and you still live! Amazing! Stupid—but amazing!"

Then, there was light—white and revealing.

In the strange light, illuminating from what looked like an egg in one hand, two bipeds stood no taller than toddlers. Both of the little people had long, dusty beards that draped down to their belt buckles. Atop their heads, both wore pointed, gray caps that offered the illusion that they stood half a foot taller. The pointy hats that covered their ears tied under their beards and brought their height to Popalia's upper thigh.

With the cave illuminated, water could be seen falling from the ceiling ten feet above. The water rippled outward to the underground shore twenty paces beyond the falls. Another ten paces upon dry surface stood the bearers of light. The one holding the illuminated egg tilted his head back and emitted a high-pitched whistling voice, "Where are your weapons? Show us your weapons, and come out from the water. It is unsafe in there!"

"We have no weapons," Popalia announced.

The light bearer's hand moved to the tip of the egg. He said, "By Regoraxoil's Dirty Beard, if you came here without weapons, you are crazy and lucky to be alive! Are you are lying? If I find you are lying, we will abandon you to darkness, surface-walker."

Katia pleaded, "We are not lying. The warriors are above us. We must get back to them."

"Well, lucky for you," patting the back of the other bearded creature, a cloud of dust puffed out from the impact, "my sister here has a few maps. If there is a connection between caverns, she can find it."

As Popalia and Katia waded closer to the shoreline, their soaked clothes hung upon their bodies. The water had expanded their garments, making them larger than normal. Dripping water from soaked sleeves, Popalia's ugly robes formed to her body.

Unexpectedly, there plunged a series of large splashes behind them. Before the second consecutive splash was heard, the tiny creature twisted the light egg in his hand, and the full darkness returned. Behind the women, there were four more rapid splashes, one following the next.

"Bane's Blood, it is dark!" Raenyl's shocked voice rang out. "Wank, Wank!" Somewhere out of the darkness came a water-logged gasp, and then a deep coughing began. Raenyl called out once again, "Are you all right? I landed on you."

Coughing and a lot of splashing, then Gregor's panicked voice sounded from over by the falls, "I can't see!"

Katia barked, "No one can see, you fool. We're making friends with little people with lights, and you just scared them off!"

"I don't believe it! Wank was right," Seth's voice boomed. "You're alive, and we came to rescue you!" Wynkkur was still coughing from somewhere close by, and Seth encouraged, "Wank, use your fire sword!"

Through a series of struggling gasps, Wynkkur sputtered, "Need breath for spell." Then, another fit of coughing followed.

Westin asked from the heavy black, "Who's got Ucilius?" Then, in the darkness, "Get off me, Gregor! He was tied to you!" There was splashing and struggling, and then relieved, Westin said, "There you are. Come on. Stand. Good."

Wynkkur coughed one more time before speaking a few words only he understood. Flame burst from the hilt of Wynkkur's sword all the way up to the sharp point. It was not a strong light, but everyone saw by it. Soaked and scrawny, Wynkkur stood aside Raenyl. Behind him, the waterfall shimmered by the sword's flame emission.

At the edge of the light, Popalia stood knee deep in water. Her wet hair stuck to the side of her face, and her soaked robes clung to every shape of her body, accenting the hidden beauty covered by ugly robes. Seth, Raenyl, and Westin looked upon her with slack jaws.

Katia stepped in front of the priestess to shelter her with some modesty. Her own blouse hung heavy with water, allowing ample cleavage and the firm shapes beneath the cloth to be seen. "Give tha' girl some respect. She is a priestess!" The men turned their heads as if they'd been slapped. Katia continued on the attack while Popalia adjusted her robes behind her. "Put yer eyeballs back in your heads, all right?"

Wynkkur's face wore a puzzled stare. *Respect the priestess? Where did Katia go? Who is this?* With an uncertainty ringing in his voice, he stated, "Thank you, Katia."

Popalia cried in joy, "Wynkkur, oh Wynkkur. What took you so long?" She chuckled as tears fell freely.

Wynkkur coughed one last sputter of water from his lungs, then said, "You know I don't like water."

Raenyl's face was a stunned mask. "We all thought you were dead, but Wynkkur knew you were not." His tone also rang reflective of his suspended belief. "How are you?"

"I was terrified, but now I am fine." Popalia laughed between joyous sobs. "I thought you were gone forever. All of you, I thought you were all gone."

From within the eternal shadow behind Popalia, a high-pitched screech announced, "Put out that flame! We could all die!"

"Ha-ha-ha," Wynkkur laughed. "That is a funny voice."

"Whoa, who said that?" asked Seth. Looking around suspiciously, he added, "Ghosts?"

"Please," the loud, reedy voice begged. "Sometimes, in the lower caverns, the air will ignite. Explode, catch fire, burn, and immolate. Do you understand me?" There was a strange, rumbly sound in the darkness before the reedy voice returned. "After the air burns, the fire makes the air poisonous. Do you need me to define poison?"

"That is not necessary," Raenyl expressed with skepticism. "We still need the light to see by." He'd planned to say more when the egg of light illuminated the stone and water world. All Raenyl could utter was, "Ohhh!" or something sounding close to that.

Wynkkur dismissed the flame from his shortsword as little, bearded folk bowed politely. Seth commented, "Look! They are like little babies with beards. Hi, babies." He waved.

In his shrill voice, the speaker said, "We are not bearded babies. We are gnomes. I am Snevilefilecin, and my younger sister Mortopingolootei. Or, if you would prefer it translated into the human-speak, Lighty-Brighty, and my sister, Brighter-Lighter."

Raenyl placed a hand to his head and admitted, "This is too weird. I need to sit down."

"Yes." The high-pitch grated, "It isn't every day we find eight humans exploring our caves." Brighter-Lighter grumbled in a low voice. Loudly, Lighty-Brighty apologized, "Forgive my oversight elf and half-elf. As your first contact with the Gnomish Rite, my sister and I wish to dispel any bad relations with you surface-walkers."

"Can you talk a little quieter, please? My ears are very sensitive," Wynkkur asked.

"That is right! A side effect of such big ears!" Lighty-Brighty remained loud. "Sorry, I cannot speak in your language and be quiet. It is impossible. See, we have a split-larynx, and I can only shout in your language. Gnomspek is low and grumbly, Humanspeak is very shouty. We speak on an inhale where your kind speaks on the exhale. It is very annoying for me, too. Annoying, see also irritating, exasperating, and trying."

"Shouty isn't a word," Raenyl informed the gnome.

"Yes it is," Lighty-Brighty reasoned. "I said it, and you understood it. Thus, it is a word."

"It is not a word!" Raenyl argued.

Popalia not so subtly insisted, "Yes, it is a word, okay?" Raenyl huffed but remained silent of rebuttal. Popalia asked both gnomes, "Could we parlay quickly, then? We really want to get out of these caves."

"Parlay—what a great word. It sounds a lot like parsley but means consultation, meeting." Stroking his gray beard and nodding, "Yes, that would be best. Lo'Lyth will have heard us by now, and we should scatter before she can find us."

"Lo'Lyth!" Wynkkur expressed almost as loudly as the gnome. Slightly unnerved by his own outburst, the elf shushed himself repetitively before adding in a lower voice, "She is here!"

Loudly, the gnome informed, "Yes, she prefers the lower caves where it is warmer. She has a *pee'el'gee* that she took from one of our miners."

Lighty-Brighty tried to explain, but it made little sense to anyone. "You see, Rocky-Docker said after Docky-Rocker was killed, Lo'Lyth shaved off his beard! How foul is that? Rocky-Docker followed the crazy elf for weeks. She carried Docky-Rocker around in a dirty blanket until his rotten body fell apart. Then, she cried for weeks. Weeks! Ever since then, we try to avoid Lo'Lyth, if you are capable of understanding."

"Yes," Wynkkur stated. "She went crazy 5,815 seasons ago. The gods banished her from the land, so she would stop eating her great-grandchildren's grandchildren."

Jumping over Wynkkur's explanation, Gregor interrupted, "I'm sorry, but what is a *pee'el'gee*?"

He waved the glowing light in his hand, "This is a *pee'el'gee*—a portable light generator. We refine Elementium into a liquid-like powder, and add it to hematite. There is a chemical reaction that results in continuous light. We then put a stylized cover over it to make it adjustable." He twisted the top to make the light dim, then twisted the other way, making the light blossom, again. "It makes our butterflies very happy, indeed!"

"Okay." Completely befuddled, Seth looked to Westin, who shrugged.

Popalia smiled as if what the gnome said made sense and replied, "That is very nice. Um, could you tell us now how to get out of here? We need to get up to the surface, and sooner is better." Her smile was shrouded with doubt.

"Well, as we gnomes say, 'A friend in need is a friend who owes us a big favor.' It just so happens my sister and I are also in a bit of a conundrum—see also puzzle, problem, enigma. We will gladly help you if you help us."

Popalia nodded, "What could you need from us?"

Loud and shrill, "Oh, I don't know. We are living our rite of passage and cannot return without bringing something back to our home. We are not permitted to come home without something usable for the whole community. We were hoping to find a deposit of hematite, but most of the tunnels have already been charted. Most veins of useful minerals have already been found by previous adolescents."

"Adolescents?" Seth remarked out of surprise. "You both look older than me."

"Why thank you, big human! But you contradict yourself. You'd said just a moment ago that we looked like bearded babies. Can you explain what you now mean?"

Still dripping, Seth stepped back a pace, but Wynkkur filled the gap and asked, "How old are you?"

"We just turned 150 years old two days ago. My sister and I have studied with great zeal to prepare for this time, but Poopah Steaky-Dinky treats us as if we were still only buddings."

Both Seth and Raenyl were removing their soggy packs as Popalia offered, "I would be more than happy to share with you the gift of spirit. It would be a pleasure to share with you the doctrine of my god, the Blessed Mystery."

Lighty-Brighty made a sour face, "That is very nice indeed, but no. The god of the gnomes, Regoraxoil...he is a selfish gnome. He is giant and can squash us if we listen to another god. The big gnome does not share views with other gods. Sometimes, sharing is considered rude."

Seth pulled out some of the leather strips from his pack. Like a handful of dripping wet worms, Seth offered the gnomes, "Here, these are useful."

"Yack!" choked the gnome. "Those are animal parts! Yack, how foul! Old cow peeled and dried, now wet again? Yack! How offensive!"

Seth withdrew his hand as if he'd burned it in a fireplace. Westin also recoiled, mumbling, "I guess offering Gregor to you is out of the question, then."

"We are not ignorant about cows!" Lighty-Brighty continued, "Big, terrifying creatures! Still, it is not nice to kill them!"

"I'm sorry," apologized Seth. "I didn't hurt the cow. I bought these at a market. It is useful for making shoelaces or repairing armor, and stuff."

"Yack!" he continued making disgusted sounds. "Why not use hemp for laces? Why use cow? Yack!" Brighter-Lighter consoled her brother by rubbing Lighty-Brighty's arm.

Wynkkur asked, "How do you have hemp? You live underground."

Clearly shaken by seeing the strips of leather, Lighty-Brighty stepped away from Seth and closer to Wynkkur. "You, too? You use animal skin!" He pointed his tiny finger at Wynkkur's bag.

"Yes, elves eat deer," he said calmly. "We use their bladders to carry water. We use their intestines for bowstrings, their antlers for arrowheads, and their skin for clothing. We honor the deer by using every part of it to keep ourselves alive."

"What do you give back to the deer?" Lighty-Brighty asked.

Wynkkur shook his head, "Deer are for us to eat. It is their purpose. My tribe only takes from the herds as much as we need and no more."

"Why not hemp?"

"We can't eat hemp," Wynkkur replied.

"We do. Makes gnomes feel dizzy and a little sleepy. It is very good medicine for rowdy buddings."

"Where do you get hemp?" Wynkkur inquired, again.

"We grow it," Lighty-Brighty yelled out. Shaking the *pee'el'gee* in his hand, he said, "We control the light, see? We have great growing rooms with over a thousand butterflies who have agreed to live with us. That is how we grow hemp."

"Fascinating," Wynkkur acknowledged.

"What?" Popalia remarked. "You have underground farms? What do you grow?"

"He said hemp," Seth reminded.

Softly, Brighter-Lighter grumbled guttural sounds beside her brother. Lighty-Brighty nodded, "Yes, my sister suggests we hurry. The cave-fishers are slow movers, but Lo'Lyth is a cunning huntress. We need to disperse. Do you know the word, disperse?"

"Yes, we would like to disperse." Popalia reminded, "We still need to know how to get out of here."

"And we need a gift for our Great Poopah."

Raenyl's voice grew stern, "Hey, that is extortion. Do you know the word?"

"Exaction, threaten, blackmail—yes, we know that word, but we are only asking for a fair trade. Something our group can use, as an exchange for something your group can use. That is very fair, we think." Lighty-Brighty stroked his dirty beard.

"I don't want to face Lo'Lyth." Wynkkur opened the flap of his bag and shoved his hand inside. "It has been many years since she's seen an elf, and seeing me could make her worse than what she already is."

Seth made tsk-ing-sounds and said, "I think we could handle one elf woman. Besides, you said she was crazy. Offing her might be a favor to her."

Still fishing in his pack, Wynkkur reminded, "She is eternal and will live forever. She cannot die, hence why my gods banished her here." Wynkkur then smiled, "Ah, there's one."

"You didn't tell me that," Seth discounted.

Katia reminded, "Yeah, he did. When he told that story about her having all those watermelon babies."

Seth patronized Katia, "He said she was eternal, not that she couldn't be killed."

Lighty-Brighty stared up at the giant mercenary, reciting, "Eternal, see also endless, undying, never-ending."

Wynkkur pulled his hand out of his bag. He wore a grin from ear to ear as he opened his fingers at eye-level for the gnomes. Lighty-Brighty and his sister's eyes lit up with what they saw in his palm. Nodding, the gnome agreed, "Yes. We can use that. How many of them can you spare?"

Wynkkur looked at the three beans in his palm, "Take them

all. If we can get out of here soon, we will not need any of them."

"Allow me to put these away, and I shall tell you the nearest way to the surface." Carefully, the gnome took each of the beans and put them in a utility pocket upon his pants.

His stubby arm pointed at one of two corridors leading away from the underground lake and falls. "Follow that cave. It will branch three times. Choose big cave, big cave, then little cave. Not far after little cave, you will come to the pit. Be very careful, and be sure to take the right side of the pit and not the left. The left is sometimes very dangerous."

The gnome looked from elf to half-elf, "After the pit, the cave will get small again, and there will be a wall and a right turn. Do not go right, go under the wall. There is a hole to get through. Don't go too far down the right tunnel. Deep to the right lives a horde of goblins. Go beneath the wall, and you will find a big room with a hole in the ceiling. It will be big enough for you to exit. Do I need to repeat?"

Popalia repeated the instructions. The gnome nodded and smiled while taking his sister's hand. "Don't forget to watch out for the goblins living in the right tunnel. We go now to avoid Lo'Lyth. Thank you for your gift, we shall return as heroes by your trade. May the big gnome shelter you beneath his beard whenever you feel small."

Chapter Thirty-Six

Time Is Lost To Darkness

Brighter-Lighter offered Wynkkur a *pee'el'gee,* saying in loud Elvish, "I'm so excited! One-Hand Against, this is so wonderful to experience you! Please take this, it will save you from the bad air."

Taken by surprise, he pronounced her name in Elvish, "You speak my language, Brighter-Lighter." It was a shocked admission, and not a question.

A pleasant smile peeked within her long beard as she shrilly fluted in a language normally considered musical, "It is an honor! By our culture, all gnomes must speak two additional languages. My twin brother was born first, and he picked to learn Human-Standard. So I, getting second pick, chose Elvish. I also recognize Orcish, but only audibly. Orcish is too primitive to enunciate." Inhaling sharply, her dark eyes sparkled, "But to actually meet you! I never thought I'd speak to a real elf...well, except to beg Lo'Lyth to leave my beard alone if she caught me."

"I'd prefer to avoid her, too," Wynkkur replied as he examined the tiny light generator. The small hematite cylinder sat in his hand no bigger than his little finger. It was lightweight, but it would require little more than dropping it to fracture. He'd need to be careful with the light source.

Fixed upon one end was a small, metallic cap that rotated. The light was inside, and all that was needed was a small twist of the cap to let some of the light out. Wynkkur nodded as he realized how the *pee'el'gee* worked. "This is amazing."

"Use it instead of fire until the second junction," she informed. "The explosive air is odorless. You will be seared badly, but not fatally. As the good air is burned away, you'll then choke to death on the poisoned air that remains. It happens every time. As you climb closer to the surface, the air becomes less dangerous. Fire will be safe to use after the second junction."

Wynkkur twisted the cap and released some of the light. He closed it again, and the light vanished. Amused and grinning, he asked, "Isn't this something you will need?"

"I have two others in my pouch," she patted her utility pocket. "My brother carries three more, and we won't separate until our rite of passage is completed. Good luck to you and your friends. We both should go before the black elf finds us. She has sharp ears, and she knows the tunnels well."

"And you are loud," Wynkkur added.

"Yes, we have two voices, or so it seems," Brighter-Lighter waved as Lighty-Brighty pulled her hand. Skillfully, with one-hand, the gnome twisted the egg-like *pee'el'gee*'s light lower, to a fraction above total dark. Wynkkur opened his *pee'el'gee* before the twin shadows moved further into the corridor.

As brother and sister were swallowed completely into the deep black, Raenyl commented, "Well, that was weird." Nudging Popalia with his elbow, "I'd say that was even weirder than your creepy episode at Dead Rik's."

Shaking her head, Popalia disagreed, "Not weird. That was a blessing. Just like at Dilligan's."

Katia added her own comment, "Looks like the Mystery had us covered on both ends. If elf-boy didn't jump down the hole, the gnomes would have shown us the way."

"Stop calling me elf-boy, or I won't dry you off like everyone else." He demonstrated on his own robe, and the wool appeared to repel droplets and dirt from within the material. Dirty water splashed about his feet, his robe now completely dry. "Who is next?"

With everyone's clothes dried, they moved quickly. Now that Lo'Lyth was no longer just a myth, this new reality made everyone anxious to leave. Wynkkur said nothing. Even Gregor was quiet. It had become their priority to avoid the Eternal Mother and escape from the confines of her grave.

They moved with a purpose, and even Ucilius seemed to move quicker, despite the cavern climbing at a steady grade. They'd climbed a short distance when they came to the first tunnel junction. There were three caves. One led deeper down, the center cave leveled off and stayed about the same size, but the left tunnel—the largest of the tunnels—continued climbing upward.

Not knowing if Lo'Lyth pursued them, Raenyl calculated her odds of finding them had fallen from fifty-fifty to one-in-six. Wynkkur reminded them that the Eternal Mother did not comprehend the language of men, so she would not understand the loud directions that the gnomes had given them. Still, Popalia prayed to cross the mad-mother's territory without an encounter.

Following the path as the gnomes had instructed, the climb began to steepen by several degrees. The precipitous path continued upward unto the point of becoming hard work. With burning muscles, they came up to the second junction, needing to clamber up the last six feet to the ledge. Seth's rope came in handy as he pulled the lame Ucilius up the last shear climb.

Heaving up and into the new pathway, the cavern split in opposite directions. Both tunnel entryways appeared equal in size, but one tapered narrow after a few paces, so they decided to follow the other. This new path leveled with a drip line of icicle-like stalactites clinging along the ceiling's center.

Tired, they eased a short way into the bigger cavern. Popalia sighed, "Let's stop here for food and rest. I don't know about the rest of you, but I've had enough for one day."

"We can use fire, again," Westin reminded. "How many torches are left?"

"Aren't they all wet?" Popalia asked. "The four in my pack are soaked."

"They shouldn't be. Check your pack, again. Everything should have dried when my spell repelled the water." Wynkkur opened his bag. "If not, it doesn't matter. I put all my torches in the pocket of my bag before we jumped down the chute."

"Jumping in that hole was crazy, man," Westin added excitedly. "I can't believe we did that."

Wynkkur waved a scornful finger at Westin. "I am not a man. Don't call me that." Softening with a grin, he added, "Yes, it was crazy."

"Poor Ucilius," Gregor sounded oddly compassionate. "He could have drowned. It is a miracle he didn't."

Seth chuckled grimly, "I was sure I'd get stuck in that tube. Then, Useless would'a drowned with all of us."

"His name isn't Useless," defended Gregor.

"He's been pretty useless so far," shrugged Seth. He gave the elf a friendly wink.

Raenyl intervened, "Relax, Gregor. It's only a pet name, like when we call Wynkkur, Wank. No harm is meant by it."

Westin cut at Gregor, "Ucilius has always been useless to you, Gregor. I don't even know why all of a sudden you've changed your mind. How many times did I hear you scorn Lissa for the man she'd chosen?"

Gregor defended, "I'll admit that Ucilius was not the best suitor for Lissa, but he did provide an heir to carry on my legacy. That alone is worth some respect."

Westin coldly reminded, "Your heir is dead. Everybody is dead, yet here you are, dragging your unwanted son-in-law through this maze of madness." Westin turned his head, his lips curling with reproach. "I think you believe saving him forgives you from being who you are."

"Don't you judge me, Westin," Gregor stood his ground. "To be good at business, you must be shrewd. My estate proves my accomplishments. Ucilius was never a strong man. His character was weak in whatever he tried to be. A businessman must be willing to make sacrifices to get ahead."

"He made sacrifices," Westin sneered. "He put up with you for loving your daughter. Like a man, he took your constant lashing and your unending disrespect. He treated your daughter like you treat your gold coins. He was an honest man and a well-liked merchant."

"He was *too* well liked!" Gregor lashed, "We'd left Magistrey two weeks ago with a full shipment of Athanian wine and silks. We came all this way in hopes of participating in the market for the full week! He'd sold our entire inventory before the first day of market, and he sold it at bulk rate! If it wasn't for his 'eager to please' sales, we'd be leaving Capitol City today and not trapped in these...damnable caverns!"

"Why are we dragging him along if this is his fault?" Westin led.

Gregor sat down, pulling Ucilius down beside him. Gregor pulled a clean kerchief—thanks to Wynkkur—from his pocket to wipe drool from the unresponsive man's chin. As he dabbed Ucilius's stubble-swathed jaw, Gregor admitted casually, "Bennae calculated our books the night after leaving Dilligan's Freepost. She'd factored all our current expenses against what our expenses would have accrued if we had sold everything at the price I'd wanted over the time we had anticipated staying in the city."

Brushing a greasy mop of hair from Ucilius's eyes, Gregor quietly stated, "After all our expected expenses were added into the equation, Ucilius made three percent over our original expectations in his bulk sale."

Westin snorted but said nothing more.

Chapter Thirty-Seven

Time Is Lost To Darkness

Popalia used the last of the carrot to split amongst everybody. The last loaf of bread in her pack has disintegrated into pasty mush. Even after the elf's "dry" spell, it was powdered crumbs sifted with dirt. Wynkkur gave the priestess all of the remaining beans—a total of twenty-nine. It didn't take a mathematician to see there weren't enough beans for another four days.

"I should have given an even eight beans to the gnomes," Wynkkur blamed himself.

"It don't matter," began Seth. "If those little guys gave us good directions, we should be outside again by sometime tomorrow."

Westin chuckled, "I'd happily eat a big pinecone just to be out of here."

Raenyl chuckled before saying, "Once we get out, we can make pine-needle stew with all the water we got this morning. That should qualify for our necessary meal, right priestess? The gods'll be satisfied, and we can all crap, again."

Wynkkur chewed his carrot slowly, savoring his last bite of chewable food. Once swallowed, he washed it down with one gulp of water. Like everyone else, he was frustrated with only one bite and a couple swallows per day. He missed the joy of eating, but he thanked Popalia's god for the blessing she'd provided through her faith. He thanked both Fenyll and the Mystery for Popalia.

Wynkkur opened his bag and withdrew the black-covered spell book. Everything he had stowed into the magical space within his bag had remained dry and undamaged. He didn't question it, and he had no answers as to why, but he was again grateful. Gratitude—a by-product of hope. They would all be breathing fresh air by sometime tomorrow.

The fear of eminent death no longer clutched the group in a stranglehold, so hope touched everyone. Smiling came easier for each of them—all of them except Ucilius and Gregor. They weren't out of trouble just yet, but hope had been restored. Life would continue and morning would eventually arrive.

They'd fallen asleep, and Wynkkur was the last to surrender. He closed his book and put it away before commanding the torch's flame to exhaust itself. Darkness and sleep joined hand-in-hand.

Waking up in darkness was now the normal routine. Whoever awakened would ask quietly if anyone else was awake, and when two were awake, they would talk quietly between themselves. When the third member awoke, they would wake Wynkkur, because he commanded the light. By then, the noise and light roused any remaining sleepers.

Quickly stowing their gear, they began down the tunnel the gnomes had directed. Raenyl took point as Seth remained with Ucilius at the flank. Popalia led behind Raenyl, and Katia carried the torch while walking beside the priestess. The common tensions shared between the two women seemed diminished. Yesterday's ordeal with the chute and the darkness had altered their dispositions.

Magical brightness poured from the *pee'el'gee* in Wynkkur's hand. The cap was twisted to only half allowance. It out-powered both the torches, held by Katia and Gregor. The portable light-generator was directional, and holding the light-tube forward drove skinny shadows stretching between legs, but the shifting, flickering torch-flames added a stomach-churning sway and awkward vibration to the wobbling shadows.

Feeling disoriented after a couple hundred paces, Westin tapped Wynkkur on the shoulder, requesting, "Would you mind turning that off? It is making me dizzy."

Wynkkur twisted the cap closed and dropped the *pee'el'gee* into his robe pocket. He heard the clank as hematite met the amber-hued crystal Seth had given to him. He then said, "The magical light doesn't mix too well with the torchlight, does it?"

"No, but it sure is nice to know we have it." The guard added, "Controllable light in your pocket—what a gift!"

Behind Westin, Gregor questioned, "Speaking of 'in your pocket', what are you going to do, Westin, now that you have left my employ? Will you try your hand at citrus farming? Fishing? Swine herding? What will you do, now?"

"You should not worry about me, Gregor." Westin's voice was amicable, and a giant shift from what it had been last night. "If I were you, I'd start trying to find a suitor for Casara."

Westin wasn't being friendly. Unknown to everyone, it was in fact, a sharp jab at the old man. Gregor tried to hide his bitterness from both guard and elf. He tried to sound unmoved but failed, "Casara? Yes, I should find a mate for my other daughter."

Wynkkur unknowingly commented, "You sound unsure

Gregor, is something wrong?"

"No, not at all. It is just that, well, Casara...doesn't seem too anxious to marry."

Westin chuckled and took another shot, "Doesn't she frequently wear men's clothes?"

Gregor replied, "At times, yes. She has." Wynkkur heard feathers ruffling behind the merchant's words. "She has done many things to discourage the fine men I've selected for her."

Westin chuckled harder, "Yes, yes. Like when that Dannon Purdee fellow came to the estate with all those flowers. It was a beautiful arrangement, Wynkkur. The poor boy was so nervous at the gate, I escorted him to the home. I saw Casara at the top of the stairs. She'd come down the stairs in a rich dress, but she faced the wall the whole time down. I figured it was her contempt for yet another suitor." He began to chuckle, "You tell him, Gregor... hee-hee-hee."

Gregor flushed and his jaw clamped tightly. He pulled Ucilius along, stiff-armed and keeping a brisk pace.

Westin continued the story, fighting his laughter, "Once she got to the bottom of the stairs, she looked to Dannon with a wide smile and half her head sheared like it was styled by a blind Athanian. The poor boy was mortified. I...tee-hee...I barely kept a straight face. There before us stood Casara, smiling gleefully with her mangy-mutt haircut. She'd done it with sewing shears, in large clumps of all different lengths." Westin lost control and laughed.

Gregor's controlled appearance snapped, "Dannon Purdee will be a very wealthy man when he inherits his father's shipping company! Cassie may have pissed away the last suitable man in Magistrey. No one wants a social-monster for a wife!"

Westin, laughing hard, added, "To fix her hair, they had to sheer her bald as a baby. Don't worry, Gregor. It'll all grow back... eventually."

"She mocks me," Gregor spat. "She resents everything I've tried to do for her. Now that Lissa is gone..." Gregor's voice fumbled. Westin's laughter stopped at the mention of the dead.

Gregor walked in silence for a little ways, refusing to look at his old guard. Then, he requested as if he'd made an order, "Don't leave my employ, Westin. What else will you do in Magistrey and be paid so well?"

Westin snorted, "I think it should be easy to figure what I'll do. I might only be a guard to you, but I listen. I know what the militia plans."

"The militia pays half what I do. Besides, the merchant navy is only talk. It is safe talking of men who stand on the shore and send unskilled boys to die at sea. That's what you've heard, and it is a fool's venture."

"You contributed 100 coins of gold to the fool's venture. You can almost build a corvette-class ship for a hundred pieces of gold—one that is fast enough to keep up with the Scarlett Marauder."

"So, your plan is to throw your life away chasing pirates? Maybe after you catch Reichmann the Scarlett. You'll then chase down Randel Grenier and his Wolf Pack? Is that your plan?"

Confidently, Westin boasted, "Someone needs to do the job. Standing around, watching your front door, is throwing my life away. Besides, you killed my future. I may as well defend my Portown."

"Enga's death is not my fault," Gregor restated, as he had a hundred times.

Popalia stopped the group as she encouraged, "Let it out, Westin. Don't keep this poison trapped inside of you."

Pointing at Gregor's chest, Westin pinned the merchant, "You should have had more guards to protect the caravan. They are all dead. Since you want to forget them, I'll name them—Tobar, Otto, Ginweck, Lissa, both your grandchildren—Uric and Vaysa—your personal guards, Kalan, 'Scabby', and Enga. All of them are dead, all because of you. You are cheap and greedy, and everyone is now dead."

"Greedy?" Gregor sneered, "I may be—but I am not cheap. I pay the best, because I expect the best. If I had doubled our guard, we still would have been overwhelmed by those orcs."

Westin growled, "I don't accept that, Gregor!"

"Anything short of a regiment of Regulators would have proven inadequate," defended the merchant. "Lissa, my grandkids, the drivers, Enga, Scabby, and Kalan would still have died, even with four more guards just as good as the four of you."

Gregor paused. Seeing Westin introspect, he added, "I was in the back of the second wagon with Bennae when the caravan stopped. I looked out the back at the last wagon as Scabby called out 'ambush'! His mouth had barely closed when he and Tobar were hit with a dozen arrows between the two of them." Gregor's lips trembled. "Don't you get it, Westin? Nothing could have changed the outcome of that ambush. Kalan, Otto, and Ginweck were already dead before the first orc charged from the forest."

Westin's eyes moistened, "I was riding beside Ucilius's wagon when arrows pinned Otto to the bench. Ucilius climbed down off the bench as more arrows whistled by. He was going to Lissa's side in the first wagon as I dismounted to cover him. I was hit from behind and never got into the fight."

Gregor, his eyes distant with revisiting the terror of that morning, honored his fallen guard, "Enga fought so bravely. She'd helped Bennae and I get free from the back of the wagon. Amazing, like a protector from the heavens, she killed three of those big alphas before being overtaken." Gregor looked away. "She gave us a chance to run and leave her to fate, but we, well..."

Westin's face twisted with torment, "The next thing I remember was being revived aside Enga. She was torn from her armor and most of her clothing. She'd been raped and beaten, her face a bloodied mess. Those animals only revived me, so I could watch what they did to the kids. I know it." Westin turned away and wiped his eyes.

Sobs cracked his voice as he said, "I cannot...I cannot give words to the horror I saw!" Westin doubled over with grief—a feeling as if his insides were being torn out with a fork. "Enga," embarrassed by his tears and covering his eyes, he sat down upon the hard floor, "I couldn't protect you. It should have been me. I should have died first."

Everyone stayed back, except Gregor. Gregor knelt next to the broken man, setting a hand upon his shoulder. Westin sobbed freely. No one spoke. Even disinterested Wynkkur and cynical Raenyl empathized with Westin's grief and loss. No one judged the fighter for his tears. All waited quietly, allowing him to let it out—every last drop of agony.

Chapter Thirty-Eight

Time Is Lost To Darkness

As the day felt late, they'd made it to the third crossing. The offshoot tunnel at first appeared barely a crevice leading downward into a wider cave. Popalia and Seth were both grateful to avoid another contortionist's nightmare.

"Was that only yesterday?" Popalia asked the large warrior.

"I think so, yeah," Seth answered in his resonant voice. "Time is hard to tell down here in all this." He waved his torch around to illuminate the surrounding area.

Gregor said with alarm, "Watch out with that torch!" Seth accidently hit Ucilius and him with the burning end of the torch.

"Watch it, you hit my torch!" Seth volleyed gruffly back to the merchant, "You break, you buy."

Westin remembered, "That little guy—didn't he say there would be a pit after the third tunnel?"

Popalia nodded, "Yeah, he said there would be a pit, then we were to stay on the right."

Raenyl challenged, "Are you sure? I missed a lot of what he said while trying to protect my ears."

Popalia continued nodding, "Yes, he said stick to the right, then under the wall, and finally out through a hole in the ceiling. I look forward to sleeping beneath the stars instead of spending another moment in this awful place."

Westin led the way as they walked a steady decline for about twenty minutes. The tunnel switch-backed, whipping from one direction, and then jaggedly around the other way. Calcite formations rippled the wall, reflecting moisture from the flickering torchlight and giving the cavern walls a wet ribcage appearance. Both Gregor and Seth used the damp protrusions as handles while easing Ucilius along.

Above Westin, the ceiling quickly rose, and torchlight vanished as the stone canopy rolled out into blackness. Before him, the cave had broadened, but the center fell away. Two paces away, the edge of the earth rolled into nothingness. The cavern may have widened on either side of the tunnel but only to make room for the great void expanding both above and below.

The trail had split, forming a walkway around the outside of the chasm. The left perch leveled wide enough to walk across with ease. On the opposite trail—along the right side of vacuous nothing—ran a narrow ledge. Below both ledges, the wall continued falling into the bottomless stomach of the world.

Standing three paces from the lip, everyone stood beside each other in a tight crescent, all of them bent forward and looking out at the obstacle of nothingness. Observing the right side of the ledge, Westin figured if he gripped the edge with his fingers, he could lean his elbow down and touch it against the wall before his arm was level. As far as his eyes saw in the limited torchlight, the trail seemed consistently narrow. From where he stood gawking into oblivion, he wondered if there was an opposite side of the chasm. If so, it was beyond his torch's range.

Noting how narrow the path looked in the limited light, Raenyl asked, "Are you sure he said right?"

Wynkkur took the torch from Katia as Popalia responded, "It looks perfectly safe, if we were gnome-sized."

"Are you absolutely sure he said go right?" Raenyl's look panned across all seven of them. "Anyone remember exactly what the little guy said?"

Wynkkur held the torch low and toward the edge while saying, "I'm pretty sure he said go right." Wynkkur gave the torch a delicate under-handed toss.

"What is wro—" Seth forgot what he was saying as the torch spiraled down into the hole. It fell, spinning gracefully, a flare that continued to fall—and it kept on spiraling ever further, reflecting smooth sides all the way into the nowhere. Then, after two more long spirals, the light blinked out. Seth closed his mouth as he shook his head, "Why did you do that? Are you happy knowing there is no bottom?"

Wynkkur scratched behind one pointy ear while squinting, "It has a bottom. I'd guess that the bottom is water by the way the torch vanished so suddenly."

"Suddenly?" Westin doubted. "It fell for ten seconds."

"No way," Raenyl disputed.

"Seven at least."

"Seven," Raenyl agreed with a slow nod, "maybe even eight, but not ten."

Gregor piped in, "I am fairly sure that little gnome said avoid going to the right. Yes, that's right. Don't go right."

Wynkkur was retrieving a second torch from within his bag.

Lighting it off the torch Gregor held, he handed the replacement over to Katia. "Go first, then."

"Why don't you flash around with that portable light-making-thing before I go?"

Wynkkur pulled the *pee'el'gee* from his pocket and acknowledged, "Wisdom." Turning the cap, he directed the light along the left trail, and it looked sturdy all the way to the other side of the gorge. Wynkkur directed the light up higher above the left ledge. Angled off the wall were twelve V-shaped rocks jutting outward.

Wynkkur announced unnecessarily for the group, "Fishers."

"Bane's Blood!" Raenyl spat out. "Three of them."

Popalia asked, "What does the right wall look like?"

The elf rotated his hand, and the light zeroed upon the right ledge. Appearing sturdy, it was a lip hanging over nothing. Above the short path, smooth stone ran the expanse of Wynkkur's projected light.

"Look, sister," Katia started, "I'm not crossing *that* chained up to you. You can go by yourself this time. If you fall, I ain't fallin', too. Not this time."

"She'll run away if you do," Gregor stated. "If you need her, don't let her go."

"What?" Katia shot out. "Hey, I'm gittin' across that little bridge! You didn't fall with the priestess last time, and I ain't falling again for anyone."

"It is a ledge, not a bridge," Raenyl corrected.

"Thank you, brother. She speaks badder than me."

"Worse than you," the archer corrected.

"That's what I said."

Gregor looked between Popalia and Ucilius, "You cannot trust her, Popalia."

Katia attacked, "You're just an old bigot, and you hate Athanians. Westin will back that."

"You're as Athanian as Raenyl is an elf, but I'm not talking about your skin or how you were raised. I am greedy, but your dishonesty is as deep as this chasm. It is the difference between who you are and who you pretend to be. I'm talking about your word, and what it means to everyone else. Like you say, 'It all comes out with a little washing.'"

"I'm not getting you," Katia sweetly stated. "Please explain what you mean."

"I think you get what I mean. You're proving what I mean by what you say."

Popalia intervened, "The chain works both ways. If she slips. I'll fall, too. Raenyl, please unlock us." Katia mocked Gregor with a boastful smirk before Popalia added, "Once we get across, we'll be chained back together."

"Aw, I thought we bonded. Didn't we get tight in all that water, together in the cave?" Katia pouted and feigned hurt as Raenyl fished his picks from his pack.

"We did," said Popalia with about as much energy as a yawn. "Once Grace is in my hands, I'll share. That is how tight we got."

Raenyl quickly depressed the tumblers in the simple lock at Katia's back. A click sounded in the lock. Katia wiggled back and forth, and the chains jingled as they collapsed upon the rock floor. Popalia pulled up the excess chain and handed it over to Raenyl.

Gregor cleared his throat before saying, "Priestess, I think we have a problem."

Raenyl stowed the chain in Popalia's backpack. He shook his head, asking, "What is it this time?"

"Raenyl, sir. This is a real concern. It is Ucilius. How will he get across?"

Raenyl cursed, shifting his stare from the catatonic man to the ledge overlooking nothing. Seeing Raenyl's thoughts, Popalia added, "Fear not, Gregor. I can heal Ucilius. He can walk across this bridge by his own freewill."

"It is a ledge, a led-je'ah," Raenyl enunciated slowly.

Seth chuckled.

"I'm talking metaphorically," Popalia lied poorly.

"Pfft, no you weren't," Raenyl continued, but Wynkkur interrupted.

"No. You will not heal him," Wynkkur sounded stern. "You must leave Ucilius with his choice."

She answered with a subjective flair of attitude, "He is without choice, Wynkkur. That is the problem! He has no choice. What is the point of being a healer if I cannot heal?" Attitude, not humility sparkled, "Besides, who are you to decide what I do with the gift my god has given me?"

Wynkkur shot back, "I am the elf who swore to protect the daughter of Ellund Saiwel. By my official charge, I forbid your healing of Ucilius."

"You cannot forbid me from performing my primary service," Popalia argued. "I've dedicated the last six years of my life to learning how to channel my god's healing love. You have no place to tell me how to exercise my gift."

Wynkkur shook his head, "I cannot imagine the degree of pain it requires to snap a mind, but it will likely happen to you. Without you, we will never recover LeSalle's Grace. So yes, I forbid you from healing Ucilius."

Popalia bit her lip, realizing Wynkkur could be right. She might only succeed in trading places with the merchant. "Wynkkur, I hear your concern, but I have to try."

Seth stepped forward, "No way. You don't have to do anything. You say your god offers questions not answers. I might not be all book-smart like you or magic-smart like Wank, but I know better than taking risks for nothing."

Patiently, Popalia addressed Seth, "This isn't a risk for nothing. I must trust my god and use gifts given in equal faith."

Growling, Seth passed over her idea, "If you go mind-dead like Ucilius, my brother and I won't get paid. I like you, Priestess, I really do, but this is about money for me and my brother." Before she could retort, Seth ordered, "Tie Ucilius to me. I'm strong enough to carry him across. He'll barely slow me down."

"No." Raenyl's tone sounded cool, "You're strong enough to do it, but that ledge is narrow. You'll need all of your balance to get across without numb-brain strapped on your back. Leave him here."

"I've been dragging Useless around ever since Bennae died, and I'm not leaving him here," Seth told Raenyl.

Raenyl's lips twisted cynically, "Well, you're stupid then. Let Gregor carry him for one of your 'promised' gold pieces and be done with it."

Seth waved his big, meaty hand at the shorter half-elf, "You're stupid, and if you want to fight about it, I'll smash your nose inside out."

"Don't threaten me, dumbass." Raenyl then dismissed Seth, "Fine, you know what? Tie him to you. When you slip and fall, you'll hear me laughing. The last thing you will hear is me shouting, 'I told you so!'—so don't cry that I never warned you."

Popalia touched Seth's wrist, saying softly, "Seth, don't let Raenyl get to you. He doesn't mean it."

Seth sneered at his brother, "You better hope I fall, because when Useless and I cross this pit, I'm gonna hurt you with my fists." Seth removed his backpack and handed it to Gregor.

Taunting, Raenyl fired back, "Well, tough guy. Why don't you do it, now?" Raenyl made a mocking face with his tongue hanging out to one side.

Seth waved his hand dismissively, and turning off Raenyl, he requested of Westin, "Tie us shoulder to shoulder, then hip to hip." As specified, Westin tied the catatonic Ucilius to the mercenary's back. It took him only a moment, and the smaller merchant dangled behind the large warrior. As Seth flexed his powerful shoulders to check his range of motion, he complimented, "Good work. It is tight, and I can still move."

"You're a back-heavy moron," Raenyl stated. "Give me the slack of your rope. I'm going to let it go and shout." Raenyl shouted with his hands cupped to amplify the words "I told you so!" While doing a quick jig, Raenyl went back to speaking normal, "Then, I'll do a little dance as you and numb-brain fall."

Seth shook his head, while slapping his palm with his fist, "You should hurry across that bridge real quick, and then keep on running."

"You know what?" Raenyl added, "I'm going to hurry across the *ledge* and taunt you. I'm gonna knock you off with Ascolan's stick."

"I'll hold the excess rope," growled Westin. "Bane's Blood, just don't fall, all right?"

Popalia called to everyone, "Stand in a circle, and take my hand." She put one hand out in front of her. "You too, Gregor... Raenyl?" Gregor shook his head as did Raenyl. Popalia expected such from the archer, but she snapped at Gregor, "By the Mystery's grace, I'm including a prayer to Stranoss, too."

Reluctantly, Gregor put his hand in the circle. Popalia prayed, "Unnamed and Stranoss, protect the servants faithful to your causes. Grant us each with a reprieve from fear. Embolden us to get beyond this chasm. Hear my words. Please, honor their sincerity. Hay'ah."

"Hay'ah," Katia, Westin, and Gregor repeated. Finally, there was one final, awkwardly spoken 'Hay'ah' by Seth.

As the others prayed, Raenyl stepped over the chasm. As they finished, he tossed one last taunt over his shoulder, "Don't fall, Seth. I doubt your prayer will catch you, dumbass."

Seth was no longer affected by Raenyl's taunts. They were all calmed as a result of her prayer—all of them except Raenyl. Raenyl didn't know this, because he didn't pray. Popalia got between the two brothers and gave Seth a sympathetic look before following the archer.

Raenyl's tone changed as he instructed the priestess, "Focus on the ledge where your feet are, and focus on the wall where your hands are. You'll get across. Just keep your eyes and mind on those two points and worry about nothing else." Raenyl reached from hand hold to hand hold, coaching Popalia from one to the next.

Katia followed, but worried none about hand holds. She carried her torch, one foot sliding, the next foot following. She brushed the side of the wall with her free hand, but this didn't challenge the practiced rogue. As archer and priestess inched along before her, she turned her head to those behind.

Wynkkur followed behind Gregor. The elf seemed nearly as confident as Katia in his ability to cross the chasm. He used the *pee'el'gee* to light the way for those around him. Gregor clung to the wall, scraping his body along, but he was moving. Katia turned back to Raenyl and the priestess.

Katia could have been across by now. Raenyl could have, too, but he was cautious for Popalia. Katia suppressed her grin, keeping her observation a secret. Katia figured out something that Raenyl would never admit. As Raenyl showed Popalia where to place her hands, and how to shuffle one pace closer to the other side, Katia witnessed the lock picker's denied respect for the red-headed girl.

She wondered if she pulled the priestess from the wall and let her go, would they all jump? Katia was sure that Wynkkur would dive in if Popalia slipped. Raenyl and Seth could jump a heartbeat later. She'd make a run for it. Under the wall, up the chimney, and she'd be back to her mission—screw Gregor and his guard. Once this job was done, she'd be done with thieving. In that order: Priestess, Thorgen, and then finally Darren—each kicked out of her life for good and forever.

Katia reached out for Popalia's dust-smudged robe. As her hand hovered over the priestess's shoulder, she envisioned Popalia plummeting in the darkness, shrieking all the way down into the nothing. It would only require a quick pull and a gentle shove.

Katia wavered. She couldn't do it. The thief bypassed the priestess's robe and took hold of a granite nub protruding over the priestess's shoulder. She'd get out of this mess, somehow—just not that way. Sometimes, the end didn't justify the means.

Raenyl reached the other side of the chasm. The priestess was next. Katia met the priestess's eye and smiled darkly before averting her stare. Stepping from the ledge onto the shelf leading into the next cavern, Katia enlightened, "Well, at least we know the goo-spitters can't pick us off from the opposite ledge."

Popalia nodded, "If we hadn't listened to Lighty-Brighty's warning, all three of us would have been dinner."

"Don't freeze now, Gregor." Wynkkur's voice drew the attention of the three who'd already made it. The merchant stood upon the edge over nothing, his body pressed against the wall.

Seth boomed, "Gregor, you better move. I'll untie Useless before I get tired from carrying him."

"I'm not frozen!" Gregor's voice piped noisily, sounding like a quieter version of the gnomes. "I just can't see where to put my hands next!"

Wynkkur gripped the edge with one hand while stretching over the bottomless pit. With the *pee'el'gee* in hand, he shined around the merchant, his dirty wig reflecting magical light. Able to see better, Gregor reached out to grab the next natural handle in the wall and slid a pace to the left. Wynkkur used the light to guide the merchant until he was closer to safety.

Raenyl took Gregor's hand, assisting him off the ledge. Once Gregor was out of the way, he patted the merchant on the shoulder before turning his attention to Wynkkur. The elf was quick after Gregor. Once he was off the ledge and a few paces from the pit, Wynkkur shined the light on the pathway, so Seth and Westin saw.

With Ucilius's dangling weight strapped behind him, Seth moved cautiously. The merchant's feet hung over the vast reaches of nothingness, his empty mind void of fear or concern. Sliding his feet slowly, Seth maintained a consistent counter-balance by gripping the wall. Slowly and eventually, Seth stepped away from the great hole of the world, pulling his living backpack up and onto the new earth.

"Whew!" was all Seth needed to say.

With Seth out of the way, Westin made the last few stretches effortlessly. Once again on solid ground, he thanked the elf for the guiding light. Wynkkur closed the *pee'el'gee* and dropped it into his pocket. Having several torches inside his bag, he wanted to use them all. They'd all be free soon, and he'd have no need for torches once they were outside. Withdrawing one, he commanded a quick flame from his hand to the oiled tip, firelight dancing brightly. Casting his known spells was becoming second nature.

The entry arch into the next dark corridor glowed brownish-orange as calcite walls redirected the torchlight. The walls looked melted and cooled into rib-like protrusions. Stalagmites—hardened piles appearing like brown ice—melded in against the moist wall. Tricks of the waving fire, long shadows stretched out into the new corridor.

"Untie Ucilius from me," Seth barked. "I'm gonna smash Raenyl's nose."

"What?" Raenyl nervously squeaked.

Seth reminded, "I didn't fall. You missed your chance to say 'I told you so'. Now, my fists got something to say to your face." Looking at each of his monstrous fists, Seth grinned while promising, "They're each gonna say, 'I told *you* so'. Now, get this brain-dead off me!"

"Hey, now. Cool off," Raenyl waved his hands, offering a crooked smile—a smile that said he'd take his chances with the big warrior, and he'd rather not. "I was only trying to help. Think of it as...motivation." Looking around and seeing there was nowhere to run, Raenyl nervously included, "See, we all made it, alive and in one piece...thanks to me."

Westin freed the merchant from Seth's back. With Ucilius's weight released, Seth advanced on a laughing Raenyl. Reaching out and grappling, Seth's hand was poised and ready to smash into the archer's head. The blow was paused only by Raenyl's locked grip at Seth's elbow. They were both chuckling as Seth shot his knee outward. The archer leapt to the side, narrowly escaping what would have been a painful blow.

Raenyl was on the defense as Seth pressed on. Seth stopped trying to hit Raenyl's face, grabbed the smaller half-elf, and gave him a good throw. Raenyl landed on even feet, laughing, "You can't beat me. You're too clumsy!"

Growling, Seth added, "You'll be clumsy red paste in a minute!"

"Hey!" Popalia interrupted, "I'm glad you two are having fun, but—" She didn't need to finish her statement. Clear to everyone, the exit was near.

Smiling, the brothers broke it off. Raenyl pointed at Seth, both sharing wide smiles, and Raenyl stated, "We'll end this later."

Seth shrugged, "I'll end *you* later."

Westin expressed in shocked amazement, "By the even hand of Stranoss, Ucilius is walking by his own will!"

Chapter Thirty-Nine

Time Is Lost To Darkness

With clumsy footfalls, knees high, and stumbling forward, his gait was reminiscent of a baby's first independent steps. An amazing spectacle for all who were watching, Ucilius was walking without a guide. Together, they shared the joy. Gregor cheered with a clap as Seth hooted with glee.

Westin asked anyone without expecting an answer, "Do you think he knows we are almost free?"

Seth, still chuckling, added, "Useless is now almost useful!"

A chipping sound skittered across the floor.

Gregor tried to make a joke, "Maybe that can be his new pet name...Useful."

After Ucilius emitted what sounded like a pained grunt, Wynkkur chuckled dryly, "Sounds like he doesn't like that, either."

Something knocked hard and bounced against Seth's boot. "Ouch!" He looked down, wondering what just happened.

"Shush!" Raenyl added, "Did anyone hear that?"

Ucilius groaned and fell face-forward to the ground as a rock clattered across the stone floor and over the side into the chasm. Another stone—smooth, disc-shaped and almost as big as a thumb and forefinger bent into a C—cracked noisily against the rib-looking calcite and landed spinning between Seth's boots. Looking from the spinning stone at his feet to Raenyl, they both knew what was happening. Simultaneously they announced, "Goblins!"

Goblins were nocturnal creatures of the forests, found outside the fringes of civilization. They were hunters who stalked during the moonlit hours using slings and javelins to take down their prey—hunters with eyes so sensitive that light blinded them. It was believed by the scholarly that goblins had eyes so attuned that total darkness was unknown to them. Now, the theory was proven.

In the past, Seth and Raenyl hunted goblins for money, and fighting goblins had made Seth and Raenyl known men for a brief time. Now, they found themselves on the other side of the hunting party. Neither archer nor warrior liked the reversal of fortune.

"Take cover!" Raenyl pointed to a wide stalagmite. "Get behind something!"

Wynkkur guided Popalia to a safe nook, then pressed in behind her. Pulling Gregor to the opposite side of the tunnel, Westin and the merchant pressed themselves with backs against the wall. Wynkkur watched Katia blend into a shadow that provided no security. Three walnut-sized stones ricocheted around the shade that hid nothing from the goblins' sharp eyes.

Raenyl called, "Katia! Get behind Wank! They can see you!"

Seth, who was closest to Ucilius, reached out and grabbed the fallen man by a foot and dragged him behind a narrow pillar beside the cave wall. Katia leapt from the ineffective shadow as two more stones bounced near the big warrior. One stone bounced at a warped angle, missing Katia's knee by a margin.

Worry creaked in his voice as Gregor called out, "Ucilius—is he okay?"

Seth called back, "Toss me a torch. I can't see." Intuitively, the warrior already knew the answer.

Westin tossed the torch underhand to Raenyl. The half-elf tossed the torch beside Seth as three more stones clacked against stone and stalagmite. Rounded stones, flung missiles from slings, bounced all around them.

Seth stretched for the torch and cursed, "Bane's Blood! Damn goblins." He angled the catatonic man out, not only as a way to examine the injured man, but also as an extra barrier from being pelted with slung stones.

As seen in the torchlight, his eyes were rolled up and back. Seth moved his ear to Ucilius's mouth where there was no breath. Between Ucilius's ear and eye, upon the left side, blood trickled from a gash. It may only have been a slow trickling of blood seeping from what appeared to be a tiny wound, but Seth assessed the real wound was far deeper. Having been hit in the temple, the softer bone had splintered when shattered by the stone. Ucilius had died from the internal wound. Outside, his wound barely bled.

"No, damn you!" Seth shook the dead man pointlessly. He shook him as if he were only sleeping and would awaken. Seth yelled, "I didn't carry you over that god-pounded pit for you to die!"

"No," Westin lamented from the other side of the hall.

Gregor added, "Priestess, please heal him. I beg you!"

Using the torch in his hand, Seth shoved the handle into the back of Ucilius's pants, so the torch was pinned under his belt and between the merchant's buttocks. Another sling-stone thumped against the dead man's back. Seth felt Ucilius's body vibrate as the stone bounced away, clattering into darkness.

"What are you doing?" Raenyl asked.

"Making him useful," growled an angry Seth. Holding Ucilius by the jerkin at mid-chest, Seth angled the merchant's body like a shield. Holding the body before him, Seth stood up and charged into the dark hallway.

"No, Seth!" Raenyl called, but his words were absorbed beneath a ferocious battle cry as the swordsman sprinted into the dark hallway. The torch in Ucilius's belt illuminated the warrior like a glowing target, drawing all projectiles to his rushing mass.

Reaching over his shoulder and withdrawing an arrow, Raenyl muttered, "Idiot. Clearly I am brother to Bane."

"Should I go?" Westin looked to Raenyl for orders, uncertain if he should break cover. Stones pelted against the human shield as Seth charged deeper into the dark hall. Bouncing against the corridor walls, flung stones skittered and spun across the floor.

One-handed, he held the undrawn bow, the arrow pinched between two fingers. Raenyl nodded, "Soon." Unsheathing his blade with the opposite hand, he tossed his weapon hilt-first across the ground to the caravan guard. "Take my sword." His eyes followed his brother's reckless assault.

Up the hall, Seth peeked between the dead merchant's shoulder and lolling head. At the fringe of his light, outlines became familiar to the warrior. Goblins—he'd known it, and now it was confirmed. In the quickly vanishing darkness, silhouettes of a bat-shaped head over skinny bodies could be seen. Their sprouting arms were long enough that they could touch their kneecaps without bending their bodies. With short legs, they appeared monkey-like, but absent of tails.

Generally, they fought in gangs no less than four and as large as mobs of fifty if a strong enough leader was present. With several war-chiefs, they could mobilize into a small army. Seth knew these things from experience. He had not known much about orcs, but he knew how to fight goblins.

Like self-conscious apes, goblins were covered in thick hair but wore animal skins sewn together to cover their loins. Goblins made their own weapons and scavenged better weapons from those they killed. Most goblins used short hunting spears and slings, but occasionally they'd be armed with man-made short-swords and daggers.

A step closer, and Seth counted five shadows materializing.

Peeking over the dead man's shoulder, he watched the furthest goblin hurtle a javelin. The sound of tearing cloth, shared with the vibration from contact, let Seth know his "shield" stopped the primitive weapon.

Another step, and Seth saw the nearest sling hunter's wide eyes being covered by narrow hands. Long fingers and dirty claws shielded black eyes, mostly pupils, from the near blinding light of the torch. Atop its head were large, membranous ears positioned out like a cat, but bigger, revealing the humanoid's vastly superior hearing.

Seth took a step closer, and the goblin sneered, feline teeth protruding beneath a pug-like snout. Another goblin, barely a pace to the right, turned its head to avoid staring directly at Seth's torch-bearing corpse.

Using his speed and raw ferocity, Seth hurled the body of Ucilius at the two goblins standing side by side. Seth watched the body he'd flung sideways slam into the first goblin, and that goblin toppled backward into the second goblin. The short spear protruding from the merchant's back added an extra limb for the two grounded goblins to be tangled beneath. Seth did not wait to see what happened next. There were three other goblins to contend with.

Pulling his sword, he pointed and speared the next closest goblin midway between navel and ribs. The sword ran halfway through the goblin, deep enough to where the broad blade's sharpness began to blunt. An agonized squeal ensued. Seth released the pommel, clipping the goblin with his shoulder as he passed, knocking the lanky humanoid solidly against the cavern wall with a scrape of steel from the sword's protruding tip.

The fourth goblin snarled, baring teeth and dropping its sling while stretching for a javelin propped against the wall. Seth shot his left hand out and at the goblin's neck, gripping tightly around its throat. He could feel wiry muscles flex beneath his grip as both long arms grabbed the attacking forearm with filth-clawed hands. The beast choked out a snarl as dirty nails began digging into Seth's skin. The warrior yanked his dagger from the back of his belt and plunged the knife up into the goblin's ribs. Pulling the blade with a spray of warm blood, he sunk the blade two more times in rapid succession.

As warm blood splashed across Seth's hand, the blade's handle became sticky. Seth continued applying pressure with his left hand, crushing the goblin's throat. As the goblin's knees buckled, the fifth goblin faded deeper into the shadows, bolting down the blackened hallway.

Seth turned to the goblin propped against the wall with his sword run through it. Gripping the hilt of his broadsword stuck within the impaled goblin, he withdrew the weapon from its living sheath. Collapsing against the wall, as if the sword was all that held him up, a final pulse of dark blood burbled as the weapon was freed. Seth faced where Ucilius lay and the goblins that were trying to free themselves from beneath.

Far behind Seth, down at the opposite end of the tunnel, Raenyl said to Westin while pulling the string of his bow, "All right, go now."

Raenyl released his arrow as the first goblin attempted to stand from beneath the tangle of bodies. The stand was short lived as Raenyl's arrow drove sideways through its throat. Clawed hands grasped at both ends of the shaft skewering its windpipe. Raenyl chuckled, pleased with his shot.

Westin stepped from cover a moment after Seth released the choking goblin. Westin saw Seth withdraw his sword from the impaled goblin. Still tangled up in Ucilius's dead body, the final goblin struggled franticly. Illuminated by the torch still snuggly poised at the merchant's belt, Seth stabbed the last goblin once, withdrew, and then shoved the blade in once more for good measure.

Westin, who'd taken about three steps toward the big warrior, stopped his hurried pace and looked over at Raenyl. Wearing a wide grin, the archer shrugged and said, "Next time, then."

Seth pulled the torchlight out of Ucilius's pants to prevent him from burning. Splattered in blood, Seth called back to his brother, "One of them got away. Why didn't you kill that one?"

"You were in the way," Raenyl emotionlessly answered.

Meeting Raenyl's calm, Seth stated, "He's gonna get more."

"Yup-yup," agreed the archer. "We should get out of here, and fast."

"Wait," Gregor stepped up. "We can't leave him here."

Raenyl shook his head while saying, "Popalia, it is urgent we move right now if we want to live."

Westin didn't wait and took Gregor, pulling him up the corridor toward Seth. Popalia and Wynkkur followed. As they walked, Westin commented, "Until we reach Magistrey, I'm under contract to protect you. If Seth and Raenyl say we go, then we go." Westin allowed Gregor the Third a moment aside his fallen son-in-law.

Westin spied and retrieved two of the primitive javelins from against the wall. One held a jagged, stone tip, and upon the dangerous end of the other a broken bone was whetted to a defined point. Both spears were wrapped firmly with sinew. The stone spear's shaft was good for throwing, but the bone-tipped spear bent slightly in two places. The guard shook his head and wished he'd kept the superior spear he'd abandoned in the upper cavern.

"No." Popalia shook her head. "You all go. Gregor is right. I must at least give last rites."

Everyone stood around looking at her, each of them with a different expression stitched upon their faces. Gregor's face wore a mask of relief and surprise, Raenyl's expression was grim and stressed. Wynkkur took Popalia's hand while nodding to Raenyl, "We've got to go, now."

Popalia shook her head, "I said for all of you to go. I'll be right behind you."

"Grrr," Wynkkur growled, but stood beside the priestess.

Seth announced, "I'll stay with them. The rest of you go, now."

"Want me to stay wit' ya too, Princess?" Katia asked as Wynkkur handed her a torch.

Katia took his torch as Wynkkur rebutted, "Go with Raenyl. He might need your help." Katia stepped in behind Raenyl.

Without wasting another protesting word, Raenyl led. The caravan survivors followed only a pace behind him. Wynkkur retrieved another torch from his pack as Popalia knelt down by the merchant and quietly prayed for the dead's final passage.

Chapter Forty

Time Is Lost To Darkness

On the run, Raenyl led the way with an arrow set on its string, but not drawn. Katia, right behind him, held her torch high. The steep walls vaulted overhead in the tall cave. Single file, they ran the narrow trail. Gregor also ran with a torch while Westin trailed, carrying a javelin in each hand. Bending ahead to the right, the tunnel continued into the black, but at the bottom of the approaching wall, a wide shadow could be seen.

"Hold one moment, right where you stand," Raenyl ordered as he stopped at the corner where the cavern veered left. Everyone stopped behind him. The torchlight lit up the corner, exposing the low shadow as being the crawl space they'd expected.

Quickly, the archer leapt into the open corridor. No more than two seconds passed, and he back-stepped into cover. He waited for another second behind the wall, anticipating the sound of sling-stones bouncing off the walls and floor. There were none, so he stepped across the opening and pressed himself next to the wall. Listening more than he watched, he waited for sounds deeper in the darkness. To Katia, he called, "Check it out."

She knelt down behind the archer, looking into the crevice. "It goes back about six feet, and then it opens up again. It'll be tight for you men, but elf-boy, the priestess, and I will get through fine."

Gregor stepped closer, but Raenyl barked, "Step back. Stay behind the wall over there. You carry light, and they'll kill you first. Every goblin hunt I've been on, the torchbearers are their first targets."

Katia dropped to her belly, crawling through the hole. Westin pointed at her feet disappearing under the wall. "Want me to follow her?"

"Yeah, make sure she doesn't leave without us." Raenyl nodded.

"What about me?" Gregor asked.

Raenyl answered, "You get behind me once Westin's boots vanish. Then, you go, but wait for me on the other side. I'll need light."

Raenyl listened as ominous sounds echoed through the darkness. Screeching and gibbering rolled from deep within the blackness. With a sigh, he commented, "They are coming back."

Gregor's eyes were wide with fright, and Raenyl jerked his head, saying, "Come on. Get behind me, and go fast."

Gregor looked back the way they'd come and saw the elf leading with the small, bright light projecting from his hand. The merchant bounded across the open space to right behind the half-elf. "The priestess is on her way."

With a snort, Raenyl remarked, "Is that what that light is? Hurry now. I don't want to be standing here when those goblins get here."

The older merchant moved slowly. As he got on his hands and knees, he muttered, "If Solander Breid only saw me down on all fours..." He shook his head and moved forward on his belly, sliding across the floor toward the promise of freedom.

Raenyl heard the goblins' high-pitched babbling accompanying a pitter-pattering of bare feet echoing ever closer. The goblins were still far enough off that, if the party hurried, everyone could still get underneath...or so he kept telling himself.

Popalia arrived as Gregor's feet vanished under the wall. She asked, "Where is Katia?"

He answered, "On the other side with Westin."

"What? She'll escape." Popalia crouched low, seeing Gregor illuminated by the torch he pushed ahead as he crawled.

"I said she is with Westin," Raenyl reminded with a sarcastic ring. "How about you and I argue when there isn't a swarm of goblins coming for us?"

Popalia agreed by lying upon the ground and pushing herself into the hole. Raenyl tapped Seth with the top of his bow, "You go."

Seth shook his head, "Uh-uh. They need your bow, and I got the wizard here."

"I'm not a wizard." Wynkkur corrected.

"Seth," Raenyl chipped in, "there are a lot of them coming."

The warrior nodded, "I ain't deaf."

"I'm *not*, I'm *not*...deaf," Raenyl rectified.

"No, you're my dumb echo. Now, hurry before they all get here."

Pausing only to offer Seth a rude finger gesture, Raenyl dropped and pushed his backpack and bow first, then pulled himself into the small tunnel. As his voice muffled in the crawl space, Raenyl informed, "Hey, Seth. It gets real tight down here."

Roughly elbowing Wynkkur, Seth grinned, "That's what his girlfriend told me." Seth laughed, trying to ignore the closeness of the approaching mob. Wynkkur rubbed his shoulder and did not look amused.

Whispering through the darkness, the first rock grazed the side of Seth's armor, spinning off between warrior and elf. A second rock clacked loudly off the wall behind Wynkkur, bouncing into his back.

"Aiee!" Wynkkur leapt and ducked at the same time.

"Light 'em up, Wank!"

Twisting the cap open fully, Wynkkur pointed the *pee'el'gee* into the dark corridor. Having crept quietly forward, two stone-slingers now pulled clawed hands to cover their big, black eyes. Turning and scampering away from the bright light, both goblins retreated, hoping to conceal themselves again in the safety of darkness.

Seth growled, "I hate sneaky goblins! Wish I had something to throw at them."

"Hold this." Wynkkur handed the *pee'el'gee* to the warrior. As Seth's huge hand took the tiny light source, Wynkkur was already voicing the words of a spell. Twin bolts of light split from the young sorcerer's hand. In the blink of an eye, both energy missiles flashed, searing one boiling burn into the hairy bodies of each retreating goblin. Dual shrieks of pain accompanied the poofs of burnt hair huffing off both goblins. The lightning fragments sent both of them retreating with a swift stride.

Seth laughed, "Yeah, that's how it should be." The noise of the mass of goblins approaching grew in intensity. "You better hurry under that wall, Wank. Even with this light-pointer, they might try and rush us."

Wynkkur was already on the floor. He quickly pulled himself beneath. Shaking his head, he remembered crawling beneath the barracks at Dilligan's Freepost. At least there'd be no spiders here. His feet scrambled, pushing him through the distance and onto the other side.

As Wynkkur crawled to the other side of the wall, Seth listened just beyond the reach of the magical light where the soft pattering of padded feet slowed. High-pitched growls from angered predators penetrated the dark halls like a mistuned chorus. *How many of them were out there, just beyond the light*? Many—and more were coming.

The chitterling, tongue-clacking boiled over into a din of animosity and hate. Seth knew there must be a leader hidden within the crowd, ordering his pack of hunters. Suspecting the gang was planning something big, he called loudly, "Wank, I hope you're out the other side, 'cause I'm coming, now!"

The first stones flung by deadly slings crackled all around the warrior. They were blind shots, taken without aim. The light was too bright for the goblins to take clear shots. Randomly trying to pelt him with lethal bullets, rocks crackled like hammer strikes against the back wall.

Seth cursed colorfully while dropping down upon his belly, shoving his backpack into the hole first. Next, he flashed the *pee'el'gee* into the crevice. Cursing again, he spat, "Bane's Blood, that *is* a tight squeeze!"

Flashing the *pee'el'gee* back at the horde of goblins, he saw the goblin's simple plan laid out. He couldn't see but the silhouettes of the slingers, but their stones were being hurtled over a wall of goblins walking backward. In the shadow of the backward stalkers, goblins crouched in the shade. Slowly, but surely, they were coming. There was nothing for Seth to do but push himself through the small crawl space.

Sliding into the crevice, the metal rivets of the protective plating on his armor scraped the ground as he slid himself sideways into the hole. Shoving his backpack further through the hole ahead of him, he crammed himself into the hole a little deeper. Holding his right hand outside, he hoped the light would hold the goblins back for a few more precious seconds. Seth pulled himself into the tight space with his left arm. Kicking with booted feet, he pushed himself along the opposite end of the crawl space.

He felt the leather cups of his pauldrons grinding across the ceiling with a gritty noise. He heard the angry hunters stalking closer. Seth pushed harder until he'd jammed himself halfway through the tiny tunnel. It was here that the grind of metal plating and the scrape of leather ceased. With a frightful lunge, Seth heaved with all the might he could muster in the narrow space. Nothing gave.

"Oh, shit! Help me! I'm stuck!"

They may not have understood his words, but the approaching goblins certainly comprehended struggle, panic, and fear. As the pattering of clawed feet hurried closer, he knew they would soon have him.

Chapter Forty-One

Time Is Lost To Darkness

Wynkkur could only see the shoes of Gregor and the boots of Westin. He crawled as fast as he could through the tiny space and took the offered hand at the end. The hand was Raenyl's, and with ease he pulled the elf out of the crawl space. He looked around to see the elbow-shaped tunnel he'd arrived in. There was a parallel corridor running along the wall he'd climbed under, and a dark hall continuing straight out from the hole he'd exited.

Excitedly, Wynkkur informed the group, "There are lots of goblins coming! They don't like light. They're afraid of it!"

Raenyl patted Wynkkur's shoulder and said, "It hurts their eyes. They will always try to kill the flame-bearers first." Handing him a torch, he patted the elf one last time as if to say, "Good luck!"

Speaking to everyone, Raenyl said loud enough so all heard, "Goblins hunt rabbits, raccoons, and small groups of people. Hear my words seriously. If we come upon any goblins, drop your torches and hope we are the better fighters. We are close to outside." Looking at Wynkkur with a wry smile, he said, "I can smell it. Once we are outside and in the sunlight, we will be safe."

Seth's pack scraped inside the crawl space. Raenyl stepped beside the opening to assist if needed. Seth's voice followed the white light pouring through the crevice, "Bane's Blood, that *is* a tight squeeze!" Then, the light cut away, ripping dark shadows in erratic sweeps while being redirected.

Raenyl could her Seth scraping inside the mini-tunnel. "Come on," he coaxed. Then, the pack pushed an arm-length closer but was still a couple inches from being clear.

Seth's voice came, again. This time, "Oh, shit! Help me! I'm stuck!"

Everyone stopped breathing.

Upon everybody's neck, cold sweat materialized. Worry froze the muscles of all as they looked from frightened face to frightened face. Popalia voiced the common uneasiness, "No, Seth."

Raenyl closed his eyes. "Gods pound-it!"

Pulling Seth's pack out of the hole, Westin bent low, tilting his head into the dark hole to see the mercenary's wide eyes looking back. Raenyl knelt, also looking underneath. Seth shouted, "My armor is caught, and there's a mob of goblins coming!"

Everybody heard, and they all knew the run was over for him. No one would speak it—a simple word so close on the tip of everyone's tongue. One word they could all see in each other's eyes, and an easy word to speak, "Run!"

No one spoke it, so no one ran.

"I can get him out," Katia stated. "Gimme a knife."

"What?" Popalia shouted. "You are my prisoner. We aren't giving you a knife!" Raenyl already offered his dagger to her hand.

Half a second later, the prisoner held a dagger. Sneering at the priestess, Katia dropped to her knees, saying to the men, "When I say pull, you two pull us out'a there, right? Right."

Raenyl nodded as Westin muttered, "Okay."

She pushed herself inside as Seth flashed the *pee'el'gee* out at the closest goblins. Stones bounced around, but he was well protected in the hole, and the slingers had little chance beyond dealing out a lucky bruise. It didn't stop them from throwing the sling-stones by hand.

Katia slid up before an angry Seth, who told her, "The little bastards are throwing rocks at me! They must really hate this gnome-thingy!"

"Is it keeping 'em away?" Katia asked.

"Sure, but how much longer?" As if on cue, a bone-tipped spear prodded near Seth's hand. He pulled back, cursing, "Damn all this! Damn it to the afterworld!"

"Hey now, relax. I'm here to get you out." Katia sounded calm until a sling stone that had been thrown by hand bounced outside and past Seth's head and thumped her hard against the top of her curly-haired head. "Ouch, buggering dung-holes! Lift your arm, so I can free you."

For a flash in time, she recalled the face of her mother. She pushed the memory away as Seth obliged. Upon seeing the blade in her hand, his eyes grew wider. She said, "I'm cuttin' your armor, not you."

She slid the blade sideways against Seth's thick bicep, between skin and leather strap. Admirably, she said, "Boy, you got some big arms."

"Everything here is big, girl." Seth grinned, his blues flashing, and she chuckled while slicing the thin, leather straps.

In that moment of forced ease, a brave or perhaps overanxious goblin took ahold of the bottom of Seth's boot. Long fingers curled around Seth's heel, and the attached arm tugged. Seth, being bigger and stronger, slammed the goblin's hand against the wall, forcing open the narrow palm. Seth mashed the hand with a second thrust of his foot, crunching cartilage and fracturing joints. The ambitious goblin retracted its broken hand with a howl.

Raenyl bent down and looked inside. "I hate rushing you, but we can hear them coming on this side of the wall, now."

Katia severed the first of three straps connecting his armor from front to back. The first strap was buckled at his upper chest, then the second under the ribs, and the final buckle above his belt. Tensely, she called back, "We are half-free."

Raenyl stood up. A moment later, she felt a hand take her foot, waiting for her call. Katia severed through the second chest strap. The rocks had ceased being thrown. Katia worked the dagger between Seth's body and the armor that trapped him. Peripherally, she saw hairy feet running through the light of the *pee'el'gee*. Perspiration sprang from her every pore as her heart beat faster.

"Um, we are about to go, right?" Seth nervously asked.

"Hang on to my arm." Katia slipped the blade beneath the last leather strap and tugged. The leather held strong, scurrying feet pattered behind Seth, and echoing shrieks of goblins began from somewhere in the dark hole behind Katia. Slicing through cured leather, the steel-edge proved sharper than the last strap holding Seth to his doom.

"Pull!" she yelled as goblins rammed their javelins under the wall. Katia felt the yank upon her legs as Westin's side pulled stronger than Raenyl's. As she slid out from the tight hole, Seth escaped from his armor like a banana stripped from its peel. The assaulting javelins caught hold of Seth's suit of armor, but despite efforts to spear through the trapped warrior, none of the thrusts drew near a drop of blood. Seth's body jerked as he was yanked out toward the side of his waiting friends. Katia saw Seth kick his armor back at the spear-shoving goblins upon his exit to freedom.

Both Katia and Seth were surprised upon exit to find it was Gregor pulling instead of Raenyl. Two paces to the right, the archer knelt with his bow extended, aiming down the tunnel parallel to the one they'd narrowly escaped. They all heard the pattering of feet coming from within the deeper dark. Firing blindly, Raenyl released his first arrow, and then reached over his shoulder to grab another. Somewhere in the darkness, there was a pained howl following the grunt of impact.

He released the second arrow, sending it swiftly. The shot

ended the howl, but deeper still announced the sound of many more feet advancing, accompanied by a high-pitched gibbering. They were still further away, but the amplification bounced the echo through the black vacuum. Seth pointed the *pee'el'gee* where Raenyl had fired his arrows, and the outline of a crumpled goblin lay on the far fringe.

"Hit 'em twice by sound not sight," Seth marveled.

"Throw the torch!" Raenyl ordered.

Popalia stood with her back against the wall. Determined and uttering a grunt, from around the wall she flung her torch outward. The flaming stick spiraled through the air for about forty paces before bouncing across the ground. Sparking in the darkness after hitting a wall, the torch abruptly stopped on its last bounce. Way up the hall, goblins shielded their eyes and made angry, hissing noises. Raenyl sent two more arrows at two different goblins, taking both of them out of the chase if not sending them into their next life.

"Bane's Blood, it just goes from bad ta' worse," Seth muttered before patting Gregor on the shoulder. "Thanks for helping me out of there—right?" He then clapped Westin on the arm adding a thankful wink.

"Let's go!" Raenyl encouraged unnecessarily.

Westin took the lead, but Wynkkur stalled. Looking to Popalia, the elf said, "Go on. I just need a second."

Not waiting for her response, he pointed the tip of his torch low. Setting the torch by the hole's opening, those still not following Westin heard the high growl of three goblins inside the hole they'd just exited through. The nasty creatures were advancing from every side possible.

Wynkkur mumbled the words to invoke another spell. Shoving the bright end into the hole, his spell went off. The end of the torch exploded outward in a jet of flame, rushing into the crawl space and filling it with fire. Terrified and agonized howls burst from under the wall as several goblins began cooking in magical flame. The reek of flash-seared hair tainted the narrow cavern annex.

The flames receded, and the torch burned normal, again. Even with the over-powering shrieks of the burning and the undertone of crackling fire, they heard the scrambling of goblins retreating from the flame-thrown hole. Wynkkur stood upright with a wide grin as Seth handed the *pee'el'gee* back.

Seth sounded upset, "Thanks, Wank. You just torched my armor."

Wynkkur smiled while dropping the hematite cylinder into his robe pocket. Magic felt too invigorating to not grin. Seth would interpret his smirk the wrong way, but oh well. Wynkkur pointed to the back of Popalia, who was marching quickly behind the thief. Everyone heard her chastising Katia about giving the blade back to Raenyl. Gregor, near the front, carried his torch right behind Raenyl and Westin, so the fighters had light to see by.

"I got the back. Go," Seth said while giving Wynkkur a penetrating stare.

Still smiling, Wynkkur did not hesitate. Not a second later, sling-stones were hurled from out of the pitch black. Stone bullets cracked noisily all around the now unarmored Seth. The big man made a hasty duck down the open hall that hopefully led unobstructed to an escape chimney beyond.

Chapter Forty-Two

Time Is Lost To Darkness

Popalia ran down the dark corridor behind Westin, her flame protesting noisily to her frantic motion. Fear ran with her as it did everyone else. Paralyzing, bone-freezing, stark-mad terror is what they would all be feeling, but by her god's blessing, the fear was diminished to the likes of a nagging mother. Her prayers may have diminished the worst of their fears, but her god did not remove the bloodthirsty mob that pursued them.

Katia had fallen two steps behind the priestess. She still had Raenyl's dagger. Popalia ran, and her mind taunted her—*Katia has a knife...my prisoner is armed.* What could she do about it? Nothing—and that tormented her more than the other fears piling up.

Ahead, she noticed the cavern was illuminated, but darkly illuminated. A new fear jumped upon the already large pile, but it remained repressed, thanks to the blessing of the Unnamed. Starlight shined down through a hole in the ceiling. No torchlight was required to see the pile of rocks leading to the chimney. Outside, the midnight domain seemed abnormally bright after spending days in the eternal darkness. The rocks had fallen into a pile and were set like natural stairs. It would be possible to scramble right up to the chimney and hopefully pull themselves out.

Popalia's thoughts betrayed her. *It is nighttime, and the goblins will follow us.*

Again, the fear was batted away by faith, and re-confirmed by Popalia's reflection, *First things first. We'll worry about that when we get to it.*

Crossing the tunnel's threshold and into the cavernous space leading to the chimney, she could scrape the ceiling above her with the torch tip if she extended her hand and held the bottom of the stock. Although she could not see the full dimensions of the cavern, she assumed she could give a sermon to at least 500 souls by the echo of their feet alone. Where her eyes had become useless, her ears had learned to compensate.

From up front, Raenyl called out, "When you no longer need your torch to see by, drop it, please!"

Westin arrived beneath the hole first. Stepping from the first rock to a higher rock until standing directly beneath the hole, he looked up. Popalia dropped her torch at the beginning of the rock pile. Aside her, Katia tossed her torch outward while saying, "Looks like it caved-in a long time ago."

Westin reported, "It's wide enough to fit us all, but it's ten feet to the top."

Raenyl stood at the edge of the rocks, calling Gregor to drop his torch. The merchant did as he was instructed. Wynkkur and Seth were approaching swiftly. Katia mentioned, "I could get up there fastest. From up top, I could drop that chain Popalia has around her so everyone can get out."

Popalia shut that down, "No way."

Thinking Popalia meant "improbable", Raenyl added, "Yeah, that chain is too small. Seth has rope."

Wynkkur tossed his torch the furthest away from the chimney, so it looked like a line of torches ran the room's floor. All except for Katia's torch had been thrown off to the side. As Seth approached, he added, "You all better hurry!"

"Katia needs rope," Raenyl replied.

"You are not giving our *prisoner* our rope!" Popalia ordered.

Seth had his pack off and his free hand shoved into it, saying, "Why not? She already has a weapon." Seth winked at Katia and tossed her the bundled rope. "Now, don't forget us down here. All right?"

Popalia turned around to face Seth. "Are you insane? She's going to leave us here!"

Katia didn't hesitate. She was already pulling herself into the chimney before the priestess could finish her protest.

The first of the goblins came into view from the furthest torch flare on the ground. Raenyl released the arrow he'd readied for this occasion. The goblin stopped suddenly as an arrow with a hundred pound push punched its way through his sternum. Knees buckled, the beast crumpled just outside the first torch, its head connecting to the ground with a melon-like thump.

Seth produced his broad blade from its scabbard. "She's our best chance at getting out of here. As of about two minutes ago, we're neck deep in shit!"

"You gave our prisoner the rope!" Popalia screamed. The chains that once connected her to Katia were still fastened around her own shoulders.

Westin, who watched Katia climb, called, "Okay, she is out."

"She is outside with a knife, and she's now free!" Popalia cried out. "Doesn't anyone else have a problem with this?"

Raenyl released another arrow. This one punched through a second goblin's hip. Shrieks, monkey-like and primitive, expressed the universal sound of pain. "Hurry up after her, then. I'm busy stopping a swarm of goblins." Nearby, goblins tried to remain in the darkness. They screeched out a noise like an unholy chorus. They were many, and more were still coming.

Westin hurled one of his javelins with a ferocious snarl. Spinning forward and ending with a wet thump, the tip tore into skin and deeper still. Low into its mid-section, another goblin fell to the ground, curling and whimpering, holding the wooden shaft like a returned umbilical cord.

Reaching up and over his shoulder, Raenyl pulled three arrows and set two at his feet, the third he set upon his string. Kneeling down he waited for the mob to rush. He assumed he still had around fifteen arrows in his quiver, and he wasn't giving up until after his quiver was empty.

The agonized goblin clutched the wooden shaft grafted into its hipbone via the razor-sharp, steel arrowhead. Rolling sideways, the wounded goblin shrieked as two new goblins leapt over him.

"Here they come!" the archer called while releasing his drawn string.

Raenyl missed, his arrow flying beyond the light's range, slamming with a wood-splintering snap somewhere unseen. Three more goblins sprang into the room, bounding over the dead and maimed. One suddenly stopped, swirling a sling over its bat-like head. There was a reflection of torchlight caught in its big, black eyes.

Raenyl whipped the first arrow up from his feet and snap-fired. He hit the slinger in the chest, but Raenyl had not sent the projectile at full pull—the arrow pierced between ribs and burrowed in finger deep. The swinging weapon opened and its stone-bullet whizzed inches from Raenyl's ear. He heard the stone clattering across the floor behind him. The goblin surrendered his sling and sat down hard on its backside, grasping at the arrow in his chest. Raenyl set the next arrow on string.

More entered the room, twelve, then twenty-two, and in a breath of time, there were thirty. Entering behind the first thirty, and being followed by perhaps thirty more, a giant of a goblin presented himself. He stood a head taller than all the others. Raenyl and Seth both recognized this goblin was important—he wore an armor breastplate of pounded bronze and had a small fencing buckler strapped to his left forearm. Except where bat-like ears were cut free, a bronze skull cap encased most of its head.

The armor had been fitted for a man, and hung loosely on the goblin's slender torso. Being bronze, the plating was ancient and had been crafted before steel was the ideal metal for armor. Seth understood it meant this suit of armor had been passed down from warrior to warrior since the day it had been acquired. It was reserved only to be used by the tribe's best.

Seth knew about tribal champions, and he knew this was the horde's tribal protector, maybe even its chief. Whichever goblin is strong enough—or crafty enough—to kill the last protector earns the privilege to replace him. The strongest goblin serves as chief until a stronger goblin usurps the power to become the next leader.

"Still no rope," hopeless Popalia reminded. "I can't believe you all just let her go."

Smartly, Raenyl added, "You take my bow, and I'll go after her."

Raenyl kept his arrow on its string and an eye on the crowd for any aggressive motion. The goblins were forming a circle, but they would not attack. Those carrying javelins held their weapons ready, but those with slings had left them empty. There was a jabbering—a nonsensical noise the goblins made amongst themselves.

A fearful Wynkkur asked, "Why aren't they attacking?"

"Ask him," Raenyl nodded toward the armored goblin.

As if the nod was the big one's cue, he stepped forward, clanking a small blackened hatchet against his breastplate. Pointing the axe like an extension of his hand, he shook it at Seth, saying something sounding like, "*Zaba-echee-grawk*!" He then pointed the axe at Westin and made a noise very similar to the first. Big black eyes stared down each of the two men, as if expecting a reply.

Wynkkur's voice trembled with unease, "I think he is calling you two out for a personal match."

Seth nodded, "Won't be the first champ I put down."

Nervously, Westin chuckled, "It'll be mine."

The armored goblin waved his lanky arms outward, chittering at his horde to step back. They backed up, but several with hunting spears spaced themselves, watching Raenyl closely. Two goblins pulled the two injured ones back to clear the "arena". Being pulled swiftly, the injured gave pained squeals, leaving black smears of blood in the dimly lit chamber. The leader of the goblins extended his long arms forward. Axe held high and buckler low, he beckoned the two challenged warriors forward.

"Think they'll let us go if we win?" Westin asked optimistically.

Stepping forward, Seth shook his head, "We'll stand proudly before our ancestors of past. The gods will applaud our arrival." Seth positioned his sword forward, turning quickly to look at Raenyl, "See you on the other side."

Raenyl smirked, "Just make him dead. We'll worry about the rest of them next."

Seth gave his brother a grim smile before facing the tribal warrior. Swerving, Seth angled to the right as Westin pounced to the left. The goblin curled its lips beneath its pug-like snout. Standing with knees bent, the goblin waved the axe high in one hand at Westin while his buckler warded against Seth. The horde surrounding spread themselves out, giving room for the combatants to scramble. This was a sporting event—a cruel pleasure they shared.

Westin jabbed outward with the short javelin, and his target twisted away, allowing armor to deflect the blow. As the chieftain pushed Westin's short spear aside with the back of its hand, Seth leapt aggressively at the goblin chief. Anticipating this offensive move, the champion deflected Seth's mighty blow with his round buckler. By the sound alone, it was easy to believe the blow must have been received painfully. Seth's thick blade added another nick in the bronze-casing enveloping the wooden buckler.

The goblin recovered unexpectedly fast by swinging the hand axe at the swordsman's face. Seth ducked the swing, but the buckler whipped back up from being battered down and was turned into a disk-shaped bludgeon. The central protuberance—the most fortified point of the light shield—caught the mercenary high on his cheekbone with a force to rattle bones. The shield emitted a hollow *donk* upon contacting Seth's face.

Stars and pain exploded in Seth's skull as his teeth shuddered with the contact vibration. Seth felt the ground strike against his butt before realizing he'd fallen backward. Holding his head, he fought against the fog wrapping around his mind. It felt like his brain banged from side-to-side in his skull. He could taste blood where the inside of his cheek had mashed against his teeth.

Determined, Westin averted what would have been the finishing blow. He swung his javelin sideways like a pointed club, connecting with the back of the lead-goblin's helmeted head. The javelin's strike vibrated the helm of the goblin, forcing a surprised,

"*Squark*!" Reactionary, the tribal champion whipped the axe back-handed.

Westin stepped back, trying to lead the goblin away from the stunned Seth. The goblin took the bait and pursued Westin, swinging wildly. Raising his hunting javelin to catch the reckless-ly swinging wedge, the axe cleaved the spear in two. The sharp-ened spear tip spun away, clattering off into the darkness. Westin stared dumbfounded at the clean-sheared shaft of what was no longer his weapon.

Fully understanding how sharp the axe blade had been honed, Westin ducked sideways as the wicked little weapon swung back toward his face. Spitting out a curse, he realized too late the deep trouble he stood in, now holding only a shortened stick.

Calling out with genuine worry, Gregor shouted, "Be careful!"

Raenyl felt helpless to only watch. He knew by raising his bow, the goblins would rain sling-stones and hurl javelins at them all. He still had an arrow ready on the string, but he couldn't bring his weapon up. He steeled himself, knowing that as soon as the vic-tor stood over the dead, he'd have barely a dozen arrows to send before accepting his own end. He called out, "Seth, you've got to get up!"

Behind Raenyl, Wynkkur looked at Popalia, who knelt be-hind the archer, hands together and lips moving. She prayed for her god's intervention. He kept his hand upon the pommel of his sword. Wynkkur knew that as soon as a victor was apparent, the blinding flash needed to save them again, but his mind kept re-peating there was no way out.

Calling the powers he needed required roughly two seconds. It would take him about a quarter of a second to clear his blade from scabbard. If the flash blinded any one of his allies, they would all die. He couldn't blind all the goblins. Those behind the blind-ed would come forward. Maybe he'd blind that wave as well, but eventually, they would advance upon them, and they would all be torn asunder—praying priestess and all. In the darkness, not too far away, Wynkkur wondered if Seth was out of the fight for good.

Seth wondered the same thing as he sat on the floor bleeding out the side of his mouth and from a deep tear in his face. He shook his head again and checked his teeth a second time with his tongue. They were all there, but the inside of his cheek was bludgeoned meat. The pain seemed to spike through his left eye and penetrate deeper into his brain. He didn't dare touch his face. Instinctively, he knew the bone was broken.

Beyond the dull ringing of his ears he heard Westin curse as the goblin champion advanced. The grounded warrior stood up despite his agony. The goblins surrounding him uttered sounds of displeasure, but stepped back to let him rise. Seth's knees wobbled once, and he stumbled closer to the wildly swinging axe and the quick-footed guard dodging death. Seth's pulverized face stabbed with shards of pure agony, but he was getting in this fight, even if the world seemed tunneled and fuzzy.

"Stranoss, help me!" Westin admitted mid-leap as the axe whipped through the air, once again only a fraction away from his nose. Holding the broken spear shaft, Westin swung back, but the goblin's buckler deflected the narrow club without effort. The goblin lunged shoulder-first into the guard's chest. Toppling backward, Westin landed hard, dropping the axe-shortened javelin, and losing it to the darkness.

Seth stumbled closer but was still too far. Westin knew Seth wouldn't make it. Scrambling backward from the advancing goblin, kicking with his feet and scampering on his palms, Westin's hand touched something wooden and rounded. The goblin stood over the fallen guard as Westin understood what his hand had found and hope exploded in his heart.

He praised, "Thank you, Stranoss."

Westin's hand closed around the severed shaft and tip of his broken spear. The caravan guard pushed himself up and forward, continuing into a mighty overhead swing. Westin plunged the sharpened bone-tip deep into the attacking goblin's leg, just above its knee. The spear tip tore through hairy skin, sinking deep into flesh and coating Westin's hand in warm blood.

Howling with unexpected pain, the goblin swung his axe-hand down. The axe cut clean into the base of Westin's skull, sinking deep above the top of his spine. The goblin fell forward onto the guard as his knee buckled. His own falling weight twisted the axe from out of his hand, but remained cleaved into the back of Westin's skull.

The armored goblin fell upon Westin's head, forcing the axe blade deeper into his brain. It mattered little—Westin was dead before his head made contact with the cavern floor. Blood gushed out the terrible wound and pooled across depressions in the uneven floor. Although his brain was dead, his heart kept pumping automatically.

The goblin howled with the spear tip protruding out his knee. He lay upon the twitching body of Westin as Seth, still dazed, stumbled closer. His face hurt, but now his heart matched the pain evenly. One thought persisted. *Kill him while he's down. Don't let him get back up.*

The goblin saw Seth coming. Rolling over, he yanked Westin's head by his bangs, working his other hand to try and free up the axe-blade wedged into the back of the guard's skull. Seth bared his teeth, determined to avenge his fallen friend. Raising his sword, the goblin freed the axe synchronously.

The goblin positioned his buckler to deflect Seth's blow, only Seth had learned from his first error. Swinging sideways like he was scything wheat, his powerful swing and heavy blade ripped between knuckles, splitting the hand in two and peeling the buckler nearly to the elbow. Sliding his sword out of the split arm, the goblin vocally expressed unfathomable pain.

Retracting his mangled hand, the goblin lay prone and open as a geyser of dark fluid shot from the cleaved arm. Still dazed, Seth fell forward on wobbly knees but aimed the tip of his sword above the goblin's breastplate. Steel scrapped against bronze as Seth's thick sword pierced though the bottom of the champion's throat. The goblin sneered ugly and swung the axe out defiantly as its own life was violently stolen. Clattering first against the bronze breastplate, the axe slid and fell into the bloody spill of two men and a goblin.

Seth released his sword's pommel to grab at his navel. He'd barely even felt the cut; it was the hollow sensation that frightened him more. He looked down in a daze, staring at his own intestines spilled out and covering the goblin beneath him. Absently, he scooped them up, trying to place them back inside the long hole in his shirt from where they'd fallen. Reality hit along with the horror of the inevitable truth. Shocked by his grievous wound, he passed out before falling forward.

Chapter Forty-Three

Time Is Lost To Darkness

Popalia's prayers were only half-focused upon her god. Wanting to open her eyes after hearing Raenyl say, "Seth, you got to get up," she felt a deep worry for Seth. She knew this fight wasn't going well, and she'd need to focus better if she expected to receive her god's blessing. Mottled thoughts ran through her mind. She was consumed with thoughts about was how Katia escaped—again. Again! She couldn't believe her friends—not friends, but her hired help—had released her prisoner.

No! She scolded herself, *focus on the Unnamed Host. All things fall under the will of the gods.*

She heard the goblins getting agitated. She knew by their accelerated chittering that the end was approaching. The noise, almost bat-like, was not as high-pitched. Behind her, she could feel the fresh, dry air flowing through the chimney. It teased her hair and kissed her cheek. Unfamiliar scents tickled her nose.

Katia was free, and Seth was going to die for letting her go—such was the will of the gods. No! Her mind fought against that possibility. *Have mercy, Great Mystery, let my friends fix their wrong-doing. Please, do not kill my...my friends. Forgive their transgressions. I beg of you.*

Westin called out in a panic, "Stranoss, please help!"

As Popalia begged her own god for divine assistance, she felt a change in the atmosphere she knew no one else could feel. She'd been conditioned to understand the subtle flux in the invisible world of spirits. The room filled with a power, calm and exact. Popalia recognized it wasn't the Unknown Host by the force of its presence. The air vibrated with the promise of order; it was the decision and the will of law that graced the cavern. Stranoss had come to the aid of His brave believer.

She heard a man-made grunt as the noise of bodies colliding touched her ears. She heard wood skittering across the stone floor, and sounds like elated cheers from scores of waiting goblins. Popalia didn't understand. Had Stranoss come to see them fail, to watch but not help?

Westin cheered, "Thank you, Stranoss!" He then followed a

screech of inhuman agony. It was terrible sound that continued on as the long shrill breath escaped. Mixed within the shrill cry, the priestess heard a meaty *thunk*.

Stranoss vanished, but the goblin's shrieking remained. She knew it was the goblin. Westin must be winning. Her heart released her own fear as the goblin's shrieks abruptly ended with a pinched gurgle.

"Praise Stranoss!" she admitted before opening her eyes.

Raenyl shouted "No!" at the same time as Gregor beside him.

Upon opening her eyes, she heard Raenyl's bow whisper "twang!" The goblins seemed confused, and their unanimous tone defined a deep uncertainty. Raenyl drew his string with another arrow ready. *Twang!* The second arrow flew into the massive crowd.

Popalia rose to her feet and saw the pile of bodies on the outside of the torch's light. It was a tangle of limbs in the darkness, but she was certain on top of the pile lay Seth. Something fleshy and wet glistened in the terribly inadequate light. Something unnatural was strung across the armor of the goblin beneath Seth. Westin lay at the bottom of the pile, as motionless as the goblin and Seth. Westin's head lolled to the side, eyes open and sightless.

A third arrow left Raenyl's string. Popalia felt coldness flowing off the half-elf's aura. Frigid was revenge. Raenyl stood emptying his quiver into an ocean of goblins, his reaction to the sacrifice of his dead brother. Popalia realized she'd been wrong about Raenyl, and fresh tears stung her eyes as she looked to the pile of the brave dead.

Sprinting forward by instinct and without any thought, she ran into the darkness toward the pile of bodies. She heard Wynkkur call out in protest, but she was deaf to any rebuttals. She could not feel her feet. Like a wisp on the wind, she crossed the distance as Raenyl's fourth arrow zinged through the air a couple feet from her head. A pained squeal uttered from the goblin nearest Seth. Arrow number five stopped the scream as the arrowhead found a way between sinister teeth, plunging deep into the back of its throat.

Popalia set herself down into the spreading puddle of sticky blood. The humid stink of copper tore at her nose, an assaulting and acidic stench. A combined mixture of warm blood soaked into her robes at her knees. Popalia blinked to eject the tears in her eyes as she rolled Seth's head to the side. She was appalled by what she saw.

His face was caved in upon one side, splinters of bone speared through the skin beneath his left eye, spilling blood down into his bearded chin. Looking down and realizing the goblin's armor was still intact, in sheer horror she realized the long tendrils spilling over the armor were Seth's innards.

The Mystery granted a miracle she'd never expected—Seth coughed.

"Oh," was all she could manage to say. For what seemed an eternity, she didn't know what to do. Never had she witnessed wounds so macabre and grievous on someone she'd cared for so closely. Priest Marcel had died so clean compared to what now lay a fraction from death, barely a cold touch away. She set both her hands onto the sweat saturated back of the warrior and prayed, "Please, Unseen. Grant to me the power to close these wounds. I accept the pain this good man has endured. I'll pay for his recovery with my own pain."

Her hands exploded in warmth, nearly hot to touch, but comforting. Pleasure unlike any she'd known before spread from within her heart to her hands and feet. The very cave seemed to explode in light—light dancing through the very air as if the room had become day. From where she prayed, the light trickled down around her. The goblins scattered, being rebuked from the place where she knelt.

Enraptured, she bent her head downward, watching the grayish-pink tissue of Seth's intestines recoil from around the armor they had been strewn over. They were being sucked back into the wound that had opened the warrior up, which by the blessing of her prayers now closed as if they'd never been.

Outlined by responsive lightning exploding from somewhere behind her, sheer joy was all she felt. She was relieved of worry or fear, experiencing divine ecstasy. Quivering, she fell over Seth, her ear pressed against his back, hearing the rhythmic beat of his heart and the steady bellowing of his breath.

Chapter Forty-Four

Time Is Lost To Darkness

Wynkkur witnessed Seth falling forward upon his sword. He heard the gurgling sound made by the goblin, enlightening the elf that Seth had finished the fight. Then, in an almost spasmodic reflex, the right arm of the goblin flung inward with axe in hand. In the low light from the grounded torches, Wynkkur watched Seth's blood spray across the goblin's bronze breastplate, followed by what seemed like slimy serpents that Seth scrambled to collect and embrace. The warrior fell forward upon the goblin that lay across lifeless Westin.

Behind him, Popalia called out, "Thank Stranoss." Wynkkur didn't understand what she was offering thanks for.

From the archer and merchant merged the word, "No!" Raenyl lifted his bow and fired into the nearest goblin. Then, he fired again and again, but Wynkkur only stared in horror at the two dead men mixing their blood with the equally dead goblin. "Thwack!" Raenyl's arrow found goblin flesh once again.

They were all about to die. Even if the horde was stunned and equally baffled by the outcome, many emitted murmuring noises, keeping the larger mob static. They would soon react and avenge their fallen leader without mercy, Wynkkur was sure of this. He looked behind him to the chimney, and there was still no rope. Katia had left them for dead. He'd had hope, as did the brothers, that she'd at least drop the rope down before running off, but their trust had proven to be poorly invested.

Unexpectedly, Popalia was up and rushing past him. He called for her to stop, but she did not listen. Straight toward the mob of goblins, she bolted. Raenyl saw it too, and he fired his next arrow at the closest goblin near the charging priestess. Being a snap-shot, the arrow sunk deep into the left shoulder of the humanoid, releasing a bubbling pulse of blood and an agonized yelp. Raenyl's fifth arrow bullseyed into its tooth-filled maw. The bloodied arrowhead punched out through the back of its skull as its limp body dropped on lifeless knees, becoming its own pile of warm goblin-meat.

As Popalia knelt beside her dead friends, Wynkkur fished the *pee'el'gee* from his left pocket. With the light source held in one hand, he withdrew his sword in the opposite hand. Side-armed with his left hand, he hurled the *pee'el'gee* upward at his fullest might. The hematite cylinder vanished into the darkness as soon as it left his hand, but a moment later, there was a soft pop, and light exploded from above where the priestess knelt.

Light, as dazzling as day, cascaded out and over the dead. Light—violent and invasive—spewed in all directions. Luminescent dust motes glittered in the air as larger pieces of the shattered *pee'el'gee* scattered across the floor, landing in the growing crimson puddles, and twirling through the darkness. Light sprayed downward from where it struck, apparently fused into the ceiling above the praying priestess.

The entire horde of goblins squealed while averting their eyes. Hating the light, their eyes burned with sharp pain. Blindly, they retreated toward the dark corridors to escape the assault of light. Raenyl didn't care if they were retreating. He fired arrow after arrow into the mob. Terrified and blind, the monsters ran.

Wynkkur was not satisfied with the retreat. Holding his sword high, he told Gregor to look away. Standing behind the half-elf, his sword burst into a blinding flash of light. A fast wave of heat caressed his face before magically charged air crackled with the soft popping of repolarizing molecules.

Keeping his eyes closed and his sword arm held high, the spell symbols danced in his mind. The sword flashed a second time, leaving a white reminder inside his closed eyelids. Heat waved, and the air snapped like canvas ripping with discharged energy.

Opening his eyes, Wynkkur informed, "I'm done."

Raenyl coldly admitted, "I'm not," before firing another arrow into the spine of a goblin feeling its way along the wall near the cave they'd come from. The punctured body crumpled with an inhuman scream.

Wynkkur wondered if the blinding they'd received would prove permanent. Their eyes were conditioned to absolute darkness, and the absolute light from his spell was meant to blind the eyes of those accustomed to daylight. Six goblins remained alive in the cavern, but they had been rendered useless. All the others had either escaped down the halls exiting to deeper tunnels, or fallen under the half-elf's barrage of arrows. The six that remained uttered terrified, helpless sounds while either stumbling along a cavern wall or crawling across the stone floor.

From the pile of bodies beneath the pouring of light, Seth's voice called out, "Popalia, let me up."

Raenyl shouldered his bow and ran over to Popalia's side. Popalia trembled as Raenyl eased her up and held her against him. As the blood dripped from the hem of her dark-soaked robe, she grasped his shoulder and laid her head against his chest. Quietly into her ear, only Wynkkur's sensitive ears heard the half-elf whisper, "Thank you." Raenyl pulled her away and out of the wide, crimson spill.

Seth got up on uneven feet, looking down at Westin. Genuine sorrow etched his tone, "He saved my life." Then for Popalia, he added, "You too, Priestess. Thank you."

Gregor stood upon the outside of the bloody puddle. Removing his wig, he wiped his hand across the long stubble upon his scalp. Quietly, he spoke to his fallen bodyguard, "I cannot recompense. I am not worthy of your sacrifice, nor can I ever repay it."

Ignoring the abandoned goblins squealing in the background, Seth retrieved the wicked hand-axe from where it lay in the sticky and coagulating puddle. Shaking the sleek weapon to release some of the blood, Seth added while looking down at Westin, "I'm keeping this in honor of you, my friend. For as long as I am alive, I'll remember what it took from you, and what you gave to me."

Trembling and uneasy, Popalia's voice mixed in with the shrieks of the blinded, "Let me give him last rites. Then, we must go."

Gregor pleaded, "Please, Priestess. I cannot leave him here. They will eat him, and he deserves a burial. At least let's take him outside, please."

Raenyl looked from the ceiling, where remnants of the *pee'el'gee* had affixed to the stone ceiling. "The goblins will never come back in here. The light is too bright. It will forever be Westin's private mausoleum." Looking over Popalia's shoulder and to the elf, he informed, "You know that thing you destroyed was priceless, right?"

Wynkkur shrugged, "What is your life?"

Gregor answered, "Nothing is as priceless as life. I'd break a thousand *pee'el'gees* for one Westin. I'd break a million to have my daughter and her family back. Too late, I understand this." He nodded to himself, repeating, "Too late."

Through the clean slice in his shirt, Seth rubbed the hair upon his scarless belly and nodded to the dead. "I'm pulling that rotten goblin off, so Popalia can do her prayer. After that, all I want is fresh air."

Raenyl nodded, "Then, we'll go after Katia. Sorry, Popalia. I really thought she would help us get out of here. She is going to die for this. We saved her life, and I trusted her with ours. Can you forgive me?"

Seth pulled the bronze-armored goblin away from their fallen friend by the clawed hand his sword hadn't mangled. Deep, dark ooze smeared across the cavern floor. Blood streaked the ground as the nearly decapitated body was drug away by Seth. He dropped the uncleaved hand and gave the cooling body a solid boot in the side of its head.

Leaving Raenyl's side and stepping as uneasily as a newborn fawn, Popalia wobbled ever-closer to the dead guard. She knelt once again in the puddle of cooling blood to give Westin a final prayer, even though she'd already known Westin's chosen deity had received him.

Wynkkur nodded, "If we are quick, I'll be able to track Katia. Her head start is only by a couple minutes. We'll catch her by the end of the day."

The elf heard something hit the pile of rocks behind him. He turned toward the chimney as one end of a coiled rope bounced against the cropping of rocks beneath the hole to the outside world. He wondered aloud, "Katia?"

Chapter Forty-Five

Unknown Day; Dusk or Dawn

Popalia screamed from somewhere below as Katia clambered up the chimney with ease, "You gave our prisoner the rope!"

Pulling herself upward, Katia noticed the air smelled different. The expected scent of pine was replaced with an arid, grassy aroma. Sage, like the spice. The sky above was freckled with stars, and her eyes adjusted easily to the deep blue of night.

Reaching outside to feel the top-soil, her fingers sifted through unexpected gravel, not the damp and musky soil expected of the forest. Pulling up and peeking outside, she spied bushes with severe, sword-like leaves, star-bursting out from thick centers. Turning her head to better see what was around her, she was shocked to see sand and aggressively pointed plants dominating the landscape. Spaced sporadically, large boulders half-submerged in sand were surrounded by an even greater concentration of prickly plants.

Westin's voice bounced up from below, announcing, "Okay, she is out." At both sides the two nearest plants promised prickly-injury if she wasn't careful. Avoiding them, she scooted out along the grainy soil.

"She is outside, with a knife, and she is free!" Popalia's echo rang out into open sky. The slivered moon hovered on the horizon—a reflection of the smile spreading across Katia's teeth. She'd never agreed so strongly with the priestess—she was free.

Standing up, she tossed the rope to the ground. Scanning the horizon, she saw a thin plane of light highlighting the edge of the world. The sun made no promises of direction to the watcher. Was it dusk or dawn? She'd know in a couple minutes. The sun always sets in the west, after that she'd know what way was north. Reverse that if the day was breaking.

She couldn't believe the forest had disappeared. In three directions, all she saw were spiky shrubs, bigger rocks, and sand. Wind, dry and with a slightly salty scent, blew from where the moon smiled over the edge.

It wasn't just sand. There were also fat, tree-like plants growing taller than she stood. One stood right beside her, standing with thick, upward prongs. It was covered with wide, bloated branches. Even without leaves, she was sure it was a plant, but could it be called a tree?

Never mind that. Behind her, tall mountains stretched in opposite directions, naked of vegetation and basking in the moon's frail light. There may have been vegetation, but none seen by light of the moon. Katia never remembered a night so bright—at least not without a full moon.

The horizon...was it brighter? Was it darker?

She looked at the rope at her feet and shook her head, "No more chains, bitch."

Katia recalled ten years, rolling backward to memories buried underneath a time long passed.

Katia remembered to an earlier time of bearing the weight of chains—always humiliating, shaming, and forever soul-stealing—*chains.* To know freedom was by working. In the plantation fields and groves was the only time the heavy chains were removed. All except the iron ring of ownership—the collar always remained fastened, constricting, forever pinching.

She had been born a slave and worked at one of the plantations south of Athania Commons, very near the deep jungle's edge. Her owner's farm produced bananas, mostly. That, and a small crop of tobacco.

The tobacco crop afforded her master a little power. That little bit of power enticed powerful people to come to the plantation before and after harvest. Some of them were more powerful than the master, and sometimes, they would take random women to the house. Sometimes, the women came back bleeding and bruised, but even if not visibly marred, the women always returned silent. Gravestones hollowed their eyes, removed was the mustard seed of a slave's pride, now R.I.P.

Katia spent the first fourteen years side-by-side with her mother as she harvested bananas with a long, sharp scythe. Mother reached up and wacked a bundle free and stepped back, letting the bunch land in the tall grasses. The slaves had to be careful when harvesting the bananas. Sometimes, aggressive spiders with poisonous bites would fall with the bunches. Their round, leathery bodies equaled two fists being pressed together, with legs thick and long, a total of eight swiftly moving spokes.

Katia, being the youngest of the harvesters, was expected to protect the older women in the event of a spider attack. She was allowed to carry a club to bat at the spider if problems arose. Mother could never touch the club. Katia had seen what happened to the older slaves when they took the club for themselves. Punishment was harsh—worse than being bit by one of the banana-tree spiders.

Oftentimes, the spiders would retreat back into the green foliage, but Katia still killed between two and four spiders per harvest. She hated the task, but having seen her mother bit once, Katia swore to never allow that to happen, again. The master lanced the poisonous boil, sparing her mother's life, but the pain her mother felt was unmatched, or so she'd thought back then. That detailed the first time mother had been brought to the master's house, or the first time in Katia's memory.

The second time came after a promising harvest of tobacco, after the city men had come to the farm. That night, it was Katia's mother who had been taken from the slave pen. They'd come drunk and released her chain from the wall. She was taken to the house by leash like a mutt. Waiting restlessly for her mother's return, Katia acted as though she slept. Upon her return, near dawn, no words came from her mother's bed—only tears as her mother cried.

Taken again the next night, upon her return, there were no tears. Shaking Katia, who'd already been awake, her mother shushed her quietly. From the master's house, she'd stolen a pair of hairpins from one of the madams.

Whispering, mother said, "I'm taking away your collar. There'll be no more chains for my baby."

Like mother promised, the collar clicked, and for the first time, Katia knew freedom. The master and his mean handlers from the house did not know she'd been freed, and this made Katia afraid. Mother set the hairpins into Katia's open hand, pleading as she did, "Now, you must free me. Please, baby."

It was there, in total darkness she'd picked her first lock—or at least what she'd thought then as being total darkness. She fumbled inside the keyhole, unsure of what needed to be done when a soft click rewarded her ears. The thrill she'd felt in that moment of freeing her mother! Mother praised, "Good baby. You've got to go. Be careful and run away from here."

As Katia pulled against her hand, mother shook her head, "I got to let all us slaves free—not only me and you. Right is right, and wrong is always wrong. You must go first baby. Don't worry, I'll find you, but never look back. You're an unwanted child of Athania, first by birth, and now forever until death. No more chains for my baby girl. When you get far enough away, they'll stop looking. Now, go. I'll find you."

Mother was right by her parting words—run far enough and fast enough, and the past will stop looking. She ran so fast and so far that when she did finally look behind, she'd already begun work for Darren Chalise. When she looked back, she never saw her mother, again. She remained behind with the slavers.

Right now, Katia needed to put some distance between her and the present slavers. She knew not why the forest had vanished, but the mountains were still there. Before being forced into those caves, she knew which way was north. She began to jog, sparing one last glance at the rope upon the ground.

Moving in the direction she believed to be north, Faradell Pass would eventually be this way. Thorgen had a great head start thanks to all the wasted time in that hole. As she jogged between two of the spiked bushes that sprouted waist high, she wondered if she'd come up further south of Dilligan's Freepost. If so, how far was she? How far south could she be from the road already traveled? One step forward, two miles backward. Could she have come out of the cave too far north?

Jogging a little ways further, she realized the sun was not setting—it was rising behind her. *No way. This is impossible*, she thought. If the sun rises now in the west, something had changed weirdly in this world while they were hidden from it. Where was she? What had really happened while she'd been underground?

The sky grew brighter, and the moon now laughed at her from over her left shoulder. She covered her eyes with her hands. In her mind, she heard her mother's voice, *Right is right, and wrong is always wrong, baby girl.*

Speaking to no one but the memory of her mother, she answered, "Momma, I didn't leave you to be put back in chains." The voice was gone and only in her head. Still, she argued, "You hear me, Momma?"

She turned back toward the hole to the cave. Wrong is always wrong. Right is right.

Chapter Forty-Six

Unknown Day; 6:30 a.m.

With the sun's piercing light burning on the horizon, any fears of the goblins taking pursuit vanished in the darkness below the land. It would be another fifteen hours before the first goblin poked its head outside whatever exit they might control. They may not even pursue after nightfall. Without a champion to lead them, the goblins would band together in smaller groups, attacking each other until a strong leader emerged to reunify them. The ordeal with the goblins ended with Seth's exit from the hole.

Having dropped the rope down the chute, Katia pulled each of them up. Wynkkur climbed up first then got behind her to help Popalia up and out. Upon exit, each party member expressed their surprise about the changes in the environment. The last to squeeze up and out of the chimney was Seth.

Katia asked, "Where is Westin?" Seth shook his head, and Katia understood. Her heart sank, "Had I been faster, would it have changed anything?"

Seth looked from Raenyl to Popalia, and this time, they all shook their heads. Relieved that she was free from guilt's excess weight, Katia stated, "We made it, then. We got out, but what you think happen't to all the trees?"

Bittersweet, it was Gregor who answered, "It looks to me that we are in the desert surrounding my home town. I swear by Stranoss as my god, I can get us to Magistrey from here. Popalia, you are truly a godsend."

Inhaling deeply, the merchant continued, "That salt smell in the air—it tells the nearness of the ocean." He pointed out into the dark, blue horizon at the edge of the desert, "With our backs to the mountains, we will walk to the ocean if we do not cross a road. If we intersect a road, it is the only road between Magistrey and Athania. Few use it. Most trade is conducted by ship not caravan. If we come to a road, Magistrey is to the northeast, and if there is no road, then we must travel southwest."

Raenyl stepped aside Popalia, and a dark look passed between the two. Popalia nodded before giving Katia a cold stare, "I didn't expect to see you. I figured you'd have been halfway across the desert by now."

The master thief smirked, "I was a quarter of the way to no-where, but I owed you one, so I came back." She coughed to clear her throat, "Had it not been for you and your gang, I'd have been raped by orcs—if not eaten by now." Her eyes skittered between Seth and Raenyl, "You trusted me without question, and I had to do what was right, all right?"

Popalia understood clearly, "So, what now? What do we do next?"

Wynkkur answered, "Let's put some distance between this hole and what it represents."

"I agree, but I mean with Katia. What is next?"

Katia shook her head, "Look Prince—I mean, Priestess. Like I told you back in the darkness, I want to make this right. That is why I came back. Don't lock me up, again. Keep the damn chains off me, and I'll follow you to the edge of the world. I promise this— I'll do all I can to help you get your scepter back. From here on, I'm with you all the way."

Wynkkur added, "If you speak truthfully, give to Raenyl his dagger as a show of good faith."

"I will," nodding, Katia exclaimed. "I am doing it. Please, Priestess. Promise to drop the chains into the hole after I give up the blade. I'm sorry about Westin, I really am." She offered the dual-edged knife to Raenyl, handle first.

Raenyl took the blade as Popalia agreed, "No one could have changed Westin's fate. I felt the presence of Stranoss before he fell. All the same, how can I trust you won't run, again?"

"I guess you're just gonna haf'ta have some faith. I swear it, I ain't never told no lies to you. I said Thorgen would go to the Golden Yoke to meet his fence. I never lied—I just didn't tell you the Yoke was in Portown Magistrey. Gregor knows I'm right." Holding her hands up in a gesture of surrender, she pleaded, "Please, I'm with you, now. Just no more chains."

Popalia cast her eyes toward Gregor. He nodded tiredly, ad-mitting, "There is a tavern named the Golden Yoke. It is a sailor's bar filled with outsiders and very few locals."

Raenyl added, "That makes sense. An outsider's bar means no questions or odd stares from the regular patrons. Barkeeps don't bother remembering names or faces in places like that."

"Katia, believe it or not," started Popalia, "I hate wearing these chains, too. You've pledged to me to see this through, now pledge it to the Unknown Host and know the Mystery is your true liege."

Katia knelt before Popalia, taking her hand and kissing her knuckles, "I am devoted to the Unnamed, and I pledge to follow your cause."

Popalia helped Katia stand, "Know this, Katia. Deceit will be returned with holy vengeance. You are bound by your word to my god, and the Mystery will hold you to it." Breaking eye contact with the risen woman, she turned to Raenyl with a smile, "Please, unlatch me from my bonds."

As swiftly as he could retrieve his lock picks, Raenyl unlocked the chains that had been wrapped around Popalia's shoulders. Keeping her promise, she tossed the chains back into the hole from which they had been found. Gravity took the links as they slipped noisily over the side and crashed into the rocks at the bottom of the forever-illuminated cavern. "I hated the weight of those chains. Your word is less burdensome."

Seth turned around and bent over. The leather strap of his belt had been severed into two lengths, both waving in the soft wind. He cursed, "Bane's Blood!" At his feet upon the ground, he picked up the hand-axe from where it laid in the sand aside a thorny shrub. Standing back up, he removed his dagger and sword scabbard before pulling the buckle of his belt. The severed leather exited the loops of his pants.

Staring at his sliced belt—a clean cut—Seth asked, "Wank, do you think this axe is magical? Or is it just cursed to cut off all my clothes?"

Katia smiled, and her eyes teased with a naughty hunger, "If I'm lucky, that axe is gonna cut off your pants!"

"If I'm *un*lucky, it may be cutting off somethin' else!" Seth added while holding his pants up.

Raenyl opinioned, "That is a wicked axe. Toss it back in the hole."

"Law's no! This thing is magic! I got's me a magic weapon, I know it."

"I got myself a magic weapon," corrected Raenyl with exasperation.

"What? I ain't giving it to you. Push off!"

Wynkkur looked at the black-bladed hand-axe held in the big warrior's fist. It was a sleek weapon and looked intended for throwing. The twine grip was completely enveloped by the warrior's meaty hand. "I don't know if it's magical, but it is sharp enough to make me ponder who might have forged it." He shrugged, "Whoever crafted that axe designed it to cut well."

"Duh," Seth mocked. "Do you think?"

Wynkkur tilted his head at the warrior, unaware of Seth's intended mockery, "Yes, I do think."

Seth laughed lightly then added, "Well, all right big thinker. Would you mind dropping it into my backpack while I hold up my pants?"

Raenyl chuckled, "Cut a length of that rope off to use as a belt, first. No one here wants to see the breakfast link you're hiding."

"Aw, come on, big man," Katia teased. "You saw mine, now lemme see yours."

Wynkkur still didn't get it. "Breakfast link—you mean you got sausage in your pants? Why have we been eating dirty orc beans for the last couple of days?" All of the humans laughed, the priestess included.

Chapter Forty-Seven

Unknown Day; 12:00 p.m.

Gregor was right. By midday, they'd reached a dirt track. Growing out from the middle of the road, weed-like brambles reclaimed rut marks in the rarely used path. They followed along the road until the sun began to set at their backs. Upon the horizon before them, a distant trail of smoke touched the darkening skyline. They'd be in Magistrey before the next full day of travel.

As the sun was setting, the nightlife began to stir. Raenyl had half a dozen arrows left, and with a couple of them, he provided more than beans to eat for the night. Two fat rabbits that were once part of the nightlife ceased to be.

Wynkkur lit a dry shrub aflame and used a spell to minimize the fire's consumption while Seth prepared the rabbits. Raenyl used the narrow tip of his longsword to spear the skinned rabbits. Holding the weapon over the fire to let dinner cook, a shiver took him. Remembering the dead woman he'd spied the orcs preparing for their dinner, he wondered if that had been Gregor's daughter. No longer hungry, he cooked the food for everyone else to eat.

Everyone quietly reflected on the ordeal they had survived while they ate, all except Raenyl. Wynkkur savored the rabbit while Raenyl asked Popalia for a blessed bean. Seth refrained from joking, his eyes contemplative and burdened with exhaustion. Even Katia kept her own silent thoughts while staring deep into the slowly diminishing fire.

Once finished eating, Gregor broke the silence, "Priestess, can I please share words with you?"

"Yes, Gregor," she nodded. "Privately, I have words to share also with you."

They stood, and she took his hand, leading him back down the road and away from all the others. When she was far enough to where she believed they were outside Wynkkur's sensitive hearing, she asked the distressed merchant, "What is on your mind, Gregor?"

Gregor looked down at his feet, and a moment later, he fumbled, "I do not know where to start." With the tip of his toe, he kicked at a small stone embedded in the sunbaked dirt along the side of the road. "I guess I seek forgiveness."

Quietly, Popalia thought about her words before saying, "What you seek, I cannot grant to you. Despite our disagreements, I have never resented you, nor have I wished ill upon you. You need not seek forgiveness from me."

Gregor focused on the rock he tapped repetitively with his foot. He spoke downward, "I sought to be a good father. Not just for my children and grandchildren, but also for my employees. Do you understand?"

Popalia shook her head. When she didn't answer, Gregor looked up at her. It was then she answered, but it wasn't an answer, it was a lead. "I have vowed celibacy. I do not know the pressures of being a parent. I'll never know about being a father—even after the conditions of my celibacy are fulfilled."

Gregor turned back to kicking the rock. "I am an honest businessman. I paid my people more than any of my competitors could. I always looked out for my employees' basic needs, and never have I compromised what I believed was right."

He stepped on the rock with the balls of his feet and shifted his gaze to the red-headed girl as young as his surviving daughter. With conviction, Gregor admitted, "I follow Stranoss, I have lived by the Law. Now, all those people are dead, all of my drivers, my guards—dead so fast that I couldn't even feel the loss. Selfishly, I have kept all my tears, but my heart, it is shattered."

He kicked the rock a little harder, and the surrounding crust of dirt cracked. "Miss Kobblepot, Westin, Ucilius, and I, we...we were forced to watch what they did to Lissa, what those monsters did to my grandchildren. I don't know if I can speak it. Katia saw it, too. She was right there with us."

Popalia nodded, "It wasn't Katia's family."

"No, it was not." One more kick, and the rock popped up, and there was more to the rock beneath the track than what had been exposed. "As soon as the fighting was over, most of the orcs in the ambushing party did what they did to Enga, and I was afraid for my daughter. I was sure they were saving her, waiting to do the same to her. I tried to help her get away, but she wouldn't leave—not without the children and Ucilius.

"My brave girl. She took a chance to free the children. We were atop the ridge when Lissa kneed her escort. Ucilius tripped the children's guard to help give Lissa and the kids a chance to escape. He threw himself at one of the big orc warriors, even with his hands bound at his sides.

"Do you understand, Priestess?" Gregor begged Popalia to understand. "The man I thought of as weak—he fought with a will so strong. My grandkids, they'd been tied together, but they ran. Then, Lissa was shot in the leg with an arrow, and my grandkids stopped. We yelled. Ucilius and I screamed for the grandkids to run faster, but then the orcs piled upon my daughter. It was but a moment later when they'd caught the children."

Gregor kicked the rock he'd dug up with his foot. The fist-sized stone bounced out into nothing, clattering across the hard road. "They impaled my baby girl. They threw her upon a spike growing out of the ground. We were all forced to watch as they tore my grandchildren apart. My babies, all dead. My daughter, bleeding to death from the stone spike rammed through her, she mouthed last words to Ucilius, 'I love you.' He faded out along with her."

Kneeling, Gregor placed his fist in the hole where the rock had been. Without looking up, he said, "I needed Ucilius to live. To carry this, I needed Miss Kobblepot and Westin to survive, but now I am the sole survivor of my caravan. How can I walk into my city tomorrow like this? How can I face my wife and my community knowing what I know?"

The desert breeze whistled though cacti and shrubs. It made harsh, lamenting sounds reflective of the pain Gregor bore. Popalia had nothing to say, and the wind spoke for her.

"I'm a selfish man. I know I am, but did I deserve this? Why am I alive? What is to become of me? I can no longer be who I was, but what am I, now?"

Popalia pulled Gregor to stand. She hugged the fragile merchant. "Stranoss arrived when Westin had called. I felt your god's presence as Westin fought to save us. The Unknown Host does not provide answers but leaves the answers for us to find."

Continuing, she helped Gregor reason with fate, "None of us who entered those caves have come out the same. The question I see for you is who will you be, Gregor? Who do you want to be when you walk into the town of Magistrey? Stranoss has given you a tremendous blessing. Forgive yourself and remake yourself in honor of those you've lost. See to the needs of those who are alive and who still love you. You have been blessed, Gregor. The gods favored you for a reason I cannot know, but you will."

Gregor squeezed the young priestess. His voice breaking, "Please, let me be selfish one last time. Please, let me cry. Tomorrow, I'll be strong for all the others. I'll be strong for those who will learn of our tragedy. Please, for now, can I cry selfishly?"

Popalia embraced the man...and his request.

Chapter Forty-Eight

Day 15, hour 10:30 a.m.

Dawn broke, and they'd already started their hike through the desert. Falling from down the side of the mountains the winds picked up as the sun rose. The gusts became gales, and upon hitting the desert floor, billowing dust dropped visibility to hazy at best.

Pelting sand raked exposed skin on the roadside travelers. The wind grabbed and thrashed long hair against already stinging cheeks, and it rippled across the fabric of filthy robes. Popalia praised the Unknown Host for having the road to guide them to Magistrey, for without it, they'd have become lost.

The previous night's smoke upon the horizon turned out to be closer than they had anticipated. Morning had barely bordered noon when the first farmhouse emerged from the dust onslaught. Once positioned downwind from the farmhouse, Wynkkur caught the scent of chicken feathers. A moment later, the acrid reek of a large population of hens struck everyone else's sense of smell.

Making a sour face and raising his voice over the howl of the wind, Gregor informed, "That is Beekron's hatchery and egg farm. Fromme Beekron is the farmer furthest south of Magistrey. You can smell why."

Gregor continued, "Normally, the wind blows from off the sea, and the odor is carried the other way. On the west side of Magistrey is Bulpug's swine farm and dairy. The center of town probably reeks, today." Gregor chuckled in self-amusement. He then added, "We will be coming up on the militia guardhouse soon. I'll most likely know the men stationed there, so let me speak when we get there."

Less than 100 paces further, through the brown haze of dust whipping across the road, a small guard shack materialized. The shape of two men standing in the road appeared next, then the cross beam. A few paces closer, it became apparent the guards wore lighter-grade chainmail than the combat chain and breastplates common to the Regulator army. The militia of Magistrey wore leather helmets with what looked like an iron bowl set over the top half of their skulls. With wind-scarfs wound around their neck and covering their mouths and noses, eyes squinted from within the view hole.

Both guards held spears, and on their belts, they wore uniform shortswords. One tapped upon the guardhouse with the back end of his spear as the other soldier stepped forward, his spear held defensively at the ready but not aggressively. Two other guards stepped from out of the guardhouse, each with a spear and shortsword. The advanced guard called out to the travelers, his voice raised over the wind, "Hello, travelers. What brings you to the Portown of Magistrey?"

A dirty Gregor, gripping his even filthier wig in a clenched hand, waved with the other, "Goodwill to you boys. It is I, Gregor the Third, and I bear the worst of news."

The guard behind the first asked, "The Third? We heard you'd gone to Capitol City. Where are all who went with you?"

"Fallen," Gregor stated through a throat thick with feeling. "Orcs ambushed us, and they took everything." Looking back at Popalia and her misfit gang, Gregor added, "These heroes saved those of us who survived the initial attack, but along the way, Westin, Miss Kobblepot, and—" Gregor swallowed hard, "and Ucilius were lost as we fought to escape."

The first guard handed his spear to the second and took Gregor's hand. With an arm over the shoulder, he pulled the merchant to where the other guards lifted the crossbar blocking the road. "That is horrible, sir. This is the worst of news." His tone rang with genuine feeling and sorrow.

"Yes, Krevill. They are all gone—all of them," Gregor repeated, a deep lament dotting his tone.

"Let us get you home, sir. I will escort you personally." Gregor's emotions nearly crippled him as the guard led the merchant.

The other guard asked, "What shall we do with your...saviors, sir?"

Gregor, his eyes heavy and tired, peered back at Raenyl and Popalia. "Take them to the Azimuth Inn. Tell whichever concierge is working that I am paying for their stay. They will be treated as if they were my own mother. I want two rooms, one for ladies, and the other for men. Baths and laundry services included."

As the guard escorted Gregor by the hand, the merchant looked back at Popalia, saying, "We part now, Priestess. Please allow me a few days alone with my family. I'll send a messenger, and we'll discuss what I can do for you, then."

Popalia nodded to the vacating Gregor as the second guard

approached her. "Hello, Priestess. I'm Corporal Naidan Polsh. After we've listed your names and documented the time of your arrival, I will escort you to our most comfortable inn." Gregor and the escorting guard faded into the gale-driven dust and sand. After documenting the names of the five survivors, Corporal Polsh kept his word and led them toward the heart of Portown Magistrey.

Several paces away from the guardhouse, outside the hearing range of the other guards, Corporal Polsh stated to Popalia, "The losses—I am reeling from all the good people who fell. I knew all of them. Westin and I enlisted a week apart."

Popalia nodded, "In the end, we knew Westin to be a reliable friend with a good heart and great faith. Knowing him for only a few days, we feel his absence."

The guard nodded, "I feel a great sadness. I knew each of them." Then, a couple paces further, he added, "Still, you saved the Third. That alone is great."

"He is just a merchant," Raenyl said loud enough for the Corporal and Popalia to hear. "I'd trade five Gregors for Westin."

The guard shook his head but did not look at the archer. The Corporal added, "No, sir. Gregor is the Third. I loved Enga and Westin like close cousins, but the Third—wait—he never told you?"

Popalia covered her eyes to shield them from debris. She and Raenyl shook their heads, and the archer asked, "Told us what?"

The Corporal explained, "Solander Breid is the Harbormaster. After him comes Martim Redcline, who is our Mayor. Gregor is the Third. He controls all land-based trade for Portown Magistrey. Our economy was built by his predecessors, and the wealth we all share is because of his influence. He is a great man—the Third. Having his blessing is nothing to scoff at. His word is worth more than all the gold he has made. He is shrewd, so having his friendship is nothing short of monumental."

The wind howled on the day Gregor the Third and his heroes arrived in the Portown of Magistrey. It was a strange wind, an unnatural wind for the season. Many in Magistrey would remember this day by its association.

Less than a week had passed since escaping Dilligan's Freepost as outlaws. Now, they were arriving in Magistrey as heroes. Only a conflict of interest could stem from such dire polarities. This dichotomy would eventually catch up to them, but for now, the life of these worthy souls should be celebrated. Tomorrow, the search for Thorgen begins.

Epilogue

Eighteen Days Since Leaving The Monastery

Slowly, Saru-Mora said the words in Elvish. Hers was a youthful face with sharp nose and chin. Softer than normal elvish cheekbones gave her face a slightly rounded appearance, but her dominantly pointed ears showed her as an elf, through and through. With dark, blonde hair tied back, her youthful face shined with relentless beauty.

Ellund Saiwel, lead priest at the Temple of Dawn's Mystery, attempted to emulate the sounds he heard. He felt as if he fumbled over an inflexible tongue. Gray eyes set under furrowed brows, his concentration focused upon the strange noises he tried to form with his mouth.

"Good, good," she excitedly complimented. "You have spoken the whole greeting in my language."

Two of the priests were learning the language of the elves. Saru-Mora, the young medicine-elf-to-be had been sent from her tribe to teach the entire clergy, but only Ellund and Geofin showed any ability to articulate the challenging language. Horace and Lemia, the other priest and priestess, had grown frustrated and opted out of trying to learn Elvish. Ellund, who believed force was a terrible form of management, permitted the others to oversee the duties of the temple to allow himself and Geofin more time for study.

Saru-Mora was now the new resident in Popalia's room. Her mother, Elanya-Mora, was the senior medicine-elf from the Zef'Lut tribe of the Whood Clan elves. She had many things to discuss with the humans. She'd insisted her daughter stay and teach the priests Elvish. Saru-Mora knew her mother could not suffer the confusion of translation. Lost information might never be recovered—the gap in the language being a dangerous chasm.

Saru found the task of teaching exhilarating. Her respect for the humans, despite their bad odor, had rapidly built upon the foundation Popalia established. She was beginning to wonder if humans, although socially primitive, may indeed be spiritual equals to the elves. She'd let her mother be the final judge once these new missionaries were capable of speaking.

Outside the temple they heard Buckley, the temple's combative donkey, braying loudly and then came Horace's pained yelp. Ellund and Geofin looked to each other as Saru stood. Horace's voice could barely be heard, "Bad, Buckley. Get in your pen."

A few days ago, Ellund had sent Horace to Ashton Hamlet to dismiss any pilgrims who may have come to pray to LeSalle's Grace. It was a dirty job, but the relic they'd come to pay homage to was gone, and as far as the clergy knew, no one else yet knew the divine artifact had been stolen. Horace, a gifted healer, could rebuke most of the ills that Grace mended. Still, it was a dirty job to send the pilgrims away.

Horace had also been sent to mail a letter to the Great Temple of the Unveiled—the central chapel in Capitol City. This had been one of Popalia's duties she'd shrugged. Ellund was not angry with his daughter for shirking this duty but was in fact grateful.

By not completing her assignment, she had bought his temple another month of time before dissolution, and by beginning missionary work with the elves, perhaps his temple and staff could remain. None of them wanted to be absorbed into the big cities. It was his faith and belief that the Unknown Host had smiled upon his temple with the introduction of Saru-Mora—an introduction arranged by his strong-willed and persistent daughter.

Ellund shook his head as the younger priest, Geofin, mused darkly, "Horace is going to want to learn Elvish, now."

Geofin was nearing thirty years of age and had Ellund's total confidence. Charismatic and intellectually clever, Geofin only awaited the revelation of his sacred task. Upon completing his task, he'd exchange his silver sash and blue ribbon for a gold sash and red ribbon like what Ellund wore. His commitment of celibacy would be ended, and he would be allowed to begin his own church whenever he saw fit. Needing only his task to be made clear, he knew with a god like the Blessed Mystery, the task could be challenging to foresee.

Upon standing, Ellund answered, "Well, let's go see how bad the damage is."

Saru followed, her blue dress flowing as she hurried to the temple's front doors. They did not reach the doors before Horace had opened one. His big body—framed by the light outside—filled the doorway. Standing there with a grimace of pain, Horace pressed his right hand over the blood dripping from his left ear. Crimson spread across the shoulder of his white robe and across the blue ribbon ringing his neck and running through nickel eyelets down the front. Covering along his right side, soil spread from where he'd been knocked into the dirt, the strongest of deposits at his knee and elbow.

Horace's hand covered his ear, and resentfully he admitted, "Buckley bit me."

"Rotten donkey," Ellund consoled. "Come here. Let me see."

Horace stood near the lead priest as Ellund nodded. "He bit a good chunk out of your earlobe. Come closer." Ellund closed his eyes and touched the top of Horace's ear. Praying, he said, "Great Mystery, please restore the damage done to Horace, for his injury was received in service to you."

Tissue that had been sheared away by strong jaws of a stubborn and spiteful donkey quickly sealed and redesigned itself. The skin and flesh rolled up and over itself, torn capillaries and veins closed, and blood trickled to a stop. The missing piece of Horace's ear had grown back, completely regenerated.

Ellund examined the new ear. Satisfied, he said, "Good as new." With a self-reflective chuckle, he added, "I haven't healed by hand since before Popalia was born. I forgot how good it feels to be the Unknown's vessel."

Horace's round face, pocked by acne-scars, looked like the moon as he grinned, "Thank you, Ellund. I agree. I'd never realized how dependent we'd become on LeSalle's Grace."

Ellund grunted an affirmation, then asked, "How did thing go in Ashton Hamlet? Were there any pilgrims?" His tone thickened on the last question—a sign of shame.

Nodding, Horace replied, "There was a young boy and his father. The boy's legs were twisted since his birth, and the boy's father needed help on the farm. They'd come for Grace's blessing, but I healed the boy with little difficulty. So long has passed since I'd healed anyone, I'd felt a little bit of pain as I laid hands. Only for a moment was there any pain, and then I felt the love of the Unnamed coursing like blood in my veins. It was revitalizing."

Geofin asked, "How did they take being turned away?"

Horace was still smiling, his brown eyes lighting up like a child's on holiday. "The father could care less after his son's legs were restored. He was genuinely grateful."

Ellund nodded, his gray eyes showing relief. "Perhaps we priests and priestesses should make a less daunting expedition for healing the sick and injured. Asunna and her servants don't expect dangerous pilgrimages for the love of their god. Anyhow, that's enough of my ranting. Have you any other news?"

"Oh," Horace exclaimed excitedly, "I received two scrolls from

Sheriff Morton. Wynkkur wasn't kidding—he is a big man. He barely fit in his chair on the porch." Horace pulled two scrolls out of his pocket and handed them to the head priest, "I wondered if he patrols the hamlet from his porch."

Geofin was the youngest of the priests who remained after Popalia had left. He chuckled at this, reminding, "I'd only ever met the deputy, and a box of rocks is smarter than that guy." Still chuckling, he looked upward, "Forgive me for my gossiping tongue."

Ellund untied the ribbon on the first scroll, saying loudly, "Lemia! Come out of the kitchen. We received a letter from Popalia." Ellund grinned, his heart lifted.

Lemia was the only priestess remaining at the Temple of Dawn's Mystery. She was a couple years older than Ellund, but had never challenged her sacred task and remained on the second tier of the clergy. Coming out from the kitchen where she was preparing the evening's meal, she wiped her hands upon a small towel. There was a grin stretched from ear to ear. They'd all been anticipating Popalia's next note.

As they all gathered, Ellund read, "Hello, everybody. Wynkkur and I have reached Capitol City. The elves gave us a ride down the river to make good time, but after we'd set camp, an allibear woke us in the night. Wynkkur was so brave. He taunted the bear away and saved all of us. I am so happy he is with me. I feel safer with him at my side."

Ellund paused to pat Saru's narrow shoulder. "That's the story you told us about."

She smiled back, saying, "That night was so—" Her violet eyes looked inward for the right word before saying, "Frightful. I'll never forget it. Please, read more."

Ellund continued reading, "Outside the Northgate of Capitol City, we saw a hanged man. A sign beneath him implied he was a thief. The king hung him dead. Since the king looks down on thievery, I should see if he'll help us. Do you think he'll share audience with a priestess of my rank? Me neither, so we found new allies."

Ellund's eyes read hungrily, savoring every word. "Sir Darren Chalise allowed us to use his suite for the night. Praise the Mystery, for he met Katia and said she was going to Portown—" Ellund stopped reading and informed, "There is a smear of ink across the parchment."

His eyes grew wide. "Oh, no!" He read, "Someone broke into

our room while we slept. Wynkkur killed two attackers. It is so awful. We had help from a couple mercenaries we'd met last night, but I don't trust them. They want gold for their assistance, and they are quite irreverent.

"Still, they saved us, but the hotel caught on fire, and we had to leave with haste. I'm finishing this letter at the Southgate General Store. We've got to hurry if we are going to catch Katia. I will send a letter from Dilligan's Freepost. Please, keep us in your prayers. We almost have Katia recaptured. We'll be back soon. Love, Popalia and Wynkkur."

"Oh, gods!" Lemia added, her weathered face showing great worry, "That girl is way over her head. We can live without LeSalle's Grace. I cannot bear the loss of Popalia."

Everyone looked pale, but no one needed to share any words, Lemia had spoken for them all. It was Horace who spoke first, "The second scroll is from the main church. I saw the emblem in the wax seal. Maybe it is good news."

Ellund nodded as he broke the wax seal. Unrolling the second scroll, his eyes moistened as he scanned the cold words written by Canon Shertlief. "Oh, no! No, Popalia, this can't be." He handed the scroll to Geofin before saying, "They are blaming Popalia for the fire at the inn. Canon Shertlief has declared my daughter as being a heretic."

About the Author:

Currently living in fabulous Las Vegas, Jake Elliot and his wife are guardians over one rather hostile cat by the name of Samson. He is a whirlwind of slashing claws and biting teeth and has inspired most of the combat scenes in Jake's books. Jake can show the scars to prove. Most writers would agree that a little pain is good for character.

A minimalist at heart and a master of traveling on a shoestring budget, Jake and his wife travel whenever they can dump vicious Samson on anyone willing to wear leather-armor for a week. For the sake of writing this book, Jake had gone to Great Basin National Park and Lehman Caves in northern Nevada. He also participated in a lower cavern tour with the rangers at Carlsbad Caverns National Park. All of this to add that extra pinch of realism into this story. He hopes it is noticed. It was eerie down there.

Also from Jake Elliot:

The Wrong Way Down
by Jake Elliot

eBook ISBN: 9781615725465
Print ISBN: 9781615725472

Dark Fantasy Action-Adventure
Novel of 82,168 words

Sometimes the right way turns all wrong.

I saw his body lying there. My teacher, my mentor, my friend - face down in a pool of his own blood. His white robes were starched brown with dried blood, his throat cut open by the thieves who'd stolen the spiritual artifact we'd been entrusted to protect.

The Blessed Mystery smiles, we caught one of the two thieves, and it is my duty to escort this foul woman to the garrison for interrogation. God, how I thirst for revenge! I cannot afford the luxury of anger, for it is my duty and responsibility to love. I am a priestess on the side of light. However, this hate, it is so heavy...it is too heavy.

Also from Damnation Books:

Phoenix and the Darkness of Wolves
by Shane Jiraiya Cummings

eBook ISBN: 9781615720552
Print ISBN: 9781615720545

Dark Fantasy
Novella of 23,379 words

Australia has been devastated by a supernatural inferno. Damon believes he is the last ash-covered survivor, a man's whose past—and future—is inextricably tied to the magick that caused the conflagration. He tracks a phoenix through this apocalyptic wasteland in the hopes of using its magick to restore his lost family to humanity. His family, in turn, have been condemned to limbo as shadow wolves, emerging for a few fleeting moments every sunset to hunt Damon in the hope his death will free them from their torment. The hunt is on!

9 781615 727599